D1589666

Fisher Ryder

All rights [...] of reproduction in whole or in part in
any form. T[...] [...]rteignment with Harlequin Books S.A.

This is a w[...] [...]acters, places, locations and incidents
are purely [...] [...] [...] to any real life individuals, [...]ing
or dead, or [...], business establishments, locations, events or
incidents. A[...] [...] entirely coincidental.

This book [...] [...] by way of trade or
otherwise, [...] [...] otherwise circulated without the[...] [...]rior
consent of [...]e publisher in any form of binding or cover other than th[...] [...] in
which it is [...]ed and without a simi[...] [...] including this [...]tion
being impo[...] [...] on the subsequent purchaser.

® and ™ a[...] trademarks owned and used by the trademark owner and [...] its
licensee. T[...]demarks marked with ® are registered with the United Kin[...] [...]om
Patent Offi[...] [...]/or the Office for Harmonization in the Internal Market, and
in other countries.

Published in Great Britain 2014
by Mills & Boon, an imprint of Harlequin (UK) Limited,
Eton House, 18-24 Paradise Road, Richmond, Surrey, TW9 1SR

THE COLTONS: FISHER, RYDER & QUINN © 2014 Harlequin Books S.A.

Soldier's Secret Child, *Baby's Watch* and *A Hero of Her Own* were first
published in Great Britain by Harlequin (UK) Limited.

Soldier's Secret Child © 2008 Harlequin Books S.A.
Baby's Watch © 2009 Harlequin Books S.A.
A Hero of Her Own © 2009 Harlequin Books S.A.

Special thanks and acknowledgements to Caridad Piñeiro, Justine Davis
and Carla Cassidy for their contribution to THE COLTONS: FISHER,
RYDER & QUINN.

ISBN: 978-0-263-91205-0
eBook ISBN: 978-1-472-04500-3

05-1014

Harlequin (UK) Limited's policy is to use papers that are natural, renewable
and recyclable products and made from wood grown in sustainable forests.
The logging and manufacturing processes conform to the legal environmental
regulations of the country of origin.

Printed and bound in Spain
by Blackprint CPI, Barcelona

SOLDIER'S SECRET CHILD

BY
CARIDAD PIÑEIRO

SOLDIER'S
SECRET CHILD

This book is dedicated to the men and women
of the military and their families, without whom we
could not have the liberties that make our
daily lives possible.

Chapter 1

Macy Ward had never imagined that on her wedding day she would be running out of the church instead of walking down the aisle.

But just over a week earlier, she had been drawn out of the church by the sharp crack of gunshots and the harsh squeal of tires followed by the familiar sound of her fiancé's voice shouting for someone to get his police cruiser.

Her fiancé, Jericho Yates, the town sheriff and her lifelong friend. Her best friend in all the world and the totally wrong man to marry, she thought again, her hands tightening on the steering wheel. She shot a glance at her teenage son who sat beside her in the passenger seat.

"You ready for this, T.J.?"

He pulled out one earbud of his iPod. Tinny, too loud music blared from it. "Did you want something?" T.J. asked.

It was impossible to miss the sullen tones of his voice or the angry set of his jaw.

She had seen a similar irritated expression on the face of T.J.'s biological father, Fisher Yates, as he stood in his Army dress uniform outside the church with his brother—her fiancé. Fisher had looked far more attractive than he should have. As she had raced out into the midst of the bedlam occurring on the steps of the chapel, her gaze had connected with Fisher's stony glare for just a few seconds.

A few seconds too long.

When she had urged Jericho to go handle the incident and that they could postpone the wedding, she had seen the change in Fisher's gaze.

She wasn't sure if it had been relief at first. But the emotion that followed and lingered far longer had been more dangerous.

Now, there was no relief in T.J.'s hard glare. Just anger.

"Are you ready for this?" she repeated calmly, shooting him a glance from the corner of her eye as she drove to the center of town.

The loose black T-shirt T.J. wore barely shifted with his indifferent shrug. "Do I have any choice?"

Choice? Did anyone really have many choices in life? she thought, recalling how she would have chosen not to get pregnant by Fisher. Or lose her husband, Tim, to cancer. Or have a loving and respectful son turn into a troublesome seventeen-year-old hellion.

"You most certainly have choices, T.J. You could have failed your math class or gone to those tutoring sessions. You could have done time in juvie instead of community service. And now—"

"I'll have to stay out of trouble by working at the ranch since you decided not to marry Jericho."

It had been Jericho who had persuaded a judge to spare T.J. a juvenile record. The incident in question had resulted in rolls and rolls of toilet paper all over an old teacher's prized landscaped lawn and a mangled mailbox that had needed to be replaced.

"After postponing the wedding, I realized that I was getting married for all the wrong reasons. So, I chose not to go ahead with the wedding and I'm glad that I did. It gave Jericho the chance to find someone he truly loves," she said, clasping and unclasping her hands on the wheel as she pulled into a spot in front of the post office.

"I told you before that I don't need another dad," he said, but his words were followed by another shrug as T.J.'s head dropped down. "Not that Jericho isn't a nice guy. He's just not my dad."

Macy killed the engine, cradled her son's chin and applied gentle pressure to urge his head upward. "I know you miss him. I do, too. It's been six long years without him, but he wouldn't want you to still be unhappy."

"And you think working at the ranch with some gnarly surfer dude from California will make me happy?" He jerked away from her touch and wagged one hand in the familiar hang loose surfer sign.

She dropped her hands into her lap and shook her head, biting back tears and her own anger. As a recreational therapist, she understood the kinds of emotions T.J. was venting with his aggressive behavior. Knew how to try to get him to open up about his feelings.

But as a mother, the attitude was frustrating.

"Jewel tells me Joe is a great kid and he's your age. Maybe you'll find that you have something in common."

Without waiting for his reply, she grabbed her purse and rushed out of the car, crossed the street and made a beeline for the door to Miss Sue's. She had promised her boss, Jewel Mayfair, that she would stop by the restaurant to pick up some of its famous sticky buns for the kids currently residing at the Hopechest Ranch.

When she reached the door, however, she realized *he* was there.

Fisher Yates.

Decorated soldier, Jericho's older brother and unknown to him or anyone else in town, T.J.'s biological father. Only her husband, Tim, had known, and he had kept the secret to his grave.

The morning that had started out so-so due to T.J.'s moodiness just went to bad. She would have no choice but to acknowledge Fisher on her way to the take-out counter in the back of the restaurant. Especially since he looked up and noticed her standing there. His green-eyed gaze narrowed as he did so and his full lips tightened into a grim line.

He really should loosen up and smile some more, she thought, recalling the Fisher of her youth who had always had a grin ready for her, Tim and Jericho.

Although she couldn't blame him for his seeming reticence around her. She had done her best to avoid him during the entire time leading up to the wedding. Had somehow handled being around him during all the last-minute preparations, being polite but indifferent whenever he was around. It was the only way to protect herself against the emotions which lingered about Fisher.

In the week or so since she and Jericho had parted ways, it had been easier since she hadn't seen Fisher around town and knew it was just a matter of time before he was back on duty and her secret would be safe again.

She ignored the niggle of guilt that Fisher didn't know about T.J. Or that as a soldier, he risked his life with each mission and might not ever know that he had a son. Over the years she had told herself it had been the right decision to make not just for herself, but for Fisher as well. Jericho had told her more than once over the years how happy his older brother was in the Army. How it had been the perfect choice for him.

As much as the guilt weighed heavily on her at times, she could not risk any more problems with her son by revealing such a truth now. T.J. had experienced enough upset lately and he was the single most important thing in her life. She would do anything to protect him. To see him smile once again.

Which included staying away from Fisher Yates no matter how much she wanted to make things right between them.

Fisher was just finishing up a plate of Miss Sue's famous buckwheat pancakes when he looked up and glimpsed Macy Ward at the door to the café.

She seemed to hesitate for a moment when she spied him and he wondered why.

Did she feel guilty about avoiding him the whole time he'd been home or was her contriteness all about her change of mind at the altar where she had left his brother? Not that it had been the wrong thing to do. From the moment his kid brother Jericho had told him about his decision to marry Macy, Fisher had believed it was a mistake.

Not that he was any kind of expert on marriage, having avoided it throughout his thirty-seven years of life, but it struck him as wrong to be in a loveless marriage. Jericho should have known that given the experience of his own parents.

Their alcoholic mother had walked out on the Yates men when he was nine and old enough to realize that if there had been any love between his mother and father, drink had driven it away a long time before.

Macy finally pushed through the door and as she passed him, she dipped her head in greeting and said, "Mornin'."

"Mornin'," he replied, and glanced surreptitiously at her as she passed.

At thirty-five years of age, Macy Ward was a fine-looking woman. Trim but with curves in all the right places.

Fisher remembered those curves well. Remembered the strength and tenderness in her toned arms and legs as she had held him. Remembered the passion of their one night which was just another reason why he had known it was wrong for his brother and Macy to marry.

He couldn't imagine being married to a woman like Macy and having the relationship be platonic. Hell, if it were him, he'd have her in bed at every conceivable moment.

Well, at every moment that he could given the presence of her seventeen-year-old son T.J.

Which made him wonder where the boy was until he peered through the windows of Miss Sue's and spotted him sitting in Macy's car. His mop of nearly-black hair, much darker than Macy's light brown, hung down in front of his face, obscuring anything above his tight-lipped mouth.

Fisher wondered if T.J. was angry about the aborted wedding. To hear Jericho talk, the teenager had been none too happy with the announcement, but to hear his father talk, there wasn't much that T.J. had been happy with since T.J.'s father's death from cancer six years earlier.

Not that he blamed the boy. It had taken him a long time to get over his own mother's abandonment. Some might say he never had given his wandering life as a soldier and his inability to commit to any woman.

From behind him he heard the soft scuff of boots across the gleaming tile floor and almost instinctively knew it was Macy on her way back. Funny in how only just a couple of weeks he could identify her step and the smell of her.

She always smelled like roses.

But then again, observing such things was a necessary part of his military training. An essential skill for keeping his men alive.

His men, he thought and picked up the mug of steaming coffee, sweet with fresh cream from one of the small local ranches. In a couple of weeks, he would either be heading back for another tour of duty in the Middle East or accepting an assignment back in the States as an instructor at West Point.

Although he understood the prestige of being assigned to the military academy, he wasn't sure he was up for settling down in one place.

Since the day eighteen years ago when Macy had walked down the aisle with Tim, he had become a traveling man and he liked it that way. No ties or connections other than to his dad, younger brother and his men. People he could count on, he thought as the door closed on Macy's firm butt encased in soft faded denim.

A butt his hands itched to touch along with assorted other parts of her.

With a mumbled curse, he took a sip of the coffee, wincing at its heat. Reminded himself that he was only in town for a short period of time.

Too little time to waste wondering over someone who probably hadn't given him a second thought in nearly twenty years.

Chapter 2

What made the drive to the Hopechest Ranch better wasn't just that it was shorter, Macy thought.

She loved the look of the open countryside and how it grew even more empty the farther they got away from Esperanza. The exact opposite of how it had been in the many years that she had made the drive to the San Antonio hospital where she had once worked.

Out here in the rugged Texas countryside, she experienced a sense of balance and homecoming. When Jewel Mayfair and the California side of the Colton family had bought the acres adjacent to the Bar None in order to open the Hopechest Ranch, Macy had decided she had wanted to work there. Luckily, she and Jewel had hit it off during her interview.

It wasn't just that they had similar ideas about dealing with the children at the ranch or that tragedy had touched both their lives. They were both no-nonsense rational women with a strong sense of family, honor and responsibility.

They had bonded immediately and their friendship had grown over the months of working together, so much so that she had asked Jewel to be her maid of honor.

Because she was a friend and understood her all too well, Jewel hadn't pressed her since the day she had canceled the wedding, aware of Macy's concerns about marrying Jericho and her turmoil over the actions of her son.

Macy was grateful for that as well as Jewel's offer to hire T.J. to work during the summer months at the ranch.

At seventeen, he was too old for after school programs, not to mention that for the many years she had worked in San Antonio, she had felt guilty about having him in such programs. Before Tim's death, T.J. used to go home and spend time with his father, who had been a teacher at one of the local schools.

She pulled up in front of the Spanish-style ranch house, which was the main building at the Hopechest Ranch. The Coltons had spared no expense in building the sprawling ranch house that rose up out of the flat Texas plains. Attention to detail was evident in every element of the house from the carefully maintained landscaping to the ornate hand-carved wooden double doors at the entrance.

Macy was well aware, however, that the Hopechest Ranch wasn't special because of the money the Coltons lavished on the house and grounds. It was the love the Coltons put into what they did with the kids within. She mumbled a small prayer that the summer spent here might help her work a change in T.J.'s attitude.

She parked off to one side of the driveway, shut off the engine and they both stepped out of the car.

One of the dark wooden doors opened immediately.

Ana Morales stepped outside beneath the covered portico by the doors, her rounded belly seeming even larger today than it had the day before. The beautiful young Mexican woman laid a hand on one of the columns of the portico as she waited for them.

Ana had taken refuge at the Hopechest Ranch like many of the others within, although the main thrust of the program at the ranch involved working with troubled children. Despite that, the young woman had been a welcome addition, possessing infinite patience with the younger children.

Sticky bun box in hand, Macy smiled and embraced Ana when she reached the door. "How are you today, *amiga?*"

"Just fine, Macy," Ana said, her expressive brown eyes welcoming. She shot a look over Macy's shoulder at T.J. "This is your son, no?"

She gestured to him. "T.J., meet Ms. Morales."

"Ana, *por favor,*" she quickly corrected. "He's very handsome and strong."

"Miss Ana," T.J. said, removing his hat and ducking his head down in embarrassment.

As they stepped within the foyer of the ranch, the noises of activity filtered in from the great rooms near the back of the ranch house and drew them to the large family room/-kitchen area. In the bright open space, half a dozen children of various ages and ethnicities moved back and forth between the kitchen, where Jewel and one of the Hopechest Ranch's housekeepers were busy serving up family-style platters of breakfast offerings.

Ana immediately went to their assistance as did Macy, walking to the counter and grabbing a large plate for the sticky buns. Motioning with her head, she said, "Go grab yourself a spot at the table, T.J."

As the children noted that the food was being put out, they shifted to the large table between the family room and kitchen and soon only a few spots were free at the table.

T.J. hovered nervously beyond, uncertain.

Macy was about to urge her son to sit again when a handsome young man entered the room—Joe, she assumed. He had just arrived at the ranch and she hadn't had a chance to meet him yet.

Almost as tall as T.J., he had the same lanky build, but his hair was a shade darker. His hair was stylishly cut short around his ears, but longer up top framing bright blue eyes that inquisitively shifted over the many occupants of the room.

He walked over to stand beside T.J. and nodded his head, earning a return bop of his head from T.J.

"I'm Joe," he said and held out his hand.

"Just call me T.J.," her son answered and shook the other teen's hand.

"Looks good," Joe said and gestured to the food on the table. "Dude, I'm hungry. How about you?"

The loud growl from T.J.'s stomach was all the answer needed and Joe nudged him with his shoulder. "Come on, T.J. If you wait too long, the rugrats will get all the good stuff."

A small smile actually cracked T.J.'s lips before he followed Joe to the table. He hesitated again for a moment as Joe sat, leaving just one empty chair beside a dark-haired teen girl.

The teen, Sara Engelheit, a pretty sixteen-year-old who had come to the ranch recently, looked up shyly at T.J., who mumbled something beneath his breath, but then took the seat.

Macy released the breath she had been holding all that

time and as her gaze connected with Jewel's she noted the calm look on her boss's face. With a quick incline of her head, it was as if Jewel was saying, "I told you not to worry."

Jewel walked to the kids' table, excused herself and snagged one of the sticky buns, earning a raucous round of warnings from the children about eating something healthy.

Grinning, Jewel said, "I promise I'll go get some fresh juice and fruit."

Heeding the admonishments of the children, she, Ana and the housekeeper helped themselves to the eggs, oatmeal and other more nutritious offerings and then joined Jewel at a small café bar at one side of the great space, a routine they did every day.

Some of the children had rebelled at the routine at first, but they soon fell into the security of the routine. Happiness filled her as she noticed the easy camaraderie of the children around the table.

While they ate, the women discussed the day's schedule, reviewing what each of them would do as they split the children into age- and need-defined groups before reuniting them all during the day for meals.

When they were done, they turned their attention to their charges. Ana took the younger children to play at the swing set beyond the pool so they could avoid the later heat of the Texas summer day. Macy took the tweens and teens out to the corrals that housed an assortment of small livestock and some chickens. They loved the animals and learning to care for them helped her reinforce patterns of responsibility and teamwork.

As the groups were established, Jewel faced T.J. and Joe who were the eldest of the children present. "I'm going to ask the two of you to go with me today. You're both new to the ranch and I'd like to show you around. Give you an idea of the chores I expect you to do."

The boys stood side by side, nodded almost in unison, but as Jewel turned away for a moment, Macy noted the look that passed between them as if to say, "What have we gotten ourselves into?"

In that moment, she knew a bond had been established and only hoped that it would be one for the better given Jewel's accolades about Joe.

"Hurry up, Mom. I promised Joe I'd get there early so I can show him those XBOX cheat codes before breakfast," T.J. said and raced out of their house. The door slammed noisily behind him and normally she would have cautioned him about being more careful, but she didn't have the heart to do it. He seemed so eager to get to the ranch.

Rushing, she hopped on one booted foot, trying to step into the other boot while slipping on her jacket at the same time. Nearly pitching backward onto her ass, she grappled for the deacon's bench by the front door and chuckled at her own foolishness.

She was just so excited to finally see her son starting to lose some of his surliness. He actually looked forward to something.

She finished dressing with less haste and minutes later, they were on their way to the ranch, T.J. sitting beside her with his iPod running. Unlike his slouched stance of a week ago, he almost leaned forward, as if to urge them to move more quickly toward the ranch.

The countryside flashed beside them as they left the edge of town, the wide open meadows filled with the whites of wild plums, the maroon and yellow of Mexican hat and mountain pink wildflowers. Ahead of them a cloudless sky the color of Texas bluebonnets seemed to go on forever.

In less than ten minutes they were at Hopechest and she had barely stopped the car when T.J. went flying up the driveway and into the house. She proceeded more slowly, stopping to inhale the fresh scent of fresh cut summer grass and the flowers from a nearby meadow.

It was going to be a good day, she thought.

Inside the house, T.J., Joe and Sara were gathered around the XBOX in the family room, where as promised, T.J. was teaching them the cheat codes.

As the women did every day, they set up breakfast, ate and after they finished, Jewel announced to the kids that they had a special treat for them that day—Clay Colton was bringing over a mare to keep at the ranch for them to ride and care for.

T.J. and Joe had been at work all week in anticipation of the mare's arrival. They had cleaned up some of the stalls in one of the smaller barns on the property, placing fresh-smelling hay in one stall and setting up the other one to hold tack, feed and other necessities.

As the ragtag group walked to a corral on the property, the younger children were in front of the pack, followed by T.J., Joe and Sara.

Macy, Jewel and Ana took up spots at the side of the group, keeping an eye on the youngest as they approached the corral. Clay Colton waited astride his large roan stallion Crockett. A smaller palomino mare stood beside him and his horse.

Clay was all cowboy, she thought, admiring his easy seat on the saddle and the facility with which he swung off the immense mount. He ground tethered Crockett and then walked the mare over toward them.

"Mornin'," he said and tipped his white Stetson. Longish black hair peeked from beneath the hat and his eyes were a vivid blue against the deep tan of his skin.

"Mornin', Clay. We can't thank you enough for bringing the mare for the children," Jewel said.

"My pleasure. How about I show Joe and T.J. how to handle her for the younger kids?"

"That would be great, Clay. It'll be a big relief for both Jewel and me if the boys can control her. What's her name?" Macy asked.

Clay pushed his hat back a bit, exposing more of his face as he waved the two boys over. "Gentlemen, come on over and meet Papa's Poppy."

T.J. and Joe scrambled up and over the split rail corral fence, stood by Clay as he took the saddle, blanket, bit and reins off the mare. The horse stood by calmly as he did so and then later as Clay showed the boys how to place all the equipment back on.

T.J. already had a fairly good knowledge of what to do since he and his dad used to ride together. He seemed hesitant at first, but then Clay said, "That's the way, T.J. Good job."

His uncertainty seemed to fade then and before long, he and Joe had ridden the mare around the corral a time or two. The younger children were calling out eagerly to have a turn as well.

Joe slipped off the horse and handed the reins to T.J.

"Me? What am I supposed to do now?"

Clay clapped him on the back. "Keep her under control while Joe gets one of your friends up on her. She's gentle. You can handle it."

T.J. took a big gulp, but did as Clay asked and before long, the two boys were giving the remaining children their turns on the mare, Clay hovering nearby protectively until it was clear that T.J. and Joe were in charge of the situation.

He stepped over to where she stood with Jewel and Ana and said, "This will work out well for you, I think. Papa's Poppy is the gentlest mare I have."

"I insist on paying for her, Clay," Jewel said, facing him.

Clay shrugged and the fabric of his western shirt stretched tight against shoulders made broad by years of ranch work. "She was an injured stray I found a year or so ago. All scratched up from a fight with some prickly poppy she got tangled up in."

"Hence the name," she said.

"Yep and to be honest, you'd be helping me out by taking her. I need room for a new stud I want to buy for the Bar None."

"Are there many strays in the area, Clay?" Jewel asked as she leaned on the top rail of the fence, vigilantly keeping an eye on the children.

"Occasionally. Why do you ask?" he said and pulled off his hat, wiped at a line of sweat with a bandanna.

Jewel dragged a hand through the short strands of her light brown hair, suddenly uneasy. "I've heard noises in the night."

"Me, too," Ana chimed in. "It sounds like a baby crying or maybe a small animal in pain."

"Yes, exactly," Jewel confirmed. "Not all the time, just every now and then."

Clay jammed his white Stetson back on his head and glanced in the direction of the two boys, squinting against the sun as he did so. "I haven't heard anything up my way, but I can swing by one night and check it out for you."

He motioned with a work-roughened hand to the two boys. "They'll make fine ranch hands. Remind me of Ryder and myself when we were kids. We loved being around the horses more than anything."

Macy couldn't miss the wistfulness in his voice as Clay spoke of his younger brother. Much like T.J., Ryder had begun getting into trouble as a teen, but then it had gotten progressively worse until Ryder had ended up in jail for smuggling aliens across the border.

"Have you heard from your brother lately?" she asked, wondering if Clay had relented from his stance to disavow his troubled brother.

"I wrote to him, but the mail came back as undeliverable." A hard set entered his jaw and his bright blue eyes lost the happy gleam from watching the children.

"Maybe your brother was moved?" Ana offered, laying a gentle hand on Clay's arm.

He nodded and smiled stiffly. "Maybe, Miss Ana. I just hope it's not too late to make amends with my little brother. I'm going to try to call someone at the prison to see what's happening with him."

"I think you're right to put the past behind you and try to make things right with Ryder," Jewel added, but then stepped away to help the boys with one of the younger children who seemed to be afraid of the mare.

Ana went over as well to help since the child was Mexican and still learning English, leaving Macy alone with Clay.

"You'll work things out with your brother," she said, trying to offer comfort. Clay was a good man and she hated to see him upset.

"I hope so. It's never too late to make amends with the people from our past, Macy. You should understand that more than some," he said, surprising her.

She examined his face, searching for the meaning behind his words. Wondering if he somehow knew about her and Fisher. About T.J.

"I do understand," she said, waiting for him to say more so that she could confirm the worst of her fears, but he didn't. Instead, he shouted out his farewell to everyone, walked over to his stallion and climbed up into his saddle.

"Take good care of her, men. I'll be back later to show you how to groom her, handle the feeding and keep the stall clean," he added with a wave to the boys before leaving.

Both T.J. and Joe straightened higher at his comment. She hadn't been wrong in wanting to marry Jericho to give her son a man's presence in his life. It was obvious from just this slight interaction that both boys had responded positively to the added responsibility and to being treated as adults.

Small steps. Positive ones.

She should be grateful for that, but Clay's words rang in her head as she stepped over to help Jewel and Ana with the rest of the children.

It's never too late to make amends with the people from our past.

As much as she hoped that he was right, she also prayed that she would not have to make amends before T.J. was ready to handle it.

Chapter 3

The mare had been a wonderful addition to their program at the ranch, Macy thought as she watched the teens working together in the stalls and adjacent corral.

She and Jewel had discussed how to incorporate the responsibilities for the mare into a program for the children. They had broken them up into rotating teams that took turns with the mare's care and feeding. In addition, she worked with the tweens and teens, including T.J. and Joe, to improve how they handled the mare. Setting up a series of small tests, she encouraged each of the teens until they were all able to take turns not only outfitting and riding the mare, but watching and helping the younger children with the horse.

When T.J. and Joe weren't with the groups, they were off finishing up some of the other chores around the ranch, including a ride with Clay Colton to attempt to track down the elusive sounds that Jewel was still hearing at night. But they returned from that expedition with little to show for it.

She was grateful that T.J. and Joe seemed to have bonded so quickly and so well. As the eldest amongst the children at the ranch, the others seemed to look up to them, in particular the tweens and Sara, the petite young teen who had recently joined them.

It wasn't unusual to see the three of them together at meals and as they took an afternoon break at the pool during the heat of the day, much as they were doing today.

As she watched them frolicking in the cool waters, Jewel stepped up beside her.

"Things seem to be better," her friend said.

"I had hopes for it, but this is more than I expected so quickly."

"Let's take a break." Jewel gestured to a small table located on the covered courtyard where someone had placed a pitcher with iced tea and glasses. A few feet away from the table in the middle of the courtyard was a fountain. The sounds of the running water combined with the scents from the riot of flowers surrounding the courtyard were always calming.

With a quick nod, she sat at the table and poured tea into the two glasses, all the time keeping an eye on what was going on in the pool.

T.J. and Joe led the younger children in a game of Marco Polo, while Sara sat by the side, arms wrapped around herself in a slightly defensive stance.

"We've still got to get Sara to open up a bit," she said.

Jewel picked up her glass and took a sip. "She's been better since the boys got here, but she hasn't been willing to say much during our one-on-one sessions."

"Nothing about the bruises or why she ran away?" she asked, thinking of the purpling marks and fingerprints that had been on the girl's arms on the day she had arrived at the ranch a few weeks ago.

"Nothing and you know our rule."

"We wait until our charge is ready to talk. Do you have another session scheduled with her anytime soon?" She sipped her tea, sighed as the cool liquid slid down her heat parched throat. She hadn't realized just how hot and dry it had been as she and the teens had worked with the mare all morning.

"I have a group session with the older children this afternoon. I was thinking to ask T.J. and Joe to join us."

She thought of T.J.'s anger at his dad's passing and of Joe's adoption by the Coltons. Certainly both of the boys had things to unload and considering how well the group had been getting along, it seemed like a good idea.

"Both T.J. and Joe might have things they want to talk about. I'd ask to sit in, but I know T.J. might be more willing to open up if I'm not around."

Jewel laid a hand on hers as it rested on the table, shifting her iced tea back and forth in the condensation from the glass. "I know that hurts, but you're right. T.J. will likely be more open if you're not around. But I'll keep you posted about what happens. This way you'll know how to deal with it."

Macy took hold of Jewel's hand and gave it a reassuring squeeze. "Thanks. I'd appreciate anything you can say without violating doctor/patient confidentiality."

"Deal," she confirmed and then they sat back and took a moment just to enjoy the peacefulness of the midday break.

* * *

Macy was working with two of the younger children when she noticed the teens walking out of the living room where Jewel often held the group therapy sessions.

The two tween boys had their arms around each other's shoulders and their heads together, talking.

T.J., Joe and Sara followed behind closely, but then split away, walking through the great space and out to the pool area. They kept on walking beyond the tract of grass with the swing set and Macy assumed T.J. and Joe were off to do the last of their afternoon chores.

Once in the great room, the tween boys headed immediately to the XBOX and she could hear them carrying on about the tricks Joe and T.J. had taught them.

She smiled at the worship of the older boys, but her smile faded as she noted Jewel's face. Excusing herself from the memory game, but urging the children to continue on their own, she approached her boss.

"You look wiped."

"Mark finally opened up today. Told the other kids about how his dad used to beat him."

Both of them suspected that Mark had been physically abused from his manner when he had first come to the ranch, but having him admit it was a good step to helping him deal with the trauma.

"How about Sara?" she wondered, thinking that maybe Mark's revelation would have encouraged the young girl to tell her own story.

Jewel shook her head. "Nothing. She just sat there, arms wrapped around herself. Silent."

"Sorry to hear that, but she is coming out of her shell. She seems to talk to T.J. and Joe a lot."

"That's a good start. Where are they?" Jewel asked as she scanned the great room and saw no sign of them.

"I saw them heading out back, probably to finish up their chores before the weekend. I'll go see what they're up to," she said and at her boss's cue of approval, she went in search of them.

As she suspected, they were at the corral, but not working. The two boys sat on the top rail of the fence, Sara between them, head bowed down.

She was about to approach to make sure everything was okay, but then T.J. brought his hand up and patted Sara's back in a familiar gesture. She had seen Tim do it more than once when comforting his young son and it twisted her heartstrings that Tim would not see the man T.J. would become.

Which was followed by a wave of guilt as she realized that maybe Fisher never would either if she didn't tell him about his son. If she didn't make amends for what had happened in the past between them.

Certain that the teens were better off without her presence at that moment, she returned to the ranch house and the game of memory she had left earlier.

But even then she experienced no relief as the children matched up the first few letters.

F.

S.

I.

Certainly someone somewhere was telling her it was time to consider what she would do about Fisher.

Fisher sat across from his dad in Miss Sue's, enjoying the last of his ribs and delicious fries.

It wasn't as if he and his dad couldn't have made themselves dinner. Since their mom had left, the three men had learned how to provide for themselves, but with it being Friday night and all, they needed a treat.

Plus, he hadn't wanted to waste time cooking when he could be spending it talking to his dad, especially since his time in Esperanza was ticking away quickly. Just a few more weeks and he would head back to the military.

As he ran a fry through the ketchup and ate the last piece of tender meat on the rib, the cowbell clanged over the door. A trio walked in—Macy's son with another boy and a teen girl.

They stopped at the door to wait to be seated. As the hostess showed them to a booth, they passed by.

"Evening, Mr. Yates," T.J. said to his dad and nodded at Fisher in greeting as well.

"Evening, T.J. Are these friends of yours?" Buck Yates asked, flicking his large hand in the direction of the other teens with T.J.

"Yes, sir, they are. Joe and Sara, meet Mr. Yates. He's the sheriff's dad and this is the sheriff's brother—Captain Yates."

Joe and Sara shook hands with the men and then the trio excused themselves.

"Polite young man," Fisher said, slightly surprised given the accounts provided by his brother about T.J.'s antics.

"He's a good kid, just a little angry ever since his pa died," Buck said and pushed away his empty plate.

"It must have been rough," he said, imagining how difficult it would have been on both Macy and T.J. His own brother had suffered greatly as well since Tim had been his lifelong best friend.

Luckily, Jericho had been Macy's best friend also and had

been by her side during the long months that Tim had battled cancer. At least Macy hadn't been alone, but it didn't stop the sudden clenching of his gut that maybe he could have been there for her, as well.

He drove that thought away quickly. Being away from Macy was up there on the list of reasons he had joined the military.

Maybe the top reason, he mused, thinking back to the night that had forever sealed the course of his life.

Chapter 4

Esperanza, Texas
Eighteen years earlier

Jericho stood at the plate, bat held high. His hips shifting back and forth, his body relaxed. He waited for the pitch.

Jericho's team was down by one. Tim Ward was on third base and another player on second with two men out. It would be the last inning unless they were able to get some runs on the board.

Fisher sat beside his dad on the bleacher and called out encouragement. "You can do it, Jericho."

His yell was followed by Macy's from where she sat a few feet away and a row down from them. "Go-o-o, Jericho-o. One little hit."

She sat beside Jericho's latest girlfriend. He couldn't remember her name because Jericho never kept a girl for too long, much like him. The Yates boys were love 'em and leave 'em kinds of guys, he thought.

Macy, on the other hand, wasn't a love 'em and leave 'em type of girl. Until recently, everyone thought she and Tim were a forever kind of thing what with them going off to college together. Except that in the past few weeks, Macy and Tim didn't seem to be a thing anymore, which meant that Tim had loved her and left her. That struck him as down-right stupid.

The crack of the bat pulled his attention away from thoughts of Macy.

Jericho had lined a rocket of a hit up the first baseline and deep into the corner of the stadium. Tim would score easily to tie the game, but as people got up on the bleachers and started cheering, it was clear the ball was deep enough to maybe score the man from second.

The outfielder picked up the ball and with all his might sent it flying home, but the man from second was already well on his way to the plate. The ball sailed past the catcher as the man slid into home to win the game.

The wild cheering and revelry of the hometown crowd spurred on the players who ran out onto the field to celebrate the victory. After a few moments of exuberant celebration, both the players and the crowd finally quieted down and the players formed a line to shake hands with the other team.

As they did so, the crowd began to disperse from the stands.

"I'll see you at home, son," his dad said, clapped him on the back and waved at Jericho on the field.

He jumped down from the bleachers and weaved through the crowd of well-wishers until he reached Jericho, whose new girlfriend was already plastered to his hip.

Tim and Macy stood across from one another awkwardly, clearly no longer a forever kind of thing and surprisingly, he was kind of glad about that.

"Hey, big bro," Jericho said as he joined them. "Tim, Cindy and I are heading to Bill's for a post-baseball bash. Want to come hang with us?"

All three of them, but not Macy? he wondered and shot a glance at her as she stood there, hands laced primly together in front of her.

"No thanks, lil' bro. Just came down to say congrats on winning the game."

"We've gotta run. What about you, Mace?" Jericho said, either clearly oblivious to the tension between his two friends or choosing to ignore it.

"I've got…things to do," she replied, peeking up at him from the corner of her eye.

"We're history, then," Jericho said and left with Cindy bumping hips with him on one side and Tim on the other.

He jammed the tips of his fingers into the pockets of his jeans and rocked back on the heels of his boots, hesitant now that he and Macy were alone. "So what's so important for you to have to do on a Friday night?"

A blast of pink brightened her cheeks before she straightened her shoulders and faced him head on, determination in her brown-eyed gaze. "Well, since it's early, I was thinking of maybe grabbing a bite at Miss Sue's. Are you hungry?" After she asked, she worried her bottom lip with her teeth, belying her nervousness around him.

He was hungry, but not necessarily for anything other than a taste of that luscious bottom lip. Years earlier he'd had a taste during what was supposed to be a chaste holiday kiss, but he had underestimated the potency of her kiss. That encounter had made him realize that like Tim, he had been smitten by tomboy Macy Ward.

"I'm hungry, but won't Tim mind, you know…you and me. Friday night. Dinner."

She cocked her head at him defiantly. "What I do is no longer any of Tim's concern. So, dinner?"

Interesting, he thought, but quickly offered her his arm. "Dinner it is. My treat."

He wanted to lick the plate of the last remnants of Miss Sue's famous apple cobbler, but his dad had raised him to be a gentleman so he held back.

Macy must have seen the hunger that remained in his gaze since she offered up the last few bites of the pie on her plate. "You can finish mine."

His mouth watered at the site of those extra pieces, but he shook his head. "I couldn't take the last of your dessert."

"Go ahead. I need to watch my figure anyway," she said, moving aside his plate and pushing hers before him.

Fisher dug into the cobbler, but after he swallowed a bite, he said, "Seems to me you're worrying for nothing, Mace."

Truth be told, she had a wonderful figure. Trim and strong, but with womanly curves in all the right places. As he thought about that, he shifted in his seat as his jeans tightened painfully. He had imagined those curves next to him once too often since that fateful kiss.

"Something wrong, Fisher?" she asked, innocently unaware of the effect she had on him.

"Not at all," he lied, quickly finished the cobbler and paid the tab.

With his hand on the small of her back, he walked her out to the sidewalk where they stood there for a moment, enjoying the early summer night. Dusk was just settling in, bringing with it the cooler night air and the soft intimate glow of the streetlights along Main Street.

"Thank you for dinner," Macy said, glad for not only the fine food, but his company. He had always been a distant fourth musketeer to their little group and tonight she had been able to enjoy his presence without interference.

As he turned to look at her, she noticed the gleam in his green eyes. The kind of gleam that kicked her heart up into a hurried little beat. She might have been going out with Tim for as long as she could remember, but she could still recognize when a man found her attractive. And considering her breakup with Tim, it was a welcome balm that someone as attractive as Fisher appeared to be interested.

He smiled, his teeth white against his tanned skin and his dark five o'clock shadow. He was the kind of man who needed to shave more than twice a day. He was a man, she reminded herself, trying to ignore the pull of her attraction to him. Nothing like Jericho and Tim, even though Fisher was only two years older. There had always been a maturity and intensity about him that had set him apart from the others.

"It's early still," he said, the tones of his voice a soft murmur in the coming quiet of the night.

"It is," she said.

He leaned toward her and a lock of nearly jet-black hair fell forward onto his forehead as he said, "Too early to call it a night, don't you think?"

She met his gaze, glittering brightly with interest, the color like new spring grass. Kicking up that erratic beat of her heart and making her want to reach up and brush away that wild errant lock of hair.

"Did you have something in mind?" she asked in a breathless voice she didn't recognize.

"How about a drive? I'll even put the top down on the CJ."

She imagined driving through the night, Fisher beside her. The scents of the early summer wildflowers whipping around them as they sped along in the open Jeep through the Texas countryside.

"I think that sounds really nice."

They drove through the open meadows and fields surrounding Esperanza, the scented wind wrapping them in its embrace while bright moonlight lit the road before them until Fisher took a dirt road to one of the few nearby hills. He parked the CJ so it faced the lights of town and the wide starlit Texas sky.

She imagined she could see the lights of San Antonio, well to the south of their hometown. She and Tim had planned on going to college together there until Tim had said he was reconsidering that decision. She gazed at the lights of Esperanza and noticed the cars parked around Bill's house where Jericho and Tim would be with the rest of the baseball team. Where she might have been a few weeks earlier if things hadn't changed recently.

"Penny for your thoughts," he said and pushed back some strands of wind-blown hair from her face. The pads of his fingers brushed the sensitive skin of her cheek, sending a shiver rocketing through her body.

"Do you ever wonder if some things happen for a reason?" she asked.

"Meaning?" He arched one dark brow in question.

"Tim and me. His breaking it off." She shrugged and turned in her seat to face him. "If it hadn't been for that—"

"Being the nice girl that you are, you wouldn't be here tonight." He once again brushed the tips of his fingers across her cheek, then trailed them down to cup her jaw.

"Is that what you think I am? A nice girl?" she shot back, slightly perturbed, which was ridiculous. She was a nice gir,l unlike many of the women with whom Fisher had been seen around town.

"Don't get so riled, Mace. There's nothing wrong with being a nice girl."

The words shot out of her mouth before she could censor them. "And boys like you don't think about doing things with nice girls."

"Boys like me?" he asked with another pointed arch of his brow and a wry smile on his lips.

Macy fidgeted with her hands, plucking at the seat belt she still wore. "You know, love 'em and leave 'em types like you."

He chuckled and shook his head, but he never broke the contact of his hand against her chin. Instead, he inched his thumb up to brush softly across her lips.

"Let's get something straight, Mace. First of all, I'm not a boy, I'm a man. A man whose daddy would tan his hide for the thoughts he's having right now about the nice girl who happens to be sitting next to him."

The warmth on the pad of his thumb spread itself across her lips and with his words, shot through the rest of her body. "Thoughts? What kinds of thoughts?"

He chuckled again, only with something darker and dangerously sexy this time. "You always were the daring type."

"He who dares, wins," she reminded him.

The smile on his face broadened and he leaned toward her until the warmth of his breath replaced that of his thumb against her lips. "Then I guess I should dare," he said and brought his lips to hers.

The shock of his hard mouth against hers was quickly replaced by a sense of…rightness which surprised her considering that this was Jericho's brother. That up until a few weeks ago, she had thought she was about to embark on a life with another man.

Another man who had rejected her. Who had never made her feel the way Fisher now made her feel.

The tip of his tongue tasted her lips, gently asked for entrance at the seam of her mouth. She opened her lips and accepted the thrust of his tongue. Joined it with hers until they were both breathing heavily and had to break apart for air.

Fisher turned away from her and clenched his hands on his thighs, struggling for control. This was Macy, he reminded himself, rubbing his hands across the soft denim of his jeans. Jericho's best friend and Tim's intended, he recalled as he held back from reaching for her again.

Only she wasn't Tim's anymore, the voice inside his head challenged and then urged, *And now she can be yours.*

He faced her and seeing the desire in her eyes, he asked, "Are you sure about this?"

She nodded quickly and he didn't second guess her decision. Reaching into the backseat of the CJ, he grabbed a blanket he kept there and stepped out of the car. Swinging around the front, he met her by the passenger side door and slipped his hand into hers. Twined his fingers with hers as he led her a few feet away from the Jeep to a soft spot of grass on the overlook.

He released her only long enough to spread out the blanket and then he urged her down.

For long moments they lay side by side on their backs, staring up at the late May moon. Listening to the rustle of the light breeze along the taller grass and the profusion of wildflowers that perfumed the air.

Fisher rolled onto his side and ran the back of his index finger along the high straight ridge of her cheek. He had known her all his life and had thought she was the prettiest woman he had ever seen.

"You're beautiful."

Much like before, an embarrassed flush worked across her cheeks as she avoided his gaze. "I bet you say that to all the girls."

He laughed and shook his head. "Now why do you think I'm such a hound dog?"

"Because I've seen you around town with all those dangerous women," she answered and the blush along her cheeks deepened.

"Jealous?" he asked, but then immediately confessed, "Because every time I saw you with Tim, I was jealous."

A little jolt of excitement rattled her body before Macy turned onto her side and cradled his cheek. His five o'clock shadow tickled the palm of her hand. As she met his gaze, made a silvery green by the light of the moon, she detected no deception there, just honesty.

"Why didn't you—"

"You were Tim's girl and Jericho's best friend. I wasn't going to be responsible for breaking up the Three Musketeers," he said and shrugged.

"And now?" she asked, mimicking his earlier move by

bringing her thumb to trace the warm fullness of his lips which broadened into a sexy dimpled smile with her caress.

"He who dares, wins," he said and brought his lips to hers.

Chapter 5

"I've never seen a smile like that one before," Buck Yates said as he signaled for the waitress, who immediately came over.

"I bet I know what you'd like, Buck," she said as she picked up the empty plates from the table. "A slice of Miss Sue's famous cherry pie and some coffee."

"You know me too well, Lizzy. How about you, Fisher? Was it something sweet that put that smile on your face?" Buck teased.

Something sweet and hot, Fisher thought, recalling the taste of Macy's lips and the warmth of her body pressed to his as they had made love that long ago night.

Shifting in his seat to readjust his increasingly tight jeans, he looked up at the perky young waitress. "I'll take a slice of that pie with some vanilla ice cream, please."

He needed the chill to cool down his thoughts.

As Lizzy walked away with their empty plates and orders, Buck once again resumed the earlier conversation. "So what had you smiling like the cat that ate the cream? A woman, and I hope a decent one at that."

With some force, Fisher shook his head. "Come on, Pa. You know I can't offer a decent woman the kind of life she'd want."

"Nonsense," Buck began and for emphasis, jabbed a gnarly index finger in his direction. "Plenty of military men have wives and families."

He couldn't argue with his dad, although he understood how difficult it was for such men. Being away from their families for months on end. The fears and dangers that each new mission brought for those left behind.

"I don't think I could share my kind of life with a woman."

His father was about to speak when Lizzy returned with the pies and coffee, but as soon as she left them, his dad continued his plea. "You could if you took that teaching assignment at West Point."

For weeks since the offer had come, he had been debating between that and returning for another tour of duty in the Middle East. As captain of his squad, he had recently led his men safely through three tours. He couldn't imagine leaving them.

"I don't want to abandon my men. Besides, I like the military life. It's orderly. Disciplined."

"Lonely," Buck jumped in. "At the end of the day when you hang up that uniform with all those medals—"

"I'll know that I helped bring home alive as many men as I could. Their families will thank me for that," he replied and forked up a bit of the pie and ice cream. The taste was wooden in his mouth because a part of him recognized that on some level his father was right.

At the end of his career, no matter how successful he had been, his uniform would hang in a closet empty of any traces of a woman or family. Despite that, he couldn't picture himself as a father or husband. Solving a family's problems instead of those of his men. He wasn't sure how to handle such things.

While glancing down at his pie, he said, "I know you'd like grandkids to carry on the Yates name, Pa. Seems to me Jericho's the one you should look to for that."

"Hard to believe it's only been a couple of weeks since he met Olivia and married her," his father said.

"I admire that Jericho's willing to claim Olivia's baby as his own and if I know my brother—"

"He'll be wanting more with her. I can see how much he cares for Olivia and it really makes me happy. I always worried after what happened with your ma—"

"Don't blame yourself. You did what you could and we all know we were better off without her," he said and yet a part of him acknowledged that her leaving had ripped away a piece of each of them. That for him and Jericho, it had made them leery of loving a woman for fear of being abandoned again.

Like Macy had abandoned him, he thought, recalling how despite their one night of incredible passion she had walked down the aisle with Tim Ward just over a month later.

His dad must have picked up on his upset. "You shouldn't let your ma leaving eat away at your gut like that. Neither you or Jericho had anything to do with that."

"You're right, Pa," he said, wanting to foreclose any further discussion. Wanting to forget anything and everything relating to Macy Ward.

He wasn't meant for women like her or for a family kind

of life. The military was what had brought order and happiness to his life eighteen years earlier.

It was what would bring order and happiness to his life for the future.

For the first Friday night in too many months, Macy felt like she could actually just kick back and relax.

The change in T.J. in a little over a week was a welcome surprise. He had clearly bonded not only with Joe, but with Sara. She hoped that friendship would help the young girl come out of her shell and talk about her problems. The Hope-chest Ranch policy was not to press for details, but offer refuge. She knew, however, that she did the most good when the children were finally able to talk about their traumas.

Maybe Sara's friendship with T.J. and Joe would help her trust them enough to share and begin the road to healing.

Much as T.J. seemed to be healing.

In addition to the bonding, T.J. and Joe had completed each and every task that had been asked of them at the ranch and eagerly helped out with the other kids during their free time. Because of his exemplary behavior, when T.J. had asked if he could go to town with Joe and Sara, she had unequivocally said "Yes."

Which meant she had time to just unwind. Rare time in her normally hectic life.

She had filled her big claw-footed tub with steaming hot water and added some fragrant rose oils that Jewel had given her as an engagement gift. She had attempted to return them after she cancelled the wedding, but Jewel had insisted she keep them so she could treat herself.

Treat herself she would, she thought, tying the lush terry

cloth robe around herself and pouring a glass of wine to take with her to the bath. On the way, she snagged her brand-new romance novel from the nightstand in her bedroom.

Tim had always teased her about her romances until she had insisted he read them to her at night before bed.

He had never complained again after that, she thought with a smile as she set the book and wine on the painted wrought iron caddy. It perfectly matched the Victorian look of her bathroom, her one touch of fanciful in her otherwise modest and plain home.

She might have taken the Victorian theme further in the house, but realized it might have made it a little too girly for T.J. and had refrained from doing so. But in here and her bedroom—her private domain—she let herself give into her fantasies.

She slipped into the tub and the heat of the water immediately began to soak away some of the aches and tiredness. She loved working at the ranch, but with half a dozen children and the two teen boys, it was always a whirlwind of activities and quite physical.

The activities, however, were clearly making progress with some of the children. In the months she had been at the ranch, she had seen noticeable improvements not only in their academic skills, but their social ones. Kids who had once been loners were finally coming out of their shells.

It was what made her career so rewarding.

Grabbing the book off the caddy, she cracked it open and began to read, only she hadn't realized it was a book with a hero in the military. It normally didn't bother her, but her emotions were too unsettled with Fisher in town and so she set the book aside and picked up her wineglass.

As she took a sip, she recalled the sight of him and Jericho standing outside the church. Jericho had been so handsome in his tuxedo, but it had been Fisher standing there in his Army uniform, medals gleaming in the sun, that had caused her heart to skip a beat.

Even if she hadn't had any doubts about her marriage to Jericho before then, that reaction alone would have made her realize she was making a big mistake.

No matter how much she tried to forget it, her one and only night with Fisher had left an indelible memory. One she had driven deep inside her heart when she had made the decision to marry Tim Ward.

The right decision, she reminded herself as she took a small sip of the wine.

She and Tim had been destined to be together, their short breakup in high school notwithstanding. Tim was kind and patient and honorable. When she had told him she was pregnant just a short time before their wedding, he had been understanding and had even talked to her about telling Fisher.

She had considered it back then and in the many years since. But Jericho had been going on and on about how happy Fisher was in the Army and since their night together, Fisher never approached her again.

Talk had been that Fisher was the kind of man who couldn't commit and back then she felt he had loved and left her. When she had heard about his enlistment in the Army, it had made no sense to ruin his life by telling him about a child he probably wouldn't want.

But then she recalled the way he had looked at her on the steps of the church. Imagined she had seen desire in his gaze along with hurt. Not that she could hurt him unless he actually had feelings for her. Something which she didn't want to consider because it would complicate things.

Forcing her mind from such troubling thoughts, she placed her nearly untouched glass of wine on the caddy and sank farther into the bone-melting heat of the water. The fragrance of roses wafted around her, reminding her of the profusion of wild rose bushes tangled amongst the small stands of trees just outside the Esperanza town limits.

Reminding her of how the night had smelled while she made love with Fisher.

She shot upright in the bath, mumbling a curse, but then the phone rang and she mumbled yet another curse.

She had left the portable phone in her room.

As it continued to ring, demanding her attention, she climbed out of the bath, grabbed a towel and wrapped it around her. She raced to her bedroom to pick up before the answering machine kicked in.

Unfortunately, the answering machine engaged just as she reached it and heard across the speaker, "Mrs. Ward. This is Deputy Rawlings."

Her stomach dropped at the identity of the caller. At his next words, sadness and disappointment filled her soul. "I've got your son down at the station."

Chapter 6

T.J. walked out of the sheriff's office beside her, his body ramrod straight and stiff with tension. He hadn't offered up much of an explanation for the speeding which had led to his running into another car just on the outskirts of town.

Luckily the damage to both cars had been minor and no one had been injured. But because of their age and the speeding, the Deputy had decided to take the boys in and call her and Jewel.

She looked over her shoulder at her boss who walked beside Joe. The teen had a hangdog look on his face and clearly seemed to be sorry for what had happened.

Unlike T.J.

As they exited the police station, she spotted Fisher strolling out of Lone Star Square. Judging from the activity in the square, the movie had apparently just let out in the theater on the other side of the plaza. Some of the people headed to the cars parked all along the edges of the central space while Fisher and another couple waited to cross the street. He noticed them leaving the police station and condemnation flashed across his features.

It made her want to go over and wipe that critical look from his face, but she plowed forward. Speaking with T.J. about what had happened tonight needed to be her number one priority right now.

As they approached the parking lot, she inspected yet again the damage to T.J.'s car—a big ugly dent along the front bumper and part of the passenger side panel of the 1974 Pontiac GTO.

The GTO that his dad had bought as a rusty heap and had been restoring for years before his death. The GTO that T.J. had also been, as he called it, "pimping."

She paused before the car and stared at the damage before she looked up and met Jewel's concerned gaze, Joe's sheepish one and T.J.'s stony countenance.

"Luckily no one was hurt and the damage to both cars can be repaired. When we get home, we'll discuss how you're going to pay for those repairs and the speeding ticket," she said. Handing T.J. the keys to the GTO, she finished, "I'll follow you home."

Turning to Jewel, she noticed her friend's concern, but also Jewel's interest in Fisher as she glanced back across Main Street toward where he still stood on the edge of Lone Star Square, watching them.

She laid a hand on her friend's arm. "Can we talk about it in the morning? It's late and we should all be heading home."

Jewel nodded, faced Joe and said, "Let's go. You and I have a lot to discuss, as well."

As the two walked away, Macy waited for T.J. to get in his car and then she went to her own late model Cherokee, starting it up and then idling it until T.J. pulled out of the parking lot. T.J.'s pace as he exited was slow.

Slow enough that it gave her yet another chance to see Fisher, the disapproval still stamped on his face as he observed them.

"Tell me again what happened?" she pressed, sensing there was something off about T.J.'s version of the speeding and accident.

"It was just an accident, Ma," he said, slouching negligently in his chair in the kitchen.

"Tell me again why you were speeding?"

His big hands, like those of Fisher, man's hands on a boy's body, flopped up and down before settling on the surface of the table. "I didn't mean to only… There was another car. It was fast. It kept getting in our face—"

"In your face? As in threatening you? Why didn't you pull over? Use your cell phone to call the police?" Macy asked as she rested her hands on the table where T.J. sat, leaning closer.

A glimmer of fear flickered across his features, impossible to miss. "No, not like that. You know like…challenging us. Trying to prove their car was better."

She understood about men and cars. Entire industries had been built about proving who was faster, better, fancier. She also understood about men and cars and girls.

"Sara was with you?"

Another small flinch rippled across his body and T.J. couldn't meet her gaze as he answered, "We had already dropped Sara off at the ranch."

She hadn't had time at the police station to ask Jewel

whether Sara had been home at the ranch when the call had come from Deputy Rawlings. She certainly would ask tomorrow because she was sure T.J. wasn't telling the truth.

"So you were drag racing? And because you were speeding, you couldn't stop when that car pulled out?"

An indifferent shrug greeted her queries, infuriating her, but she knew she had to keep her cool. Nothing would be gained by anger.

"You've already earned enough at the ranch to pay me back for the coach's mailbox. What you earn from now on will pay for the repairs to both cars and the speeding ticket. Do you understand?"

He nodded without hesitation, but never raised his gaze to meet hers.

"You're also grounded for a month. You come home after your work at the ranch. On the weekends, I'll have chores for you to do around the house. Understood?"

A shrug greeted her punishment.

"I'm going to bed. It's late and we both need to go to work tomorrow," she said, but she didn't want the night to end angrily.

She kneeled before her son, cradled his jaw with her hand and gently urged his face upward. Reluctantly, he met her gaze. "*You* are the most important thing in the world to me, T.J. You can trust me with anything. Anything," she said in the hopes of having him tell her the truth about what had really happened that night.

A sheen of tears glimmered in her son's eyes. He gulped, holding back emotion before he said, "I know, Mom. I love you."

"I love you," she said, sat up and hugged him, believing that all would be right with him as long as they still had love to bind them together.

* * *

She was a coward, she thought, not looking forward to speaking with Jewel about what had happened the night before. Because of that, and knowing Jewel's sweet tooth, she was on her way to Miss Sue's again for yet more sticky buns.

Luck was on her side as there was an empty parking space directly in front of Miss Sue's. But then she noticed that Fisher was once again sitting at a booth in the restaurant.

Didn't he ever eat at home? she wondered with irritation as she took a deep breath to fortify herself, exited the car and entered the cafe.

As she passed by the booth where he sat finishing up a mound of Miss Sue's scrambled eggs with bacon, cheese and hash browns, he met her gaze. Rebuke filled his green eyes and within her, annoyance built. At the counter, she forced a smile to her face as she ordered the sticky buns.

The waitress smiled warmly and offered her sympathies. "Boys will be boys, Macy. Don't let it get to you."

She nodded, but said nothing else. She also didn't turn to brave the rest of the people in the restaurant, although she sensed their stares as she waited. In a town the size of Esperanza, Miss Sue's was Information Central and everyone already knew about what had happened the night before.

Her sticky bun order came up to the counter. She paid quickly, eager to make her exit, but as she headed out, she noticed Fisher's attention was on her once again and something inside of her snapped.

In one smooth move, she slipped into the booth across from him, surprising him with her action. Calmly she said, "You don't know me or my son, so don't presume to judge us so quickly."

Fisher slowly put down his mug of coffee. Lacing his fingers together, he leaned forward and in soft tones said, "And I don't intend to get to know you…again. Once Jericho returns and I'm sure all is right with him, I'll be off and out of your way."

Out of her way, but also in harm's way, it occurred to her guiltily. "There's no need to rush back to the Army on my account."

He tossed up his hands in emphasis. "The Army is all I know and need. Discipline. Order. Respect."

The condemnation lashed at her once again. Discipline, order and respect clearly being things that he seemed to find lacking with her and her son. Sadly, she acknowledged that she, too, wished she had more of those traits in her life. Because of that, she tempered her response.

"I'm glad the military makes you happy. I hope you stay safe when you go back."

She didn't wait for a reply. She swept her box of sticky buns from the booth's table and hurried out the door.

In her Cherokee, she handed the box to T.J., who placed it in his lap and said, "What was that?"

"Excuse me?" she said as she pulled away from the curb.

"You and Captain Yates. It looked…intense," her son said and she realized that T.J. had seen everything through the plate glass window of Miss Sue's.

Striving for a neutral tone, she said, "Nothing important. I just asked him if he'd heard from Jericho. I expect he and Olivia will be back soon from their honeymoon."

T.J. snorted loudly and shook his head. "You're not a very good liar, Mom."

Her hands tightened on the wheel, but she said nothing else

which prompted T.J. to add, "Maybe you should practice what you preach. Maybe you should talk about what's up with you and Captain Yates."

What was up with her and Fisher was more than she suspected T.J. could handle at the moment. He'd been walking a very fine line lately and she was concerned that telling him the truth about Fisher would push him over the edge. If he crossed that line, she worried that the next trip to the sheriff's station would result in more than community service or a speeding ticket.

Because of that, she kept her silence as they drove toward the ranch.

T.J. also kept silent, guarding his own secrets she suspected since she still believed he was not telling her the whole truth about what had happened the night before.

At the ranch, it was Jewel who opened the door when they pulled up in the driveway. There was no mistaking the look on her boss's face that said she intended to get to the bottom of things.

Taking a deep breath, Macy braced herself as she approached the door to the ranch.

Chapter 7

The sticky buns became an after lunch treat as she joined Jewel and Ana in the shade at a patio table near the pool.

Jewel had opted to say little to the boys other than to assign them a mess of chores that would keep them busy until she intended to speak to them. That kept Sara with the other children rather than with her two new best friends. During their absence, the young girl retreated more deeply into her shell.

Ana's face was flushed by the midday heat as she slowly lowered herself into a chair at the table.

Macy placed a tall glass of milk before her, but two iced coffees before her spot and Jewel's. Then she set a sticky bun at each place before sitting beside Ana. Jewel came by a few minutes later after reminding the children in the pool about the rules.

Jewel's face was also flushed from the heat and wisps of

her short wavy brown hair curled around her face. Dark circles marred the fragile skin beneath her cocoa brown eyes.

"I'm sorry about last night. I know you couldn't have slept well afterward," she said.

Jewel nodded, her lips in a grim smile. "I didn't. The call about the accident brought back painful memories."

"You were in an accident?" Ana asked, leaning forward and examining Jewel's features.

Jewel looked away and gripped the glass of iced coffee. With her thumb, she wiped away the condensation on its surface and said, "My fiancé and I were in an accident on the night he proposed to me. He was killed. Although I survived, I lost the baby I was carrying."

"*Perdoname.* I didn't mean to pry," Ana replied and dipped her gaze downward to her own pregnant belly. Almost protectively, she ran her hand across the rounded mound.

"It's all right, Ana. You couldn't have known," Jewel reassured her. "I was lucky to have Joe and Meredith Colton by my side, otherwise I think I might have lost my mind."

"The Coltons seem like wonderful people," Macy chimed in.

Jewel nodded emphatically. "They are which is why I'm so happy that with Daniels being exposed and jailed, Joe's presidential campaign has taken off. His nomination seems like a sure thing now."

"Definitely. I can't imagine how Olivia must have felt when she regained her memory and realized it was Daniels who was trying to kill her," she said and a sudden screech from the pool snagged her attention, but it was only two of the kids engaged in a splashing match.

Jewel had also whipped around at the noise, obviously on the edge. But when she realized it was nothing serious, she returned her attention to her friends. "Olivia's lucky to have found Jericho only… How are you dealing with canceling the wedding? Are you—"

"Convinced it was the right thing to do. It wouldn't have been right for me and Jericho to be together. Even though we love each other as friends, he deserves more from a marriage and Olivia will give him that," she admitted. She grabbed her glass of iced coffee, light with milk and sweet with sugar and took a big gulp. The cool helped chase away some of the heat of midday.

"Do you think what happened with T.J. has to do with you and Jericho? That he's angry about it?" Jewel pressed and then quickly tacked on, "Or is it about Fisher Yates?"

The heat that pressed down on her now came from Jewel's inquiry and her own guilt about both the Yates men. "T.J. was upset with my decision to marry Jericho. He said he already had a dad."

"And Fisher?" her friend repeated.

She recalled T.J.'s words about how maybe she should talk about it, but she still wasn't ready to reveal the secret she had kept for so long. "That's a complicated story. Plus, I don't think that it has anything to do with the boys and last night."

Taking another bracing sip of her drink, she met Jewel's too perceptive gaze and realized her friend knew it was time to back off about Fisher. That she would talk only when she was good and ready. "I'm sorry about last night, Jewel. I've talked to T.J., but I feel as if he's only telling me part of what really happened."

"I've spoken with Joe as well, only…" Jewel hesitated and then picked up the sticky bun, tore off a piece. "There's something not right about their story," she finally said.

She nodded. "I agree, although I can't put my finger on what's wrong."

"They say they dropped Sara off, but I don't remember if she was home when I got the call. Do you, Ana?" Jewel asked.

Ana rolled her eyes upward as she tried to remember, but then shook her head. "I do not know. She was home later. When you and Joe came home."

"So maybe Sara was with them when the accident happened?" Macy said and glanced over at the young teen, who deprived of her two friends thanks to their chores, was sitting alone on the edge of the pool.

"If she was with the boys, why didn't the police see her?"

"And if she was with them, why would they lie about that?" Jewel wondered aloud.

"She has many secrets, I think," Ana added and absent-mindedly rubbed her hand over her belly once again.

"If she doesn't want to be found, she wouldn't want to be involved with the police," she said, considering the police were bound to discover who she was.

Jewel took another piece of sticky bun and motioned with it as she said, "But that doesn't explain why they were speeding, does it?"

"T.J. said there was another car out on the road. One that was challenging them to prove their car was better."

"A drag race? Joe says they didn't realize they were speeding. That they didn't see the other car until it was too late to stop," Jewel said, but then she turned in her seat to glance at the pool and Sara in particular. "I don't know what to believe, but my gut says it involves Sara."

"Boys, cars and girls. A familiar mix, don't you think?" she suggested, remembering her own teen years and the many times that mix had caused problems in town.

"I hope that's all it is," Jewel said, finishing off the last of her sticky bun and pointing at Macy's, which remained untouched before her. "If you're a true friend, you'll eat that," she said.

"Why is that?" she asked.

"Because otherwise I'm going to devour it and you don't want me to get fat." A hesitant smile spread across Jewel's face and Macy realized she was trying to lighten the moment.

As another playful shout came from the pool, Macy grabbed her sticky bun and with a playful snort said, "Fat. Right. That's why Deputy Rawlings is always making goo goo eyes at you."

"Goo goo eyes?" Ana asked, slightly confused by the expression.

"That means he's interested in Jewel," she explained and Ana smiled broadly, nodded with some spirit. "Definitely. I've seen how he looks at you whenever he visits."

The blush that now blossomed across Jewel's face wasn't from the warmth of the day. "I've tried my best to discourage him. I'm just not ready for another relationship."

Neither was she, although she had been hard-pressed to forget about Fisher during the day thanks to their encounter that morning. "Me, either," she chimed in and finished off the last of her sticky bun.

Ana was done as well with her treat and as Macy glanced at her watch, she realized their lunch hour was almost over.

"Do you want me to work with the older children on their study skills while Ana and the younger kids do some craft work?"

Jewel nodded. "I know school is still some time away, but it would be good for them to be ready. It'll also give me some time to talk to the boys."

The three women split up to finish their work for the day.

As she aided Sara and the two other older children with their study exercises, her mind was half on what was happening with Jewel, T.J. and Joe in the library where Jewel often met with the children privately.

It came as no surprise to her later that Jewel had not been able to get any other information from them.

It also didn't surprise her to see T.J., Joe and Sara huddled together by the corral later that afternoon, clearly engaged in some kind of animated conversation. As soon as the rest of the group neared in order to take some rides on Papa's Poppy, the conversation stopped.

Their actions worried her, but with T.J. grounded for a month due to the speeding and accident, the trio was unlikely to get into trouble anytime soon.

Anytime soon hopefully being long after Jericho had returned from his honeymoon and Fisher had left town.

She knew which Yates brother she could count on to help her and it sure wasn't Fisher, she thought.

Relative quiet ruled over dinner that night.

T.J. didn't have much to say about either his discussion with Jewel or what he, Joe and Sara were talking about at the corral.

In truth, she didn't push too hard for the information. If she did, T.J. would become even more tight-lipped and remind her that she had something she needed to get off her chest as well.

Namely Fisher.

She hadn't been able to get him out of her mind all day and as she slipped into bed that night, he once again invaded her dreams as if to remind her that she had been about to marry the wrong Yates brother.

* * *

A small crowd gathered around the steps of the church. Jewel and Ana. An assortment of Coltons. Jericho and a pregnant Olivia, her rounded belly larger than it had been just a few weeks before. Buck Yates stood beside them, a broad smile on his face.

As she neared the group, she stumbled on something and looked down.

She had stepped on the hem of her dress—her wedding dress.

Confused, she paused and stared back up at the gathering of friends and family, only everyone had disappeared, leaving only two people on the steps—Fisher and T.J.

T.J. looked solemn and too grown-up in his dark blue suit—the suit she had bought for him to wear for her wedding to Fisher.

No, not Fisher.

Jericho, she reminded herself, but as she stared at her son and the man standing next to him, she realized just how much T.J. looked like Fisher, his father.

It was there in the squareness of their jaws and the lean build of their bodies. T.J.'s hair was darker than hers, closer to Fisher's nearly black hair much like T.J.'s eyes were a mix of Fisher's green and her brown.

The physical similarities between the two men was undeniable.

She wondered why she hadn't seen it before. Why others hadn't seen it over the years. Suddenly, she realized everyone had gone.

Everyone except Fisher who stood there, lethally handsome in his Army uniform. The dark blue of the fabric intensified the green of his eyes while the fit of the jacket lovingly caressed the broad width of his shoulders and leanness of his waist.

She remembered those shoulders, she thought as she took a step toward him and the distance between them vanished.

Suddenly in his arms, she braced her hands against those strong shoulders only they were bare now beneath the palms of her hands much as she was now bare, the wedding dress having evaporated into the ether of her dreams.

His skin was warm against hers as he pressed her to his lean muscled body. A man's hard body, she thought, recalling the strength of him on the one night they had shared so long ago. Remembering the emotions he had roused that had shaken her to the core of her being.

She met his gaze, her own likely confused as she said, "I've never forgotten our one night."

"Neither have I," he said and lowered his forehead to rest against hers. His tones soft, he said, "Why did you marry Tim?"

She had loved Tim with all her heart. Loved him in a way that was different from how she felt for Fisher and yet…

She had loved Fisher as well after that night. And because of that emotion, she hadn't been able to ruin his life when she had heard of his enlistment and excitement to be leaving Esperanza.

At her hesitation, he smiled sadly and said, "Still not talking? You didn't want to talk after that night either."

No, she hadn't wanted to talk. She had wanted to show him how she cared in other ways and so she did that now, rising up the inch or so to press her lips to his.

Fisher groaned like a man in pain at that first touch, but then he answered her kiss, meeting her lips again and again. Tenderly breaching the seam of her mouth with his tongue to taste her. To unite them until every move and breath became as one between them and just kissing wasn't enough.

He gently lowered her to the ground and the softness of well-worn fabric, smelling like her mama's detergent, dragged her eyes open.

It was night out and they were lying on a blanket on the overlook, much as they had done eighteen years before.

The sky above them was a deep endless black dotted with hundreds of stars and a bright summer moon that silvered all below as it had so many years earlier.

As she met his gaze, he cupped her cheek and ran his thumb across the moistness his kisses had left behind on her lips.

"I never forgot that night," he said once again.

"Neither did I," she admitted and gave herself over to his loving.

Chapter 8

Macy bolted upright in bed, breathing heavily. Her body thrummed with unfulfilled desire.

She yanked a shaky hand through her hair, troubled about the dream. Troubled because it had hit too close to home regarding her feelings for Fisher.

No matter how hard she had tried to forget him during the last eighteen years, he had always been with her. In her brain and in her heart.

Tim had known and understood. Had realized that her love for him was strong and true, but that Fisher had touched a part of her that could not be his.

She had admired Tim for that and for claiming T.J. as his. It had allowed both her and Fisher to get on with their lives in the ways that both of them had wanted.

And what about T.J.? the niggling voice of guilt

reminded. What about Fisher not knowing he has a child? it lashed out.

Shaking her head as if to clear out that nagging voice, she slipped from bed and walked down the hall to T.J.'s room.

The door was open and as she peered at her sleeping son, the guilt flailed at her repeatedly. T.J.'s features were stamped with Fisher's, she thought again. If Fisher had stayed in town, or visited more often than during his occasional breaks between tours of duty, she would not have been able to keep her secret for so long.

It made her wonder why the other Yates men hadn't seen the resemblance, or if they had, why they hadn't said anything?

With such thoughts dragging at her, she returned to bed only to find sleep was impossible.

Grabbing her romance novel from her nightstand, she read, knowing it would give her the happily-ever-after that she seemed unable to find in her own life.

Fisher sat before the fireplace in his father's home, staring at the pile of logs ready to be lit when fall came and brought with it the cooler weather.

He had been tempted to light the fire tonight to chase away the chill from the jog he had decided to take earlier that evening. That chill had registered in his thirty-seven-year-old bones, he told himself, but the annoying voice in his head chastised him. Warned him that what he was feeling was something else.

Guilt, maybe?

The hurt look on Macy's face that morning had chased him throughout the day, especially when despite that hurt, she had wished him to stay safe.

Safe. A funny word.

For the eighteen years he had been in the military, he had regularly kept himself and his men safe. Not that there hadn't been injuries or times when he had thought he'd never see home again. But through it all he'd kept his head and made sure each and every man had come home alive.

Coming home being so important except…

He didn't feel safe here.

Being near Macy reminded him of all that his home lacked. Hell, it wasn't even his home, but his dad's, he thought, glancing around at the place where he had grown up and to where he returned after each tour of duty was over.

He rose from the couch and to the breakfast bar that separated the living room from the kitchen. A single bottle of bourbon sat on the bar and he poured himself a finger's worth of the alcohol and returned to sit before the fireplace.

After a bracing sip of the bourbon, he winced and considered what it would be like to have his own home. Wondered what it would be like to have someone like Macy to come home to. Not that Macy would be interested because she hadn't been interested eighteen years earlier.

Not to mention there was T.J. to consider.

As he had seen Macy and her son leave the police station the night before, he had thought, much as his brother and father had said, that what the boy needed was a strong man in his life to help set things straight.

He chuckled as amusement set in because he had no doubt that the headstrong and independent Macy would tan his hide for such a chauvinistic thought. Not to mention that it was ridiculous to consider that he might be that man. He wasn't the kind to settle down into the whole home and hearth thing.

Of course, his brother Jericho hadn't seemed like that kind of man either. He took another sip of the liquor, leaned his head back onto the couch cushions and considered his surprise at how happy his brother had looked marrying Olivia.

That look had confirmed to him that maybe his brother was the marrying type, but also that his brother's plan to wed Macy had been totally wrong from the outset. For starters, you didn't marry out of obligation and you sure shouldn't plan on having a platonic relationship with your wife.

A bit of anger built inside of him at both his brother and Macy at that thought. Macy for relying on her friendship to even consider the marriage and at his brother for agreeing to it, especially since he couldn't imagine lying next to Macy in bed and having it stay platonic.

His gut tightened at the thought of his kid brother making love to the only woman who had ever managed to break her way into his heart.

Since his mom had left, he hadn't had much faith in women and had sealed shut his heart…until Macy had somehow slipped through a crack.

Of course, after her abandonment, he had walled off his heart from hurt once again, but the memory of her had stayed locked behind those barriers. And now with her involvement with Jericho, it had roused all those old memories.

Slugging back the last dregs of the bourbon, he rose from the sofa, went to the kitchen and washed the glass. Slipped it into the dish drain sitting there holding an odd assortment of china and cutlery.

A single man's mix of mismatched items, he thought.

A woman would have made sure all the cutlery and plates were the same and that something wouldn't be sitting in the dish drain for days. It would be washed, dried and put away in anticipation of the next family meal.

Like when Macy and T.J. sat down to their next meal, he thought, but couldn't picture himself there beside them. She and T.J. had too many issues and it would be best for him to lay low until Jericho came home.

Once his brother returned, he would be back on his way to the Army, although he hadn't decided whether it would be to another tour of duty in the Middle East or the instructor's position at West Point.

The former was familiar, but he understood the importance of the latter. Even acknowledged how it could be a new adventure for him. A different mission.

Teaching up and coming officers was as significant as being out in the field with his men. After all, the nation needed excellent military men to lead and his many years of experience could help those cadets become better officers and save lives.

But as Fisher walked to his bedroom—the same one in which he'd slept as a child—he wondered if he would grow bored with living in one place and having the same basic daily routine. For nearly eighteen years he'd avoided that and he couldn't imagine changing now unless…

It would take something really special for that kind of change, he realized as he stared at his cold and lonely single bed.

Fisher drove from his mind the picture of Macy waiting for him in that bed because he feared that maybe Macy could be that something really special to change his life.

As he undressed and slipped beneath the chilly sheets, he reminded himself that Macy needed more than a man in her life. Her son needed a father figure and once again it occurred to him that he wasn't the right man for that job.

But as he drifted off to sleep, visions of her seeped into his dreams, reminding him of just how much he was missing in life.

Chapter 9

Macy awoke tired and grumpy. Her night's sleep—or lack of—had been dominated by thoughts of both Fisher and T.J.

None of her deliberations had been good, she thought as she and T.J. drove to the ranch. But then blushed as she remembered her dreams of making love with Fisher.

Of course, any pleasure had been wiped out by her son's surly mood. That morning he had complained about how hard he and Joe had worked the day before until she had pointedly reminded him of how much it had cost for the speeding ticket and repairs.

His cold silence had replaced the complaints during the short ride to the ranch.

When they entered the house to share breakfast with the others, he became slightly more animated, taking a spot by Joe and Sara and striking up a conversation with them.

She watched their camaraderie and was more convinced than ever that Sara had something to do with the speeding and accident.

Her intuition was confirmed when she sat with Ana and Jewel and her boss leaned over and said, "Some of the kids mentioned that they thought Sara wasn't home when the Sheriff phoned about the accident."

"She was with the boys?" Ana asked softly, keeping her tone low so that the conversation would remain with them.

"I thought so. Boys, cars and girls just seem to create problems when you mix them together," Jewel replied and took a sip of her coffee.

Macy ran a finger along the rim of her cup as she considered Jewel's words, so similar to the thoughts she'd had herself. T.J. had been working hard on restoring the muscle car and quite proud of not only the vehicle's looks, but the power beneath the hood. And even though she had thought that, she also sensed there was more to it.

Meeting her boss's gaze, she said, "That may be true, but I would feel a lot more comfortable if we knew more about Sara. About why she's here and why all three of them would be lying about her being with them that night."

Jewel paused with her mug in midair, then slowly lowered it to the table. "You know the Hopechest policy. We offer refuge without qualification. Without making any demands that our residents reveal anything."

She was well aware of the Hopechest policy. They had taken in each of the children and even Ana without question.

She nodded and said nothing else of it as they finished breakfast, instead turning to a discussion of what Jewel wanted them to do that day with the children. As she had done the day before, her boss piled on a load of chores for the two boys and after breakfast, they all went their separate ways.

Despite the work assigned to them, she noticed that the two boys managed to spend their free time with Sara. At the midday lunch break and then again during the afternoon rides at the corral, T.J. and Joe were engaged with Sara, their heads bent together in discussion.

She had hoped to speak to T.J. about it on their way home, but he was exhausted and irritated once again, not to mention smelly from mucking out the mare's stall. Wrinkling her nose, she said, "Please shower while I make dinner."

He yanked one iPod earpiece out and angry music blared from it as he faced her. "What if I'm not hungry?"

Considering how hard he had been working, she couldn't imagine him not needing to refuel his growing body, but she wouldn't get into a war of words with him.

"Then I'll eat alone."

His mouth flopped up and down like that of one of the sunfish they used to pull out of the small pond behind the high school, but he said nothing else.

He did shower as she had asked and met her at the dinner table where he silently shoveled in the burger and fries she had made. He even deigned to sit with her for a slice of a home-baked apple pie, à la mode of course.

But after that, he excused himself, saying that he was tired and planned on going to bed early.

She didn't argue with him, recognizing that the space might help him get over his pique.

After he left the kitchen, she turned on the small television tucked into a corner cabinet and took her time cleaning up. Washing the pans and dishes by hand, slowly and methodically since she found the simple work relieved her mind of thinking of more complex things.

It was barely eight when she finished, went up the stairs and passed by the door of T.J.'s room. His door was ajar and she peered within. As her son had said, he was in bed and asleep.

Relieved at the momentary peace that his slumber brought, she retired to her room where she changed into her pajamas, slipped beneath the covers and grabbed her book, intending to finish it.

A few hours passed and she was near the end of the novel when she thought she heard a noise.

T.J.? she wondered and eased from her bed to check on him.

He was still tucked safely in bed and she returned to her own, finished off the last few pages, smiling at the ending.

It was with those happy thoughts that she turned off her light and lay down to sleep.

She drifted off in that blissful state, her mind turning to thoughts of happier times. With T.J. and her husband Tim before the cancer had robbed him of life. With Fisher on the one night that had forever changed her destiny.

Her memories muddled together in dreams, becoming ones of her, Fisher and T.J. together until the phone rang beside her, rudely pulling her from her dreams.

Barely awake, she grabbed the phone, raking her sleep-tousled hair away from her face as she realized that it was barely six in the morning.

No good news at such an hour.

"Macy?"

It was Jewel on the line and she came instantly awake.

"What's wrong, Jewel?"

"Sara's missing."

* * *

The police combed every inch of the ranch house looking for clues as to Sara's disappearance.

They questioned everyone on the ranch, including T.J. and Joe who unfortunately, had little to offer as to Sara's possible whereabouts or why she would run away from the ranch.

When the police had left, Jewel and she had questioned the two teens once again, but they had little information to offer. Sadly, she knew as did Jewel that the two boys were being evasive. Despite that, hope remained within her that T.J. was not involved. He had eaten dinner with her and gone to bed early. She had seen him in his bed last night not just once, but twice.

Twice because she had heard something, she thought.

As she watched T.J. and Joe during the afternoon break, she wondered what it was that she had heard. If there had been more to it that she hadn't realized.

Her worst fears were confirmed when Deputy Rawlings returned to the ranch shortly after four.

As he walked toward the corral where they were offering the children rides on Papa's Poppy, she understood it was no social visit and so did the children. They stopped what they were doing and huddled together by the split rail fence. In the corral, T.J. and Joe helped the one child down from the horse and then also stood there, clearly anxious.

Deputy Rawlings dipped his head as she and Jewel approached him and removed his hat. "Miss Jewel. Miss Macy."

"Do you have news, Adam?" she asked, striving for a friendly tone.

He looked down for a moment, seemingly ashamed before he lifted his face and looked at her directly. "We started asking some of the Hopechest's neighbors if they had seen anything."

He continued with his report, his tone hesitant. "About a half mile up the road, one of the neighbors heard a car door slam. It was late so she looked out the window to see who it was."

A cold chill filled her as he motioned to T.J. and Joe with his hat. "She saw a young girl getting into a car with a dented front fender. From her description of the girl it seemed like it could be Sara. When we showed her pictures of the boys, she picked T.J."

Jewel laid a hand on her shoulder and stepped closer in a show of support. "You don't think T.J. had anything to do with—"

"I'm afraid I'll have to take him into custody. Ask him a few questions and find out why one of your neighbors thinks that she saw him last night with Sara."

"Can't you just question him here?" she said and he shook his head.

"There's procedures to follow and—"

"Jericho wouldn't do this," she insisted.

A strong flush of color filled his cheeks and a muscle ticked along his jaw. "Sheriff Yates isn't here and he left me in charge. There's procedures I have to follow, Mrs. Ward."

Without waiting for her, he once again motioned to the boys and called out, "T.J. I need you to come with me, son."

Her stomach clenched as she waited, hoping that he would be obedient. That he wouldn't give the deputy anything else to use as ammunition against him.

Blessedly, he did just what Deputy Rawlings asked.

With a worried look that he shot at Joe, who clapped him on the back, T.J. turned the reins of the horse over to his friend and walked to the edge of the corral. Easing beneath one of the rails of the fence, he approached the officer and said, "I haven't done anything wrong."

But she realized that with those words, he also wasn't denying any involvement with Sara's disappearance.

"Thank you for cooperating, son."

"I'm not your son," T.J. said with gritted teeth.

Deputy Rawlings nodded, laid a hand on T.J.'s shoulder and walked him around the side of the house toward the driveway.

Macy glanced at Jewel out of the corner of her eye and said, "I need to follow them into town. Find out what Adam plans to do."

Jewel squeezed her shoulder reassuringly. "I'll go with—"

"No, you stay here. The kids will need you to talk about this and so will Joe," she immediately said, appreciating Jewel's offer. The children were clearly upset by what was happening which was understandable. Some of them may have had run-ins with the law or been disappointed with the systems put in place to protect them. They would need Jewel's reassurance about what was happening.

"I'll call you as soon as I know anything more," she added and without waiting, rushed after T.J. and the police officer.

As she caught up to them, Deputy Rawlings eased T.J. into the backseat of the cruiser, then he took the wheel.

Macy quickly got settled in her own car and followed a safe distance behind the cruiser. She followed it into the parking lot for the police station and got out of her car, but as she headed toward the door, Deputy Rawlings stopped and faced her.

"It might be best for you to go get a coffee while T.J. and I talk."

She thought about her son being interrogated by the officer. She didn't like the thought of it, but she also didn't want to anger the deputy. Taking a deep breath, she looked away and realized Fisher and his dad were across the street in front of Miss Sue's.

They watched intently, clearly aware that something was up. A condemning look immediately came to Fisher's face, but Buck's features were more supportive. A second later, the older man took a step toward them and after some initial hesitation, Fisher followed his dad.

Shaking her head, she returned her attention to the police officer and decided to voice her concerns. "I'm not sure it's such a good idea that T.J. speak to you alone."

Chapter 10

Deputy Rawlings' lips tightened into an ascetic line as he ripped off his hat, frustration and anger evident in every brusque movement. "Why do you want to make this difficult? I'm not taking T.J. into custody. I just want to ask him a few simple questions."

"Is there a problem, Macy?" Buck Yates asked as he stood beside her.

She glanced up at Buck, avoiding Fisher when he took a spot just to the right of his dad. "One of the teens has gone missing from the ranch and Deputy Rawlings wants to speak to T.J. about it."

Buck nodded and pushed his hat back, adopting a stance that was more casual than that of the officer. "I'm sure the deputy understands how troubling this is for both you and T.J. That he needs to handle this carefully. Right, Deputy?"

A muscle clenched along the officer's jaw, but he nodded slowly. "Certainly, Buck. I know how to deal with this."

"Good. How about you join Fisher and me for dinner, Macy? Give the deputy and T.J. some time just to chat."

Protest gathered within her, ready to erupt, but Buck slipped his arm around her shoulders and hugged her so she kept her tongue. When the deputy took her son away, she forced a weak smile at the older man.

"Thank you for the invite, Buck, but I'm not sure I could eat a thing right now."

"I won't take no for an answer," he said and applied gentle pressure to turn her around. He guided her in the direction of Miss Sue's, Fisher quietly following behind them.

Inside the restaurant they were quickly seated at a booth. Buck took the one bench and sat in the middle, giving her no option but to slide along the vinyl of the other booth bench until Fisher could sit beside her.

The waitress came over and handed them menus.

She had intended not to take one, lacking any appetite, but Buck's half-lidded look brooked no disagreement.

After a short perusal of the menu, she ordered a soup and a half of a fresh roasted turkey sandwich, earning a satisfied nod from the older man.

Neither Fisher nor he seemed to have any problem with their appetites since they ordered the blue plate specials, which included not only the soup of the day, but chicken-fried steak with white gravy, squash and cheese casserole, green beans and a choice of dessert.

After taking their orders, the waitress brought over tall glasses of iced tea, a dish of summer slaw and a basket heaped with warm corn bread and sweet cream butter.

The enticing smell of the corn bread made her stomach growl. She placed a hand above her belly, but Fisher picked up the basket and offered it to her. "Would you like some?"

She smiled and thanked him. After buttering the corn bread, she took a bite and sighed as the dulcet flavors of the corn and butter filled her mouth.

"This is good," she said, but then quickly added, "but not as good as that jalapeño corn bread you used to make for us when we were kids, Buck."

"That was really tasty with your five alarm chili, Pa," Fisher said, but then stuffed a big piece of buttered corn bread in his mouth.

Buck laughed and forked some of the summer slaw onto his bread dish. "The four of you could sure eat," he said with a chuckle.

Fisher nodded, recalling the many nights that Macy and Tim had joined his family for a meal. "Those were good times."

"Yes, they were," Macy said. A sad sigh followed, however.

"It'll be okay, darlin'. Don't worry about T.J.," Buck offered, but Macy dipped her head down until her chin was nearly burrowing a hole in her chest.

Upset by her dismay, Fisher reached beneath the table and laid his hand over hers. "It will be okay," he also reassured.

With a long inhale and a sniffle, Macy nodded. "Yes, it will be okay. I'll make it okay."

He had no doubt of her sincerity, but worried about whether she could make good on it. T.J. seemed to be bringing her nothing but trouble and possibly the boy needed a man's influence in his life. A man who would be there for him.

When the waitress brought their meals, he withdrew his

hand from hers and they all dug into their dinners, hunger bringing a long stretch of quiet to the table.

Macy finished her meal quickly, but he and his dad had quite a lot to eat. While he ate, he offered Macy a small piece of his steak and she tried it, murmured her approval. Slowly he and his father finished their meals and by the time dessert came, they convinced Macy to get some peach cobbler.

When they were finally finished, Macy offered to pay to thank them for their company, but his father insisted it was their treat and that they should do it more often.

"I'd like that, Buck," she said.

Then something inside of him—something Fisher didn't understand and didn't want to acknowledge—had him saying, "I'll go with you to the sheriff's office."

Her mouth opened as she prepared to refuse him, but then she abruptly snapped it shut. "I'd appreciate that," she said instead.

In front of the restaurant she hugged Buck and thanked him again before the two of them silently walked side by side to the sheriff's office.

Inside the police station, one of the other deputies manned the front desk. As he realized who had entered, he sheepishly glanced down at the papers on his desk, but Fisher wasn't about to be dissuaded.

"You know me better than that, Bill. Where's Deputy Rawlings?"

Bill shuffled the papers into order before addressing them. "Deputy Rawlings is still with the suspect."

"The suspect?" Macy nearly croaked. "When did he become a suspect?"

Before the other man could answer, Deputy Rawlings stepped from one of the back rooms. He grimaced when he noticed them standing by the front desk, but swaggered over, his shoulders thrown back. Hands cocked on his hips.

"Macy. Fisher," he said with a curt nod.

"Evening, Adam. I came to see when I could take T.J. home," she said, bracing her hands along the edge of the front desk.

Adam looped his thumbs through his belt loops and swayed side to side on his feet for a moment. "I'm sorry, but I've decided to keep T.J. overnight while we continue our investigations."

The other deputy rose from the desk, wisely making himself absent for the discussion that would follow.

"Excuse me," Macy said, her voice rising with each syllable, prompting Fisher to reach over and place his hand on her shoulder to try to calm her.

"We need to be sure there's no foul play," the deputy said and beneath his hand, the tension escalated in Macy's body.

"Come on now, Adam. There's no reason—"

"A young girl is missing. We have a witness who claims to have seen your son with her on the night she disappeared."

Macy inched up on her toes, ready to erupt, but he applied gentle pressure to keep her in control. Macy didn't normally have a temper, but when it involved her family, he didn't doubt that she would tenaciously defend her son.

"You know Jericho wouldn't do this," she urged and he had no doubt about that. Jericho would not be handling this situation as badly as Deputy Rawlings, but he could see that the man was not responding well to being challenged.

He opted for a different approach, hoping that he could calm the deputy until his brother returned in a day or two. "No one doubts your concerns, Deputy, but wouldn't it be possible to release T.J. into his mother's custody? I'm sure she can—"

"Handle him?" The deputy chuckled harshly and shook his

head. "Mrs. Ward hasn't done a very good job of controlling T.J. so far. Until we know that there's been no foul play, I'm going to hold him overnight. Maybe even longer."

Macy's body trembled beneath his hand, but she somehow kept her cool. "Please don't do this, Adam. I promise to bring T.J. back in the morning—"

"I don't think so," the deputy said and Fisher was about to jump in and offer his assurances, but bit the words back. He knew little about T.J. other than that both his brother and dad believed he was good, but confused. Worse yet, he knew nothing about how to deal with the boy and even if he did...

He would be gone in another couple of weeks.

Becoming involved in their lives not only made little sense, it would be cruel since he could promise nothing of permanence. But he needed to help Macy now.

"Let's go, Macy. We'll come back in the morning."

Macy shot a worried look at him and while glancing her way, he said, "The deputy knows what he needs to do. He'll take good care of T.J."

He faced the other man and left no doubt about his words. "You will take good care, right?"

Adam stalked the remaining distance to the front desk and leaned over the barrier toward him. "That's not a threat, is it?"

"Just a reminder," he said, dipped his head and smiled, making sure that the other man understood it was a promise of what might happen if T.J. wasn't cared for. Then he urged Macy back from the desk. "We'll see you bright and early, Adam. Have a nice night."

Slipping his arm completely around Macy's shoulders, he steered her out the door of the station and onto the steps, where she shrugged off his touch and wrapped her arms around herself.

"Jericho wouldn't do this. He would know that T.J. could never hurt that girl," she said.

"But is T.J. involved in her disappearance?" Fisher asked, but as Macy's face paled at his words, he cursed beneath his breath.

"I'm sorry," he said and took her into his arms.

She was tense at first, but then she slowly relaxed and embraced him. Laying the side of her face on his chest, she said, "Thank you. I was a little tired of going it alone."

He suspected that up until her cockamamie idea to marry Jericho, she had been going it alone ever since Tim's death nearly six years earlier.

As she raised her face and her brown eyes, shimmering with unshed tears met his, he wanted to tell her that she didn't need to go it alone anymore. That he would be there for her, but he couldn't. But he also couldn't resist the pull of that emotional gaze or the desire to soothe the spot on her lower lip that she was worrying with her teeth.

He bent his head as she rose up on tiptoe. Licked the abused spot on her lower lip before covering her mouth with his.

She pressed into him, cupping the back of his head with her hand and he dug his fingers into the silky lushness of her shoulder-length brown hair.

When she opened her mouth to his, he pressed on, sliding his tongue along the perfect edge of her teeth before dancing it against her tongue. He wrapped his one arm beneath her buttocks and brought her full against him and with that dangerous full body contact, sanity returned.

They pulled apart abruptly, both of them breathing hard and obviously shocked by the intensity of the emotion they had unleashed with one simple embrace.

"Macy, I'm—"

She raised her hands to stop him. "Please don't say you're sorry because I'm not. There's no need for apologies or regrets. All I want to say is thank you for being here for me."

He dragged a hand through the short-cropped strands of his hair and held back on telling her what he wanted—that he wanted her again. Wanted her next to him. Wanted her lips beneath his, opening to his invasion. Inviting him to take it further.

Instead, he took a deep breath and stuffed the tips of his fingers into the pockets of his snug jeans to keep from reaching for her again.

"You're welcome. I'll see you home."

She wrapped her arms around herself once more and shook her head roughly, sending her hair into movement with the action. "You don't need to do that—"

"I do. Until Jericho is home, I want to make sure you're okay."

She looked away then, but he couldn't fail to see the tear as it slipped down her face and she said, "I understand, Fisher. I won't mistake what just happened for anything else."

He longed to take her into his arms and shake her until she did understand, only he wasn't sure he knew why they were both standing there, trembling with desire. Hungry for another taste, but fighting it.

Because of that confusion, he said, "How about I just watch you walk to your car. If you need me in the morning—"

"I'll call," she said, but as she walked away, he understood that she wouldn't.

Chapter 11

Macy spent the night tossing and turning, worried not only about T.J., but about the kiss that shouldn't have happened. The kiss that had rocked her world, reminding her how Fisher continued to move her. That she was still immensely attracted to him.

But she wouldn't call him.

Her life was complicated enough without adding Fisher to the mix. But the little voice in her head kept buzzing in warning. Guilting her that Fisher should know T.J. was his son. Urging her to explore the emotions he roused.

She ignored that stubborn buzz and focused on what she had to do that morning.

Rising early, she made herself some coffee, but was too nervous to eat. After showering, she phoned Jewel and asked for the day off so she could head to the sheriff's office to deal with Deputy Rawlings and T.J.

Sympathetic and supportive, her boss offered to meet her there to help in whatever way she could, but Macy couldn't accept it. She needed to deal with her problems on her own, much as she had since Tim's death.

With that focus, she rushed to the sheriff's office in the hopes of securing T.J.'s release.

Bill was at the front desk again, looking as uncomfortable as he had the night before.

"Good morning, Macy," he said, rose and held up his coffee mug. "Can I get you a cup?"

"Will I be here long enough to need one?" she said with a forced smile.

"I hope not. Let me go get Deputy Rawlings." He walked away, cup in hand, and to one of the offices, where he knocked.

Someone ripped the door open and Bill jumped back.

Deputy Rawlings stepped out from the office. As he realized she was there, he tempered his attitude. He walked to the front desk and swung open the waist-high door in invitation.

"Why don't you join me in my office?" he said and held his hand out.

"Can I take T.J. home now?" she asked as she passed by him and walked toward his office.

"Let's discuss this in private," the deputy replied, his tone obviously annoyed.

She wondered why they needed privacy much like she was still questioning why it had been necessary to keep T.J. overnight. She guarded her tongue since it would not accomplish anything if she lost her cool.

In his office, she sat before his desk and kept quiet, waiting for him to set the tone of the discussion.

He leaned back in his chair and laced his fingers together

on his flat stomach. "I spoke to T.J. at length yesterday. He clearly knows more about Sara's disappearance than he's saying, Macy."

"Sara and he are friends, Adam. He wouldn't do anything to hurt her. If anything, he's probably trying to protect her."

"I don't doubt that. In fact, our investigations so far seem to indicate that there isn't any foul play." He shot forward in the chair, opened a file on his desk and quickly moved some papers around.

"At least a week ago, Sara may have been at a local honky tonk about ten miles from here—the Amarillo Rose. One of the bartenders remembers a young girl being there and getting into a truck with someone."

She shifted to the edge of her seat and said, "So it's possible she's gone off with the same person again?"

The deputy shook his head and chuckled harshly. "Could be, although I'd put my money on T.J. But there's nothing so far that says she didn't go willingly or that any harm has come to her. Because of that, I'm going to let T.J. go—"

"Thank you," she said and popped up out of her chair, eager to go get her son.

Deputy Rawlings picked up his hands and waved for her to sit back down. "Easy now, Macy. Don't be in a rush because even though I'm letting T.J. go for now, you need to keep an eye on him. Make sure that if he knows anything about Sara, he lets us know before something bad does happen."

As angry as she was at the deputy's heavy-handed tactics, she couldn't argue with what he was asking. "If I find out anything, you'll be the first to know."

"Good to hear. I'll go get T.J. Why don't you meet us out front?"

Dismissed, she rose and headed to where Bill sat at the desk, sipping his coffee. As she approached, he said, "So you're taking T.J.?"

"I am," she answered, grasping the handles of her purse before her.

The sound of metal grating against metal snagged her attention—the jail cell opening. A second later, her son popped out, looking tired and haggard. As he saw her waiting for him, however, a smile quickly flashed across his face before he controlled it. He walked toward her slowly, hesitant, but when he stood before her, she reached out and hugged him hard. His body relaxed and he returned the embrace.

"We're going home, T.J."

She stepped away, but kept one arm around his shoulders, reluctant to lose contact with her son.

He didn't battle her but kept close to her side as they walked out the door of the sheriff's station.

She shot her son a sidelong glance. Relief washed over her as he met her gaze and another timid smile blossomed on his face. Everything would be okay, she thought until she nearly walked into the man standing before them on the steps of the sheriff's station.

Fisher.

In wickedly tight blue jeans, a chambray shirt that hugged his lean chest and abs, and a black Stetson that made his green eyes pop brightly in the morning sun.

"Fisher," she said out loud, a little more breathlessly than she liked.

"What are you doing here?" T.J. said and came to stand before her, placing himself between her and Fisher in an obviously protective gesture.

She placed her hand on T.J.'s shoulder and urged him back to her side. "Fisher and his dad were nice enough to keep me company last night. We had dinner together at Miss Sue's while I waited to see if Deputy Rawlings would let you go home."

T.J.'s mouth quirked with displeasure before he mustered some politeness. "Thank you for taking care of my mom."

Fisher seemed taken aback by the unexpected gratitude, but quickly recovered. "My pleasure. I'm sure Jericho would have done the same if he were here."

Disappointment stung her ego followed by confusion at the disappointment. Snagging her keys from her purse, she handed them to T.J. and pointed to where her car was parked across the street.

"Fisher and I need a moment alone. Why don't you go wait by the car for me?"

T.J. nodded, but before he left, he chanced an assessing look at Fisher. Then he did as she had asked, walking down the steps of the sheriff's office and to the corner, where he waited for the light to change so he could cross.

Macy shifted her attention to Fisher. "What are you doing here?"

He shrugged, looked away and dragged off his hat, bouncing it back and forth in his hands. With his head hanging down, he said, "I wish I knew."

She wished she knew as well and was about to press him for another answer when the squeal of tires rent the air. Loud, harsh and angry.

Both she and Fisher whirled toward the sound in time to see a large black sedan lurch wildly toward T.J. as he was crossing the street. Smoke came off one of the tires as the car burned rubber with the driver's haste to pick up speed.

"T.J.," they both shouted in unison and sprinted toward him, intent on getting him out of the path of the oncoming car.

He had noticed the car as well, but for a moment he stood there, stunned as the vehicle accelerated toward him. Then in a blur, he raced for the side of the street, trying to avoid the sedan which made no attempt to avert hitting him. If anything, it picked up speed, veering toward where T.J. had run to escape.

At the last minute, her son sidestepped the car like a matador might a bull as the vehicle traveled past him, but it still struck him a glancing blow. He flew into the air and against one of the parked cars as the sedan hurtled down the road, its engine racing as it continued to pick up speed.

She and Fisher rushed to where T.J. lay sprawled in the street as did a number of other pedestrians who had witnessed the accident.

When they reached his side, T.J. was attempting to rise, but Fisher laid a gentle hand on his shoulder. "Stay down, son. You could have some broken bones."

T.J. didn't argue, clearly dazed. A large gash on his temple bled profusely and he had a number of other cuts and scrapes along his face and arms.

Her hands shook as she passed a hand along T.J.'s forehead. As she glanced up the block, she noticed the flashing lights of an approaching ambulance and it filled her with relief. "Take it easy. Help will be here soon."

T.J. nodded, but even that small action seemed to hurt. He closed his eyes and lay there quietly, his face pale, frightening her.

Fisher sensed her fear. He placed his hand at the nape of her neck to steady her and said, "Don't worry. He'll be fine."

She sucked in a shaky scared breath and it rocked him all

the way to his gut. He wanted to make her feel better, but he was failing miserably.

Luckily, the EMTs arrived a second later and urged them both to move away.

He kept his contact with her as she stood there, arms wrapped around her waist. Her body tight with anxiety as they waited for some kind of word from the paramedics.

The young man finally looked up at them over his shoulder. "Nothing serious from what I can see, but we'll take him to the hospital just to confirm that."

The EMT quickly had the rest of his crew getting T.J. ready for transport. At the periphery of his vision, he noticed that Deputy Rawlings and one other officer were talking to the crowd, getting witness statements, he assumed. He wondered if anyone had gotten the license plate number. He had been too rattled to think about it, which shocked him. He was a man of action and trained to stay in control in stressful situations.

That he had lost that control scared him more than he wanted to admit.

But despite that, he knew he had to be in charge now for Macy and her son.

As the paramedics finished getting T.J. on a gurney, he took command. "Can his mother go with him in the ambulance?"

The EMT nodded. "Yes, but there's only room for your wife, sir."

"I'll follow in the car, Macy," he said and she nodded, murmured a strained, "Thanks."

He stood by her until T.J. was loaded into the ambulance and then he helped her climb up into the back. One of the paramedics came by and closed the door of the ambulance, leaving him standing there awkwardly until the sirens kicked in, reminding him he had something to do.

He had to follow them to the hospital and be there for them.

He had to do that, but not because it was what Jericho would have done.

He had to do it because his heart told him it was the right thing to do.

Chapter 12

Macy held T.J.'s hand as the paramedic placed a temporary bandage on the cut along his temple. When he was done, he strapped T.J.'s head in place to keep it from moving during the drive.

Apparently comfortable that T.J. didn't have any major injuries, the paramedic slipped into the seat beside the driver and left them alone in the back of the ambulance.

"How are you feeling?" she asked.

"A little sore, but I'll be okay," he said and squeezed her hand.

Macy thought back to the moment when she had heard the squeal of the tires and the car hurtled forward toward T.J. The fear of that moment fled, replaced by questions.

"I didn't recognize the car, did you?" Esperanza was a small town and almost everyone knew what kind of car everyone else drove.

"I didn't," her son replied, but something in his voice didn't ring true.

"Do you recollect anything about the car? The make or model? Did you see the face of the driver?"

"No, Ma. I was too busy trying not to get run over," he answered, the tone of his voice part annoyed but a greater part evasive.

"Are you sure—"

"I'm sure I was trying to get out of the way," he shot back and withdrew his hand from hers, bringing it to rest on his flat belly.

She focused on that hand, skinned along the knuckles. Drops of blood had congealed at various spots and there were more abrasions on his other hand. As she swept her gaze up and down his body, she noticed the angry road rash along one arm, from his elbow down to mid-forearm.

In her brain came the recollection of the low thud as the car caught him along one hip and he went flying, smacking into another car before falling to roll along the ground from the impact of the blow. A chill took hold in her center and she tried picturing the sedan again. Closed her eyes and attempted to remember what she could about the car, but it had all happened too fast.

The image of the vehicle was just a black blur as it sped toward T.J.

She was sure of that. The car had intended to hit her son. She had no uncertainty about that which made her wonder why T.J. might be lying to protect someone who had tried to hurt him.

The ride to the nearby hospital was blessedly short and the emergency room relatively empty. It didn't take long for them to examine T.J. and determine that there were no broken bones or a concussion. Although he would be bruised in a number of spots, especially along the one leg where the car had clipped him, there was no reason for the doctors to admit him.

Macy sighed with relief as the doctor made that pronouncement and finished sealing the cut on T.J.'s head with some butterfly bandages before taping a gauze pad over the wound. Another large bandage covered the road rash that they had cleaned while yet more gauze was wrapped around the knuckles on both hands.

As T.J. noticed her examining his various injuries, he barked out a short laugh and said, "You should see the other guy."

She chuckled and embraced him as he sat on the edge of the bed. "I was so scared."

"I'm okay, Mom. Really."

When she stepped away, he eased from the bed to stand upright, wincing as he put pressure on the leg which had taken the brunt of the hit from the car. It took him a moment to fully straighten and his first step was a little gimpy until he seemed to stretch out a kink.

With her arm around his shoulders, they walked out into the emergency room waiting area.

Fisher sat there, bouncing his black hat in his hand. He shot up out of the chair when he saw them and approached. Grimacing as he noted the bandages on T.J., he forced a smile and said, "I hope the other guy looks worse."

To her surprise, T.J. grinned and nodded. "He does."

Fisher motioned to the exit. "I brought your car from town. I'll go get it and drive you home."

The accident had rattled her nerves and having Fisher drive them would be a welcome respite. Concern remained about why someone would try to hurt T.J. and why he would cover up the fact that he might know who was responsible. As she and T.J. followed Fisher out of the hospital, she realized that she needed to tell someone about what was up with T.J. Needed to confide in someone who could help her deal with the problem.

As she watched Fisher pull up to the curb and saw how carefully he handled getting a sore T.J. into the car, she realized that Fisher might just be the someone she needed.

At seventeen, T.J. wouldn't have normally needed her to get him settled in bed, but he was aching enough now to require her assistance. She helped him take off his jeans. Managed to control her reaction at the sight of the large bruise which had already formed along his hip and thigh in addition to the smaller purpling marks along his other leg and ribs.

"Get some rest," she urged as she tucked him beneath the covers.

He nodded and closed his eyes, obviously drained by the events of the day.

She walked into the hall and left his door open, wanting to be able to hear him if he needed anything. She began to walk down the stairs, but paused a few steps down, peering through the open doorway of his room just to check on him again.

He seemed to be asleep already.

She breathed a sigh of relief that his injuries had been so minimal and finished her walk down the stairs. At the landing, she proceeded a few more steps and then turned into the kitchen.

Fisher stood at the counter by the coffee machine, pouring water into it. He slipped in a filter and then the coffee. Hit the button to get it going.

His actions were so domestic that it seemed incongruous

until she remembered how often she had seen Jericho do the same thing both in her home and his. They had grown up in a household full of men and such routine activities would likely be almost second nature to them.

She allowed herself the pleasure of watching him finish up the task, his movements sure and totally comfortable. Totally masculine. When he finished, he turned and realized she was standing there.

Fisher leaned back against the counter while he examined Macy. She appeared in control and he admired her strength in the midst of yet another crisis. Her strength being one of the things that had always attracted him.

"How's he doing?"

"Tired and sore. He's already fast asleep," she said and went to the small island in the middle of the kitchen, bent and retrieved two mugs and a sugar bowl which she placed on top of the island counter.

"And you?" he asked, raising one brow to emphasize the question.

She braced her hands on the edge of the counter, suddenly uneasy it seemed to him. She took a deep breath, held it before releasing it in a rush. Then she met his gaze directly and said, "I need your help."

"Just what kind of help?" he asked and from the corner of his eye he noticed that the pot of coffee was almost done. He took it from the machine, walked over and poured them both a cup of coffee.

She picked up the mug, her hands slightly shaky. She blew on the coffee and took a sip before placing the mug down. Bracing her hands on the counter once again, she looked away and said, "I think T.J. knows who was driving the car that hit him, but he's not admitting it. Normally I would have asked Jericho—"

"I'm not standing in for my brother, Macy. I'm not Jericho."

Her head whipped up and she nailed him with her gaze. "You're right that you're nothing like your brother. But you can't refuse to help."

He snorted and shifted his brow ever higher. "Really? Please tell me why I can't refuse."

No sign of emotion or distress marked her face as she said, "Because T.J. is your son."

Chapter 13

Sucker-punched.

That was the only way to describe how he was feeling.

She had sucker-punched him years ago with her first kiss and then again the night they'd made love.

Now she had done it again.

"Excuse me?" He came round the corner of the island until he stood directly beside her. She had looked away immediately after her pronouncement. Now he grasped her arms and applied gentle pressure to turn her in his direction. Placing his thumb and forefinger beneath her chin, he angled her face upward so that she couldn't continue to avoid him.

"T.J. is my son? My flesh and blood?" His tone was deliberately calm, displaying nothing of the maelstrom of emotions churning through his gut.

"The one night that you and I—"

"We used protection," he reminded her and she nodded, bit her lower lip as he had seen her do so often when she was upset.

"We did, but it must not have worked. I found out I was pregnant right before I was supposed to marry Tim—"

"And you didn't tell him?" he said and ripped away from her, pacing across the room with a ground-eating stride or two before facing her once again.

Her brown eyes sparkled with indignation at his attack. "I could never mislead someone like that," she said, but then pulled back, obviously acknowledging that she had misled him. That he had a right to be angry and he definitely was angry. Probably more furious than he'd ever been before—except possibly on the day that he had learned Macy had decided to marry Tim.

Sucking in a rough breath, he walked back toward her, but stopped when he was about a step away. He didn't trust himself to get any closer at that moment. Fisting his hands tightly, he kept them at his sides, struggling for control.

"Why didn't you tell me?"

She shrugged and looked down once again before lifting her face. Her eyes glimmered with tears as she said, "Jericho was going on and on about how happy you were to join the Army. How you were looking forward to seeing the world and leaving Esperanza behind."

"And you assumed—"

"I didn't want to stop you and…you never called me again and Tim… He was a good man. I knew he would be a good father." A tear finally leaked out and trailed down her face, but she did nothing to swipe it away.

Nor did he. Instead, he took the final step to bring him close and leaned down until they were nearly nose-to-nose. "*I'm* a good man—"

"I know you are. You're a real hero. One who's made a difference to so many other people. Saved lives. That wouldn't have happened if you had stayed here…with me," she said and reached up, cradled the side of his face.

Her tender touch nearly undid him, but he couldn't leave it at that. "Did you love me? When you walked down the aisle—"

"I loved Tim with all my heart."

He had thought he was over the pain of losing her to another man, but the ache deep in the center of him told him otherwise. Her words were creating as much hurt now as her actions had eighteen years earlier.

But he couldn't retaliate and wound her, even if he was in agony with her admission.

He also couldn't let her continue to hide behind her love for Saint Tim.

Cradling her cheeks with both hands, he finally wiped away the trail of tears on her face with his thumb. Stroked the soft skin of her cheek and bent that final inch so that his lips were close to hers. He whispered, "You wanted me then and you want me now."

Then he kissed her like there was no tomorrow because he knew there might not be. As honor-bound as he felt to help Macy now that he knew T.J. was his son, he was also sure that he was not cut out for family or civilian life.

There was just too much uncertainty unlike the orderly military life that had worked so well for him, he told himself even as he kept on kissing Macy. Opening his mouth against hers over and over until it wasn't enough and he finally slipped his tongue within to taste the sweetness of her breath.

She responded to him willingly, going up on tiptoe to

continue the kiss. Pressing against him until he needed more. He slipped his hands beneath her buttocks and lifted her until her backside was on the edge of the counter and her legs were straddling him.

Macy shivered as the hard jut of his erection brushed the center of her, awakening a rush of desire that dragged a moan from her.

The sound penetrated the fog of want that had wrapped itself around them, tempering their kisses. Creating a short lull during which she managed to murmur a soft, "I'm sorry. I should have told you about T.J."

The reminder of her deception stilled his actions and he lifted his lips from hers, but remained close, his hands tangled in her hair. His body intimately pressed against her.

"Macy, I wish that things could be different, only—"

"Ma, I'm hungry," they heard loud and clear from T.J.'s bedroom upstairs.

The typical teen moment shattered the emotional angst and lust that had overtaken them.

Fisher released a rough sigh and stepped away while she called up to her son, "I'll be up with something in a minute."

She slipped off the counter and gestured to the oak kitchen table. "Will you stay for lunch?"

He nodded, but quickly added, "Let me help you with it."

She sensed that the hero in him intended to help her with more than lunch, much like she had asked. As much as she appreciated that he would do so, she also hoped that she wasn't making a mistake that would not only break her heart, but hurt her son.

When she acquiesced to his request, she quickly pulled out a can of condensed tomato soup from one cabinet and handed it to him. "Can you make this while I put together some sandwiches?"

"Can do," he said and she headed to the fridge for the fixings for lunch. She had some leftover roast beef that she could slice up for sandwiches and as she prepared them, she kept half an eye on Fisher as he made the soup.

He went into the fridge and removed a bottle of salsa and some shredded cheddar cheese. After opening the can and adding the water, he proceeded to put in a few heaping spoonfuls of the salsa to the soup. As she plated the sandwiches, he poured the steaming hot soup into bowls and topped them off with some of the shredded cheese.

Grabbing a tray from beneath the island counter, she prepped T.J.'s lunch, added a glass of milk to the tray and took it up to him.

The short nap he had taken seemed to have made a difference. He appeared more alert and not as pale as before and so it was with a lighter heart that she went back to the kitchen.

Fisher had set the table, laid out the soup and sandwiches for each of them along with fresh mugs of coffee.

"Thank you," she said and offered him a tired smile as she sat down beside him.

"You may not be thanking me when this is all over," he said and picked up half of his roast beef sandwich.

"Why's that?"

Fisher thoughtfully chewed the bite of sandwich before responding with, "Because if I'm going to help you, I intend to make sure that T.J. is being totally upfront with you, me and the sheriff."

She paused to consider him as he resumed eating and realized that he was in his military mode, where there were rules that needed to be followed and the failure to do so had consequences. She had tried to follow the same basic principles in raising her son, but too often since Tim's death, she had cut T.J. slack about the consequences part. In retrospect, she had done so to try and soften his father's loss, but had Tim been alive, he wouldn't have put up with T.J.'s behavior.

Fisher wouldn't either and that might be a good thing. "I agree that we need to get to the bottom of why T.J. isn't telling us what he saw today."

Fisher paused with his soup-filled spoon in mid-air, clearly surprised by her agreement. When he realized she was on board with him, he said, "And what's actually up with the missing girl. Sara, right?"

"Sara Engeleit," she confirmed and finally took a spoonful of the soup. The salsa and cheese had transformed the simple soup and her stomach growled noisily in appreciation.

"It's delicious," she said and quickly ate another spoonful.

"A bachelor's got to know how to take care of himself," Fisher said, but knew he had made a mistake when Macy's eyes darkened with sadness. Despite that, he had no doubt that it made sense to remind her of what he was and what he would continue to be once he was done helping her.

"Tell me about Sara," he said in an attempt to draw her attention to something besides their confusing and basically non-existent relationship.

With a shrug, she said, "Not much to tell. She came to the ranch about a week and a half ago. Right before T.J. and Joe started working at the Hopechest."

"Do you know where she's from?" After he asked the question, he took a bite of his sandwich.

Macy likewise took a bite, rolled her eyes upward as if

trying to gather all that she knew about the girl before responding. "She's sixteen and from Dallas, we believe. When she arrived at the ranch, she had some bruises on her arms and hands, but she seems to be from a family that's fairly well-off judging from her clothes and behavior."

"What about your boss? Does she know anything more?"

"Yesterday morning Jewel mentioned hiring a private investigator since Sara was missing. She was supposed to get a name from Joe Colton, but I haven't talked to her since then."

"Maybe after lunch—"

"I'll call her," she said and after that, the two of them quickly finished up the last of their soup and sandwiches.

While Fisher cleared off the table and tackled the dishes, she phoned Jewel to fill her in on all that had happened, beginning with the hit-and-run incident with T.J.

"Is he okay?" her friend asked, her concern evident in the tones of her voice.

"Bruised and banged up a little, but nothing serious luckily."

A heavy sigh filled the line. "I'm not liking this, Macy. There's just too much going on for it all not to be related."

"I agree, but without any more info—"

"Actually, Joe Colton was able to provide me some information about the man he believes to be Sara's dad—Howard Engeleit," Jewel said and relief flooded through Macy that they might finally have something to go on.

"Mr. Colton knows him?"

"When I mentioned Sara's last name, it rang a bell with Joe. Apparently Howard Engeleit had once worked with him. He says he didn't care for the man and that they'd had a falling out. He left Joe's company some time ago," Jewel recounted.

"Does he know where Howard is now?" she asked as

Fisher finished washing the dishes and stood there, drying his hands on a towel as he listened.

"Howard started his own company and made a good chunk of money. He and Joe see each other occasionally. The last that he had heard, Howard was in the middle of a nasty divorce battle, but Joe couldn't recall whether or not Howard had any children."

Although the information wasn't yet complete, she was relieved that at least now they might have something more to go on in their search to discover what was going on with her son and Sara. "Thanks for all the info. Fisher and I—"

"Fisher and you? Are you a team now?" Jewel said teasingly, unaware of just how problematic being together with Fisher was for her.

"We're going to check into some things and keep you posted. If you find out anything else, could you call me?" she responded, steering clear of any further discussion of her and Fisher.

"I understand, Macy. When you're ready to discuss it…"

"I'll let you know. Talk to you later," she said and hung up.

Fisher had walked back to the table and now he stood there, hands braced along the top rung of one of the kitchen chairs.

"You've got something to go on," he said.

"Something, but we need a little more. Seems like there's one sure way of finding out more about Howard Engeleit," she said, picked up her hands and mimicked that she was typing.

"The Net is bound to turn up something. Where's your computer?"

Chapter 14

Their Internet search on Howard Engeleit immediately revealed hundreds of hits on the man.

As Macy skimmed through the various Web search results, it became apparent that Joe Colton wasn't kidding about Howard making himself money as a mover and shaker. There was account after account of Howard's business dealings, including some questionable ones. Much as Joe had said, Howard was in the midst of a difficult divorce but as luck would have it, the news articles mentioned a young daughter. Sara.

On one Dallas gossip page, there was even a picture of Howard, his wife Amanda and their daughter Sara. Howard's presence dominated the photo and Macy immediately got vibes from the submissive body posture of both his wife and daughter.

With Fisher sitting beside her and reading along, she gestured to the two women in the photo and pointed out how they seemed to be uneasy. "See their body posture and their eyes are downcast. Howard's clearly the one in control here."

Fisher nodded and agreed. "I've seen the same kind of body language on fresh recruits. He's definitely the one calling the shots."

"It may be more than that. Sara had bruises on her arms and hands when she first got to the ranch. If Howard was responsible, Sara might feel powerless to say anything about the abuse."

Fisher leaned back in his chair and rubbed his hand across his lips, thoughtful for a moment. "He's wealthy and connected, so who would believe her?"

She nodded emphatically. "Exactly. And if he's suing for custody of her—"

"He would have free rein to keep on abusing her." Fisher shook his head, sat up in the chair and clasped his hands together tightly. "It's sad that a father would do that to his child. That she feels there's no one there she can turn to."

"It's probably why she came to the ranch."

Fisher glanced up the stairs toward T.J.'s room. "Do you think he knows about the abuse? Is that why he's protecting her?"

She thought of T.J. and how much he was like the man who had raised him. Tim had been good-hearted and prone to helping others. But also, deep within her son were the genes from the man sitting beside her. A man of action. A hero. Combine the two and it was starting to make sense that T.J. was somehow involved with helping the young woman.

"I think that T.J. believes he's doing what's right for Sara, but the best thing would be to tell us what's happening so the authorities can handle this," she admitted.

He nodded, but then his gaze dropped down at his hands for a moment before he faced her. "There are times when a man has to make his own stand no matter what the rules say about what's right."

She heard him, but couldn't agree. Laying her hand on his tightly clasped ones, she said, "But he's not a man, Fisher. He's a boy. A scared and confused young boy."

Fisher eased his hands away from hers and pointed to the monitor. "You said that the deputy mentioned that Sara had been at a place up on the highway before she came to the ranch. We should print out that picture of her and check out that honky tonk. She might have run back there again."

She felt dismissed much as she suspected his men might feel when he gave them an order. She tried not to take it personally, telling herself that he was a man used to being in charge and making decisions.

But she was also used to being in control of her own life. Some might say she hadn't done a good job of it—heck, she even felt that way at times—but she had tried her best.

Her silence must have registered with him since he shifted his attention from the monitor and the prints he was making and back to her.

The strain on Macy's face was evident and Fisher struggled for a moment with a reason for it until it finally came. "Do you want to go that place on the highway or is there something else you think we should do?"

"I know you're used to taking control—"

"It's a hard habit to break," he freely admitted. In his life a delay in decision-making could cost someone their life, but he understood this wasn't the military.

"I didn't mean to order you around only...I feel like you and T.J. are my responsibility now." He paused as the strain on her face increased and sadness crept into her eyes. He wondered at it once again, although she was quick to make the reasons clear.

"Is that all we are? A responsibility?"

He mumbled a curse beneath his breath, regretting that his time alone and in the Army had seemingly cost him so many of his skills with women. Needing to reach her, both physically and emotionally, he cupped her cheek and tenderly ran his finger along the ridge of her cheekbone.

"I'm so not good at this, Macy," he confessed.

"This? As in—"

"Family life. Personal relationships. I don't know how to deal with the kinds of things you've had to handle. Difficult things like Tim's death and T.J.'s problems."

"I've done the best I could," she replied, defensiveness in every line of her body and the tight tone in her voice.

"You have and asking for my help isn't a bad thing...I don't think. But there's a lot I have to deal with also and I'm trying to do it the best that I can as well." He couldn't say it, but his reawakened feelings for Macy and the surprise announcement that he had a son were creating doubt within him. Doubt about the decisions he had made in his life. Doubt about the future he had thought to be fairly certain.

Now nothing seemed sure anymore except for the fact that he had to help Macy and T.J. His honor demanded it. He just hoped his heart would be intact when it was all over.

Macy nodded and after a shaky inhalation, her words came out on a rushed breath. "We'll do the best we can together for now."

Together for now. It seemed like the best thing they could hope for at that moment.

"Do you want to go to this honky tonk?" he asked again, trying for that togetherness.

The tension ebbed slowly from her body. "I think that's a good idea. I just want to check on T.J. first. Is that okay?"

"That sounds fine."

She laid her hand over his as it rested on her cheek, the action achingly tender and causing a funky tightening in his heart.

"Thank you for trying."

He bit back the words he had been about to say—that it was the least he could do. He had never believed in doing the least of anything in his whole life and Macy and T.J. certainly deserved more from him. Instead he said, "I will give it my all to make sure this comes out right."

A glimmer of a smile came to her face. "I'm certain you will."

Her trust in him moved him once again, choking his throat tight. Unable to say more for fear of what he might say, he nodded.

"I'm going to go check on T.J. and then we'll go, okay?"

"Okay," he managed to eke out and returned his attention to printing out larger pictures of Sara, both alone and with her parents.

He heard the tread of her steps going up the stairs and past the whir of the ink-jet printer, the soft and loving way she called T.J.'s name. A moment later, she descended the steps again and reentered the kitchen carrying the tray with the empty plates and glasses with T.J.'s lunch.

"He's sound asleep again. I left him a note that we were stepping out for a little while," she advised and went to the sink to clean the plates.

"That's good. It'll give us some time to visit this place and try to figure out where Sara may have gone." With a final *thunk-thunk,* the printer spit out the last sheet of paper with the photo of Sara.

He stood, picked up the papers, folded them neatly and tucked them into the pocket of his chambray shirt. Macy joined him just a second later.

"Are you ready to go?"

She nodded. "As ready as I'll ever be."

The Amarillo Rose sat on one of the smaller county roads, but one well-traveled by truckers avoiding the some-times more crowded state highways. Sitting smack dab in between Esperanza and another rural town, the location made it a great watering hole for the truckers who were headed from the Corpus Christi area to Lubbock or other northern cities.

The paint on the sprawling one story structure was a faded color which had probably once been yellow based on the name of the place and the slightly more colorful neon sign of a yellow rose close to the roadway. A couple of tractor trailers were parked off to the side of the building and a Chevy Silverado that was at least a decade old sat near the door.

As they walked by the truck, they noticed the name of a fish company painted on the door along with a Dallas address.

Macy took it to be a good sign.

She entered first, her eyes adjusting to the dimmer light. A small podium stood by the door and beyond that, a long bar to the left. In the center of the space were dozens of tables and chairs and to the far right, a small dance floor and bandstand.

Plastic bunting in red, white and blue emblazoned with

the name of a local beer hung from the ceilings. The walls were adorned with yet more ads and neon signs for an assortment of beers.

At the bar, a bartender was filling a glass with beer while a waitress laid out a plate for one of the three customers seated at the counter.

Fisher placed a hand at the small of her back and after a quick exchange of gazes, urged her toward the bar. She took a seat as did he and the bartender approached after setting the beer in front of one of the patrons. He slapped down paper coasters on the relatively clean surface of the bar.

"What can I get you folks?" He inclined his head in Macy's direction.

"An iced tea for me," she answered and Fisher immediately added, "And another for me."

The bartender quickly shifted away to get their orders and the waitress came to their side, held the menus before her as she said, "Can I get you folks some food? We've got a mean five alarm chili today as well as a to die for peach cobbler."

Fisher met her glance for only a second. "Peach cobbler for me. With vanilla ice cream if you've got it."

"We sure do, honey. What about you, ma'am. Same thing as your husband?" the waitress asked.

Macy was about to protest her mistake, but then thought better of it. If the waitress thought they were concerned parents searching for their daughter, she might be more inclined to help them. "I'll just have the cobbler, thanks."

The waitress walked away to fill their orders while the bartender came by with their drinks. "Here you go, folks. Is there anything else I can get you?"

Fisher pulled the photo of Sara from his pocket and as he

did so, she quickly spoke up. "My husband and I are looking for our daughter, Sara."

Fisher masked his surprise well, she thought, as he pushed forward the picture they had taken off the Internet.

"We think she might have come through here. Maybe a couple of weeks ago," Fisher said.

The bartender peered at the photo and then called out to one of the men sitting farther down the bar, "Maybe only... Hey, Billy Joe. Didn't you say that you gave a young girl a ride a few days ago?"

Billy Joe, a grizzled older man sporting a trucker's hat, slid off his stool and approached them. Leaning toward the picture on the bar, he placed his hands on his lips and tipped the hat back, exposing his Marine-buzzed salt and pepper hair.

"Yep. Picked her up just outside of Esperanza on..." The man rubbed the thick graying stubble on his cheeks as he tried to recollect. Finally, he said, "I think about two nights ago. She was on the road all by herself trying to get back to some ranch just outside of town."

"The Hopechest Ranch?" she asked and the old man nodded.

"I think that was the place. Dropped her off at the end of the driveway and she hightailed it up to the front door and went in."

"Your company's from Dallas, though, right. Do you do the drive from there regularly?" Fisher asked.

"I do. Funny you should mention that," the old man said, still rubbing at his cheeks. "When the young lady saw the name on the truck, she asked me if I was headed to Dallas. Seemed to me she didn't want to go back there if she could avoid it."

"Have any other strangers passed through here recently?" she asked, glancing back and forth between the bartender and truck driver. The waitress came over at that moment with their cobblers as the bartender said, "Have you seen any new faces around, Alice?"

A frown created a ridge above the older woman's eyebrows as she considered the question. "Just that salesman who said he was on his way to San Antonio. Didn't seem like much of a salesman to me."

"Why's that?" Fisher questioned.

"Got the most expensive thing on the menu. Didn't ask for a receipt and left a lousy tip," she said and wiggled her fingers to indicate that she wanted to see the photo.

After Fisher handed it over and she examined it, she said, "Don't remember the girl."

He pulled the other photo from his pocket and passed it to the waitress. "Was this the salesman?"

She glanced at it, but shook her head and placed the photo on the counter of the bar. "Don't recognize him."

"Me, neither," said the truck driver as did the bartender.

She exchanged a glance with Fisher, who handed the bartender the photo of Sara. "Do you think you could keep this just in case Sara comes by again? We can give you a phone number where you can call us."

"Sure." The bartender plucked a pen from inside his apron and jotted down the cell phone number that Macy provided.

Although they had ordered the desserts, she had no appetite thanks to the disappointment of discovering virtually nothing about Sara. The only worthwhile information they could pass to Jericho when he returned in a day or two would be the name of the company that the truck driver worked for and the license plate number. It wouldn't be all that much harder for Jericho to get the man's name based on that and their description of the truck driver. She didn't believe the older man had done anything, but Jericho could hopefully confirm that the man had no prior record.

Fisher bent close to her and whispered in her ear. "Do you want to go?"

"I'm not really very hungry," she admitted.

He brushed a kiss along her brow and laid his arm around her shoulders. "Let's go home then. Maybe T.J. will be able to tell us more once we tell him what we know about Sara's dad."

The tenderness of that caress chased away some of the disappointment. "Let's go home," she confirmed.

Chapter 15

They were on their way to Macy's, but it must have occurred to her that they would have to go past the Hopechest Ranch to reach her house.

She laid a hand on his arm as he drove the Jeep along the country road. "Do you mind if we drop by the ranch and speak to Jewel? I'd like to share what little we have and see if she maybe has some information for us."

"Not a problem." He slowed the Jeep as they neared the driveway for the ranch, then turned onto it and drove up to the front of the house.

After he had parked, he said, "Do you want me to go with you?"

"Of course. Together, right?"

Together for now, he thought, but couldn't disappoint. She had been too discouraged after their visit to the roadside canteen. Because of that, he nodded and followed her as she walked to the front door and entered, calling out Jewel's name as she did so.

A very pregnant woman—Mexican, young and pretty—was the first one to respond.

"Macy. Miss Jewel is in the library with Joe," the woman said.

"Is something wrong, Ana?"

Ana wrung her hands together and glanced toward the back of the house. "Joe said he had to talk to Miss Jewel. That he had something to tell her about Sara."

Macy placed her hand over her stomach and wavered on her feet. Fisher was immediately there, his hand at her shoulder to offer support and comfort.

"Let's go see if Jewel can talk to us," he said and squeezed her shoulder.

She reached up and placed her hand on his, seeking his solace and he offered it, easing his hand down so that she could grab hold of it.

Together they walked the few steps back to the library, a moderately sized room filled with books, a leather sofa and chairs as well as a small table where the children could read or study with some measure of quiet.

The door was ajar as they approached and Macy could hear the gentle tones of Jewel's voice as she spoke to Joe.

She knocked on the door, but no one responded. She was about to knock again when Jewel came to the entrance to the library.

"Macy. I'm so glad you're here." Her sharp-eyed gaze immediately went to Fisher behind her, down to where their hands were joined and then back up to her face.

"You have news?" Jewel asked.

"Not all that much unfortunately. And you?"

Jewel opened the door wide and held out her arm. "Why don't you come in. You need to hear what Joe just told me."

Her stomach did a little flip-flop, sensing the news would not be good. She tightened her hand on Fisher's.

They entered the room. Joe was seated on the maroon leather coach, but stood as he saw them. He nodded his head in greeting and said, "Mrs. Ward. Mr. Yates."

As anxious as she was, she couldn't muster the energy for niceties. "Your aunt tells us that you've got something we should hear."

The boy shifted from foot to foot and stuffed his hands in his pockets. He inhaled deeply and held it before finally speaking. "I saw Sara and T.J. together the afternoon before she disappeared. They were by themselves at the corral and Sara seemed upset."

"Upset with T.J.?" Fisher asked, but the boy quickly shook his head.

"I don't think so. It seemed like T.J. was trying to make her feel better. I think he has a crush on her," Joe said.

Jewel came up to stand by Joe and placed her arm around his shoulders. "Tell them what else you heard."

Joe fidgeted once again, clearly uneasy about what he would say and possibly, about betraying a friend's confidence. Macy understood that and so she tried to relieve that concern.

"I know you want to protect your friends, but if it's something that could get them hurt—"

"T.J. was telling Sara not to worry. That he would take her to a place where no one could find her."

"Was there someone Sara was afraid of? Someone who had found her here at the Hopechest?" Fisher asked.

"Maybe," he began and shrugged. "The other night—the night of the accident—another car started following us. Sara got worried and that's why T.J. was speeding, to get away from that car."

She recalled T.J.'s explanation that the other car had been challenging them, but this made a great deal more sense. If Sara's father had sent someone to try and find her, they might have spotted her in the car with the boys and decided to follow them to see where she might be.

"She was with you the night of the accident," Macy said, wanting to confirm her suspicions.

Joe exchanged a pained look with Jewel and nodded. "She was with us, but after we got into the accident, that car that had weirded us out was driving by. Before T.J. and I realized it, she had slipped out of T.J.'s car and somehow got back to the ranch without us."

Macy sensed something even more troublesome approached and at the thought of it, her knees began to shake. If Fisher hadn't already been gently guiding her toward one of the wing chairs, she would have sagged into one ignominiously.

"There's more, isn't there?"

Joe dropped his head until the only thing she could see was the tousled mass of his dark brown hair. He mumbled something, almost beneath his breath, but at Jewel's prodding, finally spoke up.

"I saw Sara getting into T.J.'s car the night before she disappeared. I'd heard some noises out by the one barn and went out to check. There wasn't anything by the barn, but on the way back, I saw a car in the distance and someone running to it."

"Are you sure, son? It was nighttime and you were quite a distance away," Fisher said.

Joe nodded and as he raised his blue-eyed gaze to them, it was filled with guilt. "I'm sorry, but it was T.J. and Sara. I saw their faces when T.J. opened the door and the lights came on."

She sighed and buried her head in her hands. If what Joe said was true—and she had no reason to doubt him—T.J. was headed for major trouble once the deputy found out. Before he did, she had to get to the bottom of what was really going on with her son.

Rising, she stepped up to Joe and her boss, her hands clasped tightly before her. "I know this is a lot to ask—"

"We're not supposed to speak to Deputy Rawlings until tomorrow and actually, I was hoping to wait until Jericho came back. He's due any day now, isn't he?" Jewel asked, her head cocked in Fisher's direction.

"Dad says he'll be back either tomorrow or the next day, although the next is more likely," Fisher replied. He laid his hand on her shoulder once again and said, "That gives us time to talk to T.J. and find out what's going on."

She nodded and embraced Jewel. "Thank you for understanding."

Jewel hugged her hard and brushed a lock of stray hair away from her face. "Call us as soon as you know anything. In the meantime, I'm going to speak to Clay Colton about those noises again. Find out if he can go out on the range to see if it's an injured animal."

"I'll call as soon as we have something." Turning, she took hold of Fisher's hand and they left the ranch house, jumped in the Jeep and raced home.

She knew something was wrong from the moment they pulled up into her driveway. There was something just too... quiet about the house. After she exited the Jeep, she immediately walked to the garage doors, stood on tiptoe and peered in through the glass windows.

T.J.'s GTO was gone.

Running to the front door, she threw it open and shouted his name.

When silence answered, she tore up the stairs, the house's old bones creaking from the force of her strides.

At T.J.'s door, she stared at his empty unmade bed.

He wasn't anywhere in the room.

Things had just gone from bad to worse.

He was getting slow in his old age, Fisher thought as he bounded up the stairs, chasing Macy after her mad dash from the garage and into the house.

He nearly barreled her over as she stood silently at T.J.'s door, her shoulders nearly heaving as she apparently struggled for control. He realized why as he stood behind her and peered over her shoulder into the room.

Her son...*their* son was gone.

Disappointment slammed into him as he thought of how T.J. had broken the rules of his punishment. He couldn't imagine how Macy felt, but he could see it in the lines of her body.

He stepped close and embraced her from behind, wrapping one arm across her waist while stroking her hair with his hand. "It'll be okay, Mace. We'll find him."

She sucked in a ragged breath while her body vibrated with tension. "Why would he do this? Why couldn't he talk to me?"

He remembered himself at T.J.'s age, all full of perceived male empowerment, but struggling with the confusing emotions about Macy, his mom and his life in Esperanza. Although he had been close to his father and brother, he hadn't been able to talk to them about all that he was feeling. He'd been too prideful, too perplexed and most of all, too angry.

"This isn't about anything you've done wrong, Mace. He's young and probably unsure of the situation he's gotten himself into with Sara. Women can do that to a man."

Another shuddering breath ripped through her body and transferred her pain to him and because he wanted to ease her anguish, he said, "I promise that this will work out. That we'll make this okay."

A big promise.

As she turned in his arms and wrapped hers around him, holding on to him as if for dear life, regret slammed into him that the promise he had just made might be one he would break because he didn't know how to make it okay. Had it been a mission with his men, he'd know the plan and what to do. Even if the plan got all messed up out in the field, he could find a way to make the mission work.

But this wasn't a mission and family things… They were far more complicated at times than a military mission and he feared he lacked the skills to be able to keep his promise.

Awkwardly he patted her on the back, held her as she cried out her frustration. He wasn't used to dealing with a woman's tears. Or a son's disobedience.

He couldn't tell her there was no crying in the military. Well, he could but it would be a lie because he had shed more than one tear over his men and their injuries. He also couldn't punish T.J. with a week in the brig for disobeying his mother.

In reality, he couldn't bring the kind of order he had in the Army to this family, but as Macy's tears finally subsided with a tiny hiccough that wrung his heart, he realized what he could do. He could bring her peace for a moment. Soothe her hurt and maybe make her smile.

As for T.J....

He needed a man's guidance to get him in line and he would try his best to help T.J. put his life in order. To fulfill his promise to make it okay before duty called for him to return to the Army.

Bending slightly, he cradled her face in his hands. Her cheeks were wet with her tears and slightly flushed. He wiped away the tears with his thumbs, brought his forehead to rest against hers once again and repeated his promise.

"It will be okay. *We* will make sure that everything is put to right."

As she nodded and gazed up at him, her brown eyes shimmering from her spent tears, he realized she believed in that promise. Believed in him.

His heart constricted again at the trust she had in him and he vowed to do his best not to disappoint her which meant that as difficult as it might be, they had to decide what to do about T.J.

Chapter 16

An open bottle of wine sat on the kitchen counter and he poured them each a small glass before making them a quick dinner.

Macy had protested, saying she wasn't hungry, but he had insisted. She needed to keep her strength up so that they would be ready to figure out what T.J. was doing and where he might have taken Sara, since both of them now had no doubt that he knew where the girl was.

Between the trip to the Amarillo Rose and the stop at the ranch, it was already dusk. T.J. had likely been gone for hours and what made the most sense was for them to refuel, get some rest and prepare to find T.J. the next day.

He also insisted on Macy helping him, hoping that the simple chores would help take her mind off things. As they worked together in the kitchen, he intentionally kept the talk away from T.J., wanting Macy to relax. If she felt more at ease, it might prompt some idea of where T.J. might have hidden Sara.

While Macy chopped onions and red peppers for the omelets, Fisher took out the eggs and found some bread to toast.

"There's only six eggs," he said, glancing down at the plastic egg tray from the refrigerator.

"There's only two of us," Macy replied with surprise.

"A man's got to get his protein," he said with a smile and rummaged through her fridge until he found a ham steak. Taking it out, he walked with it to the island counter where she was working and laid it before her.

"If the veggies are ready—"

"They are," she said and handed him the cutting board with the chopped peppers and onions. She grabbed another so she could cut up the ham.

"I'll get them cooking up," he said and little by little, with the two of them working side by side, the omelet and toast took shape.

Within less than half an hour, they were seated at the table, eating a delicious omelet. Silent as they finished the simple meal and sipped the last of the wine in the bottle. After, they cleared the table and cleaned the dishes together at the sink.

By the time they had finished, Macy was obviously more in control. More relaxed and truthfully, so was he. Being beside her…

It made him imagine what it would be like to have a family of his own. To do everyday things together like they had tonight. Simple things which somehow brought a peace to his heart that he hadn't experienced in some time.

She walked him to the door, but then they both stood there,

awkward. Uncertain. Lingering at the door, heads hanging downward. He wondered if she was as reluctant as he about all that had happened that day. About leaving her, although he was hesitant to admit that.

"Fisher," she said, her voice rising in question although she didn't pick up her head.

He bent a little, trying to see her face, but couldn't in the dim light of the bulb at the front door. He placed his thumb and forefinger beneath her chin and gently tipped it upward so that he could see her face.

"Macy?"

She kept her eyes downcast as she said, "I don't want to be alone tonight. Would you stay?"

Stay. With her?

It tightened his gut to imagine being with her. Lying beside her and yet…

She was vulnerable and he was…decidedly too puzzled about what she made him feel. Regardless of all that, as she finally tipped her eyes up shyly and the need there slammed into him, he realized he couldn't deny her request.

"I'll stay."

As they walked back into her home, he finally took the time to appreciate her house's simplicity. No fripperies or excessive feminine touches. He wondered if she had kept this home simple and feminine-free for Tim and T.J. If it was the kind of house she wanted or one she had settled for because of the men in her life.

Was this the kind of house they would have shared if things had been different or if she would have taken the time to stamp their home with her unique personality.

As she opened the door to her bedroom, he finally saw traces of her.

He knew little about design, so the best he could do was call it feminine. Lacey things adorned the rich mahogany furniture in the room. Floral curtains were at the two windows and a bedspread with a similar pattern of roses covered a queen-sized bed. To the far right of the bed sat a big soft chair and ottoman in a floral chintz pattern. A romance novel sat on the ottoman. The cover was up with the open pages facing the ottoman, marking the spot where she had stopped reading.

Macy paused in the middle of the room and gestured to a door at the other end. "The bathroom's in there in case you need to…you know."

He didn't need to do anything, but decided to give her a moment to collect herself. With a courteous nod, he went to the bathroom and shut the door behind him.

The decor of the bathroom was even more feminine. Lace decorated the one window and the light rose-colored towels were adorned with beige lace. A painted wrought-iron stand by the bathtub was fanciful as was another by the window which held an assortment of African violets blooming in shades of purple and pink.

He smiled at the flowers, which added so much life to the space, and walked over to touch the velvety surface of one bloom. Soft and lush. Like Macy's skin.

Wrong, wrong, wrong, he reminded himself. He needed to be in control if he was going to survive the night.

He walked to the pedestal sink, turned on the cold water and splashed his face with it over and over again until he had restored control.

Drying his face and hands with one of the very feminine towels, he then folded it neatly and laid it on the rack to dry.

When he walked back into her bedroom, her door was closed and the room was dimly lit by one small lamp on a nightstand by the bed. Macy was on top of the covers, fully clothed, her back turned toward the bathroom.

He wrung his hands nervously, then wiped them up and down on his jeans before taking a stutter step toward the bed.

She turned at the sound he made, leaned back on one hand as he approached. Her brown-eyed gaze looked him up and down, hesitant but hungry as he stopped at the edge of the bed.

"Are you sure?" he asked.

"I don't want to be alone tonight. I haven't been alone in this house since…"

"Tim died?"

Shaking her head vehemently, she said, "I bought this house and everything in it a couple of years after Tim died. T.J. and I…we needed a change. There were just too many sad memories at the old place."

Relief washed over him then. Relief that he wouldn't be lying in another man's bed. Beside another man's memories.

He sat on the edge of the bed and pulled off his boots. Tossed them aside and they landed with a thud on the polished hard wood floor.

Facing her, he copied her pose, leaning back on one hand as he considered her. "It must have been hard for you."

She lay down on her back and nodded. "I didn't want to believe it at first—that Tim was really going to die. Since we found out that he…"

She shuddered and closed her eyes before shifting to grab

the crocheted throw at the foot of the bed. She pulled it up around her, as if she was cold.

It tugged at him with the vulnerability it exposed and he shifted quickly, moving to her side and embracing her. Bringing her to rest beside him as he stroked his hand up and down her side, trying to soothe her.

"I know I said I was sorry at his funeral, but—"

She slipped her hand over his mouth. "Can we talk about something else?"

He frowned, confused until she said, "Could we talk about you? Why you chose the Army?"

He wanted to say "Because of you" but bit the words back. He had already been considering the Army before what had happened with her. What had happened with her had only cemented the decision he had already been about to make.

"My dad did a great job of giving Jericho and me stability after Mom left and I needed that after high school. Community college just wasn't doing it for me. I needed more."

"And the Army gave you that?" She cradled his cheek and stroked her thumb across the roughness of his afternoon beard.

He nodded, but it seemed to not be enough for her.

"Did you ever miss Esperanza while you were gone?"

He should have lied. It would have made things that much easier, but he was a man of honor and couldn't lie to her.

"I missed home more than I thought I would."

Macy told herself not to read anything into his words. "Jericho and your dad miss you a lot. They worry about you. So do a lot of people in town—you're our hero."

He smiled tightly, clearly uncomfortable with the praise. "I'm just doing my job."

"A job that could get you killed." She shifted her hand

down to rest on the hard muscles of his chest. Beneath her palm his heart beat strongly. Steadily, much like the man beside her.

He covered her hand with his, his palm rough on the back of hers. The thin white line of a scar marred one knuckle and another larger one was close to his wrist. The hand of a warrior.

"Almost more than anything, I want you to be safe and to be happy," she said, finally admitting to what had been in her heart for far too long.

"Almost more? Can I guess that what you want even more is to see T.J. safe and happy," he questioned, tenderly rubbing his hand back and forth against hers.

"Definitely."

He slipped his hand from hers and slid it into the short waves of her hair, softly cupping her head. "And what about you?"

"Me?" she asked, slightly befuddled until she met his brilliant green-eyed gaze and his meaning was clear. "What do I want?" she asked, just to be sure.

"Yes, what do you want for yourself?" he said, leaving no room for doubt about the answer he expected from her.

What did she want that was only for herself? she wondered, but then the answer came too swiftly to be denied any longer.

"I want you."

Chapter 17

A tremor rocked through the hand in her hair and beside her his body tensed.

"Macy," he said, his tone low and tinged with an odd combination of exasperation and need. He rolled onto his back, breaking contact with her.

She raised herself up on one elbow. "You were right when you said that I wanted you back in high school and that I want you now, but you know what else?"

He looked away, unable to meet her probing gaze as he asked, "What?"

"Want without love is empty. That's what I realized back in high school. That's why I married Tim," she finally confessed, thinking that he deserved a complete explanation after so many years.

The pain in his heart was almost more than he could bear

and so strong that he wanted to lash out at her. Before he could control himself, he had flipped and pinned her to the mattress, his body holding her down while he held her hands above her head.

"You never even gave me a chance to prove to you it was more," he said, his breath ragged in his chest from his distress.

"No, I didn't and that was wrong. I should have given you a chance, especially when I found out I was pregnant with T.J., only…"

"Only what, damn it! I deserve an answer as to why you kept my son from me for his entire life," he barked out.

"I was afraid of what I felt for you. I was afraid that if I gave you my heart, you'd break it when you left." Tears shimmered in her eyes, but she battled them back, biting her lower lip in a gesture that was all too telling and all too tempting.

He slowly loosened his grip on her hands and bent his head, bringing his lips to a hair's breadth from hers. "Maybe if you had asked, I wouldn't have left," he said and then closed the distance between them and kissed her. Put all of his heart and soul and eighteen years of frustration into showing her just what might have been between them.

The shock of his kiss, filled with such need and yearning, overcame any doubts Macy might have had about whether it was right to explore this. She opened her mouth to his and pressed her body upward, meeting the hardness of his muscled physique. The short strands of his dark hair were soft against her hands as she held his head to her, urging him on.

Over and over they kissed until they were both trembling. Until it wasn't enough and she lifted her hips against the press of his erection, so full and hard against her belly.

She shuddered and between her legs, her muscles clenched

on the emptiness there, but she reminded herself of her earlier words to him. About how empty want was without love.

She had no doubt she cared for him. About him. She had no doubt she could be falling in love with him. With his strength and goodness.

But she also knew that if that love was to grow true and strong, taking this any further tonight would be wrong. Fisher must have sensed it as well since he gave her one last kiss before slowly pulling away.

"I'm willing to wait until you're ready, Macy," he said, brushing away a tousled lock of her hair.

She nodded, but had to ask him. "What happens then, Fisher?"

Fisher wished he knew what to tell her. He wished he knew whether she ever would be ready for a relationship with him or whether he could commit to her if she was. Commit to having a wife and family after so many years in the military.

"I'm not sure," he confessed.

She faced away from him as she said, "Jericho said you might not sign up for another tour of duty. That you might teach instead."

Damn his brother for being such a busybody, he thought. Hadn't Jericho ever heard the old saying that loose lips sink ships?

"I've been offered a teaching post at West Point."

"And had you given any thought to it?" she asked, turning toward him once again, the resoluteness in her brown-eyed gaze drilling into him, daring him to lie to her, but he couldn't.

"I had given it some thought," he admitted and that seemed to be enough for her for the moment.

"I think it's time we got some rest," she said and flipped onto her side.

He nestled against her, his front to her back, spooned as close as he could be, and dropped his arm to rest across her waist while pillowing his head on his other arm.

"Good night, Mace."

"Good night, Fisher," she said and laid her arm over his.

For long moments he lay there, listening to her breathe until the rhythm of it deepened and lengthened, confirming to him that she slept. Even then he clung onto wakefulness, trying to experience this peaceful interlude. Wondering how it might be if she lay beside him every night. What it would be like to sample the passion he had experienced but for a brief moment earlier that night.

As he drifted off, the taste of her on his lips and the memory of her pressed close, it occurred to him that maybe family life might not be such a bad thing.

That maybe it was worth giving that teaching position more than just a thought.

He awoke to the smell of fresh coffee and Macy. Her scent lingered on the sheets long after she had left the bed.

He took his time to snuggle her pillow close and savor that rose-filled scent. Maybe even memorize for the future if it turned out to be that his nights were meant to be without her.

Realizing he couldn't dawdle for long, however, he rose and went to the bathroom where he relieved himself and after, washed his face and hands. Put a little of her toothpaste on his finger and scrubbed his mouth out the best he could.

Thankfully, it took just his fingers to rake smooth the short strands of his hair and then he was on his way downstairs and to the kitchen, where Macy was standing at the counter, fork-splitting some English muffins.

"Good morning," he said and came up behind her, dropped a quick kiss on the side of her face.

"Mornin', Fisher. I walked over to the corner store and got some more eggs. Figured I'd make us a bite to eat while we decided what to do today."

"Let me help," he said, grabbed the muffins and brought them to the toaster while Macy cracked the eggs.

After he popped the muffins into the toaster oven and got it cranking, he leaned back against the counter and asked, "Have you given any thought to where T.J. might have taken Sara?"

She shook her head as she scrambled the eggs and said, "I've been thinking about that ever since yesterday. Joe said T.J. thought no one would find her there..."

Her voice trailed off and she stopped whipping. She put down the fork and bowl and said, "We used to go hiking and camping about thirty miles from here in the Texas hill country."

Wiping her hands on her apron, she headed toward a side door in the kitchen and he followed.

The door opened into the two-car garage which had a recessed area on one side. Shelves and a large plastic storage bin were tucked into the recess and Macy immediately went to the storage bin and pulled up the top.

"The camping equipment and knapsacks are gone. T.J. must have taken them and if he did that...I bet that's where he took her. We used to go up in the hills and camp. We even found a cave one time."

"Was the cave big enough for someone to hide in or stay for any length of time?" he asked.

"Definitely. We slept there one night when it was raining,"

she said with a quick bob of her head. "T.J. and his dad used to go there often until... I only went a few times, though. Hiking and camping were not my thing."

"Do you think you could take us there? Find the trail that T.J. would be most likely to use to get to the cave?"

"I think so. It's been a while, but I'm good at remembering places. We'll need some supplies—"

"I've got camping gear back at Dad's house and we can stop by the feed and supply to pick up some MREs."

"MREs?" she questioned, clearly unfamiliar with the term.

"Ready to eat meals. Dad has everything we need in his camping section," he explained.

"I'll get changed and pack some warmer clothes. It can get cold in the hills."

"And they're predicting heavy rains. I hope T.J. knows enough to stay to the high ground and away from those arroyos. They can be dangerous if there's a flash flood."

Macy paled a little, but kept her cool. "I hope he knows that as well. I'll be down in a few minutes."

"I'll finish cooking breakfast. The food will help us to be prepared for a long day."

As Macy walked back into the kitchen and he went about finishing the meal, he only hoped that by the end of the day, they would have a better idea of where T.J. and Sara might be.

Fisher had called Buck Yates ahead of time and his dad had a few days worth of rations as well as some maps of the area ready for them when they arrived at his feed and supply store on the outskirts of town. Combined with the camping equipment that Fisher had picked up at his dad's house, they would be well-prepared for a trip into the hill country.

As Buck helped them stow supplies in their knapsacks, Fisher asked, "Is Jericho still due home tomorrow?"

Buck nodded. "As far as I know he is."

Fisher shot a look at her and said, "Tell him that we think T.J.'s helping Sara and that they're hiding up in the state park. We'll check in with the park ranger when we get there, but Jericho should try and reach me on the cell phone as soon as he can."

When their bags were packed, they tossed them into the back of Fisher's Jeep, climbed in and started the ride to the state park. It was about thirty miles away in the hill country and easily reached along a small interstate.

The weather station had predicted torrential rains for that afternoon. Macy hoped that they could reach the park and pick up T.J.'s trail before the rains came and obliterated any sign of him and Sara.

The weather forecast was on her mind during the entire ride along with concerns about what would happen if Deputy Rawlings decided to come by the house to question T.J. Would he assume the worst if he found them all gone? If he did, would he issue an all points bulletin for T.J. as if he were a fugitive?

At her prolonged silence during the ride, Fisher glanced at her out of the corner of his eye. "Don't worry. We'll find them before there's any more problems," he reassured her.

"If Deputy Rawlings—"

"Jericho will be home soon enough and I think Rawlings is smart enough to know that Jericho would be less than pleased with the kind of grief he's already given you. He's not going to escalate this."

She shook her head, recalling the dour look on the deputy's handsome face when she had gone to pick up T.J. "He seemed pretty determined to me."

"Focus on what we'll do once we get to the park. Which trail we'll take and where T.J. might have hidden Sara," he urged and she did, forcing herself to remember the two or three trips she had taken with Tim and T.J. up into the hills. Trusting that between that and Fisher's military expertise in tracking, they could find where T.J. and Sara might have gone.

Hoping that whoever it was that had tried to run down T.J. or had been asking questions back at the honky tonk would not already be on the teen's trail.

Chapter 18

When Fisher pulled into the main lot of the state park, her heart skipped a beat.

Stationed at the farthest corner, beneath some thick oaks, was T.J.'s GTO. She pointed at it and Fisher drove to the car and parked beside it. As she stood beneath the canopy of the oaks, she realized why he had chosen the spot. It would be difficult for anyone searching from above to spot the car.

Fisher kneeled by the driver's side door, observing some impressions in the gravel by the car. He tracked the impressions to a dirt path besides the gnarly pines surrounding the parking lot. "The footprints lead from the car to here, but there's only one set that I can see."

"From last night when he came back to where he'd hidden Sara," she said.

He nodded, lifted his hand and pointed to the small ranger

station about thirty feet away on the opposite side of the lot. "Why don't you stay here while I talk to the ranger?"

If someone was chasing the teens, they might also have a picture of her and be showing it around. Better she lay low as well, she thought and eased back into the Jeep to wait for Fisher's return.

Nearly half an hour went by as she sat there, tapping her foot and fidgeting with her cell phone. She was on the verge of calling Fisher when she saw him via the rearview mirror, exiting the ranger station. He had a piece of paper in his hand which he glanced at once or twice as he came closer.

When he reached the car, he eased back in and laid out the paper—a map of the park areas—in the space between the two seats. "The ranger says there's at least three trails into the hills. One of them starts right here where T.J. parked."

He pointed to a spot on the map and she leaned over, followed the meandering uphill path of the trail on the paper until it arrived at an overlook.

She remembered such a spot at which she, Tim and T.J. had stopped on at least two of their hikes. Thinking back on it, the scenic hillside site had taken them nearly three hours to reach and she mentioned that to Fisher.

He examined the map and said, "Assuming you were only walking about two miles an hour, this overlook would be about six miles away so it seems as if this might be the trail T.J. would take since he was familiar with it."

Trailing her finger along the path, she stopped and circled one area on the map. "The rock face around here had a lot of openings. That's where we found a cave that one time and stayed inside overnight."

"Could be where T.J. stashed Sara," he said and then his

mouth tightened to a grim line as he jabbed at another spot on the map. "This is a bridge over an arroyo. Let's hope that it's more than a foot bridge and that they have the sense to stay away from it if the rains are as bad as they say they'll be."

Her stomach turned at the thought of how bad a flash flood could be high up in the hills. The water would come churning down the arroyos, sometimes ripping up small bushes and trees. Cascading with powerful roughness against anything in their path. Anyone caught up in the way of the raging waters faced serious injury or death.

"He'll know better," she said, but it was almost as if she was trying to convince herself.

"Are you ready to go? If we're lucky the rains will hold out until we've got a solid grasp on where T.J. was headed."

"I'm ready," she said. As she eased on the knapsack and adjusted its weight on her shoulders, she worried about why Sara had run away and why T.J. would have found it necessary to hide the young girl.

But then she remembered the bruises on Sara's arms when she had arrived at the ranch and T.J.'s comments about the driver who had challenged him a few nights ago. The teens had clearly been afraid of whoever was responsible for both.

Because of that, she hoped she and Fisher would find the teens before anyone else did.

Although heavy rains were expected later that day, it had been at least a week since it had rained and the ground was hard and dusty. Despite that, Fisher was able to track the impressions in the gravel by T.J.'s car to a distinctive set of sneaker treads on the dirt path leading to the trail.

"What size shoe does T.J. wear?" he asked.

"A thirteen," she responded and stood by him as he kneeled to examine the footprints.

"That's about the size of this shoe which confirms that T.J. probably went up this trail."

He rose and adjusted the straps on the knapsack, making sure they were tight so that the pack would not shift as they headed up the trail. From the trunk, he removed a rifle, eased the strap over his head and settled the weapon securely beside the pack on his back. Then he faced Macy, reached for her straps, but paused by the bindings on her knapsack.

"May I?" he asked.

She nodded and he quickly adjusted her pack to keep it from shifting and then gestured to the trail. "I'll lead the way. If I'm going too fast—"

"Believe me I'll let you know."

He smiled, ripped out a baseball cap from his back pocket and plopped it on her head. "Put this on. There'll be glare on the footpath and once it starts raining, it'll keep you dry."

"Thanks."

He grabbed his cowboy hat from the backseat of the Jeep and also put on a pair of polarized sunglasses which would help cut down on the glare. Taking the point, he focused on the sneaker tread pattern and followed it up the trail.

T.J. had not tried to hide his tracks. The footprints were clearly visible along the path. He had been in a hurry, however, judging from the wide distance between his steps. If he recalled T.J.'s height correctly, the space between the footprints indicated that he had been almost jogging up the trail.

If Macy hadn't been with him, he would have done the same, eager as he was to find the teens and put to right what was happening so Macy could have some peace of mind. But she was with him and so he kept his pace reasonable, his mind focused on tracking T.J., but also aware of how she was doing as she followed behind him.

About a mile up the path, T.J.'s stride began to shorten and about a quarter of a mile after that, they became the length of a normal walking step. He paused then and perused the path ahead of them as well as the open country all around.

Pines and oaks dotted the rolling hillsides. In between the stands of the trees were patches of grass and larger meadows which in the springtime would be awash with the colors of Texas wildflowers. Even now there were spots of bright color from some of the later blooming plants and stretches of prickly pear cactus. Up ahead of them, the trail wound through stands of trees before a limestone rock face rose up to the left, leading to the overlook Macy had identified on the map.

"It's beautiful, isn't it?" she asked as she stood beside him.

"It is," he said and pointed to a herd of fallow deer feeding on grass in one distant meadow, their almost white coats bright against the dull brown of the parched grasses.

Macy leaned against him and took hold of his hand as she witnessed the sight. "I wish that one day…"

He didn't need her to finish. He knew what she wished and inside of him, something had been slowly taking root since last night. Something that said maybe what they both wished wasn't so far apart.

Looking up the trail, he said, "You mentioned a cave?"

She nodded. "There's quite a few of them up ahead, but I think the biggest one is quite a ways up. Probably past the overlook and closer to the bridge."

Once again concern rose in him as he cast his gaze upward at the thickening clouds above. Inhaling deeply, he could smell the coming rain and hoped the forecasters were wrong about the force of the storm.

"Let's get going. The rain will be here soon," he said and they once again set off, following T.J.'s sneaker prints in the dust of the trail.

They had been on the winding path for another half an hour when the first fat raindrop plopped on the brim of his cowboy hat. He quickly removed two large rain ponchos from one of the pouches on his pack and helped Macy ease hers on over the backpack. Then he slipped on his own as the drops grew more frequent and quite heavy in a matter of seconds.

There was little shelter on the trail as they continued upward, just an occasional stand of oaks here and there, but they couldn't pause for any delayed shelter under the trees. The impressions of T.J.'s sneakers vanished quickly beneath the onslaught of the rain. The trail in front of them became a difficult morass of mud.

As they struggled ever onward, he kept his eyes trained on the areas around the trail to make sure T.J. had not detoured off the path. There wasn't any sign that he had deviated from continuing up the trail. If anything, up ahead he found an impression protected by a thick oak beside the trail. Bending down, he examined the footprint more closely just to make sure. It was T.J.'s.

Beneath the canopy of the oak, he offered Macy a drink and short respite from the mud and pounding rains they had been battling for nearly an hour.

She took a deep draw from the canteen and pulled off her baseball cap to wipe away a line of sweat from her forehead. "We're not even halfway to the overlook."

No, they weren't, he thought. He cradled her cheek and

said, "Don't worry. If we're moving this slowly, so is T.J. He won't get that much farther ahead. For all we know, he's taken refuge in one of the caves to wait out the storm."

Macy considered his words and prayed they were true. That would give them a chance to catch up to her son and Sara.

She dragged her hand across the back of her neck. She had tucked her hair up into a ponytail to try and stay cool, but with the rain the ponytail was dripping wet. Beneath the plastic of the rain poncho and heavy backpack it was hot, although once the sun went down, the temperature would cool quickly.

She glanced at Fisher who seemed as fresh as he had when they had first started the trek. Of course he would. As a soldier he was used to exercises like this. It was why he had taken the bulk of the supplies in his pack. She appreciated it since even the lighter weight in hers began to feel like a ton of rocks.

"How much farther will we go today?" she asked although she was determined to follow Fisher even if she had to crawl up the trail.

"Depends on how bad the footing becomes and how quickly it gets dark. We can't risk losing our balance once we're higher up on the trail."

She eased the baseball cap back on, pulling her dripping wet ponytail through the hole in the back. "I'm ready to go."

He smiled and tenderly passed his fingers down the side of her face. "I know you are."

Turning, Fisher once again set off up the trail, but as they cleared the protection of the oak, the rain pounded them once again. Beneath their feet, the ground was even more unsteady and their boots sank into the mud, making each step that much harder. At one point she slipped and fell to one knee. The cold of the rainwater soaked through the fabric of her jeans and she prayed T.J. had been sensible enough to take shelter from the storm.

As she struggled to rise in the muck, Fisher was there to help her up.

She took hold of his hand, but he didn't release it as they continued onward, slipping and sliding. Pressing ever onward until dusk came and darkness threatened. By that point, they were beside the limestone rock formations that held an assortment of crevices and breaks.

Fisher stopped at one, examining the size of the opening which was big enough for someone to slip through.

He turned to her and as he removed his pack, he said, "I'm going to check inside."

Leaving his pack propped up against the face of the limestone hillside, he easily sidestepped into the opening and exited quickly into a small cave. Clearly, someone had stayed inside. The cold remains of a firepit were in the center of the area and a small pile of tinder and wood sat along the wall.

He could barely stand upright, but there was enough space for a few people to comfortably sit or sleep. He snared a small penlight from his belt loop and flashed it along the edges of the cave. The exterior wall was fairly straight and toward the back of the cave another opening led deeper into the rock hillside. Stalactites had formed near that opening from beyond the sounds of dripping water echoed from deep within the cave.

Although the cave smelled damp, there appeared to be fresh air flowing through it, which would explain how they could build the fire within the small space. As he turned his penlight on the dirt floor of the cave, T.J.'s easily identifiable sneaker tread was visible in several spots along with a much smaller footprint.

T.J. and Sara had been there recently. Maybe last night, he hoped, thinking that if the two teens were up ahead they were also finding a dry place to spend the night. If he and Macy got an early start in the morning, they might be able to make up some ground on the teens.

He eased back out through the opening to where Macy stood huddled against the rock face, the rain pounding against her.

"T.J. and Sara were here recently. We can stay in the cave tonight."

Stepping beside her, he helped her slip off her pack and then led her through the opening before heading back out to bring in his own supplies.

Inside the cave, he gestured to the firepit. "Think that you can get a fire going?"

She pulled off her baseball cap and then her poncho, setting them by the entrance to the cave opening to dry. "My Girl Scout skills are a little rusty, but I think I can manage," she said, reached into her pocket and pulled out a small package which she wiggled in the air. "Your dad handed me some waterproof matches on the way out of his store."

He grinned and nodded. "There may be some deadfall just off the trail. It'll be wet, but should still get dry if we get a good fire going. There's some tinder and a small supply of wood just over there," he said and motioned to the far side of the cave wall.

He had left his pack and the rifle by the entrance of the cave as well and stopped to remove a small hatchet from the main storage area on the pack. Exiting the cave, he carefully eased down a side of the trail that had some small brush, saplings and luckily, the deadfall from an oak tree. With a few sharp strokes, he chopped away some larger branches which he carried back up to the cave before returning once again to gather some more wood.

When he had a good enough pile, he returned to the cave, set the hatchet by his pack and slipped off his dripping poncho and cowboy hat. His boots were soaked as well and so he took them off and placed them besides Macy's.

Turning, he realized she had a nice fire going. The smoke from the fire was being drawn back toward the interior of the cave. He suspected there was a break somewhere allowing the air to vent. Macy had also laid out a tarp on the cave floor and had their sleeping bags ready for later use. A cooking frame was set over the fire and she heated water in a small kettle beside another pot where something was steaming flavorfully.

"Smells great," he said as he placed the damp wood close to the fire to dry.

"Thank your dad for the prepackaged stew." She stirred the mixture in the pot before reaching beside her and grabbing a plastic bag. "We've got some biscuits I'll heat up as well."

"Do you mind?" he said and motioned to his wet jeans.

Macy gulped as she imagined what lay beneath the faded denim, but it made sense. She had planned to remove her own wet jeans as well once the meal was closer to done.

"Go ahead." She kept her eyes trained on the stew and once it bubbled, she tore open the package with the biscuits and laid them on the grate of the cooking frame to heat.

Before she knew it, Fisher was kneeling beside her, his sleeping bag wrapped around his hips.

"Why don't you get out of your wet things while I finish this up?"

She handed him the spoon for the stew and stepped away only long enough to peel off her damp pants and set them on top of her pack to dry. As he had done, she wrapped her sleeping bag around her waist and returned to sit by the fire.

Fisher gingerly flipped over the four biscuits with his fingers and he shot a quick glance at her. "Would you rather have tea or coffee?"

"Coffee would be great." After he had sprinkled grounds in the pot with the boiling water, she picked up the two divided plates she had removed from his backpack, held them out to him.

He snared the biscuits from the grate and placed them on the plates, then quickly spooned up the stew into one of the sections of the dish. As one they shifted away from the fire and sat, using the cutlery that came with the mess kits to eat.

Hunger took control and it was quiet as they both savored the meal. The heat of the fire helped chase away the damp and chill of the rain.

Macy watched as Fisher sopped up the stew sauce with the last of his biscuit and took pity on him, handing him her second biscuit.

"Are you sure?" he asked even as he was reaching for it.

"I'm full," she said and she was. The stew and first biscuit had been surprisingly filling. She grabbed a pot holder and picked up the coffeepot, swirled the liquid and grounds around before setting it back down on the grate to continue brewing.

While she did that, Fisher rose and removed a large thick plastic bag from his pack and placed the dirty dishes inside. "We'll wash them up later."

She nodded, grabbed the two mugs she had put by the fire earlier and poured them both steaming cups of coffee. She opened a plastic bag which contained dry creamers and sweeteners. After they had fixed their coffees, they sat and quietly sipped them.

The sound of the rain coming down continued outside and Macy grimaced. "Do you think it will let up soon?"

He blew on his cup of coffee and took a sip before answering. Shaking his head, he said, "Weatherman said the storm front would be with us until tomorrow night, but it shouldn't be as heavy during the day tomorrow."

Macy cradled the hot tin mug in her hands, enjoying the warmth of it more than the coffee within. When she finally took a sip, the coffee was strong and sweet. She peered over the edge of the mug to where Fisher sat, drinking his coffee and adding some wood to the fire.

The wood was still damp and as it heated; it began to snap and pop. Hissed as steam escaped from the log.

The heat grew pleasantly in the intimate space of the cave and she unzipped the sweatshirt she had put on, allowed the heat of the fire to soak in. But her growing comfort made her guiltily think about the kids and how they might not be as restful.

"Do you think T.J. and Sara—"

"They were in this cave. Probably last night. I'm sure they took shelter again today."

His words reassured her, until it occurred to her that she would once again be sleeping beside him. Sharing intimate space and given last night's talk, trusted feelings.

A scary and exhilarating realization.

Chapter 19

As he looked up from where he had been poking at the fire, trying to get it banked for the night, he didn't fail to notice the battling emotions on her face. He could even understand.

He would be sleeping beside her tonight. Again.

It scared him. Each time that he was beside her made it harder to think about leaving. And it terrified him to think about what would happen if he released the control he had exerted last night and finally explored his feelings for her.

Which brought an unwelcome tightening to his gut which he had to tamp down like the fire he was so diligently managing.

Yanking his attention back to the flames, he said, "Do you want any more coffee? I'm going to go clean the mess kits."

"I'll help—"

"No," he said more forcefully than he had intended. Repeating it softly, he said, "No, just stay warm and get comfortable. I think Dad packed some inflatable pillows in your bag."

She handed him her mug and he piled up everything from the mess kits. Balancing it all, he went to the opening of the cave and the flow of air through that gap chilled the bare skin of his legs. Lucky for them, however, since that ventilation kept the cave free of the smoke and other toxins from their fire.

Easing through the gap, he used the rainwater to rinse off their plates and after, to clean the coffee pot and refill it for the morning.

His shirt was damp by the time he was done and he shivered. At his pack, he pulled off his shirt and grabbed a dry sweatshirt, slipping it on.

Macy had also changed into a different sweatshirt and lay by the fire, watching him. Her gaze was wickedly tempting as he imagined lying beside her and shedding the clothes they were both using as defenses against their emotions.

He padded back to the fire and gave it one last poke. He would have to keep an eye on it during the night to make sure it was under control. Then he slipped into the sleeping bag beside her and lay his head on one of the pillows she had inflated.

A nice comfort considering the hard ground beneath them and the tarp which crinkled noisily as they moved about. Of course, he'd slept in worse conditions.

"It's not so bad. We're warm and dry," he said, striving for neutral.

"I'm still a little chilled," she admitted.

"We could zip the bags together and share our body heat," he said before his brain had a second to think about the consequences of those actions.

Her eyebrows shot up in surprise at the suggestion and

worry settled onto her face. She bit at her bottom lip and mulled over the suggestion before finally saying, "Do you think that's a good idea?"

He thought about lying beside her. Remembered the press of her body against his last night and the softness of her cheek beneath his hand. He imagined the softness of her in other spots and immediately answered.

"It's probably the worst idea I've ever had."

She chuckled, shook her head and toyed with one of the ties on the sleeping bag. "I always knew you were an honest man."

Honest? An honest man might confess to what he was feeling and the conflicting emotions she roused in him. But then again, he was an honorable man and surprisingly, honor sometimes meant being less than honest.

"I guess I should be glad you feel that way about me."

Macy sensed hurt in his words and hadn't meant to cause it. Cupping his cheek, the rough beard on his face rasped the palm of her hand. "I didn't mean anything bad by it. I always admired you."

"Did you? Lots of women thought I wasn't a happily-ever-after kind of guy," he said.

She thought back to those days and the women he had dated—none of them had been the kind to have lasting relationships with. Except her. Which made her wonder aloud, "Why me?"

A flush stained his face and he looked away at her perusal. "Why you? That night, you mean? Why you and not someone else?"

The words escaped her on a tortured breath. "Yes, why me?"

He met her gaze then, his resolute and hard. "I dated the kind of girls who didn't want commitment, but I knew you were different. I knew you and Tim… I had wondered for a while what it would be like if it was you and me."

Much as she had questioned afterward what being with Fisher would have been like.

"Do you ever think about it now? I mean, with the teaching offer and all?"

She couldn't bear to look at him as she finished and concentrated on the ties of the sleeping bag, twirling them around and around her finger as she waited for his answer.

And then waited some more.

Finally, she had no choice but to meet his gaze.

"What do you think?" he asked.

"I'd like to think that maybe you had thought about it. About us," she finally admitted, deciding that after eighteen years of doubt, it was time to put an end to it.

"I have, only now there's T.J. to consider as well. A son that I didn't know I had."

"I'm sorry that I didn't tell you before. With Tim's death and all that started happening afterward, I wasn't sure T.J. could handle that kind of revelation," she admitted.

"And now?" Fisher asked and tipped her face up so he could search her features. "What makes now any different?"

Tears filled her eyes. "I always worried whenever you went on a mission. I prayed for you to be safe so that maybe one day you and T.J. could get to know one another."

"Did you maybe pray a little for yourself? That maybe one day you and I—"

"Yes, I did," she blurted out and shifted closer to him. Cupped his cheek and brought her lips close. "I prayed that one day you and I could finish what we started."

"Then let's finish it," he replied and kissed her, taking

her lips over and over again until she was clinging to his shoulders. Pressing her body tight to his except the thickness and tangle of the sleeping bags kept them from really being close.

Without breaking the kiss, he unzipped both bags and dragged her body to his, his hands splayed against her back. The bare skin of their legs warm as they twined their legs together.

He needed to feel more of her skin and inched his hands beneath her sweatshirt. The flesh at the small of her back was damp. Slick as he moved his hands upward.

She copied his actions, shifting her hands beneath his shirt to grasp his back. Moaning impatiently before reaching back down for the hem of his shirt, in one swift move she had pulled it over his head, baring him to her gaze.

She stilled then as she laid her hands on his chest. They trembled for a moment before she eased her one hand down to the scar along his ribs—a stray piece of shrapnel and a minor injury. She ran her finger along that scar before shifting to another on his arm.

"Don't think about them. I'm here and I'm alive. I want to explore the feelings between us," he urged, knowing that if she focused on those old wounds for too long, her fear would overwhelm everything else.

"How about I think about the way your heart skips when I do this," Macy said and moved her hand to cup his pectoral muscle. Beneath her palm, his nipple hardened into a tight nub. She shifted her hand so she could strum her thumb across the hard peak.

He sucked in a breath and at her back, his hands clenched against her skin.

"Not fair, Mace."

"All's fair in love and war, Fisher. You should know that," she teased, bent her head and took his nipple into her mouth.

He cupped the back of her head to him and murmured his approval, but even as he did so, he slipped his hand between their bodies and cupped her naked breast. Rotated her nipple between his thumb and forefinger and she gasped against his chest.

"That feels good," she said.

"Then this will feel even better," he said and pulled her shirt up and over her head, encircled her waist and brought her breasts to his mouth, where he greedily suckled, shifting his lips from one breast to the other as he pleasured her.

She held his head to her, kissing his forehead and encouraging him with her soft sighs and the press of her hips against his hard body.

"Touch me, Mace," he pleaded.

She reached down between their bodies with her one hand and covered his erection. The cotton of his briefs was smooth over the long hard length of him. She ran her hand over him, but when he bumped his hips forward, she answered his silent plea.

She slipped her hand beneath the cotton and surrounded him with her hand. Stroked the smooth soft skin of his erection as he teethed the tip of her breast, yanking a harsh moan from her.

The sound of her passion and the gentle caress of her hand nearly undid him.

Fisher eased her onto her back and while he continued suckling her breasts, he moved his hand downward until he encountered the edge of her low-rise panties. She sucked in a breath and held it, creating a gap between her skin and the panties and he pressed forward, delving beneath the fabric. Moving beyond the soft curls between her legs to the center of her, where he stroked her with his fingers. Felt her swell and grow damp beneath his fingers until he shifted his hand downward and eased his finger within.

She arched her back and called out his name in a satisfied surprise. "Fisher. Please tell me this is about more than want."

"It's about more," he said.

Smiling, she brought her lips to his and said, "Then make love to me."

Chapter 20

He groaned, so loudly that it made his body rumble against hers. He jerked beneath her hand, clearly at the edge and threw his head back with a shuddering breath.

"Damn, Mace. I don't have any protection."

Tenderly she stroked him while with her other hand she cradled his jaw and urged him to face her once again. "I've been on the Pill since Tim got sick and just never stopped taking it, hopeful I would find love again. I'm safe."

"I'm safe also," he confirmed and there came a flurry of movement as they dragged off their underwear.

Spreading her legs, she guided him to her center where he poised for a moment, the tip of him brushing her nether parts. Her muscles clenched in anticipation of welcoming him. Accepting him into her warm depths.

He looked down to where they were about to join, leaving

her staring at the short dark strands of his hair. She needed more. She needed to see the look in his eyes as they took that step. As they started to finish what had begun eighteen years earlier.

Asserting gentle pressure on his jaw, she urged him to meet her emotionally the way he would soon join her physically.

His green eyes glittered brightly and a slight flush worked across his cheeks as he breached her center with just the tip of him, holding himself away from her with shaky arms.

"Are you sure?" he asked, almost as if he needed to convince himself as well.

"I've never been more sure of anything in my life," she said and flexed her hips downward, surrounding him as she did so.

They both held their breath at that union. Held steady as their bodies reunited and their minds processed the fact of that joining.

He was thick within her and hard. All of him was hard against her, she thought as she laid her hands on his shoulders. Stroked the broad width of them, broader even than he had been at twenty. Stronger.

"You feel..." She stopped, unable to find the words. How familiar and yet different in a way that was exciting, she thought as she ran her hands all across his well-defined arms and shoulders. Across the deep muscle in his chest and down the six-pack abs that came from real honest work and not a gym.

He held himself steady, allowing her that exploration before he braced his weight on one hand and picked up the other to caress her breast. He ran his thumb across the tip of her and then took her nipple between her thumb and forefinger, tenderly tweaked it, creating a pull deep within her legs that caressed him. Urged him to move.

Slowly he did, easing out with almost agonizing tardiness

before he stroked deep within again, pleasing her with the fullness of him and the friction of his movement.

Fisher gritted his teeth and held on for control. Nothing had prepared him for how good it would feel to be inside her. To have the warm wet depths of her hold him as he moved in and out of her body. As he stroked her breast and knew that just touching wasn't enough. He had to taste…all of her.

He bent his head and sucked her nipple into his mouth as he continued his tarried penetrations, drawing her ever closer to a release. She clutched his head to her, shifted her other hand down to his buttocks to urge him on, but he withdrew from her, wanting that taste.

At her protest, he trailed his mouth down the center of her. Over the softness of her flat midsection and the sweet indentation of her navel. He paused there to tongue that valley before quickly moving past the nest of darker brown curls between her legs and to the center of her.

She yanked in a ragged breath as he tongued the nub between her legs and eased his fingers into her. Stroking her as he then kissed her there and sucked, building her desire with his hands and mouth. Feeling the pulse of her passion intensify beneath his mouth and fingers until her back arched up off the ground and she came, calling his name and holding tight to his shoulders.

He feasted on that release with his mouth, but before it had ebbed, he quickly shifted upward and joined with her again.

"Fisher," Macy cried out, holding onto him as his penetration brought her to the edge again and she shuddered.

He smiled, bent his head and kissed her. She could taste herself on him and realized that now she wanted a taste as well.

Pushing on his shoulders, she urged him onto his back and

straddled him, increasing his penetration and her pleasure. It was all she could do not to come again, but then he cupped her breasts. Tweaked her taut nipples and urged her on.

"Come for me, Mace. Tell me how much you like this."

She shuddered and climaxed, the explosion of damp and sensation ripping deep between her legs.

"That's it, Mace," he said, but then groaned as she rocked her hips up and down on him, dragging all that moist pulsing heat along the hardness of his erection.

He brought his hands to her hips to guide her, helping her set a rhythm. Picking up his head to lick at her breasts as she rode him and built toward another climax, but she still wanted that taste before it happened.

She eased off him, earning a strangled protest until he realized her intent and then he lay back, offered himself up, laying his hands to his sides. Exposing every bit of him to her.

She started at his chest, licking and biting his deliciously brown male nipples while she encircled him and stroked him, the wet of her from her possession of him slick beneath her hand. As the trembling in his body increased with her caresses, she trailed her mouth down the center of him, but she paused to kiss the scar along his ribs and murmured.

"I never want you to be hurt again," she said, but even as she did so, she worried that she might be the one to cause that hurt if things didn't work out with them again.

Shifting downward, she traced the edges of his defined abdomen with her tongue before playfully biting the skin over his nearly flat navel. He chuckled and cupped the back of her head, urged her downward until her mouth brushed the tip of him.

His big body jumped beneath her and she slowed the stroke

of her hand, tightened her grasp as she finally took the head of him into her mouth.

He groaned then and closed his eyes, arched his back to ask for more and she gave it to him, sucking him deep into her mouth while continuing to fondle him with her hand until he inhaled roughly and held his breath. She tasted the first hint of his release, but knew she wanted him deep within her when he came. Wanted to come with him and share in their passion for one another.

She held him tight and straddled him again. Guided him to the center of her and then sank down on him.

Their gazes locked at that union and she leaned forward, grasped his hands where they rested at his sides and brought them up and over his head. Twining her fingers with his, she watched his face as she began to move. Welcomed the surprise and acceptance in his gaze as their bodies strove toward the same goal. As the rush of pleasure and satisfaction drew them closer and closer to release.

Her body was shaking as was his when she finally bent her head and brought her lips close to his. With her eyes locked on his intense gaze, she whispered, "Love me, Fisher."

"God help me, but I do, Mace. I love you," he said and released the explosion of passion between them.

The muted call of an early morning bird filtered into her brain followed by the hard warmth of him spooned against her. The cadence of his breath changed, confirming that he, too, was awakening. His body definitely was, she thought as his erection stirred against her buttocks, arousing fresh desire within her.

She hadn't thought it possible given how often they had made love throughout the night, but she couldn't deny it now.

Pressing herself against him, she waited expectantly.

"Are you sure?" he asked as he splayed his hand against her belly.

When she nodded and urged his hand downward, he eased his thigh between hers and then pressed his erection into her.

She was slightly dry and the friction of him was rough at first, but he stilled to allow her time to adjust. Found the center of her with his fingers, caressing her. Bringing his other hand around to tease her nipples until she was wet and throbbing around him.

He let her set the pace, murmuring encouragement as she rocked her hips back and forth, her movements slow at first, but growing more determined as he brought her to the edge with his hands.

As her strength flagged, he somehow rolled and brought them to their knees. She braced her arms on the ground and accepted the strong thrusts of his body which pushed her ever closer to her release.

When he leaned over her and cupped her breasts from behind, rotating her tight nipples with his fingers, she came roughly as did he. But he was still there to hold her. Support her as her body shook with the force of her climax until they both dropped to the ground, bodies still joined.

The passion ebbed from their bodies, but the comfort of being beside him remained. Bittersweet because she knew there were still many tests their reborn love would have to survive.

From outside came more morning sounds as the hill country awakened, but mixed in with those sounds was the distinctive patter of rain against the ground and rock face. Inhaling, she smelled the rain in the air and hoped that T.J.'d had the sense to remain in whatever shelter he had found.

She and Fisher would not have the same luxury.

They had to find T.J. and Sara and return to Esperanza in order to set things right. She hoped that by now Jericho had returned from his honeymoon. Before she could say anything, Fisher said, "I can feel you drifting away."

Almost prophetically, his body slipped from hers, breaking the physical connection of their bodies. Trying to deflect his concern, she said, "Only until we have time alone again."

"Will we have that kind of time again?" he pressed, not falling for her attempt to avoid any serious discussion.

She flipped onto her back and he pillowed his head on one hand, braced his elbow on the floor so he could face her. "I want to. Once we find the kids and deal with whatever is going on with them—"

"We'll deal with us? With telling T.J. the truth?"

She thought about how difficult that might be, but recognized it was well beyond time to confront that past history and heal those old wounds so they might build a future. If he wanted to build a future, that was.

"Will you think about the teaching position?"

He nodded. "I already had, but now it seems as if I have even more reason to consider it."

She wanted to press for more, but decided she already had received more of a promise than she had ever expected. Rising up, she dropped a kiss on his lips and afterward said, "We should get going."

As she went to move away, he eased his hand around the nape of her neck and dragged her close for a deeper kiss. She clung to him for a second before he finally broke away.

"Just to make sure you know" was all he said as he rose

and went to the fire, tossing on some kindling and firewood to ignite it once more.

Once a small flame sprung up, he kindled it while she dressed and stowed away their sleeping bags and pillows. By the time she turned back to him, he had also dressed, gotten the pot of coffee going and had some oatmeal with fruit cooking on the campfire grate.

"Smells good," she said and sat down on the tarp beside the mess kits he had cleaned the night before.

"It'll provide solid energy and chase away the chill from the rain."

It wasn't much longer before they were eating the delicious warm oatmeal and drinking the coffee. He had made enough in the pot to fill up a small thermos he had in his pack. With the ever present rain, it would feel nice to have something warm to drink once they were back on the trail.

She helped him clean up and finish putting away their supplies. Once again they slipped on the ponchos, careful that the plastic covered their packs. Using the hoods and their hats to shield their heads from the worst of the rain.

Outside the downpours from the night before had abated somewhat, but the ground beneath their feet was sloppy. It was immediately clear their climb today would be arduous.

Despite that, they pressed on, Fisher in the lead, constantly alert to the ground and area around them in the hopes of finding any sign of the teens. About two-thirds of the way up, almost within sight of the overlook, Fisher held up his hand and motioned for her to stop.

A few feet ahead of him was another gap in the rock face along the left of the trail. A big enough gap that he was able to enter with his pack on his back. She followed.

As in the earlier cave, a firepit rested in the middle of the space and beside the firepit, something heartbreakingly familiar.

She rushed to the stones near the pit and picked up the piece of bright silver foil. "It's T.J.'s favorite granola bar," she said.

Fisher knelt and motioned to the footprints all around the foot of the cave. "T.J.'s tread and Sara's smaller shoes from the looks of it."

He held his hand over the ashes and remnants of burnt wood surrounded by the stones of the makeshift firepit. "Still warm. They can't have left all that long ago. Maybe they were waiting during the morning for the rain to let up—"

"And when it didn't, they left. So maybe they're not so far ahead."

"Maybe," he said and jerked his head in the direction of the gap in the rock face. "Do you think you can pick up the pace?"

Her legs ached from the constant sucking and pulling of the mud as they hiked, but if it meant finding T.J. faster…

"I'll go whatever speed you want."

With a nod, he rose and walked toward the break, but he stopped before her, cradled her cheek and said, "I always said you were a hell of a woman."

She smiled at the compliment, gratified by his praise. Back out on the trail, however, she was sorely tempted to curse him as he took her up on her word and pushed her at a grueling pace. Finally the trail leveled off a bit. Luckily, the sun was trying to poke through the clouds. While it would bring heat and humidity, it would hopefully dry up the ground for an easier hike.

They were near a bend that would put them on the final part of the trail to the overlook when she heard what sounded like a shout and the sudden intense roar of rushing water. Fisher must have heard it as well since he hurried around the bend.

She followed and smacked into him since he had stopped dead on the trail. As she glanced ahead, she realized the reason why.

Barely twenty feet before them was a wide arroyo spanned by a rickety wooden footbridge.

On the footbridge were two people—T.J. and Sara—hanging onto the flimsy wood and rope balusters of the bridge as it swayed and bucked from the force of the water cascading across it and down the arroyo.

"T.J.!" she shouted and rushed toward the bridge.

Chapter 21

Fisher took off after Macy, fearful that she would attempt to cross the bridge to reach the teens.

He had barely gone a few feet when a sickening crack and groan filled the air as the moorings for the footbridge closest to them gave way.

The end of the bridge rushed downward, propelled by the flood waters while T.J. and Sara bravely clung to the ropes and what remained of the bridge. The remnants of the bridge, with them hanging onto it, slammed into the far side of the arroyo, nearly unsettling the teens. The rush of the water covered them and the bridge pieces and then with another loud snap, the other end of the bridge likewise collapsed, plunging the teens into the flood waters.

Since the water sluicing down the arroyo actually brought them closer to where he stood, he jumped off the trail and careened almost wildly down the slope toward the edges of the arroyo. Seconds later, as he reached the bank and searched for T.J. and Sara, he heard Macy pound down the slope behind him.

"Do you see them?" she shouted over the loud noise of the raging flash flood that continued to surge down the arroyo.

On the opposite bank was a tangle of wood and rope from the footbridge, caught up in some tree roots and rocks. He thought he saw a glimmer of a red jacket amongst the debris, but couldn't be sure.

Tossing off his poncho and pack in the event he would have to go in after the teens, he waded into the edge of the waters. The immense force of the current pulled at him. Cursing under his breath because he doubted he could make it across the flood waters to the remnants of the footbridge, he withdrew back to drier land.

As he did so, some of the remaining bits of bridge gave way and were swept down the arroyo, but luckily, it revealed that T.J. and Sara were directly opposite them, clinging to each other.

When he looked at them more closely, he realized that T.J. had managed to grab hold of a sapling that had been along the edge of the arroyo. T.J. had one arm around the sapling and another beneath Sara's arms. The young girl was clutching him frantically, holding on to his arm and the fabric of T.J.'s red windbreaker.

He had to act and quickly. Sara looked like she couldn't hold on for much longer and the torrent of the waters was quickly eroding the ground securing the sapling.

He untied his rope from his pack and formed a lasso. He was a bit rusty, he thought, as he twirled the rope round and round, building up enough force to then toss it out across the twenty or so feet separating them from the teens.

It fell short of the mark but was in the right general vicinity.

He quickly reeled the rope back in, once again twirled the lasso over and over until he let it sail and it landed smack between the teens.

T.J. shouted at Sara to grab the rope and she did, but Fisher had other ideas.

"Tie it around the two of you—"

"The water's too strong and we'll be too heavy," T.J. shouted back. "Take Sara across first."

"T.J., please," Macy shouted from beside him, but he glanced at her and said, "T.J.'s right. It'll be too hard and we'll lose them both."

Macy hated that the two men were right. She also hated that by pulling Sara across first, they might risk T.J.'s life if he lost his shaky grasp on the small tree. But continuing to argue only increased the risk of that happening.

"Hold on tight, Sara," she shouted out and watched as one-handedly, her son somehow managed to get the rope up and around Sara's arms, securing her to the lasso.

Fisher had tied the other end of the rope around a tree on the bank and as T.J. released Sara, the waters carried her downward. Fisher began to pull her in, the muscles in his arms straining as he battled the force of the waters.

He had her halfway across the arroyo when a shot rang out.

By his head, a bit of bark flew off the tree beside him.

Someone was shooting at them, she realized, but she hadn't even finished the thought when Fisher blocked her body with his and continued reeling in Sara.

Another shot rang out, close to his head once again. He mumbled a curse, pushed her back behind the protection of the tree trunk while he held on to the rope, fighting to not lose his grip on it.

"Can you handle the rope?" he said and she immediately grabbed it, sensed the pull of the water and Sara's weight threatening to drag it from her hands.

She dug in forcefully, firmly planting her feet in the wet soil and leaning back to get the leverage she needed while Fisher grabbed his rifle. As she pulled in the rope, dragging it in hand over hand, Fisher used the scope to search for the shooter.

Another shot rang out, dangerously close to Fisher, but he grunted with apparent satisfaction.

"Now, I've got the bastard," he said and opened fire.

Her arms trembled from the force she was exerting, but she kept at it, protected by Fisher's body and shooting.

As Sara neared the bank of the arroyo, the muddy dirt by her feet flew up.

The shooter had turned his attention to her.

Fisher reacted immediately, rushing to block Sara's body with his and urge her in the direction of the tree.

Sara plopped down behind the trunk, shivering from the cold of the water. Her hands shook as she slipped the rope from around her body and handed it to Macy.

Wet hair covered most of her face, but her fear was evident. Her teeth chattered from the cold as she said, "Y-y-ou n-n-eed t-t-o get T-t-J."

She peered across the surging waters cascading down the arroyo. T.J. was still holding onto the sapling, but he was deeper in the water as the roots of the tree began to give way.

She didn't have much time to save her son.

To save their son.

While Fisher continued to pin down the shooter by returning fire, she undid the rope from around the tree and stepped toward the bank of the arroyo. Fisher shifted his body to keep her covered. She swung the rope as hard as she could and when she thought she had enough momentum, released it.

It flew across the waters but landed below T.J.'s position.

Mumbling a curse, she quickly pulled the rope back in and gave it another try, aiming for a spot well above him.

As the rope flew across the waters this time, it landed a half a dozen or so feet above and was quickly carried downward by the waters.

With a sickening knot in her stomach, she watched T.J. lunge outward with one hand for the rope. As he did so, the sapling in his other hand gave way and he surged down the arroyo. She feared she had lost him, but suddenly there came the rough pull of the rope in her hands. Strong enough to almost upend her, but she braced herself and wrapped the rope around her arm.

T.J. had managed to grab the rope.

Using all her might, she made her way back to the tree and braced herself against the tree. She used the trunk to help her, inching around the tree with the rope. Suddenly Sara was beside her, helping her to tie the rope to the tree.

Then another shot hit the trunk beside them, gouging a deep wound in the wood, but Fisher was immediately shooting at their assailant, trying to protect them.

As Fisher returned fired, she and the young teen began to reel in T.J. Together they managed to bring him onto the bank and once he was there, he slogged out of the water and mud and rushed to their side.

The happy reunion was short-lived, however, as the shooter opened fire on them again.

The three of them ducked down behind the meager protection of the tree and Fisher.

Fisher kept firing on the location of the shooter. It was only a matter of time before someone got hurt since they were too exposed on the banks of the arroyo. If he could backtrack on the trail and get behind the shooter, he could disarm them.

Glancing back at Macy where she huddled with the two kids, he said, "Can you grab the rifle and cover me? I need to take out that shooter."

Macy vehemently shook her head. "I'm a suck shot."

"I'll do it. My dad taught me how to shoot," T.J. said, standing up and holding out his hand for the rifle.

He ignored the ache in his gut at T.J.'s mention of his dad. Of Tim. Of how it could have been him who had taught T.J. to shoot the same way his dad had taught him and Jericho.

Driving away the pain, he handed T.J. the rifle and then stood beside him to point out the location of the shooter. Luckily, their attacker decided to fire, providing a needed view of his muzzle fire to confirm his position. T.J. immediately returned fire, his shot striking on the rock right by where he had seen the muzzle fire.

"Great shot. Keep that up, son," he said and patted the teen on the back. "I'm going to double-back along the trail and then come up behind the shooter."

"I'll cover you."

He nodded. "As soon as I've got a hold of him, I'll signal you so you can come down."

T.J. confirmed that he understood and then Fisher shot a look at Macy as she huddled next to Sara behind the tree trunk, trying to comfort the young girl. As their gazes met, he gave her a look that hopefully communicated his intent to stay safe.

At her nod, he rushed back up the slope and to the trail. While he did so, he whipped his cell phone out and called down to the ranger station, advising them of what was happening. Although the ranger immediately answered, he gave Fisher the answer he suspected.

"The sheriff and I won't be able to reach you any time soon," the ranger advised.

"I understand. He's got three of us pinned down and I need to get this shooter under control."

"Understood. The sheriff and I will be on our way shortly."

"I'll keep you posted," Fisher said and tucked the phone back into his pocket.

During the conversation, he had managed to make it halfway down to where the shooter was located. Moving as quickly as he could along the sloppy trail, he kept his eyes focused on the shooter. Listened as the ping and ricochet of gunfire echoed through the hills and arroyo.

Well aware of the shooter's position, he slipped from the trail, careful to stay out of view of their attacker, but unfortunately, he knew he might be out of view of T.J. and Macy. It meant he would likely need to deal with the shooter on his own, but he was well-prepared to do that.

In retrospect, it was the only way to keep them safe which was all important to him.

Important enough to risk his life.

With that awareness, he forged ahead.

Chapter 22

T.J. had his one arm propped against the trunk of the tree which shielded the bulk of his body from the shooter. The rifle was up against his other arm and he kept up a steady, but careful return of fire. Macy nestled with Sara behind the tree.

The girl was shivering in her arms and softly whispering, "It's all my fault."

Macy did what she could to comfort and reassure her. "It's no one's fault, Sara. Don't worry. We'll be fine."

She suddenly heard the hollow click as T.J. fired. The rifle was empty. Ducking down next to them in the meager protection provided by the tree trunk, he quickly reloaded the weapon with the ammo she had removed from Fisher's pack. Then he rapidly reassumed his position and began a brisk return of fire.

When he paused for a moment, she glanced up at him and asked, "Is something wrong?"

"I'm not sure. I think I saw Mr. Yates for a moment." He kept his weapon trained on the attacker, but held his fire.

She only hoped the shooter had not seen Fisher as well. When there was a continued lull in the shots from down below, T.J. dropped back down next to her and said, "We should head down. See if Mr. Yates needs our help."

"I'll go for the trail first. If it's clear, then you and Sara can follow," she instructed.

As she was about to move back up to the footpath, T.J. resumed his position at the tree, ready to fire, but no one shot at her as she headed up the embankment and back to the trail.

The ground was slippery and the weight of her pack made speed of any kind laborious, but she couldn't delay.

Fisher might need help.

Ironic how in all the years that she had worried about him being killed while on a tour of duty, he was probably in greater danger right here at home because of her and T.J.

She forced such negative thoughts from her mind and focused on the trail, remembering where she had last seen Fisher before he left the footpath to double back on the shooter. From behind her came the sounds of T.J. and Sara plodding along, gaining ground on her.

The lack of shooting was almost as scary as being fired upon. *Had Fisher subdued their assailant?* she wondered, refusing to consider the other possibility as she paused at the edge of the trail. She peered back up at where they had been pinned down by the shooter. It seemed far enough down and as she took the first step off the trail, she noticed that a few feet away, the brush and soil was torn up, as if someone had recently come that way.

Fisher, she thought, and rushed downward, at one point

losing her footing and ending up on her backside, sliding down the muddy bank of the trail. The weight of the pack dragged at her as she struggled to rise and she opted to release the bindings keeping it on.

She could move more quickly without it and if Fisher needed her help …

Free of the encumbering weight, she charged forward and came upon a small clearing where Fisher was fighting with a bigger, but slightly older man. A man who still held a rifle and was trying to bring it around to shoot.

"Fisher!" she called out and raced ahead.

Macy shouted his name and from the corner of his eye, he saw her plowing toward them, heedless of the fact that their attacker still had his weapon. Putting herself in danger.

The larger man took advantage of that millisecond of distraction and sharply hammered the butt of the rifle into his ribs. The blow drove the air from him, but he couldn't let the pain or lack of breath hold him back.

He had been tempering his actions up until now, keeping from using deadly force in the hopes of subduing the man, but Macy's presence had changed all that.

His years of military training took over.

When the man swung around to try and raise the rifle to fire, he unleashed a roundhouse kick to the man's head which dazed him for a moment. He followed up with a penetrating jab to the man's solar plexus, but the man somehow kept his hold on the rifle.

Charging him head on, he tackled their assailant to the ground and the impact of the landing finally loosened the man's hold on the weapon which went sailing a few feet away.

"Mom," he heard as he wrestled the man to his stomach and got him in a choke hold. Applying pressure, the cartilage in the man's neck crunched beneath his arm. With just a little more pressure it would give and end the battle. But as he shot a look out of the corner of his eye, he realized that T.J. and Sara had arrived. T.J. had shouldered the rifle again and now had it trained on them, ready to fire.

"It's okay, son. I've got him under control," he said and loosened his grip on the man's throat while grabbing hold of the arm he had twisted behind the man's back.

"Get his rifle, Mace," he instructed and she did so, picking up the discarded weapon before resuming a spot a few feet away beside the teens.

"Get up," he commanded the man, although he dragged him upward as well and maintaining his grip, made him face Macy and the teens.

"Dad!" Sara exclaimed, stepping from behind T.J. to stare at the man he had subdued.

He finally allowed himself the luxury of examining the man and realized he was one and the same as the picture that he and Macy had found online of Howard Engeleit.

Macy realized it as well. She stepped forward and looked up at him. Shook her head and said, "You're Sara's dad. You were shooting at your own daughter? Why?"

Engeleit sneered at Sara and said, "Because that little bitch is just like her mother. She was going to ruin my life."

Fisher increased his pressure on the man's arm, forcing him up onto his tiptoes to avoid the pain. As he did so, he asked, "Care to explain in a little more detail?"

"Sara saw my wife and I arguing—"

"You were always screaming at us and then you hit her. I

had to do something and realized I had my cell phone camera. I recorded him yelling and hurting my mom."

Howard sagged in his arms and his tone was pleading as he said, "You didn't understand what was going on, Sara. It was all a misunderstanding."

"I know what I saw," she shot back. "You were abusing mom and you were lying to the judge about her being unfit," she immediately continued and advanced on him until she stood right before him. She was petite and Howard's big bulk nearly dwarfed her, but she got up on her tiptoes until she was right in his face and said, "You only wanted custody of me so you could keep her quiet about how you mistreated us. But now I have proof of what you are."

Even though Fisher had a firm hold on him, the man lunged at his daughter. He yanked him back and T.J. took a protective step forward, the rifle pointed right at the man's head.

Howard stepped away and as if finally realizing that he was defeated, drooped in Fisher's arms until he was on his knees, his head downcast as he bemoaned his likely fate. "You're going to spoil everything, Sara. Once people see that video, I'll be ruined."

It was T.J. who spoke up next. "The night of the accident, someone chased us. Sara thought it was you."

Howard shook his head. "It was one of my investigators. I had him trying to find Sara. I just wanted you home safe and sound, honey," he cried, his tone cajoling, but Sara remained unconvinced.

"What you wanted was my cell phone with the video, that's why you tried to take it from me. You said you'd kill me if I didn't give it to you."

She faced Macy. "That's why I ran away and why I had those bruises on my arms—from fighting him off." She reached into her pocket and pulled out the cell phone. She had put it into a plastic bag and despite her soaking from the rain and flood waters, the cell phone appeared undamaged.

She dangled the bag with the phone in front of her dad. "Even if you take it now, it won't do you any good. T.J. and Joe helped me upload a copy of the video. It's safe now and I'm going to give it to Mom. I hope the judge gives her everything she's asking for in the divorce."

"And we're going to show it to the police," Macy said, coming to stand beside the young girl. She placed her arm around Sara's shoulders and said, "It's going to be all right now."

The young teen nodded. "It is. Thanks to T.J. and all of you, I finally feel safe."

From across the distance separating them, Macy met Fisher's gaze and the pride on it was evident. Their son had only been trying to keep Sara protected all that time. She only wished he had trusted them so they could have avoided a lot of misunderstandings and the risk to their lives.

"We should get down to the ranger station," she said and Fisher inclined his head in T.J.'s direction. T.J. had shouldered his pack for the trip down the trail.

"There's cable ties in the top pouch to the left, Macy. If you can get some, I'll get ol' Howard here trussed up for the trip down the hillside."

While T.J. continued to keep his rifle trained on Howard, she quickly removed the cable ties and handed them to Fisher who expertly secured Howard's hands behind his back.

After he was done, he said, "I'll take the pack now, T.J."

"I can handle it. Why not take Mom's?" he said and with a nod, Fisher shouldered the smaller pack as well as Engeleit's rifle which he used to prod the man and get him moving down the trail. As he walked, he called ahead to the ranger station to apprise the ranger of what had happened. When he hung up, he said to them, "The sheriff will be waiting for us down at the bottom of the trail."

She nodded and took up a spot just behind him while T.J. brought up the rear, Fisher's rifle cradled in his arms.

The downhill journey took a few hours, but it was much shorter and easier than the uphill climb. The sun had finally emerged, bringing with it the heat and humidity which she had expected, but also drying the ground somewhat, making their footing and journey less severe.

At the end of the trail, the local sheriff and park ranger were waiting for them. The sheriff took Howard Engeleit into custody, promising them that he would make sure Engeleit was held without bail in light of the threat he posed to Sara and his attempt to murder them along the trail.

With the sheriff gone, the ranger offered them the use of the ranger station to rest a spell before they went home.

Macy wanted nothing more than to head to Esperanza and clear up things about T.J., hopefully with Jericho and not Deputy Rawlings. But before she did that, she realized something else needed to be done.

She faced Fisher and held out her hand. He took it with his and smiled gently, although a hint of confusion colored his features. "I want to thank you for everything you've done for us."

T.J. stepped up to his mother's side, placed his arm around her shoulders and said, "Yes, thank you for taking care of my mom and me, Mr. Yates. I know my dad would have appreciated all you did also."

A pained look crossed Fisher's features and Macy knew it was the right time to act. Turning to her side, she took hold of her son's hand and said, "There's something you need to know, T.J."

Before either she or Fisher could say anything else, T.J. surprised them by saying, "Mr. Yates is my biological father, isn't he?"

Once again pain flashed across Fisher's features, but he schooled his emotions quickly. With a nod, he said, "Yes, I am. How did you know?"

Sara jumped in at the moment to say, "I think you all need some time alone. I'll be waiting in the ranger station."

After she walked away, T.J. said, "While we were on the steps of the church, I overheard someone say how handsome father and son looked. They were talking about you and me. Then I realized how much we looked alike. How we were standing alike."

And as they stood there facing one another, Macy once again noted the physical similarities between the two that marked them as father and son. Guilt swamped her, creating a knot in her stomach. She took a deep breath and slowly released it before she said, "I'm sorry you learned the truth that way. Your dad… Tim and I should have told you."

"Tim Ward was my father," T.J. began, his voice shaking with emotion.

Fisher laid a hand on T.J.'s shoulder and the young man didn't pull away. A good sign, he thought.

"Tim Ward was a good man. I never want to replace him in your heart, T.J. But I would like to get to know you."

Beneath his hand, tension radiated in T.J.'s body, but then the teen relaxed a bit. After a moment's delay, T.J. nodded and said, "I'd like that."

He didn't know how it happened, but a second later, they

were embracing and his heart swelled with love and pride at the fact that this young man was his son. "I'm proud of how you protected Sara and helped me up on the trail."

"Thank you for all that you did for us. For helping Mom, Sara and me," T.J. replied again before easing away to stand before Macy.

She slipped her arm around his shoulders and gave him a hug. "You're welcome to visit any time you'd like, Fisher. I know that with your military life that may not—"

"Actually, I may be seriously considering that job up at West Point," he said, wanting her to know that things had changed between them. Aware that in time, he might be asking her and T.J. to go with him, although he kept that to himself for the moment. Too much was happening right now to add that to the mix.

"I'm glad, Fisher. I always worried about you when you went on tour," she said and added, "It's time we all headed home."

"Let's go get Sara and maybe get the two of you into some dry clothes," Fisher suggested.

"I lost my pack with all our stuff when the bridge gave out," T.J. said.

Fisher motioned to his bag and Macy's which were on the ground by T.J.'s feet. "The clothes may be big, but you and Sara can take stuff from our packs."

T.J. immediately grabbed one pack and went off in the direction of the ranger station, his long strides quickly putting some distance between them. Fisher picked up the other pack and together, and much more slowly, he and Macy strolled to the station.

As they walked, she glanced up at him, almost shyly. "You were serious about considering that teaching position?"

He thought about leaving the life he had known for so long. A life that had brought him order, discipline and stability. But as he met Macy's gaze, he thought about all that he had missed with her and all that they could still have. With a smile and a nod, he said, "I've never been more serious about anything in my life."

Her smile was the only answer he needed.

Chapter 23

"I don't know what's going to happen with my mom and dad, so I'd like to stay on the ranch for now," Sara said, her brown-eyed gaze skittering over each of them before finally settling on T.J. as he sat beside Joe on the couch.

Jewel Mayfair contemplated Sara's request a moment before responding. "I hope the three of you realize how much danger you put yourselves in by not trusting us with the information about what was happening."

Macy watched as if almost orchestrated, the heads of all three teens bobbed up and down in unison. Bodies slouched, they were clearly aware of how their behavior had jeopardized not only their lives, but hers and Fisher's.

Jewel continued. "I have no problem with you staying as long as you'd like, Sara, but we need to let your mom know what's happened, and also Sheriff Yates."

"I've already talked to Jericho," Fisher offered from his spot beside her. "I phoned him from the ranger station, plus the local sheriff faxed him a copy of his report a short while ago. He'd like to interview all of you tomorrow so that he can complete his part of the report on Howard Engeleit's activities."

T.J. perked up and said, "Does that mean I'm no longer in trouble with the law?"

"You're out of trouble with them, but not with me," Jewel advised. Facing the two boys, she said, "Starting tomorrow, I expect both of you to get back to work bright and early. Even though you did what you did for a good reason, T.J. still needs to pay off his mom for the damage to the two cars and the speeding ticket."

Jewel then faced Macy, "Don't you agree?"

"Wholeheartedly," she said with a nod.

"I'm glad that's settled. I'd like to talk to Macy and Fisher alone for a moment, but afterward we're going to call your mom, Sara."

The young girl nodded and the three teens rose and went off to the family room to join the other kids, while Fisher and she remained behind in the library.

Jewel rose and closed the door, let out a tired sigh. "Am I glad that's all over."

"So am I. I'm sorry about how T.J. acted," she began, but Jewel waved her off and sat back down in her chair.

"He was confused and trying to help. Luckily it worked out well, only…I had actually thought we'd find him and Sara somewhere on the ranch property."

Fisher shifted to the edge of the couch and leaned his elbows on his thighs. His large hands were clasped before him as he said, "Why do you say that?"

"For several nights I've been restless with worry about T.J. and Sara and have been going for walks outside. For the past few nights I've heard noises while I walked. What sounded like crying—"

"Like what you heard before that you mentioned to Clay Colton?" she asked.

Jewel confirmed it with a shake of her head. "Similar, only this time I thought I heard hushed voices as well which is why I thought it might be the teens."

"Did you call Jericho and tell him?" Fisher asked.

Jewel shrugged and said, "I figured he had enough on his plate what with his just getting back from his honeymoon and all that was happening with the kids. Besides, when I mentioned it to Clay again, he said he would check around once more."

Fisher shifted back onto the sofa beside her. "If it continues, you should mention it to Jericho. It could be nothing or it could be—"

"Serious. I know. I should listen to the advice I gave the kids and talk to the sheriff about it."

Macy considered what her friend and boss had said and grew concerned that the noises might truly be something to worry about. "Do you want Fisher and me to stay here tonight? Help you keep an eye on things?"

Jewel shook her head. "No need right now. Clay is going to look around, but if it keeps up, I'll call Jericho. Besides, I figure the two of you need some time together. Or am I wrong about that?"

Hesitant, she risked a glance in Fisher's direction, but there was no uncertainty there. He quickly answered, "You wouldn't be wrong about that, Jewel. There's a lot for me and Macy to work on."

A broad smile came to Jewel's face. "Well, I'm glad to hear that. If you need to, take another day or so, Macy. Ana and I can handle the kids."

She appreciated her boss's offer and thanked her as she rose from the sofa. Turning to Fisher, she said, "I think it's time we took T.J. home and let Jewel get some rest."

Fisher stood up and eased his hand into hers. "I'd like to go home with you, if that's okay."

Macy grinned. "It's better than okay. It's what's right."

Fisher was used to sitting down to dinner with his men or his father and brother. Maybe it was because they were generally taciturn men that he found the back and forth between Macy and her son—no, their son—to be so lively.

T.J. was busy filling her in on what Joe had to report about the goings on during his absence.

"He says Deputy Rawlings was totally pissed off when Sheriff Yates told him that he was assuming control over Sara's case."

Macy carefully and methodically cut into the steak on her plate, clearly thoughtful about T.J.'s comments. "I think the Deputy is interested in Jewel, so maybe he had hoped to spend some more time around her thanks to the case."

"I don't like him," T.J. said without hesitation and then stuffed a chunk of sirloin in his mouth.

"That's understandable," he offered. "He was kind of rough on you."

"Damn straight," T.J. replied with a determined nod while he chewed the steak.

"T.J.," Macy warned, but the teen quickly swallowed and renewed his protest.

"He wouldn't cut me any slack, even when I told him the accident wasn't my fault."

"Let's just say he had past history to consider. Sometimes it's tough to overcome that kind of past although what you did for Sara will count for a lot," she said.

T.J. glanced over in his direction as if waiting for his take on things and then Macy looked his way as well. Considering T.J.'s actions that day, there was only one thing he could say.

"You were a hero today. You helped keep us all safe, only... Next time you should trust your mom more. Tell her if you or a friend are in trouble."

"What about you? Can I tell you if I'm in trouble?" he challenged and at his words, Macy looked away, obviously uncomfortable and possibly nervous about the answer.

To quell her discomfort, he laid his hand over hers as it rested on the table and said, "You can count on me, T.J. I'll be there if you need me."

"Will you be here for my mom?" he pressed and Macy's hand tensed beneath his.

"Your mom and I...there's lots for us to discuss and whether I'm here, that's for your mom to decide."

T.J. shot a glance between the two of them, without a doubt wondering about them, but he kept silent and resumed eating.

He and Macy did the same, polishing off the rest of the quick and simple steak and potatoes meal they had prepared.

After dinner, T.J. helped clear off the table and then walked to the door of the kitchen. "I'm kind of tired, so I'm going to my room to turn in early."

Fisher thought about saying goodnight. Thought about leaving the two of them that evening and every evening thereafter. It was more difficult to imagine than he had expected.

Macy solved the problem for him, coming to stand by his side while addressing T.J. "Would you mind if Fisher stayed with us tonight?"

"With us?" T.J. echoed and then picked up a finger and pointed it between the two of them. "You mean, like with the two of you like a mom and dad kind of stay with us?"

Heat flared across his face and as he shot a glance out of the corner of his eye, he realized Macy was likewise blushing at T.J.'s directness. Despite that, she nodded and answered, "Yes. As in Fisher and me staying together tonight like a mom and dad."

T.J. thought about it for a moment before he said, "Could I speak to Mr. Yates for a second, man-to-man?"

With a nod, Fisher walked up to him and then the two of them stepped outside the kitchen and into the hall. T.J. stood face-to-face with him and he was struck once again by how much the boy looked like him and wondered why no one had ever noticed before or if they had, why they hadn't said anything.

"What can I do for you, T.J.?" he asked, his voice pitched low so that Macy would not hear.

"You do mean to do what's right for my mom, don't you?" the boy asked, his tones seriously adult.

"I do, but I also want to do what's right for you. I've been thinking about whether to accept a teaching position at West Point—"

"I think Mom would like that," T.J. said and then quickly added, "And so would I. It would let me get a fresh start somewhere and get ready for college. That is if I'm included in your plans."

He imagined what T.J. might feel like, being faced with so much change in so short a time. So much life altering change, but then he realized he didn't have to imagine so hard. He had lived through such upheaval when his mom had abandoned them. He was living through the same abrupt change now with the discovery that he had a son and was still in love with Macy.

Even with his own confusion about the recent changes, he had no doubt about the answer to T.J.'s question.

"You're my son and I want what's best for you. If you and your mom wanted to stay here until you finished high school—"

"I'll do whatever will make Mom happy. I know I haven't made her life easy lately, only...I really missed Dad...Mr. Ward..."

"Your dad. Tim Ward was your dad, T.J., but I'd like for us to get to know one another. For your mom and I to possibly share our lives as well."

T.J. nodded and before Fisher could anticipate it, the teen hugged him hard, but then just as swiftly, turned and raced up the stairs.

Emotion swelled up in him, so strong it nearly choked him. Taking a few steadying breaths, he walked into the kitchen where Macy had just about finished cleaning up. As she dried her hands on a dish towel, she faced him. Worry clouded her features as she asked, "Is everything okay?"

He smiled and said, "Better than I could have expected."

"Really?" She walked toward him, stopped about a foot away and looked up at him. "T.J. is...okay with things?"

"As long as you're okay with things, only you and I really haven't decided what the future holds for us."

Macy was nearly strangling the dish towel in her hands and he stepped up and took it from her. "Why don't we go up to your room and talk."

She narrowed her eyes, as if taking his measure. "Is talk all you want to do?"

He grinned. "What do you think?"

Taking the final step to close the distance between them, she slipped her index finger beneath the waistband of his jeans and tugged him even closer. "I think that if you don't plan on kissing me soon, I may go crazy."

Clay Colton glanced out over the Hopechest Ranch from the small hill at the edge of the Bar None. All seemed quiet down below and he had yet to hear the strange noises in the night about which Jewel had complained.

Pressing forward, he headed down the incline to the metal fence which separated the two ranches and helped keep his livestock from wandering off. He followed the fence line, thinking that possibly one of his animals or even a wild animal had gotten caught up in the fencing. Or maybe they had been hurt by the barbed wire and lay injured nearby, accounting for the crying sounds that Jewel had heard.

Riding slowly along the fence, he kept his eyes trained for signs of any animals or possible problems and then something caught his eye in the bright moonlight.

He eased off Crockett and ground tethered the horse as he approached the fence. Squatting down, he realized there were boot prints near the fence and also, a few cigarette butts close by. He picked up one of the butts. There was something familiar about it, although he couldn't quite put a handle on what it was.

Taking a bandanna from his back pocket, he slipped that butt and two others into the bandanna, intending to show them to Jericho. As he stood and tucked the bandanna into his pocket, something glinted in the moonlight once more up ahead on the fence.

As he approached, he realized that the bottom line of barbed wire had been cut. Recently, since the ends were still silvery and unrusted like the rest of the wire. With the bottom wire cut, it would be easy for an animal or a person to slip through and as he looked around more carefully, he noticed more boot prints on the Hopechest side of the fence.

Strange, he thought and rose, searched out the countryside for signs of any strays or humans, but saw no one. He did notice, however, that he was near some caves where he and his kid brother Ryder had used to play as children. They would head down into the caves to avoid the heat of the summer day and had even camped out overnight in one of the larger ones a time or two.

He and Ryder had sure shared some fun times back then, before the problems.

His baby brother Ryder, he thought once again as he had often thought about him in the past few weeks. He'd had no luck reaching him in the prison where he was being kept. No luck finding out anything about how his brother was doing.

As he let out a low whistle for Crockett and the horse came over, he thought about writing to Ryder once more, but then decided that it would probably be another futile endeavor. Grabbing Crockett's reins and hoisting himself back up in the saddle, he decided he had to do something more if he was going to find out what was up with his little brother.

Tomorrow he would phone the prison and after, head into town to tell Jericho about his findings along the fence. He hoped his friend would be able to help him figure out what was going on between the Bar None and the Hopechest and possibly decide what to do about Ryder.

Chapter 24

Macy held Fisher close, arching her back as he slowly shifted in and out of her, slowly building her climax.

As she reached the edge and sucked in a rough breath, he stopped and arms braced on either side of her, looked down at her. "Are you okay?"

She was more than okay, but there was T.J. to consider just a few doors away. Reaching up, she cradled the back of his head and urged him down until she could murmur softly against his lips, "More than okay, love."

He kissed her then and whispered, "I understand, Mace."

He continued kissing her as he began to move within her again, dragging her to the edge time and time again, holding his own release back until his body was shaking above her. Raising her hips, she deepened his penetration and dragged a rough moan from him which she muffled with another kiss.

"Come with me," she urged against his mouth and with a few stronger strokes, he did, joining her as her release washed over her. Swallowing her small scream of satisfaction with another kiss before he lowered himself onto her, breathing heavily.

It took a minute or so before they could move, easing onto their sides so they were facing one another. It took less than that before they were touching each other again.

As Fisher cupped her breast and shifted his thumb back and forth across the tip of it, he said, "I can't get enough of you, Mace. I can't imagine how I survived all this time being without you."

"I'm here now, Fisher," she said and ran the back of her hand over the ridges of his abdomen before moving lower and encircling his softness which immediately began to harden beneath her hand.

He stilled his motions and as she glanced up at him, he asked, "I want more than now, Mace. Can you give that?"

"Whatever you decide, I'll be here for you, Fisher. I don't want to lose you again."

He groaned once more and his body shook against hers from the force of his emotion.

"You won't lose me, Mace. I promise," he said and pressed her down into the mattress as he began loving her anew.

Macy held him tight, her hands clasped on his shoulders. Her body welcoming his as they tried to make up for all the time they had lost. As she tried to store up the memories to keep her in the event he decided to go back on another tour of duty.

He must have felt her stiffen in his arms since he bent his head and repeated his earlier promise. "You won't lose me."

As she released her heart and body to him, she prayed that was a promise he could keep.

Jericho flipped through the pile of envelopes that Clay had handed him. Each bore Ryder's name and cell number neatly printed in Clay's handwriting. He noticed that the postmarks on the envelopes went back for several months. Leaning back in his chair, he rubbed his finger across his lips and contemplated the man sitting before him.

Clay Colton sat tensely on the edge of the hard wooden chair, juggling his Stetson between his large work-worn hands.

"You say the warden had nothing to tell you."

Clay nodded and released a heavy sigh. "Warden said he wouldn't tell me anything about Ryder and couldn't give me a reason why the letters had been returned unopened."

Even though Ryder's actions years earlier had created a rift between the two brothers, Jericho had no doubt that Clay sincerely wanted to make amends and was concerned about his younger brother. Unfortunately, there wasn't much he could offer for the moment.

"I'd take a ride to the prison and demand to speak to the warden and Ryder. Hear what they've got to say to your face. In the meantime, I'll make some calls and see what I can find out."

A tight smile came to Clay's lips. "I'd appreciate that." He juggled the hat up and down once more, clearly uneasy.

"Something else you want to say?" Jericho asked.

"I hate doing this to you so soon after your return, but I'm a little worried about something I found up at the border between the Bar None and the Hopechest."

The other man explained about Jewel's concerns about the

crying noises in the night and how he had gone out and discovered the boot prints, cigarette butts and the recently cut fence.

"Rustlers, you think?" Jericho asked, but Clay emphatically shook his head.

"All my horses are accounted for and I've asked around. No one's missing any livestock or seen anything out of the ordinary."

A relief, Jericho thought. With him and Olivia just back from their honeymoon and still recovering from their run-in with Allan Daniels, he had been looking forward to a little quiet at his return. Of course, given all that had been going on with T.J., Macy and Fisher, quiet was the last thing that it seemed he was going to get.

"I'll send the deputy to make some extra rounds at night and take a ride up myself to see what's happening. I'll let you know what I make of things."

Clay rose from his chair and held out his hand. "I'd appreciate whatever you could do on both counts."

He stood, shook Clay's hand and nodded. As Jericho was sitting back down, he noticed Fisher coming through the front door of the sheriff's office.

"Welcome, bro," he called out and waved his brother over to his door.

Fisher seemed tired and considering what had happened during the last few days, it was understandable. But as Fisher approached the door, he noticed the happy gleam in his brother's eyes. When they embraced, there was something more relaxed in his brother's normally militarily rigid posture.

"It's good to have you home, Jericho," Fisher said and after, sat in the chair before his desk.

"You seem to be doing okay, all things considered."

Fisher leaned his elbows on the arms of the chair and laced

his fingers together before him. "All things considered, I'm doing better than okay although…"

His brother surged forward in the chair, his hazel eyes glittering brightly. "There's a lot I've got to say and I'm going to ask you to let me finish it all before you start asking any questions."

Jericho nodded and leaned back in his chair which squeaked from the weight of his body. As he grasped the arms of the well-worn leather chair, the bright gold of his new wedding band caught Fisher's eye.

Once again he thought about how his brother hadn't seemed like the home and hearth type, but then again, until lately, he hadn't thought of himself that way.

That was, until lately.

"I'm thinking of taking the teaching position at West Point instead of signing up for another tour of duty in the Middle East. I'll miss my men and worry about them, but I think I can do a lot more good teaching new officers."

He waited for Jericho to comment, but his brother just sat there, although a broad smile slowly leaked onto his face.

"Nothing to say?"

"You told me not to say anything until you were finished and I suspect that's the start of your announcements."

He chuckled. His kid brother knew him all too well. Shaking his head with amusement, he met his brother's happy gaze and continued. "Do you know why I was angry about your planned marriage to Macy?"

"'Cause you wanted her for yourself?" his brother offered, surprising him.

"You knew that?"

"I suspected, but she needed my help—"

"And you were always one to help a friend. Much like Tim helped Macy when she told him she was pregnant," he said, but before he could continue, Jericho jumped in.

"I always thought she and Tim kind of rushed things. Her being pregnant out of wedlock explains—"

"No, it doesn't explain everything, bro. Macy was pregnant with *my* child."

Silence followed for long moments until Jericho plopped forward in his chair and splayed his hands on the top of his desk, his eyes wide and a look of shock on his face.

"T.J. is your son? And you never knew?"

"Never. I suppose you never suspected it," he said and examined his brother's features as the surprise slowly faded from Jericho's face.

"Never. I mean, T.J. didn't look that much like Tim, but I always thought he favored Macy." He paused and shook his head in disbelief.

"You have a son. I have a nephew," he said with a dazed tone in his voice.

"I have a son and yes, you have a nephew. Not to mention that Dad…well, Dad's a granddad."

"And he'll have another grandchild soon. I imagine the old man will be as pleased as a racehorse put out to stud. His family's growing by leaps and bounds," Jericho said and once again shook his head as he thought about everything.

"What do you and Macy plan to do? I mean, you've told T.J., I assume—"

"We have," he said and bounced his joined hands up and down nervously. "He seems to be handling it well. He says he'll do whatever will make his mom happy."

Jericho covered his mouth with one hand, his actions thoughtful as he rubbed his hand across his lips.

"What will make you happy, Fisher?"

"I can't imagine being without Macy again, Jericho. I think I'm going to ask her to marry me."

Jericho let out a small whoop, hurried around the desk and wrapped him up in a powerful bear hug. "I'm glad to hear that, Fisher."

He returned the embrace and when they parted, Jericho sat on the edge of his desk and picked up one of the envelopes there. Holding it up, he said, "Seems like we're not the only ones in a marrying kind of mood."

He held out the fancy off-white envelope and Fisher took it, removed the invite from within—one to Georgie Grady and Nick Sheffield's wedding. The event was barely a week away and he chuckled as he thought about good ol' Georgie Grady finally tying the knot after so many years.

"Seems like Cupid's been busy in Esperanza lately."

Jericho eyeballed him intently. "Are you complaining, big bro?"

He thought about going home to Macy later that day and warmth and happiness filled him.

"Not at all, lil' bro. Not at all," he confessed.

Chapter 25

A week later, they gathered for Georgie and Nick's reception at the local catering hall. The wedding had taken place earlier that day at the church where less than a month before she had planned on marrying Jericho. Where Jericho had married Olivia three weeks ago.

She held Fisher's hand beneath the table where they sat, listening as Clay relayed the information he had been able to obtain about Ryder after visiting the prison.

"The warden wouldn't see me at first, but I insisted. That's when he finally let me into his office and told me that Ryder had died a few months ago," he said and beside him, his wife Tamara covered his hand as it rested on the table and tenderly twined her fingers with his.

When Clay spoke once again, his voice was tight and slightly hoarse from holding back his emotions. "It's hard to believe he's gone. I feel like he's still alive. I still feel as if one day I'll be able to make amends for the distance between us over the last few years."

Jewel, who was sitting beside Jericho and Olivia at the table and her date, Deputy Adam Rawlings, leaned closer as the music from the band grew a little louder, making conversation slightly more difficult. "I know how you feel. When I lost my fiancé and baby…it took a long time for me to really accept that they were gone."

She had experienced the same emotions after Tim's death. For the longest time, she would roll over in bed, expecting him to be there. She would even smell him sometimes and recounted those sentiments in an effort to comfort Clay.

"Tim used to have this funky aftershave that T.J. had bought him for one Father's Day. For months after he was gone I imagined that I could still smell it," she said and Fisher tightened his hold on her hand, offering her solace.

Clay's eyes narrowed at her comment. "I thought I smelled Ryder the other day. He used to smoke these fancy cigarettes that had this weird odor…" His voice trailed off, but then he quickly added, "I think they were like the ones I found by the fence separating the Bar None and the Hopechest Ranch. You have the butts, right, Jericho?"

"I do, Clay. I sent one of them on to the state police for analysis."

"We appreciate you doing that. It'll be nice to know there's no worries to have about the kids," Jewel said and glanced in the direction of a large table at the other side of the room where T.J., Sara and Joe sat together with Georgie's little girl and the other kids from the Hopechest.

"They're having a nice time," her boss said and suddenly the band launched into a Texas two-step.

Jericho stood and pulled his newlywed wife Olivia to her feet. "Come on, darlin'. I've got to teach this city girl how to dance before you get too big to move around."

Macy smiled as Olivia eased into Jericho's arms and the two of them hurried to the dance floor. It pleased her that Jericho seemed so happy and as she shot a glance at Fisher, there was no doubting the contentment on his face. Even Clay, with his sadness over his brother's loss, seemed to have an easier burden with Tamara beside him.

As her gaze skipped to Jewel, she wished her boss would find happiness and as if some fickle Cupid somewhere was listening, Adam leaned toward her and said, "Would you mind taking a spin with me, Miss Jewel?"

To her surprise, Jewel's lips tightened with displeasure. "Thanks, Adam, but I think I'll sit this one out."

The deputy's face went white with anger before flushing red from embarrassment. His jaw clenched tightly, he dipped his head, rose from beside her and walked away to the bar at the side of the room. He stood stiffly while waiting for a drink.

"You okay, Jewel?" she asked.

Her friend shrugged and looked away from the deputy. "There's just something about him lately… I guess I'm a little angry about how he handled everything with Sara and T.J."

She understood completely. She'd had her moments of hostility about the deputy's actions, but she didn't want that to create problems for her friend. "I understand, but don't be mad at him on my account. I kind of thought he had a crush on you."

"Which I guess explains why he asked me to be his date for the wedding, although I'm wondering why I agreed to come with him. I mean, he's nice and everything, but the more I think about it, the better it is to wait for the right person. I mean, just look at Graham Colton over there," she said and motioned to where the older man sat, watching all the goings on, but physically and emotionally alone.

"He never was one to join in, but I think he really did love my mom," Clay said, surprising everyone with his comment.

"Too bad he didn't know how to show it," Fisher said and glanced her way, his gaze hot and intense, leaving no doubt that he knew how to demonstrate his affections for her.

As heat pooled in her center at just how he would show her once they were home, she leaned close to him and whispered a warning. "Fisher, please. You'll have to wait until later."

Jericho and Olivia returned just then, slightly sweaty and winded from their two-step adventure. As Jericho glanced their way, he said, "You two have a secret?"

Fisher chuckled and wrapped an arm around her shoulders. "Actually, it seems as good a time as any to make this announcement—Macy and I are getting married. She and T.J. are going to join me at West Point where I've accepted a teaching position."

Congratulations and hugs erupted all around the table and she found herself going from one person to the other, accepting all their good wishes. She finished making her rounds by going to Jewel, who hugged her hard.

"I'm so happy for you, Macy. Fisher seems like a wonderful man."

"He is," she said and brushed back a lock of her friend's

short light brown hair. "I know that one day, you'll meet a wonderful man, as well."

Jewel grinned and playfully tugged on her hand. "I hope you'll let me be your bridesmaid again."

"Without a doubt. Fisher and I will be setting a date shortly and finalizing all the plans soon. I'll stay as long as you need me at the ranch."

"Don't worry about that. Ana and I can handle things for a little longer," her boss reassured her, but Macy didn't want to leave her in a lurch.

"With Fisher accepting the appointment, we'll have some more time in Esperanza and I'll help you find my replacement. Get things settled at the ranch before I go."

"I'd appreciate that," Jewel said and after, they all sat back down around the table to enjoy the rest of the wedding.

As Fisher took her hand in his again and they shared an intimate glance, she realized that soon they would be gathering to celebrate her wedding to Fisher. Her son…no, their son would be standing beside them, blessing their union. Making them a family finally.

Her secret was out in the open and as she faced Fisher and brought her lips to his, she whispered, "Are you sure?"

His grin erupted against her mouth, calming any of her fears. "I'm sure that our being together is about eighteen years overdue. And you?"

She chuckled against his lips and said, "I'm sure that if I do want I want to right now, Jericho will have to lock us up."

He joined in her laughter and closed the distance to her lips, kissing her deeply until an amused cough drove them apart.

"Bro, I think it's time you and Macy went home," Jericho said, his eyebrow arched in amusement.

Fisher jumped to his feet, her hand in his. "For once, I'm not going to argue with you."

The deputy's patrol car had passed him along the edge of the road, but he had flattened himself to the ground in a small ditch and gone unseen. When the car returned on its rounds and skipped by him on its way back to town, he waited for a few more minutes before rising from the ditch and making the nearly mile long trek to the cut in the fence.

He moved swiftly and quietly, slipped through the cut barbed wire on his way to the small stand of trees and the caves where he and Clay had played as kids.

Clay, he thought, thinking about his older brother and how he had looked the other day when he had come out to inspect the area and noticed the cut in the fence.

Ryder had been hiding by the trees, watching him. Wanting to reach out and let Clay know he was there, but he couldn't do it just yet.

He paused by the fence along the edge of the Bar None and Hopechest, glanced down toward Esperanza. He had noticed the traffic around the church earlier in the day and later, the gathering of cars and people at the one big hall in town.

Another wedding in Esperanza.

There seemed to be a lot of them lately and he wondered who was getting married today. Wondered whether any of the people at the wedding were aware of what was happening right beneath their noses.

Of course not, he told himself, pushing away from the fence and heading toward the caves. Not even the sheriff had a clue about what was going on or that the big bad little brother was back to get to the bottom of it. To redeem himself for all the wrong that he had done as a young man. The wrong that had driven a wedge between himself and his older brother Clay.

As he paused at the edge of the trees, he looked back toward town again and smiled at the thought of returning home.

"Soon," Ryder told himself and slipped into one of the caves, intent on completing his redemption.

Jericho and Fisher waited on the steps of the church, T.J. beside them much as they had stood there nearly a month earlier. Only there was no doubt now about who Macy was wedding and that this would be a real marriage.

Clasping his hands before him tightly, he rocked back and forth on his heels, prompting T.J. to ask, "Are you nervous?"

Nervous. Excited. Happy.

"I am," he confessed and examined his son. "Are you?"

T.J. shrugged, but the fabric of his dress blue suit barely moved since the jacket was slightly big on him. Not for long, he knew, thinking back on how both he and Jericho had filled out in their senior year.

Clapping a hand on T.J.'s shoulder, he said, "I'm glad we'll have the time to get to know each other."

"I'm glad, too," T.J. responded.

A second later, a limo pulled up in front of the church. Jewel stepped out first, looking beautiful in a pale pink bridesmaid's dress that hugged her slender figure. As she noticed them waiting on the steps of the church, she waved at them.

"Time for you to head inside. It's bad luck to see the bride before the wedding," she called out in warning, but before they could take a step, Macy slipped from the limo.

The dress she wore this time was nothing like the one she had purchased for her wedding to Jericho. This one was …

Amazing, he thought, taking note of the intricate skirt of the pale ice blue dress with its yards and yards of palest white lace. The bodice hugged her curves, accentuating her tempting shape and her shoulders were bare, making him want to touch her.

As his gaze skimmed up to her face and hair, he realized that she had gone all out. Makeup expertly done and her shoulder length brown hair stylishly cut and set in a tousled style that screamed sexy.

"Fisher?" his brother prompted.

He faced him and T.J., blushed as he saw the look on his brother's face and T.J.'s amused look as he said, "Aw, come on, Fisher. That's my mom."

"She's beautiful, isn't she?" he said and with a wink at Macy, he once again clapped T.J. on the back.

"Ready to become a family?"

T.J. shot a quick hesitant look back at his mom, but then a wide grin erupted on his face. "You love her, don't you?"

"I do. With all my heart."

"Then I guess it's okay," T.J. said. "I'll go get Mom."

Fisher watched as he walked away, went to Macy's side and slipped his arm through hers.

He was about to head into the church when T.J. shouted, "Wait up, Fisher."

To his surprise, T.J. hurried Macy over and then slipped his arm through Fisher's. "A family, right?" T.J. said as he stood between them.

He met Macy's gaze which was shimmering with tears of happiness. Grinning, he said, "A family, T.J."

Looking up at Jericho, who was waiting beside Jewel, he said, "Come on, bro. The three of us have places to go."

As they followed Jewel and Jericho down the aisle of the

church, he felt the secrets of the past slip away, replaced by the excitement of his new tour of duty—building a life with Macy and T.J.

It was a mission he knew would bring nothing but happiness for the three of them.

* * * * *

BABY'S WATCH

BY
JUSTINE DAVIS

Justine Davis lives on Puget Sound in Washington. Her interests outside of writing are sailing, doing needlework, horseback riding and driving her restored 1967 Corvette roadster—top down, of course.

Justine says that years ago, during her career in law enforcement, a young man she worked with encouraged her to try for a promotion to a position that was at the time occupied only by men. "I succeeded, became wrapped up in my new job, and that man moved away —never, I thought, to be heard from again. Ten years later he appeared out of the woods of Washington state, saying he'd never forgotten me and would I please marry him. With that history, how could I write anything but romance?"

Chapter 1

Cops, federal agents and the people who wrote glamorous stories about them, were all crazy. There was freaking nothing glamorous about undercover work, Ryder Colton mused as he stubbed out his last cigar.

In fact, he thought wryly, the only difference between his life right now and his life seven months ago was that now he was sitting in the dark in a stand of scrub brush, unable to leave, instead of in a cell at the Lone Star Correctional Facility, unable to leave.

Well, that and the cigar, he amended silently. He'd missed the taste of the Texas-born Little Travis cigars he'd gotten attached to when he'd started running with the older and greatly admired Bart Claymore at fifteen, and bummed them from him.

Bart was one of the men who'd left him holding the bag the night that had started him on the road to prison—an irony that wasn't lost on him. Then there was the irony of his entire situation: that he, the bad boy of the Texas Coltons, was here pretending to be one of the good guys. Near the end—or so he hoped—of his search. A search that had brought him back to, of all places, the Bar None ranch. Now that was irony.

And *irony* was a word he'd never used in his life before now. He only vaguely remembered a discussion of it in some class in school, before he'd landed himself in juvie detention the first time. He must have paid more attention than he'd thought, because now, all of a sudden, it made perfect sense.

You're smarter than you want to believe.

Boots's words echoed in Ryder's head. The first time he'd said them, Ryder had laughed in his face; he never would have pegged the leathery, prison-toughened convict as a do-gooder. But Boots Johnson hadn't been the first one to tell Ryder he was smarter than he was acting. He'd heard the litany countless times before, from teachers, counselors, and family—especially Clay.

Ryder winced inwardly at the memory of his straight-arrow, stiff-spined brother. Clay had done his best when their mother had died, leaving the eighteen-year-old with a fourteen-year-old sister and a sixteen-year-old brother he had tried to take care of. Georgie had turned out okay, her only mistake was falling for that city slicker. But that had given her little Emmie, the pride and joy of her life.

His niece.

He remembered the moment when he'd told Boots about her.

So, you're an uncle, the old man had said.

He'd blinked, opened his mouth to say "What?" then shut it again. Emmie had been born well over a year before he'd landed here, and until that moment he'd never thought of himself as an uncle. A relative. Connected.

Not that his sister would want her now five-year-old little girl connected to him. Georgie was too determined that her little girl have a good life, and somehow he doubted that plan would include an uncle convicted of a felony who'd been in the federal pen most of her young life.

He considered lighting another cigar and decided against it; he only had a few more, and they were hard to come by. If nothing else, he'd learned in prison that his live-as-if-there-were-no-tomorrow philosophy wasn't always the best policy. And his motto—have your fun today—had landed him in a very tight spot.

Thankfully, the sky was getting lighter now, so he had to pack it in. He was tired from lack of sleep, also from the endless hours of sitting, watching, waiting for something that didn't happen.

And thinking. Most of all, he was tired of the thinking, the contemplating, the pondering. His brother had been the thinker of the family—not him. But sitting out here all night long, there was nothing else to do.

And he knew now why he'd always avoided it. It was much easier to just live his life, doing what seemed like a good idea at the time...

"And look where that landed you," he told himself as he buried the stub of his last cigar and headed back to the ten-year-old, battered pickup he was driving these days. They'd offered him a standard-issue, plain-wrap sedan, which he had wryly told them would stand out in Texas ranch country like a neon sign.

"Why don't you just paint Narc on the side and be done with it?" he'd said, earning him a frown from Furnell, his main handler.

Handler. That's actually what they called him. That had been the sourest bite in this whole stupid meal. Ryder Colton, the man who never let anybody, man or woman, "handle" him, not even his own family, was now owned by a dark-suited, overly tense type A. At least, he was for now.

And if that wasn't bad enough, he wasn't even watching for drug runners or murderers, nothing dramatic or exciting like that.

No, Ryder Colton, the bad boy of the Texas Coltons, was on baby patrol. Now *there* was some irony.

He got into the truck and started it, the smooth purr of the motor belying the battered exterior, exactly the reason he'd wanted it. He, the guy who'd worked so hard at not doing what his father had done, leaving a string of bastards across the country, was now trying to earn his way out of prison and a felony record by helping some über-secret government agency crack, of all things, a baby-smuggling ring.

If they'd purposely searched out someone less suited, they couldn't have found him, Ryder had thought when they'd first approached him. Not only had he never had anything to do with babies, his life experience didn't include any knowledge whatsoever of what it would be like for a loving parent to lose a child. He'd never known anyone like that.

Well, Georgie. He had to admit that his sister obviously loved little Emmie. But he couldn't help thinking that was because she'd had the same experience he had, and was trying to make up for it. Or maybe she loved Emmie like she loved her horses, only…more. Maybe that was what it was like.

God, he was going slowly insane. He'd laugh if he weren't so tired. And bored.

He drove carefully—and as quickly as possible— through Esperanza, on his way back to San Antonio, where he was staying. He hadn't wanted to take the chance that someone in Esperanza might recognize him. While he looked a little different now—his hair was shorter and he'd filled out a bit—he'd been too well known, even notorious he supposed, in this little town to skate by unrecognized. It was much safer to lose himself among the million-plus population of the second largest city in the state.

The thought of doing it for real, taking this chance and just losing himself, dumping this crazy assignment he'd taken and making a break for it, starting over somewhere else, occurred to him, and not for the first time. East, to New York and the big city? Hell, he could lose himself forever there. Or L.A., maybe, warm, and thankfully dry weather, the beaches, paradise, right? He could lose himself there, too.

You can lose yourself anywhere. It's finding yourself that takes effort. You throw yourself away often enough, and one day you don't get it back.

Boots hadn't been talking about New York or L.A., but his words echoed in Ryder's head all the same. He didn't think he'd forgotten one single thing the older man had ever told him.

He'd thought at the time that it was just typical of his misbegotten life that he'd find the first human being who really gave a damn about him—the real him, not the impossible ideal Clay had always expected him to live up to— in a place like the Lone Star Correctional Facility. And that it would be a reformed armed robber who'd drawn the max because two people had died as a result of his crimes.

But regardless of all that, for the first time in his life, he started to see the way he was living it as a waste. He'd never worried about that before, rarely thought about it, but somehow Boots made him care. Made him want to change, to try another way.

He'd just never figured it would be such damn hard work. And he wasn't thinking about the job he'd taken on. That was the easy part.

He shook his head wearily, and drove on into the rising sun.

Ana Morales stood on the front porch of Jewel Mayfair's precious Hopechest Ranch house. She rubbed at her aching back with one hand as she gazed out over the ranchland bathed in the morning sun. To the east was San Antonio, she knew, although she had not ventured into that city the whole time she had been here. She could not risk it.

To the north was the vast, rolling, beautiful hill country of Texas. She would like to see it someday; she had heard so much chatter about everything from inner-tubing down the Guadalupe River to Saturday nights at the state's oldest honky-tonk. She smiled with a linguist's pleasure at the word; and Americans thought Spanish was odd!

Her pleasure at the word faded as she wondered if she would ever get to explore her love of languages again. Becoming a teacher had been her dream since childhood…and now here she was, nearly ready to bring a child into the world herself.

And by herself.

She turned to go back inside, back to the room Jewel had given her, no questions asked, at Ana's request; the room that looked out onto this porch—and gave the occupant a chance to see anyone who arrived. Before being seen herself.

She had been useful here. She had found purpose, something to focus on as she waited for the precious life within her to come into the world. And she had found someone else to worry about, she admitted; Jewel had been kindness personified to her, but Ana knew Jewel was deeply troubled. Too often, when Ana got up in the nighttime hours, suffering from the inability to find a comfortable position for her expanded body, she would find Jewel already up and walking the house. Sometimes Jewel had clearly been up for a while, sometimes she had the slightly wide-eyed look that told Ana she had been jolted awake by one of her nightmares.

It was those times that Ana felt rather small; this woman, who was working so hard here to provide the hope of the ranch's name to troubled kids, had had so much tragedy in her life. And yet she found solace in her work here—although not peace.

Or sleep.

Ana instinctively smoothed a hand protectively over the mound of her belly; she could not begin to imagine the horror of losing this child before it had a chance to live, as Jewel had lost hers. This life within her had been the impetus for everything she had done in the past seven months, since the day she had first suspected that she was pregnant.

"Getting heavy, that little one?"

Ana whirled around as quickly as she could, given her current bulk, chastising herself for getting so lost in her thoughts that she was caught off guard. That Jewel sometimes moved like a wraith around this place was no excuse in her mind.

"Sorry, I didn't mean to startle you."

"It is all right," Ana assured her. "I was actually just thinking about you. Did you finally get to sleep last night?"

"Some," Jewel said, but her weary brown eyes beneath the tousled cap of golden-brown hair told Ana that "some" had not been enough.

Doctor, heal thyself, Ana thought, although strictly speaking she knew Jewel was a psychologist, not a physician.

"Is there any more word?" Ana asked, turning to the subject that concerned her most; the very thought that a baby-smuggling ring was operating in the area terrified her. More than once she had thought she should move on, take her unborn child to a safer place, but she knew the folly of that; she had found shelter here, in a climate where most looked upon her as an enemy, just another illegal come to milk the American system. Of course, she was nothing of the kind.

She was secure here at the Hopechest Ranch, and it was simply up to her to keep her baby safe.

"Not that I've heard," Jewel answered. "But Adam will probably stop by later, and then I'll know for sure."

Ana smiled at the woman seventeen years her senior, and painfully wiser. "He is visiting more and more, Deputy Rawlings."

At first the sheriff's deputy had made Ana nervous, given her shaky immigration status. But the tall, strong man with the perfectly groomed dark hair and the always razor-creased uniform seemed only to have eyes for Jewel, which suited Ana just fine. Jewel deserved some happiness and his attention provided her benefactor—and herself, she admitted—with firsthand information on the ongoing investigation.

Jewel smiled, but absently. "Yes, he is."

"You do not like him?"

"Of course I do. He's been very kind to me."

"But…?"

"I'm not ready for that."

She didn't clarify, and Ana didn't ask. She had her own problems and wasn't about to counsel anyone in an area where she had made so many mistakes herself. She had trusted where she shouldn't have, and now she was paying the price. That one of the men she had trusted had been her own father didn't absolve her. Once she had found the evidence of his true character, it seemed the signs had been so clear she couldn't forgive herself for having missed them.

As for Alberto…she could not forgive herself for that, either. Yes, he was smooth, convincing, but so was her father.

Her baby kicked, mightily, as if the thoughts of traitorous men were unsettling to more than just her. She smiled as she put a hand over the spot.

"Kicking?" Jewel asked.

"Yes," Ana said, her smile widening. And then, suddenly remembering, her smile vanished. "Oh, Jewel, I am so sorry. It must be terribly hard for you to have me here, to see me, with my baby."

Jewel waved her to silence. "It's all right, Ana. I will never get over the loss of my baby, but I don't expect the world to stop turning and other women lucky enough to be pregnant to hide, just to spare my feelings."

Ana studied the benefactor who was rapidly becoming a friend. "You are very wise," she said.

"What I am," Jewel said frankly, "is very tired."

"I know," Ana said. "Is there anything I can do for you? Something else I can take over, so you can rest? Perhaps you might have better luck sleeping in the daytime?"

If Jewel was offended at the suggestion, or bothered by Ana's knowledge of her sleepless nights, she didn't let it show.

"I'll let you know. Thank you." A smile flashed across Jewel's face. "Unless you want to go riding with the older girls over at the Bar None this afternoon. I'm sure Clay can find a nice, gentle horse for you. You haven't left the ranch since you got here."

Ana was sure by Jewel's laugh that her fear must have shown in her face.

"Even if I could get this—" she gestured at her own bulk "—into a saddle, I wouldn't. Horses and I...no."

"You're in Texas now, girl. Better learn to love them."

"I do," Ana said. "They're beautiful creatures. But I prefer to admire them from a distance."

"You'll get over it," Jewel predicted. "It's in the water. And soon," Jewel warned her with a smile, "I'm going to make you take a break and have some fun."

Ana retreated to her room after that, wondering if the word *fun* would ever again be in her lexicon. It seemed a very, very long time since she had done anything but worry and plan and pray.

She stretched, trying to ease her aching back. If Jewel wouldn't take her advice about a nap this afternoon, perhaps she herself would. Along about three she was usually beginning to feel the strain of the extra weight she was carrying. Her feet would swell, her back would throb, and there would be nothing more welcome than to lie down for a while.

Except then there would be no distraction, nothing to keep her from dwelling on the unpleasant facts of her situation. She was twenty-two, unmarried and not likely to marry. She was about to become a mother, with a past in shambles behind her. But she was determined to build a life for herself and her baby.

She had never felt more alone.

And then the baby moved again. Ana set her jaw and her courage.

She was not alone. She had a tiny, helpless human being depending on her. A child she already loved beyond measure. She would make sure that child had a chance.

She would do whatever she had to to make that happen.

Chapter 2

By the time he reached his small, nondescript motel room, Ryder was feeling the too-familiar sensation of physical weariness coupled with being mentally amped up. It would be another day of restless sleep. He was definitely a night owl and used to sleeping in daylight—that was, according to Clay, one of his biggest failings—but doing nothing made him crazy.

"Buenos dias, mijo."

With his key—no modern card key for this old place—still in the door to his room, he looked over his shoulder to see the source of the "Good morning." It was Elena Sanchez, the tiny, round woman who ran this place with her husband, Julio. They'd been married, she had told Ryder at one point, nearly fifty years. The concept of being with one person that long boggled him.

"Hola, mamacita," he said, teasing her about her

tendency to mother him, even though she'd only known him a week. She also had amenably adapted her cleaning schedule to his, so that she never disturbed him when he was trying to sleep, but his room was always scrupulously clean; he appreciated that.

"You have been out all night again," she said.

"Working," he told her; something about the woman and her easy concern for a stranger made him want to reassure her.

Yeah. Like she'd be really reassured, considering how she feels family is everything, knowing you were out spying on your own brother's ranch. Better yet, tell her you're doing it because it got you out of prison, that ought to stop her worrying in a hurry.

"Have you eaten yet?"

"I just got here," he explained.

"Then you come eat with us. There is plenty."

"Thank you, but—" He stopped as she waved him to silence. And realized with a little jolt that he *liked* her worrying about him. That revelation put him off his game, and she won.

"You must eat," she said briskly, and bustled off, leaving him shaking his head at how neatly she'd trapped him. There was no way for him not to join the couple at their breakfast table yet again without being, in Elena's eyes, unforgivably rude.

And when the hell did you start worrying about being rude? he asked himself.

He supposed he could chalk that up to Boots, too. For all his rough edges, the man worked hard at doing what he'd never been able to do on the outside—be a decent human being. And that had included befriending a wild, out-of-control kid who'd landed in the adjoining cell.

Ryder's idea of learning hadn't included Boots's lectures, but with him in the next cell, he hadn't been able to avoid hearing the man. He'd taken to working on his collection of prison-style weapons. This, at least, he saw the need for; the looks and youth that had been a benefit on the outside earned him attention he could do without in prison. He learned fast, and was starting with a shiv made out of a toothbrush handle, since he wasn't allowed a belt with a buckle to hone to an edge. The work helped him tune out Boots's seemingly endless supply of reasons to turn his life around.

And that had included, later, convincing him to take the chance he'd been offered to clear his record and get out of prison before he was hardened beyond redemption.

A chance to do something good with his life.

A chance to help put away some guys doing some very nasty things.

A chance that had ended up with him coming full circle, back to Esperanza, where he'd grown up and gotten into trouble in the first place.

A chance that landed him, after following a trail that led all over the Southwest, where he was now. Spying on the Bar None ranch.

Home.

Not that he'd ever felt that way. All he'd ever felt at the Bar None was out of place. And a disappointment to his big brother. His little sister had been better; she had enough fire in her to understand Ryder's restlessness.

And look where that got her, he told himself. With a kid at eighteen, after she fell for some handsome, sweet-talking city dude. He'd have thought his sassy little sister would have been too smart for that, but some women were just suckers for a pretty face.

Lucky for you, he thought with a wry grimace, knowing that, except for the city part, he could have been talking about himself. He'd loved—well, in the here today, gone tomorrow sense—and left more than one woman, although after Georgie had turned up pregnant at eighteen he'd taken the lesson to heart and been very, very careful. Up until then he figured if a pregnancy ever happened he'd do just what his father had done—have nothing to do with it.

But after seeing what Georgie, the one sibling he could almost relate to, had gone through, the last thing he ever wanted was a baby to muck up the works, so he'd taken every precaution. His plan from early on had been to have as much fun as he could for as long as he lived, and that included taking advantage of how much women were attracted to him. That they weren't the kind of women who stayed didn't matter; he wasn't that kind of man, either.

"You are quiet this morning, *chico*," Julio said after they'd eaten, one of Elena's usual vast spreads of eggs, beans, and fresh tortillas made and patted out by her own hands.

Ryder wasn't sure how to respond. "I say fewer stupid things that way," he finally answered.

That earned him a smile from the usually taciturn Mr. Sanchez. "More should do as you do."

By way of thank you—and habit; there had been no one to clean up after them in their house, whether they were Gradys or Coltons—he helped clear the table. And he *was* thankful; the full, warm meal might help him actually get some sleep before he had to start in again.

Back in his small but clean and tidy room, Ryder took a quick shower, wrapped a towel around his waist and sat on the edge of the bed. He reached into the nightstand drawer and took out his pay-as-you-go cell phone. He had the other one, the one they'd given him to use, the one they paid the bill on. But there were some things Ryder preferred to keep private, and his talks with Boots definitely fell into that category, for both their sakes. The convict had gruffly made him promise to stay in touch, which, according to him, meant to take the weekly call Boots made.

That was a lot more staying in touch than Ryder was used to, but he hadn't been able to say no to the older man. Not after everything he'd done. So for the past seven months, when the phone rang on Wednesday mornings, he answered it.

Right on cue, the cell rang.

"How goes it, boy?"

"Not backward," Ryder said dryly.

Boots chuckled, that raspy, wry sound Ryder always associated with the older man. He could picture him, on the phone in the dayroom, lean, wiry and leathery. After fifteen years in prison, his ability to laugh at all was a marvel. Ryder thought his own three years had leached all humor out of him, and left him with only that new appreciation of irony.

"Sometimes," Boots said, "that's the best you can hope for."

"It's not enough."

"Depends on who's doing the grading. You always did want more faster."

Boots didn't point out that that very trait had been what had landed Ryder in trouble so many times—okay, most times—in his life. Perhaps he assumed it was obvious, even to Ryder, that he didn't have to.

Perhaps it was that obvious. Ryder jammed a hand through his thick, dark, and still shower-damp hair.

"So no progress?"

"I'm running out of cigars," Ryder said. "Is that progress?"

"Of a sort," Boots said with another chuckle.

Ryder had to consider his words carefully. After all, he wasn't supposed to be discussing his new "job" with anyone. But since Boots already knew about it—he'd been with Ryder when the men in the dark suits and the government-issue sunglasses had shown up in the first place—Ryder didn't figure he was giving away any state secrets talking to him, as long as he was careful.

"It's strange. To be out there, but…not to be. To have to hide."

He'd managed to let Boots know how the trail he'd been following had led him to, of all places, his brother's Bar None ranch.

"You don't think he's involved, do you?"

At the very thought of straight-arrow Clay being involved in anything illicit, Ryder had to smother a laugh. "No way in hell," he said succinctly. "I'm the problem child in that family."

"Were," Boots said gently.

"You'd be hard-pressed to convince my brother of that, I'm guessing."

"I won't have to," Boots said. "You will. Once you're free of all this."

This was old ground; Boots was determined that Ryder would reunite with his family, once this was all over. Ryder had tried to tell him Clay had washed his hands of him, and once Clay made up his mind, it took heaven and earth to change it. While Ryder believed in earth—at least the six feet of it he expected to be under before he was forty—heaven? No.

Somewhat to his surprise, Boots, a deeply religious man now, didn't push it on him. He believed enough for both of them.

"I've got to get some sleep, if I'm going to go out and play spy again tonight."

"You're not playing," Boots reminded him. "If this is for real, it could be dangerous."

Ryder couldn't quite imagine baby smugglers as armed and threatening.

As if he'd read his thoughts—Boots was good at that, even over the phone—the man chided him gently. "You're not taking this seriously enough, Ryder. Don't let the nature of the contraband fool you. There's a lot of money at stake in this venture. Probably more per ounce than any you'll ever come across."

He'd never thought of it that way. He really had no idea how much it cost to buy a kid, and he hadn't asked. Maybe he should. Because Boots was right; where there was money, there were men who would fight to get it and keep it.

"Something's coming," Boots said. "You watch your back."

"You been talking to the Boss again?" Ryder teased; Boots spoke to God as if he were a poker buddy sometimes, making what he called "suggestions," most of which of late seemed to involve the salvation of one Ryder Colton. And no matter how much Ryder tried to talk the old man out of it, Boots never gave up on him.

More than I can say for my brother, he thought as Boots ignored the jibe.

"More the other way around. Just a feeling, Ryder. Be watchful."

With that Boots's phone time was up, and the call ended.

That was what drove him craziest about Boots and his beliefs, Ryder thought; no matter what happened later, the man would nod wisely and say, "I told you." If what happened was something good, it was straight from his

God. If it was something bad, God's intervention had lessened the blow.

Yet, Ryder thought as he pulled the thankfully room-darkening curtains of the small motel room closed, he couldn't deny that the man's pure, shining faith had had an effect on him. He'd fought it, resisted fiercely, but Boots's quiet determination to save him from himself had made inroads.

He'd finally decided that the principles underlying Boots's beliefs were good no matter what the foundation. And when Boots had laughed and told him he didn't have to believe to live by them, the result was the same—Ryder had felt a sudden sense of relief he'd never known before. And in that moment he'd determined to give it a shot, for the sake of the man who had seen something in him worth saving, a man who would never see the outside again, but still found hope.

To his surprise he slept well, for nearly seven hours. More than enough to keep going. He got up, dressed, grabbed his last box of Little Travis cigars and headed out. He wasn't hungry yet; Mrs. Sanchez's hearty breakfast was still holding. So he headed instead to the local library branch.

It wasn't as foreign territory to him as he supposed many might think, given his capacity for trouble. There had been times when he'd wanted information, and had wanted to get it without his big brother hanging over his shoulder. Esperanza's tiny library was just that, tiny, and his presence would be noticed—and reported on to Clay within hours—so he'd avoided that. But there were other towns, other libraries, and he spread it around.

His official cell phone rang as he pulled into the parking lot of the library.

"You didn't check in," a stern voice said.

"I did," Ryder countered. "I left a message. Not my fault you didn't answer. I needed sleep."

His alternate handler—an agent named Gibson—apparently decided to let it go. "Developments?"

I'm about out of cigars and my ass is tired of sitting all night in the dark, waiting for nothing, he thought. But he knew better than to bitch, at this guy in particular. He was a little more human, and sometimes even unbent enough to commiserate with the frustration Ryder felt. Ryder didn't want to blow that.

"Nothing. No movement, no sign of movement, and nobody who shouldn't be around. They go lights out around here early, and it stays that way."

Work started very early on a ranch, and Clay Colton was serious about work. Ryder had chosen to ignore his brother's work ethic and this had always been the biggest bone of contention between the two brothers.

That, and the fact that Ryder had been born for trouble.

"The biggest thing that's happened around here is people keep getting married," Ryder said. "The sheriff, his brother…"

Ryder clammed up before he let slip something that gave him away. It wouldn't do to mention that he knew his ex-sister-in-law was back on the ranch, or the even bigger shock of learning that his little sister had married some overtense suit.

As far as his handlers knew, he had no family. None of them really wanted to claim him, so he'd done the same. On anything that had required listing next of kin, he'd put "None." And that's how it would stay. For all he knew, that's why they'd picked him for this job. Maybe Boots was right, and this was more potentially dangerous than he'd realized.

Not that it mattered. He could get blown away tomorrow, and it would barely cause a ripple. Boots might shake his head sadly, but that was the truth. No one else would really care. Not that he expected them to; there was something inherently wrong with him. If even his own father and brother wanted nothing to do with him, why would anyone else?

"We need to get this wrapped up," Gibson said. "The Colton campaign is on its way to San Antonio soon, and we do not want to try and run this operation with all that going on."

The casual reference gave Ryder a jolt. He'd been so focused on his little bit of work here, the bigger happenings in the world hadn't even registered. Not that he ever paid much attention to politics, not even presidential politics.

He wondered what that cool, commanding voice on the other end of the phone would think if he realized that he was speaking to a man who was, technically if not officially, the nephew of the man who could well become president of the United States.

Wasn't there some branch of the feds who investigated all the family members of people who aspired to the highest office? It only made sense. And the fact that Joe Colton's ne'er-do-well brother had fathered a crop of kids outside his marriage wasn't exactly a secret.

For the first time, it hit Ryder that he was, by blood, connected to a very famous family. Not that they would claim him any more than his own father had, but still, if he were mercenary enough...

He could almost see Boots's frown. Could hear the old man's stern warning that that way lay hellfire. Could even hear himself answering, "Don't worry, Boots. That'd mean I'd have to claim Graham Colton as my father, and that ain't ever going to happen."

That much was the truth. No amount of money or

famous family would make him do that. He might feel a bit of wistful sadness about losing his brother and sister—they'd once been a tight-knit group—but his father meant less than nothing to him.

As he meant less than nothing to his father.

"Don't forget to check in when you're in place tonight."

"Yeah," Ryder said absently, locking the truck as he headed for the library. He could have asked how much money they were talking about here, but caution won out; he didn't want them thinking he was pondering going over to the other side.

He didn't think his recruiters had believed him when he'd told them, just as he had told the court at his trial, that he'd never intended to smuggle illegals into the country. That he'd merely been paid to drive a truck, that as far as he knew was full of computer equipment. No one had believed him back then.

In fact, it had barely bothered him that he'd ended up in prison for something he hadn't intended to do. As he'd told Boots later, when the man had begun to talk to him about his future, he'd done enough intentionally to land him here anyway.

"It's just karma catching up with me," he'd said. "No big deal."

"But a big chance," Boots had said, already launching into his crusade to salvage Ryder's life.

Ryder hadn't been listening to the older man, though. Not then. This situation wasn't going to change anything, not really. To his way of thinking, it was just a speed bump on his racetrack, and he'd be back at full tilt as soon as he got out. Older and wiser, maybe. Hopefully wise enough to keep from getting caught next time trouble irresistibly called his name.

Once he'd spent a couple of hours in the library researching, he was a little stunned at what he'd found. At how much people would pay for a child they knew nothing about. At how long this had been going on, seemingly forever. At how many ways it happened, from the simple theft straight out of a hospital nursery, to unethical doctors who arranged black market adoptions, to unscrupulous lawyers who facilitated all of it.

He was stunned most of all at the fierce desire for a baby that drove it all.

He headed back out to the ranch to start another evening of surveillance and endless waiting. He made his usual circuit to check the tunnels suspected of being used by the ring, but his telltales—small things he'd placed that would be pushed aside or stepped on unknowingly by anyone who went through the openings—were undisturbed, as they had been for days now. This obviously wasn't a high-volume operation.

Or he was on the wrong track altogether, which he didn't like contemplating.

When he was done with his inspections, he settled in in a key spot and waited for full dark before moving in closer to the ranch.

Once more, Ryder found himself sitting and watching, with nothing to do but think. He tried all sorts of distractions, from taking Boots's theory and trying to figure in his head what a six-pound baby would cost per ounce at the going rate, to deciding what approach to use on that cute waitress at the diner down the street from the motel. Nothing seemed to work very well. And he kept coming back full circle, thinking about the family who'd cut him off.

Although, to be fair, he'd done the same thing.

Was he luckier to *know* his family? Luckier than a kid

who'd been sold, but at least to people who wanted him? Or worse, stolen, maybe from a parent who actually loved him? He wasn't sure.

As darkness fell around him again, Ryder worked his way slowly down toward the new building that had been put up since he'd been gone, the building he suspected might be a stop on the smugglers' route. How different his life might have been if he'd been stolen as a baby. Better? Maybe. Easier? Probably.

But then he felt a jab of guilt. Clay had sacrificed a great deal, trying to keep them all together. Ryder hadn't ever wanted to admit that, but he couldn't deny it any longer. Clay had tried harder than anyone had any right to expect. It wasn't his fault that his little brother was a screwed-up mess. But knowing Clay, he probably blamed himself. Ryder grimaced inwardly.

The only language you seem to understand is trouble. And when it calls, you come running.

No sooner had the words formed in his mind than he heard it. A low, agonized whimper of sound.

He froze. Instantly his brain discarded the possibility that it had been a baby's cry; this was someone older, an adult. He tilted his head, trying to triangulate the sound.

Inside the house.

It came again, harsher this time, a cry of pain and anguish that stabbed at him.

A woman. It was a woman.

Instinctively he took a step forward, then stopped himself.

The only language you understand is trouble. And when it calls, you come running....

His thoughts taunted him. Somewhere in the back of his mind a little voice told him to walk away, all the while laughing, knowing he wouldn't.

Knowing he couldn't.
Trouble was calling.
And, God help him, he was going to answer.

Chapter 3

Ana knew she was in trouble. Jewel had taken the Hope-chest children into town for a treat, a movie and then ice cream at Miss Sue's. Although Jewel had asked her to accompany them, Ana's back had been aching fiercely all day. She had seized the chance for some quiet in the empty house; with Macy Ward, the recreational therapist at Hopechest, away on her honeymoon with the sheriff's brother, Fisher Yates, Hope chest was completely deserted—and peaceful—tonight.

She had dozed fitfully through the ache and awakened after an hour to the empty house. She had panicked, knowing now the reason her back had been aching so.

The baby.

When the first contraction ripped through her it caught her off guard and she screamed. The sound echoed off the walls of the deserted house, and she bit her lip in the effort to stop another cry.

As the pain ebbed, for a brief moment she allowed herself to hope it was only a false alarm. Surely she would not be so unlucky as to give birth at the worst possible moment, when she had no one here to help?

And why would this surprise you? she asked herself sternly. Your judgment in life has been so sterling thus far.

Slowly, she sat up, relieved when she was able to do so. Her water had broken, she couldn't deny that, but perhaps the baby would wait at least until Jewel returned. She thought about calling the Bar None, but she was certain Jewel had mentioned that Clay Colton was out with his ex-wife.

It seemed like an odd thing to her; she could no more imagine going back to Alberto Cardenas than she could imagine stopping this baby from coming. Not now that she knew he was as bad as her father. But she knew not everyone was as unlucky—or unwise—as she was.

On that thought, a second contraction hit, shocking another cry out of her. This time she had the presence of mind to look at the clock; timing was important, was it not?

Tears brimmed in her eyes and she told herself it was the pain. She would not cower and whine, she simply would not. Determined, she tried to stand. If she could walk, perhaps she could stave this off until help arrived.

Her first steps convinced her of the folly of that notion. She made it to the chest of drawers a few feet away before another pain struck, sending her to her knees; she barely managed to cling to the heavy piece of furniture and keep from falling.

In the process she pulled over the small statue of a road-runner Jewel had so kindly given her when she had arrived here. She had seen it in the library and exclaimed that it reminded her of home. Thinking that Ana was homesick, Jewel had offered the piece. Ana had accepted it, temporarily, thinking it would serve as a good reminder of all the reasons why she had left.

The statue shattered on the tile floor, having just missed the colorful rug in front of the chest. Ana barely had time to regret the miscue before another pain hit. She did not have to look at the clock to know it was too soon; the pains were too close together to pretend.

Her baby was coming.

She was alone.

She was going to have to do this herself. Somehow.

And she would, she told herself fiercely. She'd gotten her baby into this, it was up to her to handle it. She—

Her self-lecture broke off at a sound from the porch. For an instant she felt relieved until she realized she had not heard the ranch van pulling up the driveway, or heard the door open to the garage, which was next to her room.

It was not Jewel.

It was not anyone who had arrived openly by car. And while it was possible, even a frequent occurrence, that a visitor would arrive on horseback, she had not heard that either. And at this hour of night, that did not seem likely.

No answer she could come up with was good.

A tall shadow shot across the tile floor, hiding the gleam of the broken pieces of the statue. Ana choked back the scream that rose to her throat. She grabbed the largest, sharpest shard of the shattered roadrunner. It was not much, but it was all she had to protect herself and her baby.

As the shadow moved closer and she found herself staring up into the eyes of a tall, dark, menacing stranger, she thought she was going to have to defend the two of them.

Trouble, he'd expected.

A very pregnant woman, he hadn't.

He'd done his homework on this place, this Hopechest Ranch. He'd been a little taken aback when he'd learned that the Hopechest Foundation that funded it was the pet project of Meredith Colton, who was his aunt. And potential first lady.

But he hadn't heard even a rumor that the place helped illegals. He considered the woman's obviously Hispanic appearance and wondered if she had run away from home. Everything he'd read had indicated the place was a home for troubled teens, not pregnant ones. Although maybe the two sometimes went hand in hand.

It occurred to him momentarily that he might well have been considered one of those teens not long ago. But he'd never thought of himself as "troubled," just determined to have fun. There'd been too little fun in his life, and he'd been set on making up for that.

And then it hit him. Was he perhaps closer than he'd realized to his goal? Had he inadvertently stumbled onto yet another aspect of the investigation, something they didn't even know?

Was this pregnant woman here not just to have her baby, but to get rid of it? Was it already bought and paid? She didn't look or act the type, but what did he know about that? Perhaps her protective posture was to save her investment, not her child.

The woman on her knees doubled over, and he heard the moan she tried to hold back. She was dressed in some flowing cotton gown in a pure white that gleamed in the moonlight. She was clutching something in her hand, something that looked like a piece of broken pottery. Suddenly she straightened slightly and waved it at him with an unsteady hand.

"*¡Salir de aqui!*" she said, her voice slightly steadier than her hand.

As she told him to get out of here, he realized she had some idea of using that little shard as a weapon. He nearly laughed aloud, but she was so clearly frightened he quashed the urge.

"No tengas miedo," he said, although he doubted that simply telling her not to be afraid would alleviate the problem. After all, from her point of view he'd turned up out of the dark, she was clearly alone, and in pain…

In labor.

Belatedly it hit him.

My God, she was having that baby now.

Even as he thought it she cried out again, hunching protectively over her swollen belly.

"Damn," he muttered. "You're going to have that thing right now, aren't you?"

"That *thing* is a baby!" she snapped in perfect English.

He held up his hands at the sudden fierceness of her tone. "Sorry," he said. "But I'm right, aren't I?"

"It is coming, yes," she said, and suddenly the fierceness vanished, replaced by an almost tangible fear. Ryder realized how young she was, even younger than he was. Twenty, maybe twenty-two?

"Now?"

He was more than a little scared himself. He didn't know a thing about this process, and at the moment wished he had stayed where he belonged, out there on that fruitless, useless stakeout.

"Right now," she said grimly, doubling over once more.

"Damn," he said again.

He bent to try to help her get up, but she pulled away from him. Instead she grabbed the edge of the heavy, carved chest beside her, and tried to pull herself to her feet. She fell back to her knees as another pain apparently hit.

Close together, those pains, he thought. That meant it really was imminent, didn't it? He'd seen movies, read stories…

But this was real life, about to happen right in front of him, and he was the only one here. No empathetic woman to take over. He should have paid more attention to his sister, but the very idea made him nervous and he'd avoided the subject entirely.

What if he called Georgie? Would she even talk to him? As far as his family knew, he was still in prison, he guessed. By now even Georgie, his sometimes partner in mischief as children, had probably washed her hands of him. She'd somehow turned very serious when she'd had a child to think about. Children really did change everything.

The woman moaned, shifting on the floor as if trying to escape the pain. The movement took her into the shaft of moonlight that came through the front window of the room. And he realized with a sudden jolt that she was lovely. Her long, dark hair fell in thick waves well past her shoulders. Her eyes were just as dark and caught the light enough to show him they were wide with pain and brimming with moisture.

She moaned again, and the helpless sound of it galvanized him. He didn't know if it was some instinctive male gene that drove him toward protecting a woman in her most helpless yet miraculous time. Or maybe something more personal. He only knew he couldn't just leave her like this. She needed help, and he was the only one around.

Unluckily for you, *chica,* he thought to himself.

He scooped her up off the floor. It was clumsy, because of her bulk and the effort not to hurt her any more, but once he had her he was a little surprised; he'd thought she would be heavier, what with the baby. It hit him that he was carrying one person back to the bed, but before long there would be two. The idea rocked him. He'd never been this close to a birth before.

"You must have done something to get ready for this," he said.

"There are…blankets and things…in the trunk." She made a gesture toward the heavy trunk at the foot of the bed. He went to it quickly, lifted the lid, found the things she'd mentioned. He got out the pile of soft cotton cloths, spotted a pair of scissors in a sealed package and grabbed those, too.

Cord, he thought. You had to cut the cord, right?

God, he was way out of his depth.

"There's no one to call?" he asked her, wanting to be absolutely certain before he committed to this.

"No one…could be here…in time."

She was panting now, and he wondered if she'd taken some class in special breathing—didn't they always say stuff about that?—or if it just happened naturally.

He laid her gently down on the bed. She cried out as another pain seized her. He reached over and turned on a bedside lamp, turned back and forgot to breathe for a moment.

She was more than pretty, she was beautiful. Her wide, dark eyes were huge, gleaming in the light. Her skin was a light, luscious olive tone—smooth, flawless, glowing. Her lips were full, soft, and slightly parted as she tried hard not to moan; he could see the ferocious effort she was making. It jogged him back to reality, and the urgent matter at hand.

"I don't know anything about this," he told her. "You'll have to tell me what to do."

"And you think…I know?" Her laugh wasn't bitter, but it wasn't amused, either. And for the first time he wondered how she'd gotten into this situation. He couldn't quite believe she'd done it intentionally, getting pregnant to sell the baby. It was feasible. But something in her dark, exotic eyes, and the way she looked up at him, made that impossible for him to believe, at least right now.

And it didn't really matter right now. Whether she was involved in the smuggling ring or not didn't change what was about to happen. Working on some combination of stories heard and movies seen, he did what seemed reasonable, starting with rolling up his sleeves and washing his hands in the bathroom just down the hall.

"How old are you?" he asked when he came back.

She looked startled, then wary.

"I'm only asking because my sister got pregnant four years ago. She was only eighteen."

The woman smothered another moan, then answered. "I am twenty-two."

Better, he guessed. But not much. "She fell for a smooth-talking city boy. He deserted her."

It wasn't a question, nor was there any emotion in the flat assertion.

"Is that what happened to you?" he asked softly. "He deserted you, when he found out you were pregnant?"

He found himself hoping she'd say yes, that she was here because she simply had no choice, not because she had the soul of a mercenary.

"No," she said, her tone still flat. "It was I…who ran."

Ryder blinked. He hadn't expected that.

A sharp cry broke from her, and he realized the pains were coming closer together, and even he knew what that meant. No more time to try and find out who this woman was or why she was here, what her motives were.

"Hot water," he muttered. They always talked about that, too, didn't they?

"No…time."

He realized she meant that literally.

"The baby…is coming."

Now. She meant right now.

Ryder stifled the urge to run. Her hands flailed wildly, as if seeking purchase. He grabbed them, startled at the strength in them as she cried out yet again.

"It's all right," he said, squeezing her hands. "We'll get through it." *Somehow,* he added silently to himself.

He had no plan; he worked strictly on instinct. He kept up a stream of encouraging words, trying to distract her— and perhaps himself—from the embarrassingly intimate position they found themselves in. He wasn't sure it helped, but when he paused she asked him to keep talking.

Until it started to actually happen.

He'd had no idea birth was such a messy thing. He'd always had some image that the kid slid out and got wrapped in a blanket and handed over. But this was wet, bloody and shockingly brutal. He didn't know who to marvel at more—the woman going through it, or the child for surviving it.

If, of course, it did.

It was when he first spotted the baby's head emerging that his gut truly knotted. Dark hair, nearly as dark as his own. He was a little startled. He thought babies were born bald.

The woman screamed then. It was a rending sound, and he touched her gently, trying to soothe her.

"It's coming," he said, even though he realized that no one knew that better just now than she did. "It'll be over soon."

She seemed to take heart from that, and sucked in a breath.

"Can you push?" he asked diffidently, wondering if that was just a stupid cliché, too.

She grunted then, a primal, earthy sound. Then again, and again.

Women, he thought. You heard about what they went through in childbirth, but until you saw it, you didn't really realize how tough they were.

To Ryder, it seemed to happen fast then, although he suspected it wouldn't be wise to say so to the straining woman. He should be paying more attention to the baby, and shifted just in time to see a tiny pair of shoulders emerge.

It did happen fast then. He reached to support the tiny thing she was expelling.

The moment he touched it, the "thing" became real to him. He stared down at the baby who barely filled his two hands. So tiny, so helpless…but it was a life, another human being, a fellow inhabitant of this glorious planet, and he'd helped it arrive.

This was big, he thought.

Huge.

How could something so incredibly small, so fragile and delicate, make him feel like this?

"It's a girl," he whispered. "A little girl."

The woman made a sound he couldn't begin to describe. She sounded exhausted, but there was something else in her voice when she instructed, "You must cut the cord."

He winced, even though he knew that. He followed her brisk instructions, glad she was able to walk him through it. She might be young, but she'd clearly done her homework on this.

Or maybe women were just born knowing, he thought, despite her earlier claim to ignorance.

"I just leave it like that?" he asked, looking doubtfully at the stub of the cord still attached to the baby who appeared to be, to his amazement, looking around. Her eyes were brown, he thought, a little numbly. Dark, rich, espresso brown, like her mother's. Her head looked a little funny, misshapen, but he guessed that was normal.

"It will fall off of its own accord later," the woman said. "You must clean her. Her mouth, nose, so that she breathes easily."

He did his best, aware that he was shaking slightly. And when the tiny child in his hands let out a protesting wail, he found himself grinning; things were working fine, it seemed.

"She's got lungs," he said, feeling a bit loopy, as if he'd downed one tequila too many. To his surprise the new mother laughed, as if she hadn't just been through hell.

When she was clean and dry, he wrapped the baby awkwardly, but with a need for gentleness unlike anything he'd ever felt before. He took a last look down into the tiny face.

"Give her to me."

The new mother's voice was shaky, and when he looked from daughter to mother he saw fear in her eyes. She reached out, as if she were afraid he would refuse to hand over the baby. Ryder wondered suddenly if she knew what was going on around here, and had the sudden thought that she might suspect him of being connected to the baby-smuggling ring.

Well, she's right, isn't she? he told himself.

Then he put the baby into her mother's outstretched arms. The look that mother gave him nearly stopped his heart cold.

"Thank you," she whispered.

For the first time in his life with a woman, Ryder was speechless. All he could do was look at her, and at the tiny bit of humanity he'd just helped bring into the world. He didn't know how he felt, only that whatever it was, it was more intense than he'd ever experienced before.

And on some level, somewhere deep inside him, he knew he would never be the same again.

Chapter 4

Maria.

Ana held her baby close, savoring the feel of her, the smell of her, the miracle of her.

She had thought of other names, but when the time had come there was no other. Maria. Her mother deserved the tribute; it was not her fault that Ana's father had not been the man she had hoped. For a long time, Ana was grateful her mother had died before she'd learned the full extent of her husband's dishonesty and evil. But now, she could only feel sad that her mother was not here to see this precious child, her granddaughter.

So she would do the only thing she could; she would name her after her grandmother and give her the life she deserved. Somehow, she would do this. She would ask for no help, no charity, she would make her own way, for herself and her baby girl.

No help…

"A hospital," the dark stranger said. "You and she need to see a doctor."

Ana shook her head. She trusted no one, especially now. She had heard too much about the local baby smuggling, had pumped Jewel daily for information, information she'd given sometimes reluctantly, for fear of frightening the soon-to-be mother.

"I am not going anywhere."

"But what if there's something wrong?"

"There is nothing wrong. She is beautiful. Healthy. You can see that."

"But what about you? That was…you need—"

"No." It sounded cold and heartless to her ears, when all he'd done was express concern about her. She hastened to add, "I—and my daughter—thank you for what you did. But you must go now."

He looked nonplussed. She supposed it was rude, but what did rudeness matter when she had her baby to protect? She knew Jewel would be back with the kids soon, then she would have help she trusted.

She did not, could not dare trust this man. She didn't know why he was here, how he had happened to arrive just as she needed help. For all she knew, he was one of them, had been watching her, a pregnant woman obviously alone, thinking perhaps to steal her baby as so many others had been stolen, ripped from the loving arms of their mothers and sold as if they were packages of cereal.

"You don't trust me, do you?" he said softly.

"I do not trust anyone," she said. "A lesson I should have learned earlier."

He studied her for a moment, and then, to her surprise, nodded. "Wise choice."

His voice was soft, gentle, but it held a harsh undertone that stirred something in her. Who was this man who had strode in out of the moonlight and helped her without questions? What had he been—what had he done—to sound like that? Was he truly one of them? Was her baby still in danger from him?

"Go," she said, her voice sharp as her fears grew in proportion to the exhaustion that was growing, threatening to overwhelm her at any moment.

"I can't just leave you here alone."

"I will not be alone for long. People will be back here soon."

"You don't have to lie to get me to leave."

"I am not lying. The woman who runs this place, she will be back with her charges soon. They only went to town for an outing."

He lifted a brow at her, and she wondered what she'd said. Her English was, she knew, nearly perfect. She'd worked hard at that in college, intending to put it to use teaching in a bilingual school.

But sometimes, she realized it was too perfect; local idioms and slang peppered the talk of others, but her college-taught skills stood out, marked her as different. But she'd long ago decided she would rather be different that way; if she was going to be judged, as people were, by the way she spoke, better too well than not well enough. That had always been her way. She saw no reason to change it now.

"Go. Please."

He hesitated a moment longer, looking down at her. He towered over the bed, so tall, long-legged and strong, she thought. His eyes were dark, piercing, and she couldn't help feeling he saw more than she wished. His jaw was stubbled with slight beard growth, as if he hadn't shaved since this morning. His hair was even darker than her own, and fell in a silky if shaggy sweep over his brow when he leaned forward. She wanted to run her fingers through it and push it back.

That thought sent a stab of shock and fear through her. She needed this man gone. She obviously was not thinking clearly in the aftermath of this life-changing experience. The very last thing she should be doing at this moment was finding a man attractive. Especially a man she knew absolutely nothing about.

Of course, she had thought she knew everything about Alberto as well.

"Go," she said again. "Please."

"You swear to me that there will be help here soon?"

His concern moved her against her will. "I swear. And I repeat, I do not lie."

She meant that. Small, kind lies to avoid hurt feelings were one thing, although she preferred to avoid those as well. But big lies about things that mattered had shaped then destroyed her world. She hated them.

For another silent moment, her rescuer, the man who had helped deliver the baby squirming in her arms, stared down at her. And then, sharply, he nodded.

"Be well," he said, in a tone she couldn't describe, some combination of command, awe and benediction. She had the oddest thought that this time had been life-changing for more than just herself. But this handsome American seemed too strong to let something affect him that much.

And then he was gone, disappearing back into the darkness as silently as he'd appeared, surprising her that a man of his size could move so quietly. It was unsettling, someone that big should make more noise, she thought. And in her exhaustion her imagination began to come up with reasons why a man like that would learn to move so stealthily—and none of them were good.

She was relieved that he had gone. She had half expected him to grab her baby out of her arms, proving himself part of the ring she so feared and that the local authorities were so diligently searching for.

But she could not deny he'd been a godsend. She did not want to think about what she would have done had he not appeared out of the darkness.

But she also did not want to think about what she would have done had he refused to go back into that darkness.

She cuddled her baby close, running through her mind all that she had studied: when to feed her, how she would know when she herself was ready for that, all the things she'd so voraciously read in preparation for this day. The pain she'd just endured was nearly forgotten already, although the gentle, encouraging touch and words of the dark stranger were not. She thought she would never forget those, or him. One day it might be a fascinating story to tell her daughter, about the unknown man who had come to their aid, and then vanished into the night.

Perhaps in time she would wonder if he had even been real, that tall, dark man. She smiled at her own silliness, a little surprised that she was still capable of such fantasy. Perhaps she was already preparing stories to tell her child at bedtime.

Instinctively she began to sing quietly to Maria, a sweet little lullaby her mother had sung to her.

Duérmete mi niña,
Duérmete mi sol...

Not that she actually wanted her little sunshine to sleep just yet, she was still too caught up in the wonder of it all. At last, she held this miracle in her arms, and she felt she must do something motherly, something to show this tiny human being she was loved and welcomed, even if she was lacking one of her parents.

"Better no father than an evil one, *mija*," she whispered, determined that the baby would hear English as much as Spanish as she grew and learned to speak.

Yes, it would be different for Maria. She would grow up speaking both, at home in both tongues in a way her mother would never be. But it was what she'd wanted, Ana told herself. She was alone, isolated by choice from the family she'd once been close to. The family she'd once trusted.

You must remember who they really are, she told herself. She couldn't help thinking some of them had to know what she had only recently learned, how vast were the criminal dealings her father was involved in. Once she herself had found out, the evidence was so obvious she could not believe she had missed it for so long. The older ones, her father's brothers, sisters, the ones she could no longer think of as aunts and uncles, they must have known.

Had they indeed known, and conspired to keep it from her? Or had no conspiracy been necessary? Was she such a naïve fool that they had managed to keep the truth from her with no such effort?

The baby stilled, seemingly calmed by the sweet song. Ana held her even closer. She closed her eyes, shifting in the bed. The big man had seen to her comfort in an unexpectedly gentle manner, cleaning her, changing the bedclothes, and disposing of the mess of the birth quickly and efficiently. For a man who claimed to know nothing about the process, she thought he had handled it with remarkable aplomb. Her mother had often told her how her own father had been worse than useless. She liked the idea that her gallant stranger was much more of a man than her wicked father. She wondered what that stranger was thinking now, if he'd already put them out of his mind, if what had been a miracle to her was simply an odd occurrence to him.

He probably thinks you're just another illegal looking for a handout, she thought.

She told herself it didn't matter what he thought, not when she herself knew the truth. She was an intelligent woman, she had an education to offer, and she was going to start a new life for herself and her daughter. She would do it herself, without charity or handouts. Anything given to her, she would repay, in some form, as she was helping here at Hopechest Ranch in return for Jewel's hospitality and kindness.

No matter what it took, she and Maria would make their way, and have a good life.

"I promise you, *mijita*. You will be safe, you will have good things, you will grow and learn, and above all else you will be loved."

Ana settled in to wait, wondering what Jewel would think when she returned to find the population of her beloved Hopechest Ranch increased by one.

Chapter 5

This was insane, Ryder thought a couple nights later.

There was no reason in hell why that woman and her baby should haunt him like this.

He'd done the right thing. He might be the black sheep of the Texas Coltons, but even he had been unable to simply leave a pregnant woman in labor without help.

So why couldn't he just chalk it up to some unexpected sense of decency, hope it might someday tip the judgment scales in his favor and move on with the job he was here to do?

He shook his head as he drove to a meeting with Alcazar. A daylight meeting for a change, which Ryder acknowledged with wry humor; rats didn't usually come out in the sunlight.

And he himself was tired, tired enough that he needed to be on guard against making a mistake. His time in prison had given him some creds with the gang he hadn't had before. He'd had to spin a tale about how he'd been released early due to prison overcrowding and good behavior—a first in his lifetime, he'd laughed as he relayed the carefully concocted story—and Alcazar had obviously checked it out before setting up this meeting today.

Ironically, the track his investigation had led him on, all around New Mexico and southwest Texas, had served to cement his position. He'd done a few jobs for people Alcazar knew, and word had gotten back.

Of course, he'd had to cover his ass with his new, government bosses, and had reported on each incident. They'd told him going in that a lot would be forgiven if he accomplished the main goal. Apparently they'd meant it; nothing had come down on him for doing exactly what had landed him in custody in the first place, joining the coyotes who traveled under cover of darkness, smuggling in illegals.

Only this time, he was doing it with full intention and knowledge. It was still unsettling even though the feds had ordered him to go along. And he'd been on track all the way.

Until that night.

It hit him again, hard, the memory of that moment when a tiny little girl had nestled into his hands, looking up at him with dark eyes like her mother's. He figured she probably wasn't seeing him, not really, but it surely seemed as if she were peering into his dark, bruised soul.

He'd been right. This was insane. It made no sense. It was only a baby, one he would likely never see again. So why did he feel as if there were some sort of connection between them, him and that tiny bit of squalling humanity? Just because he'd had the misfortune of being there at her birth? Just because he'd been the first one to touch her, hold her, because he'd been the one to make sure she was breathing and clean and dry and warm?

It made no sense, he repeated to himself.

Now, her mother, that made sense. She was a beautiful woman, a woman any man would take notice of. Even here, where olive-skinned beauties were common, she stood out.

But this puzzled him, too. Because it wasn't simply her looks—she had been swollen with child and under the worst of circumstances when he'd first seen her—but her quiet courage under those circumstances had him thinking about her often. Too often. She was occupying his thoughts unlike any woman ever had.

And he didn't even know her name.

He was so lost in his contemplations that he nearly missed his turn. He yanked the wheel left and headed into the brush along a barely visible track that wound into the back country, where anything could be lost forever.

As he got closer to the selected meeting place, he checked the cubby in the door of the truck where he'd hidden the handgun, a Glock 17, they'd given him after the crash course in using it. But going armed into a meeting with Alcazar would be the height of idiocy, and he was hoping he was past that kind of foolishness. It was secure, and they'd have to literally tear the truck apart to find it, so he felt reasonably sure they wouldn't.

His government-issue cell phone rang. He reached for it automatically, then stopped. That was one advantage to working out here in the vast expanse of empty space; he could always claim he hadn't gotten the call due to lack of signal. He supposed they had ways to verify that, but unless he abused the excuse, he doubted it was worth it to them. And he usually called them back before too much time had passed.

It was a silly, perhaps childish game, but it gave him the

illusion of some kind of control, and right now he would take what little he could get. He didn't want to tell them about what had happened at the ranch.

He wasn't even sure why, if he was afraid they'd chew him out for violating what they called protocol, stepping out of his undercover role and being seen, or if he just wanted to keep it to himself. It almost felt as if telling anyone would violate a promise he hadn't even made, to a courageous woman and a newborn he'd helped bring into the world.

And that made less sense than anything, he thought as he checked the truck's odometer and began scanning for the small building he'd been told to look for.

When he spotted the ramshackle shed, he thought he must be wrong; this wasn't a building, it was a lumber pile in the making. Alcazar wouldn't hang out here. But then, would the man trust him enough to let him know where he really hung out? Ryder knew if he were in Alcazar's position, he would trust no one.

Just as she trusted no one, he thought, the image of that dark-eyed beauty snapping vividly into his mind once more.

Annoyed at himself, he shoved the image away, forcing himself to concentrate. Hadn't it been hammered into him during his weeks of training at that super-secret facility, that lack of focus could be fatal?

So focus, he ordered himself silently.

As he drove up to the tumbledown shack, he spotted a gleam of silver from behind it, the bumper of another car. So it *was* the right place, he thought, unable to imagine any other reason for a car to be all the way out here.

And then, seemingly out of nowhere, the truck was surrounded by armed men. Four of them, automatic pistols at the ready, and all trained on him. His gut knotted, but he kept his hands on the steering wheel in plain sight. The last thing he wanted was to give them an excuse to shoot. And with these guys it wouldn't take much.

The other vehicle was, absurdly, a stretch limo. But then Ryder remembered something he'd heard long ago, before he'd been tossed in prison—that Alcazar liked to conduct his meetings in what he called his "mobile office." This had to be it.

The biggest of the welcoming committee gestured him toward the limo. One of the others opened the passenger side rear door. When he didn't move quickly enough to please the third man, he got a jab with the barrel of the weapon he held.

For a split second, Ryder considered taking the man's head off. Only knowing it would be the last thing he'd ever do stopped him, at least long enough to rein in his temper.

He climbed into the back of the limo.

"Wise choice," said a voice from the far corner.

Ryder didn't pretend not to understand. "Patience is one of my new virtues," he said, but added with a glance back at the man who'd shoved him, "along with a very long memory."

Laughter, rough but tinged with genuine amusement, echoed in the car. Ryder could see Alcazar now, dressed to perfection in a light gray suit and a hat that was a cross between Clay's white Stetson and something a pimp on the streets of Dallas would wear.

"Duane is a bit…energetic, but he's also useful."

"I'm sure. For now." That earned him a jab with the deadly weapon. Ryder merely glanced at it. "I prefer an old-fashioned revolver, myself. It never jams, so you never need to stall, pretending to negotiate with a rattlesnake."

The man being discussed muttered something under his breath, which got him a sharp rebuke from the man in the hat. At further orders, the armed men retreated, shutting the limo's door after them.

"Carbone in Laredo tells me I can trust you."

"He did. It paid off for him."

"So he says."

Ryder said nothing more. He learned never to volunteer more information than was asked for. Besides, he had little else to say on the subject. He wasn't about to let Alcazar know that the man whose word he seemed to value was one of theirs, a government agent going into his third year of undercover work along the border.

The silence stretched out until finally Alcazar said, "You're the silent type, aren't you?"

"I'm not a salesman," Ryder said with a shrug. "Either you trust me or you don't; you have work for me or you don't. You're the boss; you decide."

The laughter came again, and this time it was appreciative. "Would that all of my men had that view."

Ryder shrugged again, this time saying nothing.

"I'm curious, Mr. Grady," Alcazar said.

Ryder lifted a brow, but said nothing. He was used to the name. He'd spent the early years of his life with it, the name of the mother who had never told them who their real father was, the father who had so little interest in them that they'd never laid eyes on him since before Georgie was born. It didn't take a genius to figure out that the name Colton in Texas—or anywhere else these days—would draw more attention than he wanted.

He could just hear Alcazar's reaction if he explained, "Hey, yeah, my bio-dad's brother is *that* Colton, the one who's probably going to be president. But don't worry, I'm still an outlaw…."

"Why would you want to get involved again in the very thing that got you time as a guest of the federal government?" Alcazar asked.

"Because I wasn't involved in it before, and I got hung for it anyway."

He knew the answer was flip, even absurd, but he also knew Alcazar was reputed to have a slightly warped sense of humor. Ryder was gambling on that.

His gamble paid off with the biggest laugh yet. "Might as well be hung for a sheep as a lamb, is that it?"

"Something like that."

"This would be different."

"Different?"

"The package to be transported would be...smaller."

Ryder's breath stopped, his brain screaming that this was it, but he masked his reaction.

"Easier," he said neutrally.

"Not necessarily."

Ryder pretended to consider this, then shrugged. "At least with you I know what I'm getting into."

"Kissing ass, Mr. Grady?"

"No. Just didn't like being a useful idiot."

There was a moment of silence before a rather bemused, "Well, well..."

Ryder said nothing, just waited. That had been close enough, he wasn't about to risk saying anything that might make Alcazar too curious about just who exactly he was.

"I may have something for you. Be ready. Available."

He stopped, as if he expected questions. Ryder asked none. After a moment Alcazar nodded in approval.

"Go. I'll be in touch."

Ryder nodded, took the words as dismissal, and moved toward the door. Then he stopped, glancing back.

"May I punch Mr. Energetic?"

A final laugh. "I would prefer that you didn't."

Ryder shrugged. "You're the boss," he said again.

"Yes," Alcazar said. "I am."

Ryder left it at that. He wasn't about to rock the boat anymore. Not when he apparently had finally broken through; a smaller package could only mean one thing.

A baby.

He was in.

Chapter 6

Ana yawned as she put Maria back to bed. It was only ten o'clock, but she was ready for bed herself. Her little girl seemed to have a voracious appetite, demanding to be fed every two or three hours round the clock. She'd read that this would ease as the baby grew, but for right now it was exhausting.

A light from the hallway glowed under her closed bedroom door. Jewel again? Ana wondered. Did the woman never sleep? She had been so concerned about Ana. After recovering from the shock of finding that the baby had arrived during her absence, Jewel insisted that Ana see a doctor, then rest as much as she could for the next few days. Yet she herself continued her string of sleepless nights.

Now that Ana had her own reason for restless nights and broken sleep, she was even more amazed that Jewel had managed to keep going, suffering seemingly endless insomnia. She did not think Jewel had slept an entire night since she herself had been here, and it only seemed to be getting worse.

And more than once this week when she had been up for a middle-of-the-night feeding with Maria, she had heard Jewel cry out in the darkness. The first time, she had run to her assistance, afraid something had happened. But Jewel had assured her it had only been a bad dream. Ana ached for her new friend, trying to imagine what it must be like for sleep to be so hard to come by, and then, when at last it did, for it to be so haunted by horrible dreams.

She hoped Maria's vocal demands to be fed in the night weren't further disturbing the already-weary Jewel. But the woman never failed to gush over Maria whenever she saw her, and always offered to take her for a while if Ana needed to rest, or do something else. It was such a relief to have someone she truly trusted at hand, yet Ana took care not to overburden the woman who was clearly already carrying a heavy load.

Ana opened her door now, and made her way down the hallway toward the kitchen where the light was. Jewel had been more than kind and generous to her, and she would do whatever she could to help.

She stopped just short of the kitchen doorway when she heard voices. Jewel's and a man's. She leaned forward just enough to see that the visitor was the handsome deputy, Adam Rawlings. And that he was holding Jewel in a comforting embrace.

Ana backed up quickly, not wanting to intrude on what seemed like a tender moment. She had guessed the first time she had seen them together that the deputy was interested in Jewel—it was hard to miss; the man watched her like a hungry cat. But she also knew that Jewel was not interested, not really. She had told Ana that Adam had been very kind, but that she was not ready.

Ana assumed that Jewel's hesitation was because of her old relationship, and had wondered if it ever got any better, if any woman could truly hope to find a man who would not leave or let her down in the end.

A picture popped into her mind, of a tall, dark stranger, with piercing eyes and a dangerous edge. She had sensed the danger about him, although his spine-tingling grin when Maria had let out her first squall had momentarily wiped out all Ana's concerns.

And when the time had come, when her little girl had arrived, he had handled her with exquisite care, with trembling hands and a look of utter awe that had somehow reassured Ana even more.

With an effort that surprised her, she pushed the vivid image out of her mind. She took care with her footsteps as she turned to go. She did not want either Jewel or Deputy Rawlings to know she'd nearly walked in on them.

And then she heard Jewel say three words that stopped her in her tracks.

"…lost my baby."

She whirled back, her heart hammering in her chest. Jewel had lost a baby. Once again, Ana's sympathies went out to the woman. She knew what it was like to lose a child. To have lost both her child and her fiancé at the same time, in a tragic accident, was something Ana could not begin to imagine. Her own loss, of a man not worth having, seemed petty in comparison. Jewel had clearly loved her Andrew, having found him after a long, confusing time in her life.

And the baby…

"So you can see," Jewel told the deputy, who was patting

her gently. The man clearly cared for Jewel, his affection was obvious. "I know what Ana is afraid of. I know what it means to lose a baby."

Adam Rawlings murmured something Ana could not hear, but she was certain they were words of comfort, consolation. For a selfish moment she hoped that he was saying they were close to cracking the smuggling ring, for only then could she breathe easy.

She might be selfish, but she was also thinking of Jewel. When it became clear the topic of the baby-smugglers was not going any further, she retreated to her room and carefully, silently closed the door.

She sat on the edge of her bed, glancing over at the crib now set up just a few feet away. Had she lost a baby so tragically, she was not sure she could bear having another woman's under her roof. Yet Jewel had never given any indication that Ana and Maria were anything less than welcome here at Hopechest. Ana ached anew for her friend.

And marveled anew at her brave spirit.

Perhaps there truly were more good people than bad in the world.

And she could not seem to stop herself from wondering which category her rescuer, and Maria's, fell into.

"I'm still on the ranch," Ryder said into the phone. "I think I'm in, and that there's going to be a move soon, but I don't want to take a chance on missing something else."

"Good thinking."

Ryder's mouth quirked; that was something he hadn't often been accused of in his life. He'd reported in on the approach from Alcazar, which had pleased his handlers, even Furnell, although he hadn't been able to stop himself from giving Ryder a lecture on how critical it was that he not do anything to blow this now.

Ya think? Ryder had muttered silently, but kept the sarcasm to himself.

He ended the call and closed the phone. They'd accepted his explanation of why he was still here easily enough.

Maybe it was even partly true.

He lifted the high-powered binoculars to his eyes, scanning the area around the Hopechest building. It sat in the most distant corner of what had been Bar None land, a piece they'd never been able to use much. Clay had often talked about selling it, although Ryder hadn't paid much attention to such things; he'd sworn early on never to be owned by duty the way his brother was.

And look where that got you, Ryder thought as he turned the binoculars back toward the adobe-and-tile ranch house.

His heart leapt up into his throat, stopping his breath.

There she was.

She had the baby in her arms, wrapped in a pinkish-looking blanket. Very girly, Ryder thought. For a beautiful little girl.

His own thoughts startled him. Again. It was just a baby. One of those squirmy, noisy, red-faced, funny-looking creatures he'd never been comfortable around. The ones who messed, spit up, drooled and woke you at all hours of the night.

Okay, so this was different. This was the only baby he'd ever been this close to. Certainly the only one he'd ever helped bring into the world. It had been an odd feeling, a new one. But he hadn't expected it to last, hadn't expected to feel much more than the lingering curiosity, speculation and mild affection he'd had for the sorrel colt he'd once helped deliver, or Daisy's pups that time.

But this was different.

And he wasn't at all sure what it was.

Maybe it was that he'd never really felt completely connected to another person before. He wasn't capable of that kind of feeling, hadn't even really missed the closeness of family, had instead felt as if he'd escaped when he'd cut all ties with them. He felt the occasional jab of wistfulness for the days when Georgie had tagged after him, but she'd clearly grown up and moved on, changed forever by the birth of her daughter.

And that scary thought brought him jolting back full circle as he watched the woman he'd shared those most intimate of moments with. She cuddled the tiny bundle in her arms. She'd been so incredibly courageous, determined to protect her baby even while doubled over in the agony of labor. She'd fought hard, without the help of drugs, medical equipment, or experienced hands.

She'd had only his hands, and had taken their help only reluctantly.

That was a lucky baby, he thought. And she could do a lot worse than try to grow up like her firebrand of a mother.

He wondered, not for the first time, where the baby's father was. He could understand how the news of a baby would panic a guy, but how the hell could a man walk away from a woman like that?

Maybe he's like you, Ryder thought grimly.

He knew he wasn't capable of being in love. He'd never even been close, wasn't sure he even knew what it meant. He knew love existed, he'd seen it in others, but for himself it was an abstract and romantic notion and he'd dismissed the possibility early on. He'd had his share of women— okay, maybe more than his share—but he'd never once found one he couldn't walk away from without a backward glance.

And he hadn't now, he told himself firmly. Certainly not a woman he'd been with for all of a few hours in the darkness—not that he hadn't done that before, too, but definitely not like this—and whose name he didn't even know.

But sitting here now, looking down at her, seeing her with the baby who'd slipped into his hands, he couldn't deny that he felt…something. A tightness in his chest, a sort of yearning.

He let out a short, sharp bark of laughter at the ridiculous word as it formed in his mind.

Yearning.

Yeah, right. Him, Ryder Grady Colton. Really a yearning sort of guy.

Not that it would matter if it were true. He was a long, long way from getting clear of the mess he'd gotten himself into, and until he finished this job and got that free pass and expunged record, he had no business doing anything but focusing on the job he had to do.

The thought that a baby that wasn't even his could change him forever, the way it had changed his sister, was the most absurd thought of all.

Chapter 7

"**Y**ou're sure you wouldn't like to come? I'd love for you to meet Tamara."

Ana shook her head and smiled at Jewel. "Perhaps in a few days. I am still very nervous about Maria."

She regretted causing the shadow that flickered in Jewel's eyes. But the woman nodded in understanding.

"Better to be safe," she said. "That baby-stealing ring is still operating, and the fewer people who know about Maria the better, until it's broken up. Some of Tamara's old CSI colleagues are at the ranch now, looking for clues."

Ana was heartened by that news, that the authorities were still working in the area. "That is good."

"I'm worried about Clay, though," Jewel said. "He's taking his brother's death very hard."

Ana frowned. "This is the brother who was in prison?"

Jewel nodded. "He wasn't a bad kid, really, just a little wild. He didn't know what he was getting into."

A bit cynical about criminals claiming innocence, Ana said nothing, not wanting to dispute Jewel's assumption.

"I think the fact that he didn't even claim Clay as next of kin, that he put down he had none on the prison forms, didn't even use their name, really got to Clay. He didn't even find out he was dead until seven months after it happened, when he went to the prison to find out why his letters came back undeliverable."

"I am sorry for his pain," Ana said. That, at least, she could honestly say.

"Tamara told me Clay tried so hard. Not many eighteen-year-olds who would take on the task of raising two younger siblings. But Clay did. And he feels responsible, guilty that he couldn't keep his little brother out of trouble."

"No one," Ana said carefully, "has more power to hurt us than the ones we most love."

Ana felt Jewel's gaze sharpen, and regretted speaking even those vague words. But Jewel kept her word, to ask no questions Ana did not want to answer, and once again Ana silently thanked her.

As she watched Jewel load up the kids for another trek to the Bar None for pony rides, Ana was very happy that her benefactor had found a new friend. And if she found it odd that Tamara and Clay Colton were by all appearances back together again, with the one-time forensics expert happily settled back at the Bar None, she kept the thought to herself. She knew nothing about their relationship.

It was a lesson she'd learned in the hardest of ways, when everyone told her she should turn a blind eye to Alberto's dealings, just as they had told her she had no right to judge her father. They were impressed by her father's polish, his education, the whole, false package. They had called her an idealistic fool to expect any man to turn his back on a lucrative career, just because she did not like some aspect of it.

The illegal aspect of it, she thought. The taking of things they had not earned, from people who had worked hard. The selling of evil, destructive things they called simply "commodities," never caring what the drugs did or the lives they destroyed. The coercion of innocent people to help in their "work," coercion by threat to families, children…

She was not sure which disturbed her more, the actual activities, or the urging of those around her to look the other way. Perhaps she was a naïve, idealistic fool, but she refused to have her baby grow up in a place where such things were accepted.

Alone again, she checked on Maria, who was napping peacefully. She decided she felt up to resuming some of the tasks she had taken on before, in an effort to earn her keep. Jewel had told her not to worry, not to push herself too hard so soon after the birth, but after nearly a week she was restless.

And really, other than feeding and bathing Maria, she had little to do; the children at Hopechest had seemed fascinated by Maria, and the girls especially were always offering to help. Ana suspected they looked upon the baby as an animated doll of some sort, but she still found their wide-eyed interest touching.

At the same time, she looked at these children with a quiet determination that Maria would never end up needing help like this. She would always be there for her little girl, making sure she always knew she was loved. For that was what she saw most in the too-old eyes in the too-young faces around her here. So few of these children had ever been certain they were loved.

"You will always know, *mija*," she told her sleeping child. "You will always know."

* * *

"You all right, boy?"

Ryder sighed, knowing it must be bad if Boots could tell even over the phone that he was in an uproar.

"Things are just…complicated," he said.

"Life is," Boots agreed. "That's why the Boss gave us brains, to figure it out."

"Yeah, well, I could use a better one just now, then."

"Nothing wrong with your brain, Ryder. How you've used it on occasion, well, that's another story."

The teasing was gentle, and Ryder took no offense. Boots had his best interests at heart, and that was something Ryder had never honestly believed of anyone before in his life. Except maybe his mother, but Mary Lynn Grady had spent most of her too-short life struggling to support her three children sired by, but never acknowledged by, Graham Colton, the profligate brother of the current presidential front-runner.

Ryder had heard some wonder if Joe Colton was fit to be president, with a brother like Graham. Ryder had never been one of them. After all, didn't Clay, straight-arrow, upstanding, good-man-to-the-core Clay, have a brother like him?

What he'd never understood was what his mother had seen in the clearly sleazy, too-slick Graham Colton.

"What are you thinking about, boy?"

Startled, Ryder chided himself for this newly born tendency to get lost in thought.

"My mother," Ryder said, "and how I wish I'd known her before."

"Before?"

Before she got tangled up with my bio-dad, he thought.

"Before she gave up the rodeo," he said. "She must have been something. All fire and sass. But all I ever knew was the woman who got up before dawn every day to work in that diner."

"And you find that less appealing than being a rodeo rider?"

"Well, yeah," Ryder said, barely managing not to add "Of course!"

"Even though she did it for you?"

"You see, that's what I hate about it. Woman gets pregnant, and her life like…ends. She gives up her dreams, like nothing else matters but the kid. Or she dies young, like my mother did. She was only forty-six."

And while that still seemed old to him, he knew that it was far too young to die.

"So why don't you tell me," Boots began, in that tone Ryder had come to know meant some heavy thinking was coming his way, "what it is that's more important than raising kids?"

"I'm not saying it's not important, I know, they turn into adults someday and they'll be in charge, I know all that, but—"

"Did you miss having a father, Ryder?"

"Not mine," he said sourly.

"Agreed. Yours left a lot to be desired. But a father like you might imagine? One who cared about you, was involved in your life, one you could look up to?"

"I guess," Ryder said.

"Do you think things might have gone differently if you'd had one?"

"Maybe."

"Do you think your brother might have been a little more relaxed if there had been a father around to do the things he took upon himself, at far too young an age?"

"Sure."

"And perhaps your sister might have avoided falling for a smooth-talking city boy?"

He'd had enough. "What's the point, Boots?"

He could almost see the leathery old man shrug, could hear in his voice that lopsided smile that meant he was about to drive it home.

"Your biological father thought everything was more important than the kids."

Ryder felt as if he'd been sucker punched. Boots was too damned good at that, led you down the path to exactly where he wanted you to go, then hit you between the eyes.

"Damn it, Boots," he muttered.

There was a moment of silence before the man asked, "What's brought this on, boy? Why are you thinking about all this now?"

He almost spilled it, right then and there. But he couldn't, he knew he couldn't. If he'd tell anyone it would be Boots, but not now, not on a cell phone, not on a phone at all. There was no way in hell he was going to try and explain what had happened the other night over the phone. Hell, how could he explain something he himself didn't understand?

I helped deliver a baby, Boots. For the gutsiest, most beautiful woman I've ever seen. And now I can't get it out of my head. Her...or the baby.

"I don't even *like* babies," he muttered. "They're messy, they throw up on you—"

Boots voice was suddenly sharper. "You haven't done anything stupid, have you boy? Get some girl in trouble?"

"No!"

There had been, admittedly, that girl in New Mexico, when he'd been out of Lone Star for less than two weeks. He'd gone a little crazy, he knew, but it had been a long time. When the sexy little blonde had laughed at him, saying he made love like he'd just gotten out of jail, he'd laughed with her, but he hadn't gone back.

And he'd been, as he always was, careful. No trail of bastards across the country for him.

"It's just this whole…thing I'm working on. It's hard for me to understand."

"Of course it is. You're a decent human being, Ryder."

Ryder laughed. "Now there's something I don't hear much of."

"Take it from a man who was not at one time. I know them when I see them."

Boots didn't often refer to his past. He'd once told Ryder that the man he had once been was dead and buried, and his evil ways with him. To Ryder's amazement he hadn't been bitter at the prospect of spending the rest of his life locked up, despite being a changed man. He didn't even make a true effort at seeking parole, something he'd once explained to a puzzled Ryder.

"Not many believe in jailhouse conversions," he'd said simply. "And I can't blame them. They see it as a criminal's way to try and get out, convince everyone you've found religion so they'll let you go. I won't belittle my faith in that way. And," he'd added, "I have a lot to atone for. Here is as good a place as any to do that."

A lot to atone for…

He remembered how that had hit him, hard. He'd always thought atonement had to be forced on you, like when Clay would order him to apologize to Georgie for teasing her, or that it was something akin to his going to jail, to make up for being stupid enough to get fooled into driving a truck in coyote territory without being sure of what was inside it.

He'd never thought about what it would take to make a

man feel that from inside himself, to feel like he needed to atone for his transgressions, and to proceed to do so in his own way, with no one forcing it on him, no judge ramming it down his throat.

Simply because it was right.

That was the turning point, he realized now. That was the moment when he'd begun to look at Boots not just as a fellow inmate who was older and wiser in the ways of prison life, not just as a man who'd done far worse than Ryder had ever thought of, but as a man who had found something Ryder had never known—a solid, unshakable center, a path to follow and the strength to walk it.

Ryder was no Holy Roller, but when it came right down to it, he didn't think the source of the strength Boots had mattered as much as how he used it. And for some reason he'd chosen to use that strength to help Ryder find his own way.

"You know what the right thing is, Ryder, whatever it is that's eating at you. You just need to let down that guard of yours enough to see the answer."

They'd hit the end of Boots's allotted phone time, and had to say a hasty goodbye. But long after he'd disconnected, Ryder sat thinking.

So what was the right thing? Was Boots right? Was the answer right in front of him—he just couldn't see it?

He shook his head sharply. It was time for him to get back to work. He needed to check the perimeter of the Bar None. There was always a chance of more tunnels that hadn't been found yet. But he wanted to be back at his usual observation post at Hopechest by 2:00 a.m.; he'd seen that somewhere around two or three, the baby usually awakened and her mother got up to feed her.

Tonight was no exception. It was 2:15 a.m. when the light in that front room came on.

Even from a distance, through the high-powered bin-oculars, the sight of that mysterious, lovely woman with the baby he'd brought into the world at her breast, was the most incredible thing he'd ever seen. It was as if all the pain she'd endured was forgotten, as if the bloody, sloppy mess of the delivery had never happened, all of it wiped away by the miracle she now held in her steady, loving arms.

Had his mother felt like that? She'd been alone, too, thanks to his useless father.

There it was again, that odd, uncharacteristic sense of connection. He'd never felt it before, and now that he couldn't seem to get rid of it, he didn't know what to do about it. He'd always thought being a loner was easier— no strings, no ties, no responsibilities. But the sight of this woman, alone and frightened and yet ready to fight for the child she hadn't even laid eyes on yet, had given him a whole different view of being alone.

And the sight of her now made him feel his own isola-tion in a way that dug deep.

That famous guard Boots had mentioned seemed useless when it came to this woman.

And to that tiny human she held.

The baby was wrapped in a different blanket this time, something again pink, but with big flowers printed on it. Girly stuff, he thought again, with a smile that surprised him. He didn't know much about that, girly stuff. Georgie had always been a tomboy of sorts, more interested in horses than dolls, and the rodeo schedule always won out over a social calendar. And he'd never been with a woman long enough to really get to know the ins and outs of all that…frilliness.

But the baby's mother didn't seem like the frilly sort. Courageous, definitely. Beautiful, obviously. Tough, absolutely. And he suspected he should throw smart into the mix as well.

And classy.

That was the word that had eluded him until now, when he was watching her tend to her baby with gentle care. Something about her made him picture her in some sleek, designer outfit, turning heads....

As he drove back to the motel in the minutes just after dawn, he thought about that. And he couldn't quite reconcile his image of her with his image of the frightened, desperate illegals that he'd discovered—at the same time as the border patrol agents—in the back of that truck he'd been tricked into driving.

Obviously, one of his assumptions, his images, was wrong.

Maybe both, he thought wryly.

Chapter 8

"...**P**residential campaign of front-runner Joe Colton will be heading to Texas, where the scandal-plagued candidacy of disgraced Governor Allen Daniels has ground to a halt. Colton and his wife, Meredith, plan a joint visit in a few weeks."

Ryder sipped his coffee in front of the small, motel television. As he watched the video clip of the surging candidate and his wife, he found himself studying them dispassionately. As if they were any other couple in the news, nothing to do with him.

Joe Colton was a tall, lean man in his late sixties. Ryder had heard some time ago that he was an accomplished and lifelong horseman. He'd thought of Clay and Georgie then, and wondered idly if such things were passed on genetically.

Colton's dark hair was peppered with gray, and pure gray at the temples, giving him a distinguished look; any hint of his age was belied by his obvious fitness and his ease of carriage.

As the video played on, Ryder shifted his focus to Meredith Colton, Joe's wife of nearly forty years. She was trim but curvy, and dressed in a classic suit that showed she still had a great pair of legs. Her golden-brown hair was in one of those chin-length cuts that swung as she moved. Her eyes were a warm brown, and sparkled with a kindness that seemed very genuine. She was a classy woman.

Odd, that wasn't a word he often thought of, and yet now he'd done it twice in a day, about two very different women. He frowned. At least, he thought it was today...he had to think to remember if it had been before or after midnight that he'd had the thought about the woman at Hopechest Ranch.

He took another sip of coffee as the report ended with a mention that several of the Colton children, both biological and fostered, would be joining them periodically on the campaign trail.

His cousins, he thought suddenly.

The coffee suddenly tasted bitter, and he dumped it down the motel sink.

Joe Colton and his wife, it seemed, had hearts big enough to take in a multitude of kids not their own. They had even taken in the daughter of Meredith's late sister, who had tried her best to destroy her sister's life.

It was that daughter who was given the chance to run the Hopechest Ranch here in Esperanza. He'd even seen her and had no trouble recognizing her; the woman he'd spotted at the ranch looked just like Meredith Colton.

It occurred to him yet again to wonder how this whole Hopechest Ranch thing had happened. Before he'd gone to prison, the place hadn't even existed. How had it ended up here, on the Bar None of all places? Had Clay somehow joined the Colton fold? Just how much had he been involved in this decision? Was there more to this than merely the sale of some land Ryder knew Clay had been thinking about unloading for a long time? Had Joe and Meredith Colton decided Clay was worthy of inclusion in the illustrious Colton dynasty?

His mouth quirked wryly at the string of questions shooting through his mind. This was getting old fast, this constant wondering and introspection. It occurred to him then that perhaps he was dodging the real question that would likely never be answered. Which was why Graham Colton, so obviously unlike his brother Joe, couldn't even be bothered to acknowledge—let alone care about—children he had actually fathered himself, Ryder thought sourly.

A Colton family portrait flashed on the screen. In it, Joe Colton was seen wearing his trademark dazzling smile. Every time he saw a picture of that smile, Ryder had felt an odd sensation, not quite uneasiness, but a sort of twitchiness it had taken him a long time to figure out. When he had—when he happened to have seen a photo of the then senator shortly before having his own photo taken for his driver's license—it had been a jolt he would never forget.

Because Joe Colton's smile, that look that charmed millions, was a dead ringer for his own.

Talk about genetics.

"Get over yourself!" Ryder snapped aloud now.

He'd had about enough of this unaccustomed pondering of the mysteries of life that he'd never bothered himself about before.

"Leave the philosophizing to Boots," he ordered, then nearly groaned as he realized he'd added talking aloud to himself to his list of new and annoying habits.

He turned off the television, starting to wish he'd never turned it on. Knowing he was connected, however tenuously, to the family that seemed to head every newscast and headline every newspaper was too unsettlingly strange for his taste.

Clay, now, he could see that. He'd fit right into that family, with his straight-arrow attitude and oversized sense of responsibility.

"More power to you, bro," he said, meaning it. For his part, he knew the best thing he could do was what he'd done—sever all ties and leave Clay in peace. He was no doubt relieved not to have the burden of worrying about his troublesome little brother.

He glanced at his watch. It was nearly twilight when he could head out for his nightly surveillance. Anticipation kicked through him at the thought of seeing her again, even at a distance. Over the past several nights he'd given up trying to fight the feeling; now he just settled for hoping it would eventually wear off.

In the meantime, he kept an eye on Hopechest Ranch and its environs for his job, and an eye on a young mother and her baby for himself.

His cell phone rang. Not the silly, chirping ring he'd programmed in for his calls from his handlers, but the sharp jangle he'd set for one caller only.

Alcazar.

He went still. This call could possibly be the beginning of the end; if he was really in, it would be a job. And if so, he was on the verge of blowing this ring wide open.

And then he'd be done here, and he didn't know whether to wish for that or not.

On the third ring, he flipped open the phone, making certain his voice was casual, unconcerned as he answered with the name he'd given them, borrowed from his mother and his legendary grandfather. He'd never known "Rattle-snake" Grady, which he'd always regretted; he'd sounded, in the stories his mother had told, like the one relative he would really have liked to have known. How could you not admire a man who could stick eight seconds on the back of a rattler-spooked bull, then kill the snake, and who wore its skin like a talisman in every rodeo he went to until the day he died?

"I have a job for you," the voice on the other end of the phone said without preamble.

Ryder's pulse jumped, but he kept his voice even. "Yeah?"

"Tonight."

"Short notice."

"Is that a problem?"

"Not for me," he said, as if it meant less than nothing to him. "Not if it's worth my while."

Alcazar quoted a figure then, a dollar amount that took Ryder aback for a moment. He'd guessed this business was profitable, but that much, just for a night's work?

"In that case," Ryder said, "you get the platinum service."

To his satisfaction, Alcazar laughed. He wanted to stay on the right side of this man. He didn't think he was the ringleader—he wasn't smart enough—but he was the best lead Ryder had. He had his suspicions about who was really running things, a man who had access and opportunity, but Ryder hadn't pointed him out to his handlers yet. His new bosses had a nasty habit of making moves they didn't tell him about until after the fact. He supposed it was one of the downsides of being a coerced agent rather than a vol-unteer good guy. Which made no sense to him. He himself would trust somebody who had everything to lose more than the innate desire for law and order some people had.

Maybe because he'd never seemed to develop that desire

himself, he thought wryly as he listened to Alcazar's detailed instructions on where to be in three hours.

When the call had ended, he wondered whether he should let his handlers know it was a go. If he did, they might move into the area and screw up everything. If he didn't, they might just yank him out and toss him back in that prison cell—not a prospect he wanted to deal with. If he had to go back and serve the rest of his interrupted sentence, that would be bad enough. But he had the suspicion that if he blew this, the powers that be would conveniently forget where the key was, and he'd be lost forever in the prison system.

He compromised and, while driving to the rendezvous point set up in the earlier call, made the official report and told them most of it.

"I don't know what the job is. Not for sure." That was true. "I have to meet with them again, then maybe I'll find out."

"Report in as soon as you know," Furnell ordered.

"Yeah."

Feeling like a puppet on too short a string, he snapped the phone shut sharply. And once again pondered the possibility of just running, leaving all this behind and taking off. He always felt like this after talking to Furnell.

But he didn't want to spend the rest of his life looking over his shoulder, slipping down into a pit of paranoia until he saw the feds behind every tree.

Running wasn't really an option; he was just flailing around looking for an escape that wasn't there. As Boots told him, he should be glad for this chance to make things right, a chance few got. If he pulled this off he'd be free and clear, his record clean and no need to check that damn little box on any form asking if he'd ever been convicted of a felony.

He made the turn as instructed and continued to drive, now on a rough, dirt, two-rut track, the truck's headlights pushing back the utter darkness out here in the remote, unlit ranch country. With the windows rolled down in the night heat of August, the scent of warmed mesquite blew through the truck's cab.

It was a familiar scent to him, although he denied feeling any kind of nostalgia for it; it was just nice to be out, and not locked up where this kind of isolation and peace and quiet was impossible. He'd never thought of himself as a loner, not really, but he'd found that the simple privilege of privacy was one of the things he'd missed most in prison.

This was a different location than the last meeting, in the opposite direction and many miles farther off the main road. It was also very close to the western border of the Bar None, near Hopechest. He hoped the world he'd left behind and the world he'd landed in now weren't going to collide before this was all over.

What he would do then, when it was over, he didn't know.

The first thing that popped into his head was an image of a beautiful, olive-skinned woman and a tiny baby. She— well, both she's—had gotten under his skin like no one ever had, and he didn't like the feeling.

Once he got out of this, got away from here, he was sure he could regain his usual nonchalance about such things. It was the forced proximity as much as anything else that had kept them in the forefront of his mind—he was sure of that. Once he took off, it would all fade away. He'd be glad to be gone, he told himself. There were too many memories here anyway.

Somehow seeing the Bar None every day, seeing life going on, knowing his little sister had gotten married, seeing his brother apparently cozying up once more with his ex-wife, just pounded home how little he belonged here. His absence obviously hadn't even left a ripple, so there was no point in sticking around.

This kind of life wasn't for him, anyway. He wasn't the kind to settle down to life in a little burg like Esperanza, getting married and raising a bunch of rug rats...

Even as the thought flitted through his mind, the images played back in his head again—of the tiny little girl, who moments before had been merely an abstract concept, but had suddenly become the most real thing he'd ever seen. And his had been the first human touch she'd known....

He shook his head, angry at himself now. He needed to be focusing on what was about to happen, not some silly, rose-colored memory probably half-imagined by now anyway.

Boots would laugh if he could see him now.

As soon as the words ran through his mind, he knew they weren't true. If Boots could see him now, and know what he was thinking, how he was thinking, Ryder knew exactly what the old man would do.

He'd sit there as he always did, smiling that annoying smile that said he saw more than you'd ever wanted him to, and nodding wisely as if he'd expected this all along.

"You set me up for this, damn it," he muttered in the darkness of the truck's cab.

And then he nearly groaned anew at the ridiculousness of trying to blame an old man locked up miles away for his own screwed-up thoughts. He'd thought he'd gotten past that old dodge, blaming others for the results of his own poor decisions. Lord knew, Boots had spent enough time hammering the lesson into his head.

Telling himself he'd do better to remember the lessons pounded into him at that secret training facility, he reached down with his left hand and pulled the Glock out of the

hidden compartment. He shifted in the truck seat and
shoved the weapon into his belt at the small of his back.

Then he settled in and drove on through the night.

Chapter 9

Ana thought the evening would never end. She had only reluctantly agreed to accompany Jewel and the younger children on this trip into town. Only Jewel's firm and caring insistence made Ana acquiesce.

She had been nervous about being seen out in public, with her uncertain status until the long, laborious process of obtaining her legal papers was completed. But Jewel was nothing if not determined and kept at her to leave the ranch. And Ana suspected she had put more than a little of her vast knowledge of human psychology to work in the process as well.

Most of all, of course, Ana had been nervous about leaving Maria. Jewel guessed this easily. Things had been very, very quiet lately, she had said, with a knowing look that told Ana exactly what she meant; there had been no further smuggling activity. Ana supposed Deputy Rawlings had told Jewel this, so it must be true.

And while she knew Nicole, the older girl who had volunteered to watch the baby, was reliable, no one could look out for her child the way she herself could.

In the end, Jewel had been persuasive. She owed so much to this generous woman with such tragedy in her past, it was impossible to say no to her.

And it was nice to get out. A little, at least. Despite her nervousness, she enjoyed meeting Becky French, the short, plump woman who ran Miss Sue's. She was a lifelong resident of Esperanza, and knew everyone and everything that happened in the little town.

"We're like that Bogart movie," the woman said, smiling widely, her blue eyes sparkling, "sooner or later, everyone comes to Sue's."

When a little—very little—bit of coaxing from Jewel got the woman to bring out the latest photographs of her grandchildren, Ana found herself looking on with interest. None of them were as beautiful as Maria. Ana laughed at herself; she had become a thoroughly blind, doting mother already.

Cautious, she did not mention Maria despite the urge to share in the joy of new babies. And she was grateful when Jewel didn't mention her either.

I know what Ana is afraid of. I know what it means to lose a baby....

Jewel's tragedy stabbed through to Ana's tender heart. It was nothing short of a miracle that this generous, loving woman could even bear to look at photographs of other women's babies, let alone take one into her home.

Ana felt a sudden, fierce need to go, to be with her baby. She was sure if she made a fuss, Jewel would cut short the outing and take her back to the ranch. But the children were so happy, these youngsters who had had so little happiness in their lives until now, and Ana couldn't bring herself to do it.

I simply should not have come, she told herself. And I will not again. I will never allow myself to be separated from my baby again. It's far too hard.

She stirred her melting ice cream into a thick chocolate soup, and waited.

This time the meeting place was a deep gully that would be a ripe pathway for flash floods after a storm. Ryder could see the advantage. You could hide a set of double trailers in there and no one would be able to see them except from an aircraft.

They'd told him to look for a half boulder marked with paint and park there. He soon spotted the bright red slash that gleamed like blood in his headlights. The sides of the gully were less steep here, but steep enough so that his four-wheel-drive truck started to slide a bit. He stopped it on the left side of the boulder as instructed, and then spotted a dark-colored open Jeep down in the bottom of the gully. The motor was still running, the headlights on and aimed his way, as if they wanted to hide in the darkness behind the lights.

Or ruin your night vision, Ryder thought.

On that thought he flicked on his high beams; two could play that game. The added, brighter light showed him two figures standing near the Jeep, and a third one sitting in the driver's seat—planning a quick getaway, perhaps?

He heard one of them swear, then yell at him to kill the lights. He smothered a grin as he hit the control.

"Sorry," he called out. "Didn't want to hit anything. It's dark out here in the boonies."

Just like the rats prefer, he added silently as one of the men called him a name in Spanish that Ryder was sure would have offended his mother, if she were still alive. Ryder smothered a grin as he scrambled down the side of the gully with as much grace as he could manage. The other section of the paint-marked boulder, an even bigger chunk, lay at the bottom.

"Stop right there. Just because the boss trusts you doesn't mean I do," the voice said, confirming Ryder's guess about his identity.

Mr. Energetic. Great.

"Let's get this done, we're wasting time," Ryder said. He wondered if they were going to send him somewhere to pick up a baby. Wondered how the hell they arranged it. Wondered where they found people to help.

Wondered how they slept at night.

Idiot. If they were the kind who'd let that bother them, they wouldn't be doing it in the first place, he told himself.

"Let's go," Mr. Energetic said, swinging a large duffel bag out of the back seat of the Jeep.

"*Let's* go?" Rider asked.

Mr. Energetic laughed, that same harsh sound. "You think the boss is stupid? I'll be coming with you."

"I work alone."

"Then you don't work with us. Which is fine with me, pretty boy."

Ryder had to make a quick decision and he could only see one possibility. He shrugged. "Your funeral," he said, earning a sharp look from Mr. E.

At the man's order he climbed back up the way he'd come down into the gully, not caring for having to turn his back on Mr. E, but hoping clambering up the slope would keep him occupied.

Once they were next to his truck, the man spoke again. "Drive back the way you came. We'll be called with directions on where to take the package," he finished, indicating the bag.

The first thing Ryder thought was that even Mr. E didn't know where they were going yet. The second was that he'd been completely wrong.

Ryder's hopes collapsed as he stared at the zippered bag. He'd obviously misjudged. And despite Mr. E's claim that the boss trusted him, obviously he didn't trust him enough to let him in on the baby smuggling. So what were they having him carry? Was the thing stuffed with coke? Meth? Worse?

He hesitated; this could be a hornet's nest for him. His handlers had let a lot of petty stuff go in the interest of furthering the investigation, but a duffel full of drugs? But he didn't see any way out, and took the handles. The way Mr. E was holding it made the bag seem light to him, as he pictured kilos of white powder or some such jammed into every corner. And he could see now that it wasn't packed as full as he would have expected.

"It's drugged. Should be quiet."

It took a moment, given his thoughts about the contents of the bag, for the odd statement to register.

"What?"

"They give it some kind of cold meds, to keep it asleep." Mr. Energetic gave a harsh laugh. "Don't want the thing crying at the wrong time, now do we?"

Ryder went cold. He wasn't sure what made him queasier, the thought that he'd been wrong, that this really was the break he'd been waiting for, or that they'd apparently stuffed a baby into this bag like so much dirty laundry.

It. The thing.

The words, his own words, echoed in his head, and made him feel slightly ill. He'd talked the same way, with the same lack of concern.

He reached for the zipper on the top of the bag.

"What the hell are you doing?"

"I went to prison for not making sure what I was transporting," Ryder answered. "Not stupid enough to do it again."

The reminder of his prison time seemed to mollify even Mr. E, who let his protest subside as Ryder tugged the zipper halfway open. He peered inside as best he could in the faint light this far from the Jeep's headlights.

His heart slammed in his chest, and his breath stopped in his throat when he saw a wad of cloth wrapped around a tiny bundle.

A blanket.

A familiar blanket.

Pink. With darker pink flowers.

In disbelief he tilted the bag, looked at the tiny face, at the gorgeous skin, the dark hair just like her mother's.

It wasn't just a baby. It was *the* baby. The baby he had brought into the world.

Ryder silently swore the same heartfelt curse the smuggler had. An image of this child's mother flashed through his mind. Of her walking the floor in the middle of the night, nestling this tiny girl to her breast. He remembered, for an instant, the moments when he'd wondered if she was here to simply have this baby and hand it over to the smugglers for a price.

Call him a fool, naive, or any of the other things he was half-sure he was right now, but he didn't believe it. Couldn't believe it.

She wouldn't.

She would not do that.

Which left only one option. Kidnapping.

Which left him only one option.

Chapter 10

Ryder knew the moment he made the move that it was a mistake.

A big mistake.

If he'd thought first—not his greatest strength—he would just played along and taken down Mr. E when they were alone out in the brush somewhere. He could have done it easily.

And probably would have enjoyed it.

But what capacity he had for thinking first seemed to have vanished at the first sight of the baby. Or rather, this baby. Her presence enraged him; the thought of her in the hands of these slime balls for any length of time was damn near unbearable.

So at the first sight of her, he'd promptly forgotten the crash training course the feds had put him through. He did what had gotten him into trouble so often before—went with his gut reaction. He grabbed for the duffel bag.

Forgetting the little problem of four-to-one odds.

He had completely, thoroughly, lost his mind.

With a shout, Mr. E dropped the bag and lunged at him. Ryder spun, took him down with a kick that should have shattered his knee and an elbow to the solar plexus. It gave him time to back up and go for the Glock at his back. Mr. E was writhing on the ground, swearing and staring at Ryder in shock.

Ryder heard the shouts, the sound of the Jeep roaring up the slope like an angry cougar.

Oh, yeah. The other guys, Ryder thought stupidly. Three of them.

He grabbed the duffel bag and backed toward the truck, the Glock trained on Mr. E. The Jeep crested the bank in a spray of dirt, and the three men leapt out.

"Don't shoot him," Mr. E yelled at them. "His ass is mine."

They were running at him, all three of them, guns at the ready. Mac 10s, he guessed from the shape. He held onto his own weapon, the only equalizer he had. He wasn't sure who to train it on. Mr. E didn't seem like the type to inspire enough loyalty to get the other two to put down their guns. Not when they'd have to explain to Alcazar later.

It looked like a standoff.

But he had the baby, and that made him the winner.

I'll get you back to your mother, little one, he promised the baby silently.

"What the…?" one of the armed men asked.

"I knew the boss shouldn't have trusted pretty boy here," Mr. E said, getting to his feet slowly.

Damn, Ryder thought. Guess I didn't break his knee after all.

Then again, when he tried to take a step, the man groaned loudly, and that leg nearly buckled. But he reached under his jacket and took out a matching automatic pistol. And now Ryder was looking at four weapons that could pump him so full of metal he'd probably reflect the Texas sun when they finally found him out here.

If they ever did.

"What the hell do you want with a baby?" the man who'd been behind the wheel asked, sounding more bewildered than anything. "No one's going to deal with you, not with Alcazar running this show."

"Shut up," Mr. E said, and Ryder was pleased to see sweat beading up on his face.

"But he's not a cop, we know that, what the—"

"Just shut up, Denny," one of the other men said, and Ryder got the feeling Denny was the driver because they didn't much trust him to react quickly enough to do anything else.

"Back off," Ryder said, gesturing at them with the Glock.

"Pretty boy can't count," the one who hadn't yet spoken said. "Four of us, one of you, jerk wad."

"Gives me four targets," Ryder said, feigning a cool he was far from feeling. The too-slight weight of the duffel felt like the weight of the world to him in that moment. "I'm not even going to tell you which one I'll shoot first."

"He had to know it was a baby, that's why we're here, so why was he so surprised?" Denny asked.

"Shut *up!*" one of the others said in exasperation.

"He was down for the deal, until he looked at the baby. I think—" that earned the beleaguered driver a chorus of derisive hoots, but he kept on doggedly "—he *knows* that baby."

The hoots of laughter continued. Obviously they weren't terribly worried about him, or his promise to shoot one of them. Not that he could blame them, not at these odds.

The laughter faded into jabs about Denny's thinking abilities, but Ryder's heart sank when he saw that Mr. E, instead of joining the chorus, was looking at him, brows furrowed.

"Shut up," Mr. E said, but this time it was directed at his men.

Ryder suddenly didn't like the taste of this at all.

"Put down that bag," Mr. E said, and there was a world of menace in his tone now.

"Guess that makes you my first target," Ryder said.

"Never mind your first target," Mr. E said. "Here's mine."

And the hand that held his weapon shifted, lowered.

Ryder's stomach clenched, sending a wave of nausea through him.

He was aiming at the baby.

"You won't shoot." It took Ryder a moment to get the words out past the knot in his throat, to pretend a casual callousness he was far from feeling. "Your boss won't like it if you kill his investment."

He hated even talking about the baby that way, but he had to in order to get through this.

Assuming he got through it at all.

"It won't be my problem," Mr. E said easily. "The story will be that *you* killed it."

Ryder's gut clenched anew.

"Put the bag down."

Ryder stared at the man. It was like looking into the cold, reptilian eyes of a venomous Gila monster. And Ryder knew in that moment, without a doubt, that the man would do exactly as he said. He would murder a helpless baby without a second thought.

Ryder set down the bag.

Mr. E gestured at him with his weapon. "Now the gun."

Ryder hesitated; once he gave up the gun, he was toast.

And the baby would vanish, likely never to be found. But if he tried to shoot his way out of here, the baby could end up dead anyway.

Mr. E shifted his aim, once more pointing the weapon at the duffel bag.

"Fifteen bullets per second," Mr. E said, with an evil glee that made Ryder feel deathly cold.

He knew what would happen to him. He felt that at least the baby would survive, in fact would probably have a good life somewhere, with parents willing to pay any amount for a healthy child.

Her mother, he thought, an image of the woman whose name he would now likely never know forming in his mind. The memory of her nerve, her steely determination, had haunted him for days now.

If it were she standing here, what would she do?

She would do whatever it took to protect her baby.

He knew that as surely as he knew his life was counting down right here. She would give up anything, sacrifice anything, to ensure her baby's safety.

He dropped his Glock into the dirt.

When two of them grabbed his arms, he thought they were going to cart him back to Alcazar to decide what to do with him. He even had an instant to plot his escape, but the baby complicated things. He couldn't, wouldn't risk her getting hurt.

And then Mr. E moved, suddenly, putting his full weight behind a pile driver punch.

Pain exploded in Ryder's gut. A starburst of light seemed to blind him for a moment. He thought his lungs must have collapsed under the force and he couldn't draw breath. A second blow made his head spin. A third glanced off his ribs, but set up a whole new kind of pain.

He jerked against his captors but they only tightened their grip, yanking his arms back until his shoulders screamed a protest. Mr. E laughed. The sound matched the look in his eyes when he'd aimed his weapon at the duffel bag.

The first blow to his head made Ryder dizzy. The next snapped his head so hard to one side he thought he felt something rip. The next set up a ringing in his ears that he thought might never go away.

Through the pain, as Mr. E laughed harder and put more power into each blow, Ryder began to realize this wasn't just punishment for stepping out of line.

This was an execution.

Oddly, the idea of dying didn't particularly terrify him. But then if he died no one would know what had happened to that baby.

He had to stay alive. He was the only one who'd gotten this far. If someone came in and had to start over, the baby would be long gone, lost forever to her mother. And her mother would never get over it. He knew that in some bone-deep way.

After Mr. E's next punishing strike, he let himself go limp. His suddenly dead weight broke their hold as he started to sag to the ground. He had to hope neither of them noticed he was keeping his feet under him.

"Our turn now?" the man on his right arm asked hopefully.

"All yours," Mr. E said. "Leave something for the vultures to feed on."

The man who had spoken laughed, and let go of Ryder's arm to step in front and add his own fists to the mix. In that instant Ryder made his move. Ignoring the excruciating pain that wracked him, he yanked his left arm free. For an instant he thought his legs weren't going to cooperate. Then he got them working.

He ran.

He heard the shouted curses. Knew he had only seconds, if that. Heard the first shot. Then a spray of automatic fire. He let out a yell of pain. Stumbled backwards to the crumbling edge of the gully. Flailed wildly. Went over the edge.

In the instant when he hit the split boulder at the bottom of the ravine, heard an ominous snap in his chest and felt a sharp stab of pain, he thought he just might have finished the job for them.

Chapter 11

Ana nearly cried when the kids decided they wanted to stop at the mini-mart, the only business still open this late. It was not that she begrudged them their candy bars, but she wanted to get back to her baby. The stress of separation was about to make her scream out loud.

Since Jewel would allow them only one candy bar each—which, she told them sternly, they would have to save until tomorrow after the ice cream tonight—they talked about getting what they all liked and dividing up the goods among them all. And when two of them discovered a tiny souvenir T-shirt that said, "I found hope in Esperanza," a play on the meaning of the town's name, Ana felt ashamed of herself for wanting to cut their outing short.

"Absolutely," Jewel said with a smile as she held up the little pink shirt. "Maria needs this. It is her color, after all."

Ana touched Jewel's arm, and the woman looked at her. "Your kindness," Ana said softly, "and your courage humble me."

"If you want to talk about courage," Jewel retorted in an equally soft tone, "let's talk about yours."

Ana felt her cheeks warm. Jewel patted her arm in turn. "Let's get you home to your little girl. You've been very good about staying away so long, so these short people here could have some fun."

The kids reacted with groans at the short people joke, but Ana sensed they were not really upset; Jewel and Hopechest Ranch had given these children a sense of belonging, of being valued, that had been sadly lacking in their lives. They were blossoming under the tender care, whether it was on an outing like this, working feverishly at some craft, or playing with the multitude of toys scattered around the ranch house.

Jewel then turned to pay the cashier. When she had the bag in her hands, she explained that she would be holding onto the loot until tomorrow, earning her a chorus of groans. Jewel was not only kind and brave, she was very smart about children, Ana thought. And Ana admired the way she was instilling confidence in all her charges, and responsibility in the older ones, like Nicole.

Ana wondered if perhaps her kindness might extend to teaching Ana what she knew; she needed all the help she could get for the days to come when she would have to raise Maria properly, teach her what was right and wrong, what was important in life.

She herself, so far, could only serve as a bad example, she feared. But that was over now, behind her, and she would never make mistakes like that again.

She would never trust so easily again.

* * *

He wasn't going to make it.

With every step, he knew it. Every time he fell, he knew he couldn't get up again. Every inch he gained, even when he was reduced to crawling through the brush, he knew was the last he could manage.

Yet he kept going.

He thought he passed out a few times, at least he seemed to remember waking up with his face in the dirt, with various insects scurrying over him, in anticipation of his certain death, or perhaps just drawn by the blood. Sometimes the thought of them feeding on him drove him a few precious yards farther. Sometimes he hurt so much he didn't even care.

He told himself that if they hadn't taken his truck and he'd tried to drive, he would have crashed it by now. It didn't make his progress any less torturous. He didn't know how long he'd been crawling. Didn't know how far he'd come. Wasn't even sure he was going in the right direction. He had to hope that his memories of the Bar None were guiding him properly. His conscience jabbed him anew. He had to tell her. Even if he died with his next breath, he had to tell her. She would do what had to be done to save her baby, he knew it. He hated that he'd blown it so badly, that it would be left to her, but it was down to that.

He had to get to her.

He kept on, for what seemed like an endless nightmare trek. Still he was startled when, the next time he forced himself to his feet, he saw the dark shape of Hopechest Ranch looming up in the darkness, just a few yards away. For a moment he thought he was imagining it, that some burst of wishful thinking had his mind seeing things that weren't there in the darkness.

But from the fixture on the front porch, there was a gleam of light near the room where he'd found the beautiful, gutsy woman about to deliver the prettiest little girl he'd ever seen.

He blinked, his dazed mind telling him, belatedly, that it was okay to blink now. It had been the hardest thing he'd ever done, not to blink when Mr. E and his men had shone a bright flashlight down on him at the bottom of the gully. He'd forced himself to keep his eyes open, trying to approximate the blank stare of dead eyes, praying that they wouldn't come down the slope, that his eyes and the twisted, awkward position of his body bent painfully back against the boulder would convince them he was already dead or close enough to it.

He hadn't been sure they weren't right, had been almost afraid to try to move when they'd laughed and gone, afraid that he wouldn't be able to.

But he had. And somehow, he'd gotten here. The sight galvanized him, and he got his feet under him and staggered forward. He was going to get it done, the one thing that had driven him. He had to last long enough to tell her what he knew. It seemed an unfair burden to drop on a woman still recovering from childbirth, but the memory of her quiet courage that night, the steely determination he'd seen in her dark eyes, was the prod that had kept him going; she would do what had to be done, he told himself with every pain-wracked step.

He collapsed in a heap in the shadows beneath her bedroom window.

With a smile, Ana accepted the hugs of the children and the gift they had picked out for Maria. As Jewel led them off to bed, Ana walked down to the family room where a light was on. Nicole was on the couch, fast asleep, the controller for the video game still in one hand. Ana frowned; she had not realized this was what the girl would be doing. She had had an image in her mind of Nicole playing with Maria, as she often did during the day, the girl smiling as her baby cooed. It was the only thing that had enabled her to leave at all.

But perhaps she had only begun to play the game after she put Maria to bed, Ana thought, not wanting to jump to harsh conclusions. She gently took the controller, studied the unfamiliar buttons for a moment until she found the way to turn it off. Then she shut off the television.

Rather than wake Nicole, she took a throw from the back of an adjacent chair and spread it over the sleeping girl. She was good-hearted, surely she would have taken good care of Maria. And she had spoken often of taking care of her little sisters before their parents had tragically been killed.

Still, Ana had to check on her baby right now.

She turned and walked back toward the front of the house. All was quiet there now. She could hear Jewel speaking softly to the young ones, who had apparently followed her instructions in record time, no doubt to make sure they got their selected treats tomorrow. The house went silent so quickly Ana was amazed.

She heard Jewel's footsteps as she went toward her own rooms on the other side of the house. Hoping Jewel would get some real sleep tonight, Ana headed down the hall and stepped into her own room, leaving the light off so as not to wake Maria. She tried hard to keep the baby quiet at night, for Jewel's sake.

She started across the room toward the crib. Her anxiety had lessened now that she was back and all was apparently well. But she still wanted to see her baby. She walked carefully; her rubber-soled sandals tended to squeak on the tile floor, and she didn't want—

The quiet groan from just outside stopped her in her tracks. She barely stifled a scream. Only the realization that whatever it was sounded like it was in great pain allowed her to keep from shrieking the roof down.

The fact that she could not be sure what it was she had heard calmed her instinctive fright a little. The sound had been so muffled, so muted it could have been anything, any kind of animal. That it had come from outside her window was unsettling, but not necessarily terrifying. She thought of calling for help, but the only other adult in the house was Jewel. She couldn't bear to disturb her when she was getting so little sleep anyway, not without knowing what was wrong.

She tiptoed toward the window, keeping carefully to the shadows, thankful she had not turned on the light to betray her presence. The big, comfortable rocking chair, a gift from Jewel, was in front of the window. She stepped around it, thinking that if anything—or anyone—tried to break the window and come in, getting tangled up in that moving chair would give her enough time to grab Maria and make an escape.

Ready to run in an instant, Ana peered out the window.

And nearly screamed again. Instead she sucked in a breath of pure shock, the sound she made tiny and strangled.

There was a man lying on the ground outside her window.

She turned, starting to back away. She would grab Maria and go to Jewel. They would call for help, maybe Deputy Rawlings and—

The man moved. She leapt back, out of any possible line of sight. He groaned again, and there was no mistaking the pain in the sound. And then something registered in her mind, something that made her frown.

His movement had revealed his face. His features were oddly dappled in the light of an ebbing moon, but they registered.

Instead of running, she leaned forward and took a second peek.

It was her white knight, her rescuer, the tall, dark and handsome cliché who had appeared as if magically out of the night and disappeared the same way.

And suddenly everything changed. She still did not trust him, but he had helped her when there was no one else to do it. He had helped bring Maria into the world, had been the first touch her baby had known, and then when she had asked him to, he had gone back the way he had come, no questions asked. That had to be worth something, if not everything.

She had certainly not been able to put him out of her mind as she had hoped. Images of him had interrupted her days and haunted her nights. She had been filled with a strange sense of longing that, no matter how she tried, she could not seem to talk herself out of with any amount of common sense.

She had wished more than once that he could have known who she really was, that she was not just looking for a handout, that she wanted to do things right, was trying to do it the legal way, that she was intelligent, educated, and had skills she could and was willing to put to good use in exchange for a safe life for her and her little girl.

She had never imagined it could matter to her so much what a total stranger thought of her. But it did.

She had tried to tell herself that it was because he had shared that most intimate of times with her, or that it was because he had been like a white knight in a fairy tale, appearing in the nick of time and then vanishing. But part of her new life was a determination to face honestly the realities of the people around her; seeing what was not there, or not seeing what was, had propelled her into this situation to begin with.

And she had realized, during one 2:00 a.m. feeding in that chair, staring out into the moonlit night as Maria suckled, that this new resolution should include being honest with herself as well. That had been the moment when she had admitted that her feelings about her unknown rescuer were much more complicated than simply gratitude for his mysterious and timely help.

And now, here he was, obviously hurt and needing her help in turn. Her need for fairness, her faith in balance and, in an old-fashioned way, her sense of honor demanded she provide it.

She should still wake Jewel, she thought as she hurried around to the front door; opening the garage would make enough noise it might draw someone curious, something she did not want until she had the chance to assess the situation. After all, here was this strange man, on the grounds of her precious Hopechest Ranch. Although Ana did not think he was a threat, that was not really her decision to make.

But first, she must see how badly he was hurt. If he needed medical attention, that would make the decision for her.

Moments later she was crouching beside him, pushing the branches of the privet bush under her window aside to reach him.

The moment she touched him he groaned again, and jerked slightly. His eyes opened, but looked oddly unfocused. Then they sharpened, and she saw that he recognized her.

He smiled.

Ana's breath caught. Never in her life had a man smiled at her like that, in a way that made her heart leap in her chest. That this man would do so now, when he was so obviously in pain, stirred a feeling buried so deep inside her she could not name it, not now. There was no time anyway, things needed to be done, and as he had been for her, she was the only one here to do them.

She leaned in closer, and smothered a gasp of shock when she realized that the discolorations on his face that she had thought were an effect of the moonlight coming through the leaves were instead patches of blood and swollen, reddened flesh. He looked as if he had been beaten, and badly.

Very badly.

"No, no," she whispered when he moved as if he were trying to get up. "You are hurt, you must stay still until we know how badly."

"Walked...forever," he said. "Can't be...that bad."

At least he could speak, she thought. A moment later she wished he could not.

"The baby...your baby."

Ana went still. "What about my baby?"

"Tried...get her away from them."

The sense of what he was saying stabbed through her. "My baby is here. In her crib."

"Saw her...pink flowers."

The blanket, Ana realized. Maria's blanket, that's what he was talking about.

Terror gripped her. Without another thought she leapt to her feet and raced back into the house. This time she hit the light switch the moment she ran into her room, thinking she would never be more grateful to hear Maria cry.

Seconds later she was standing beside her baby's crib, her hands clenched around the rail until every knuckle was white.

Maria was gone.

Chapter 12

Ryder saw the scream forming in her throat.

"Don't," he said.

He'd been able to get up and follow her inside, feeling not quite so horrible after his unintentional rest outside her window. For a brief moment, he'd even allowed himself to hope he'd been wrong, that it hadn't been her baby. How would he know, after all? Barring obvious differences, one baby looked pretty much like another to him.

But he'd known. In his gut he'd known, with a certainty that stunned him almost as much as Mr. E's first punch had.

She whirled then, her dark eyes wide and full of panic. And accusation. She flew at him, her fists up. He held up his hands to ward her off; she might be more than half a foot shorter than he, but he knew her strength, and, coupled with her emotional state, she could do some real damage.

Especially when he was wobbly on his feet already.

"You took her!" the frantic woman spat out, but she stopped in front of him without striking a blow. Lucky for him, he thought. "You are one of them, those despicable men who traffic in innocent babies."

"I'm not. I'm trying—" he had to stop to take in a breath that hurt his ribs "—to stop them. I've been working on cracking the ring."

She didn't look much less suspicious. "I am going to call the sheriff."

Ryder swore inwardly. He was so close, and if she called the sheriff now, it would all be over. He'd be back in the slammer and Maria would be lost forever somewhere up the evil railroad these slimeballs had built.

"We'll lose her," he said, desperate to get through to her but not knowing how. He didn't know how to deal with this kind of fear and anger. This kind of love.

"I will call Jewel's friend, Deputy Rawlings. He will find out the truth." Rage and fear boiled up in her eyes again. "But I already know it. You stole my Maria!"

For an instant, his brain still too sluggish, all Ryder could absorb was what she'd named the baby.

"Maria," he said softly, trying it out. "Maria. It fits."

He wasn't sure what happened next. Or why. But he knew her expression changed. She took a half step back, cocked her head at an angle as she studied him. He didn't know what he looked like, but judging by the soreness of his face, it wasn't pretty. He was confused when he realized that the suspicion, the accusation had faded from her eyes. All he'd done was repeat what she'd named her baby.

He shook his head, trying to clear away the fog. Pain jabbed from his jaw up to his left temple, effectively sharpening his thoughts.

"I didn't take her—" He stopped, grimaced, before adding, "I don't even know your name."

"Nor I yours," she pointed out sharply, clearly not pleased with the distraction from the matter at hand.

"Ryder," he said. "Ryder Grady." He was at least thinking clearly enough not to say "Colton," not here in a house on Bar None land, run by a woman named Jewel who was connected to his brother, by business and by blood.

Means she's connected to you, too, a small voice in the back of his battered brain said, but he shoved it aside.

After a moment, the woman finally returned the nicety, albeit tersely. "Ana Morales. Why should I believe you did not steal her? No one else even knew she was here."

Ana. He tried it out in his mind, aware that if he'd spoken it aloud his voice would likely have held the same wondering tone as Maria had.

"Everybody in this house knew," he said.

"Children," she said with a wave of dismissal. "You accuse children?"

"There are adults here, too." He was finding it a bit easier to talk, now that he was upright and not lying on his ribs.

"Jewel? Macy? You think to blame them for this?"

"I'm not blaming them. Or anyone here. I'm just saying…it's natural they would talk. A new baby, delivered here at the ranch, they would talk. And anyone could have overheard them."

Ana Morales frowned at that. He could see that she was considering his words. For all her justifiable emotional upheaval, she was still thinking. He was grateful for that; otherwise she'd probably be hammering him with those small, hard fists. He knew her strength too well from that night, and didn't doubt he'd have paid a price had she kept coming.

"Ana," he said, "I'm working with the government on this. I know who has her."

She went very still. "You are the police?"

"I'm more of a…private contractor."

"What does that mean?"

"It means I knew some of the men involved. They approached me to help."

She studied him for a moment. "And what do you get in return?"

He winced inwardly. It was the kind of thing he himself would ask, and he wondered what had happened in her young life to make her so cynical. Funny, it seemed only normal to him, but in her, it bothered him.

She wound up pregnant and alone in a strange country, and you're wondering what made her cynical? he asked himself.

But he knew better than to lie to her. Not now, when her emotions were in full flood and her maternal instincts roaring; he sensed she'd know it instantly.

"It was a deal," he admitted, afraid if he told her the rest, she'd never believe him about anything else. "But that doesn't change the facts. I know who has her, Ana. And I can get her back."

"Why should I believe you?" she asked again.

Ryder let out a compressed breath. Even that simple act caused his bruised ribs to ache. And that added pain made him snap, "How about because I trekked halfway across freaking Texas, like this, to tell you?"

He knew he sounded like a petulant child, wanting credit for one of the few noble things he'd ever done in his life, but he didn't care. He was tired, he hurt all over, he thought a couple of those ribs might in fact be cracked, and he wanted nothing more than to lie down and sleep for a week.

"What happened to you?"

He frowned, which hurt nearly as much as a deep breath. "Told you. I tried to stop them."

"And they did this to you? If you work for the government, do you not have a gun?"

"I did. They had more."

And one was aimed at Maria, by a man who wouldn't hesitate to use it, he added silently. He wondered at himself for a moment. He knew instinctively that that, of all the things he could tell her, would stir her to his side. But he couldn't tell her, and he didn't quite understand why.

She would completely lose it, he told himself.

He even believed that. If he told her how close her baby had come to death, she might be unable to function, and right now he needed her thinking hard. It had nothing to do with protecting her—he had never cared about any woman enough to worry about that—nothing at all.

"They?" she finally asked, looking him up and down.

"Four of them," he said, strangely unwilling to let her think he'd been beaten by merely one or two. Thinking his brain must be scrambled, he strove to take charge. Time was wasting and the trail was getting colder by the second. "I need a phone. I have to call my—" He hesitated on the word *handler.* "My contact," he said instead.

She hesitated.

"Ana, please. The longer we wait, the less chance we have of finding Maria."

Again, her daughter's name seemed to turn the tide. "Jewel gave me a cell phone when Maria was born, in case of emergencies," she said, and walked quickly to the dresser and dug into an outside pocket on a large canvas bag. Pink, Ryder noticed, girly again.

She handed it to him. He checked the phone readout for the number. At this hour chances were he'd have to wait for a call back, he explained to Ana. He dialed, keyed in his code and the cell number, then disconnected.

"How long?" she asked.

"A few minutes has been the longest, before."

She stood for a moment, rubbing her arms with her hands as if she were chilled, despite the hot August night. Ryder felt the ridiculous urge to hold her, to take her in his arms and warm her with his own heat, to comfort her…

He even took a step toward her, stopping only when he realized the foolishness of the thought, and realized he was in no shape to comfort anyone.

"Wait here," Ana said, and turned.

Was she going to call for help anyway? "Ana, don't—"

She waved him to silence. "I will not do what you are thinking. There is a first aid box in the children's bathroom."

He'd asked her to trust him, so he guessed he had to trust her as well. He let her go. He heard the distant sound of water running. Moments later she was back, with a wet washcloth, a large towel, and a well-stocked plastic case of bandages, antiseptics and various other implements. He supposed that was a necessity with lots of active kids running around. He should be grateful.

He'd thought she would simply hand it to him and leave it at that, but instead she directed him to sit on the edge of the bed. He did, warily, the movement tugging on bruised rib muscles. He bit back a grunt of pain, telling himself he had no right to complain about a few twinges, not here in this room where she had gone through such agony to bring her baby into the world.

The intimacy of the memories unsettled him.

She began to work without comment, and he noticed with a little surprise that she'd used warm water on the washcloth; he'd expected the shock of cold. Or maybe it was just August in Texas, he thought wryly, and the water never really did get cold.

She was amazingly gentle, her touch soft and compassionate. It still hurt, but he did his best not to show it. When he couldn't manage that, she apologized. He sat there for what seemed like endless minutes, his awareness gradually shifting from the pain to her closeness, and another sort of forced intimacy was suddenly upon him.

She leaned toward him to reach his split lip with the warm cloth. Her breast brushed his arm, and while she didn't react, it took all his focus for him not to jump. An image shot through his mind, of the picture she'd made, sitting in that rocking chair by the window, nursing Maria. In the late-night hour and the privacy of her room, she hadn't covered up, and he'd known even then that he would remember the sight for the rest of his life, the baby's tiny fists kneading that soft, generous curve.

As she moved again, he realized that even through his bloodied nose he could smell a faint scent of soap or shampoo.

Had she been out on a date?

The idea made him frown, which made her apologize. He let it go; he certainly didn't want to explain that it was his thought, not pain, that had caused the expression.

But then a vague, hazy memory came to him, of lying outside her window, safe in the shadows of the house, and hearing first the ranch's van, then the excited laughter of children for a brief moment before the garage door had settled heavily into place.

She'd been out with the children, not a man. And he didn't like how relieved that made him.

"This needs stitches," she said as she swabbed at the most painful spot, on his left temple, about even with his eyebrow.

"It'll keep. Just use those," he said, gesturing at the small packet of butterfly bandages in the first aid kit.

To his surprise she didn't argue with him, just did as he asked. Then he realized he shouldn't be surprised; she was likely only doing this to keep herself distracted when everything in her must be screaming to go after her baby.

It hit him, the enormity of the trust she had put in him. He didn't know if it had been the weight of his government connection, or if she simply trusted him to help her as he had the night Maria was born. It was hard to believe that much faith could be built in so short a time, but he had to admit it had been transforming even for him.

And if it convinced her…

"Your ribs are hurt," she said.

He grimaced. "My dramatic exit was a bit…costly."

He explained to her how he'd faked a fall into the gully, and played dead when they'd peered over at him. He didn't say it was likely the only reason he was still alive, but he saw in her eyes that he didn't have to; she might be young, but she wasn't a fool. He hadn't mistaken the keen intelligence there.

"Take off your shirt."

He blinked. Then connected it, belatedly and feeling foolish, to her comment about his ribs.

"There's nothing to do about them."

"But you are bleeding there as well. It should be cleaned, stopped. You will do Maria no good if you collapse."

She had a point. He took off his shirt. And closed his eyes, telling himself it was so she couldn't see the flash of pain in his eyes, not so that he could concentrate on the feel of her fingers on his bare skin.

The stupidity of such thoughts when he was hurting so much, when there was so much at stake, wasn't lost on him, and he made a fierce effort to regain his focus.

The cell phone rang. He stared at it for a split second, disconcerted by the ring. She'd obviously programmed it for the baby, a quiet, simple lullaby. Recovering, he grabbed it, checked the readout and answered.

Thankfully, it was Gibson and not Furnell.

He explained quickly, leaving out his personal connection to the baby. They didn't need to know. Better that they didn't; if they thought he had a personal stake in this, they might pull him off the mission.

"Why didn't you just play along?" Gibson asked.

Clearly, instead of mooning over Ana, he should have been thinking of answers to questions he should have known were coming. He could hardly explain it all now.

"It just went haywire," he said. "Alcazar's main man, he decided he didn't trust me."

Gibson's voice was suddenly sharp. "Did they know you were working for us?"

"I don't think so. The guy just didn't like me. Maybe he thought I was trying to move in on his spot."

It was lame, but the best he could come up with. Quickly he went on, hoping Gibson would drop the questions he couldn't answer for the moment.

"I don't know where they were taking her. We were supposed to get a call with further directions."

"A cell call?"

"Probably." Something else occurred to him. "They told me I'd be driving back the way I came. First cell reception should be about at the west corner of the Bar None where it meets the county road. It drops to next to nothing after that."

"Hold on." There was a minute or two of dead air, and Ryder wondered if they had a way to check on any cell calls made in the area.

They're the feds—of course they do. What good would they be if they didn't?

"Three calls around the right time," Gibson said without preamble when he came back. "One from a local prefix, two with Del Rio prefixes."

Ryder went still. "The limo, the one Alcazar was in when we met up…it had one of those metal logos attached. Some dealer in Del Rio."

"Right on the border," Gibson said. "That could be the start of their network. We may have been looking in the wrong place for that end of the operation."

Ryder spoke quickly, before the man could bolt too far in that direction, away from where Ryder needed him to focus.

"We've got to find that baby," he said. "She's our best chance at breaking up this end of the ring."

"She?" the agent asked.

Ryder ignored the curiosity. "We've never been this close before, Gibson."

If the agent was surprised by Ryder's unaccustomed use of his name, he didn't let on. "I know. We've never been on them this soon after they've picked up a kid."

It's not some anonymous kid, Ryder shouted in his mind. It's Maria, damn it!

"They'll be moving her for a while yet, if we're right about how far they like to get from the border before they hand off to the next link."

"We are," Gibson said. "You know we've been working this from the other end, too."

Ryder knew they had, that they had located at least three couples who had obtained their babies through this operation. The last he'd heard, none of them had been very cooperative, fearing the loss of the child they considered their own.

Bought and paid for, Ryder thought sourly.

Did they ever think about the parents, the mothers like Ana, grieving endlessly?

He knew that wasn't quite fair, that the couples were likely told by the operators of the ring that the children were discards, unwanted, that they were giving them a much better life than they would otherwise have had. And maybe in some cases it was true.

But not in Maria's.

"Have you gotten anything out of them?"

"Not yet. But we think one of the men is about to break. I'll let you know."

"Immediately," Ryder said, not caring if Gibson took offense at being ordered by his ex-con recruit. But Gibson sounded more amused than offended.

"Those Del Rio calls have to be the right ones," Ryder said. "Can you track them back, isolate the phones they came from, and track those?"

"Maybe, if I can commandeer the resources. Sit tight, I'll be in touch. This number?"

"Yes," Ryder said, not explaining that he meant only to the last part; he had no intention of sitting tight and waiting. Not when Ana had put her trust in him.

Not when he had promised a tiny little girl that he would bring her back to her mother.

Chapter 13

Ana set her jaw.

"No."

She said it firmly. She had somehow found the backbone to face down her father, and her fiancé. She had had the courage to sneak out when they'd tried to confine her. She'd had the nerve to make her way on the perilous path out of her country to a different, strange, wonderful yet frightening place where she was determined to make a new life for herself and her baby.

She certainly was not going to back down now just because this man had told her to stay here and let him handle this. She was through blindly trusting the men in her life to do the right thing.

She had put her trust in this man, that was true.

But not blindly.

"Ana, you can't. You need to stay here, wait for me to—"

"I will not."

"It's only been two weeks since Maria was born. You can't go chasing off—"

"I am fine. And that is for me to decide."

"These are dangerous men."

She glanced at the bloody washcloth she had used to clean his face, his ribs, then met his gaze.

"Do you truly think I do not know this?"

"That's not what I meant."

"They have my baby," Ana said simply, as if there was nothing else to be said.

And for her, that was true.

Ryder studied her for a long, silent moment. She returned his gaze levelly, masking her instinctive sympathetic response to his battered face. And hiding the unwanted appreciation she was feeling for the beautiful way this man was put together. Hard and lean, not soft like Alberto. Just looking at his bare chest made her feel odd longings, made her wonder what it would feel like pressed against her.

She wished he would put his shirt back on.

She was not unaware that, if he was telling her the truth, he had already sacrificed a great deal for Maria. But her past experience had taught her the value of that simple word *if*.

"I appreciate what you have done," she began, then stopped when a sardonic expression flitted across his face.

"If I'd done what I should have," he said as he did as she'd silently wished and pulled his bloodied shirt back on, "I'd have been bringing Maria home to you, not just dragging my own sorry ass here."

The bitterness in his voice startled her, and despite her doubts, she found she believed that it was genuine. He truly blamed himself for not rescuing her baby right then, outnumbered or not.

She still had reservations, and deep inside she feared she might regret going against her better judgment, but her judgment had told her for too long to ignore the obvious about her father, and then about Alberto.

"You say you can find her."

"I've never been so close to cracking the ring. Never known when they had…a baby in the pipeline, only found out afterward. This is the time, when the pathway they've built is in use."

Ana listened. It made sense. But when it came down to it, much as she might hate the idea of what these men were doing, only one thing mattered to her.

"I do not care about them. I cannot afford to care about them. I care only about Maria."

"Then stay here, and stay safe for her."

"I have decided to trust you, Ryder," she said, using his name for the first time since he'd given it to her. "But I am not a fool. I believe a great man in this country once said 'Trust, but verify.' I intend to follow that advice."

"Ana—"

She held up a hand to stop his protest. "I made a promise to my little girl. I promised her that I would build a new life, a better life for her, that I would never give up on that dream. And I will not."

Ryder was looking at her with a touch of amazement, which puzzled her. She did not find what she was saying so strange, or different. It was what any true, loving parent would do, was it not?

"And besides," she said, "you are injured. You may need help."

He lifted a dark brow, then winced at the movement. Ana managed not to react to this obvious sign proving of her point, but his wry grimace told her he had gotten it.

"And I may be of use in other ways," she added. "Women can sometimes go unnoticed where a man cannot."

He blinked, looking startled this time. "I suppose."

She pressed her case. "I am coming with you," she said firmly. "The only question is how much energy you will waste in trying to stop me."

She saw the moment when he gave up. Without a word she turned and began to gather some few items that she tucked into the pink bag that had served her as a diaper bag but carried all the other baby accoutrements as well, plus her own small store of things she would ordinarily put in a handbag.

"What are you doing? You want to lug all that?"

She looked over her shoulder. "This is the trusting part. You say you will find Maria, so I will need her things."

Were it not for her deep, gnawing fear for her little girl, the look on his face, even through the swelling on his jaw and around his eye would have made her smile.

Ryder felt a little like he'd been caught up in a tornado. Or maybe a flash flood. There was no stopping either, and there was obviously no stopping Ana Morales.

He thought about slipping out now, starting out on his own, while she was changing clothes in the bathroom. But he had the distinct feeling that if he did, she would merely follow him anyway. And he would rather have her where he could keep an eye on her than out poking into dangerous territory by herself.

Which, he thought ruefully, is exactly what she'd do.

He shook his aching head, but cautiously. He sat there, trying not to imagine what she looked like, shedding one set of clothes for another. How had this woman, in such a short time, become the focus of his world? He'd already admitted the obvious, that she was a strikingly beautiful—

and clearly intelligent—woman. And that he admired her determination wasn't so hard to acknowledge. That he was slightly in awe of this kind of fierce, maternal love, was a bit harder, but he couldn't deny it.

He was having trouble with the realization that the combination made him incredibly, ridiculously hot. Beautiful, sure. That was always a plus, although it hadn't always been a requirement. But the rest? Hadn't he always shied away from smart, determined women? The kind who wouldn't settle for the little he was able—or willing—to give?

Or was it just that you knew they wouldn't have anything to do with you? That any woman with smarts would see right through you?

That little voice in his head was starting to annoy him. He'd never been troubled by it before, and didn't think it was a coincidence that it had started nagging him shortly after he'd been stupid enough to let Boots get to him. The old man had a lot to answer for, and Ryder was going to let him know it when this was all over. With no small amount of pleasure.

Ana came back, dressed in a pair of black jeans and a sleeveless black turtleneck. The clothes made her look impossibly slender for a woman who had just given birth two weeks ago. Yet the full swell of her breasts and the womanly curve of her hips reminded him, as if he'd needed any reminder.

In one hand she carried a lightweight jacket. In the other, puzzlingly, she had a glass of water.

She held the glass out to him. He took it, looking at her curiously. Then she held out a small bottle that had been hidden by the glass.

Aspirin, he realized.

"Bless you," he said, meaning it, and powered down four in a hurry.

"Take them with us," she said. "There are children's aspirin for the little ones."

He'd already planned on it, and stuffed the bottle into a pocket. He was going to welcome the relief they gave him before this was over.

"I'll need to keep your phone."

She nodded without comment.

"They took my truck," he said. "We're going to need a vehicle."

"There is a truck here. Besides the van Jewel drives. She said I could use it any time."

It seemed she had a answer for everything. "They took my gun, too. I don't suppose there's a weapon in this place?"

"With all the children?"

"It's Texas," he countered.

"Jewel would never take the chance." Then, after a moment, she added, "I am sure there would be weapons over at the Colton ranch."

She didn't, he knew, realize the jolt she'd just given him. But she was sharp, and quick, and he didn't want her to guess, so he muttered, "I don't think so," and turned away.

I can just see myself, knocking on Clay's door. "Hey, bro, yeah, I'm out, and just when you thought you were rid of me for good, here I am. And by the way, I need to borrow your scattergun…"

No, the Bar None was not an option. Not that he wouldn't be above sneaking in and grabbing what he needed from the gun rack, but Clay had never been a sound sleeper—all that worrying and responsibility—and Ryder didn't want to risk it.

Wouldn't risk it.

The last thing he wanted right now was to have to explain himself and what he was up to to his brother. Clay would likely never believe him anyway. Clay had washed his hands of his irresponsible, troublesome little brother when he'd gotten into the scrape that had landed him here, and Ryder didn't blame him.

At the sound of a drawer sliding shut Ryder snapped out of his reverie, annoyed that anything had the power to take his mind off the crisis at hand. More to lay at Boots's door, he thought. The old man had harped on him endlessly about mending the breach between him and Clay. That had to be what had him thinking about even an unpleasant confrontation, when before he would have laughed off the idea before the image even formed.

Apparently he hadn't quite succeeded in cutting himself off completely, at least not in his mind.

You can't ever pry your family out of your heart, boy. No matter how hard you try.

He'd laughed at Boots then. "Maybe not, but you can freeze them out," he'd said, knowing it was true, because he'd done it.

Assuming he had a heart to begin with, of course.

"I have this, if you wish it."

He turned, and his eyes widened as he saw what Ana Morales held out to him.

It was a knife.

But not just some small, useless, ladylike pocketknife.

This was a blade. In a tooled leather sheath, it looked to be at least six inches long, with the hilt adding another four. And what a hilt it was; some dark, exotic-looking wood carved into curves to perfectly fit the hand that gripped it, and inlaid with something white and gleaming that had the sheen of pearls. The butt end of the hilt was set with what looked for all the world like a real ruby; it winked blood red in the light.

Almost in awe, he reached out and took it. He slid the knife out of the sheath. The grip seemed a little small to him, but the polished blade of clearly fine steel glinted. A quick touch with his thumb told him it was honed to the kind of fine edge that had given rise to the expression "splitting hairs."

The knife was meant for damage, the tip a fine point for stabbing, and the deadly curve that came after for slicing with ease.

And it had to be worth a lot, he thought, knowing instinctively that this was something a collector would prize. It was an elegant, almost dashing kind of weapon, and the old-fashioned word didn't seem silly as he held the perfectly balanced knife.

"Where in the hell did you get this?"

"It was my great-great-great-grandmother's."

He blinked. That explained the size of the grip, then. "Your great-great-great-grandmother?"

"That is correct? The mother of my mother's mother's mother's mother?"

He wasn't even going to try to work that one out. "Close enough," he said. "It's beautiful."

Ana smiled, the first he'd seen from her tonight. The first he'd seen from her since the moment he'd handed her her baby.

"My great-great-great-grandfather did not think it so beautiful. She tried to kill him with it, the first time they met. She tells of it in her journal, which was handed down to me."

He stared at her. A smile of his own started to curve his mouth; she'd come by that courage and nerve honestly, it seemed. Whatever he'd thought about her when he'd first seen her, the idea that she was simply another illegal in a long line had vanished now. There was much more to this woman than he knew. This little bit of her history proved that.

He wanted to hear that story about her great-whatever grandmother, but he knew there wasn't time.

He wanted to hear all her stories.

The realization jolted him even more than the sound of the name Colton coming from her had. He wanted to know everything about her, what had made her the incredible woman she was. He wanted it all, and he had never wanted to know such things about a woman. He never wanted to know anything beyond what he needed to figure out how to get her into bed.

He told himself that he was thinking this way because he knew that was not an option, given the short time since Maria's birth. It was a comforting theory, but he wasn't sure he believed it. Because he still wanted to know everything about her.

But the first thing he was going to need to know, he thought, was the most important.

Was she running to this country simply for a better life, or was she escaping something unbearable in her old life? And what—or who—was it?

Then the thing that was truly the most important belatedly hit him. Whoever or whatever it was…was it coming after her?

Chapter 14

It was right, Ana thought, that her ancestor's gleaming weapon be used in this hunt. She knew in her heart that Elena Maria de la Costa would approve; she would count no cost too high for family. That it was a great-times-three granddaughter would make no difference; blood was blood, and you took care of your own.

Unless and until they betrayed you.

She had wondered if the ancestor she most admired, would have been ashamed of her for what she'd done, for leaving her father and the father of her child.

More likely, for being fool enough to be taken in by them in the first place.

But then she had gone back to that treasured diary, read again the tales of an older time, and of the spirited life Elena had led, and what she had thought of what went on around her. Elena's true character, bold and smart and fearless, had shone through the pages, and as she had since the first time she had read those pages as a girl, Ana felt as if she'd known this long-ago woman who was forever linked to her.

And she realized that Elena Maria de la Costa would have understood.

And probably would have sliced Alberto before she left, Ana had thought then.

Like Ryder was about to slice the man whose throat he had under Elena's blade now. The man who had been so obviously stunned to see Ryder when he had pulled him out of the car parked behind the roadhouse tavern.

"You're dead!" he'd exclaimed then.

"Exaggerated claim," Ryder had said smoothly as he'd searched the man for weapons, jamming the lethal-looking handgun he found in the man's waistband under his shirt into his own belt.

Ana's reaction hadn't been so calm. The man's words told her Ryder's story had been the truth; he had tried to save Maria and they had killed him for it.

Or rather, thought they had.

The tentative trust she had put in him got a bit more solid in that moment. And she felt an odd ache inside, over and above her worry for Maria, an ache at the idea that this man had risked his very life for her little girl. She wished to reach out and touch him, to thank him, but now was not the time.

Nor was it time to follow the other, unexpected and unlikely urge she felt; kissing this man would be intriguing, she was sure, but hardly appropriate just now.

Instead, she studied this thing—she hesitated to call him a man—who had helped steal her little girl. She found her fingers curling, wishing it was she who held her ancestor's blade to his scrawny throat.

"You can talk to me now," Ryder was saying, "or I can see that you never talk again."

"I tell you, I don't know!"

"Then you're no use to me, are you?" He shifted, as if in preparation for that fatal slice of the blade. The man screeched.

"If I knew, I'd tell you!"

Ryder seemed to consider this. He glanced her way. She saw the question in his eyes, as if he were asking her if she was satisfied this was the truth. But there was something more there, an uneasiness it took her a moment to understand.

He expected her to be horrified by what he was doing.

She nearly laughed; if only he knew the anger she harbored, the craving to punish this man and all his partners in these heinous acts.

The craving to slaughter, painfully, the man who dared lay his hands on her little girl.

"I mean what I said," she told Ryder softly. "I will stop at nothing. *Nothing.*"

The man under the blade was watching this exchange, bewilderment on his face.

"Who is this bitch? Who the hell are *you?*"

"Me? I'm the guy you killed back there in that gully, remember?"

The man looked at him warily. He scoffed, but there was a touch of uncertainty in his voice. Did he truly believe he was looking at a ghost? Ana wondered. Then she realized he was drunk enough that his thought processes were tangled. If they were ever clear, she thought, reminding herself again of what this man had done, what he did to make his money.

And she, who had been a gentle loving child, thought

she would relish nothing more than to see this man's throat laid open like a filleted trout.

"You some kind of cop after all?"

"You'll never know," Ryder whispered, and shifted the gleaming blade.

The man screamed, broke.

"I swear," he babbled, choking out the words as if fear were throttling him, "I don't know anything. I got my orders from Duane, I just did what he told me. I just rode shotgun on the first leg, mostly, I never handled any of the brats. I hate 'em."

"Who took the next leg?"

Ryder shifted the blade again, and Ana saw blood begin to trickle down the man's unshaven neck. Funny how the stubble of beard looked simply unkempt on this man, but had looked oddly attractive on Ryder that night. Even then she'd wanted to touch, to feel the stubble rasp against her fingers. Another urge that was unexpected and startling.

Right now, of course, his face was still swollen and reddened from the beating he'd taken. The beating he'd taken for her little girl.

Yet he was still a very attractive man. Even now.

Perhaps even more attractive now, she thought. Now, when he was so fiercely intent on the mission, on finding Maria.

The trust she had put in him suddenly shifted form, as unwanted emotion slipped into the mix, making her nervously aware that she was letting things get confused in her mind and heart.

That way lay disaster, and she tried to quash the feeling. She would focus on nothing but the search, think of this man as nothing more than the best tool she had at hand to use to find her daughter.

"Marco," the man finally gasped out, believing at last

that Ryder would do what he threatened. "He lives in the motel, east end of Esperanza."

Ryder didn't back off a millimeter. "Room?"

"Nine."

Ryder moved quickly then, using the man's own belt to fasten his hands tightly behind him. He instructed Ana to find the trunk release on the car. She leaned into the vehicle, her nose crinkling at the smell of stale food she couldn't see, and the faint odor of urine. She found the latch labeled with a drawing of an open trunk, and pulled it.

Ryder searched the trunk first, thoroughly, and after pulling out the spare tire to look beneath, handed her a box of ammunition, which she assumed was for the gun the man carried.

"I don't want him warning anyone. Any problem with leaving him here?" he asked as he dumped the protesting man into his own trunk.

"Only that he is still alive," Ana said bluntly.

Ryder chuckled. "He may not be, if no one finds him by tomorrow morning. It's August in Texas, and it probably gets hot enough you could roast a chicken in there."

"That would be justice," she said.

The man looked at her as if he realized she was the biggest threat. "Who are you?" he wailed, looking at Ana.

"Haven't you guessed?" Ryder said, stuffing a greasy rag he'd found into the man's mouth, thankfully stifling any further wails. "She's an avenging angel, straight from God, and it's judgment day."

He slammed the trunk lid down, cutting off the muffled scream.

"Will you truly leave him there?" Ana asked after they had moved the car. They'd put it in a secluded spot in the strip mall's parking lot, where any sound the man made would likely not be heard, until the world started to wake up again. Ryder had searched until he'd found the man's cell phone, and a check of the number told him this was not one of the Del Rio ones.

"Does it matter?" Ryder asked.

She didn't waste time pondering. "Not really."

"I didn't think so," he said, although he suspected should the man really die, she would feel a qualm of remorse. Ana Morales was a very complex woman, he was beginning to realize.

And a very good one, in an old-fashioned sense of the word he'd never applied to a woman before because it had never mattered. A good woman had never been something he'd hankered for; give him a party girl, out for fun, with no strings, every time.

He'd go back to that, he assured himself. As soon as this was over, and Maria was back with her mother and these scumbags were where they belonged. He'd finish his job, break the ring, and go on about his life with a clean record. No need to get too drastic about changing. He'd just be smarter this time.

"I'll call my contacts, eventually," he said. "Tell them where he is."

He didn't explain that he couldn't call them now, because they likely would try to rein him in, tell him to wait until they had agents in place. They might even pull him off altogether, now that things seemed to be on the verge of breaking loose.

And there was no way he was letting anyone pull him off this now. Not until he had personally put that baby back in Ana's arms.

An image of what that would be like shot through his

mind, of seeing that tiny bundle safely back with her mother, of the joyous expression that would spread across Ana's face. It made him smile, even though it hurt his split lip.

"You are smiling," she said into the darkness of the truck cab.

"I was thinking of your smile, when you have your baby back."

He didn't know why he'd admitted that. Something about this woman seemed to make him run at the mouth.

When she spoke, her words were soft. "You are a good man, Ryder."

That pronouncement, coming from a woman like Ana Morales, nearly made him laugh. But he couldn't bring himself to correct her. He didn't want her knowing just how wrong she was. He'd never really cared before, had known his bad-boy reputation attracted exactly the kind of woman he preferred, but this was different.

Everything with this woman was different.

When she reached out and gently put a hand on his arm as he drove, he just about jumped out of his skin.

"Thank you," she said quietly.

"I haven't found her yet."

"But you will. I believe that."

As he slowed for a turn he glanced at her. She was watching him with a steady look that stabbed through to his soul as surely as if she'd used her blade on him.

This was a woman who'd have your back. Forever.

He nearly jumped again as he realized he'd actually thought the word *forever* in relation to a woman. But as he stared at her, feeling somehow bigger, stronger under the unwavering gaze of her dark eyes, he realized she was a woman who deserved nothing less.

Marco was sound asleep when Ryder rousted him out

after silently and easily breaking into the seedy motel room. It seemed clear that he was not living high on the proceeds of the smuggling ring, but then, that was typical. Alcazar drove a limo, the peons lived in dives like this.

Marco was even more astonished to see Ryder alive. And thankfully for Ryder's rapidly diminishing patience— he was hurting, damn it, and thanks to these bastards he had to grit his teeth and keep going—he broke much more easily.

"Denny," the man sputtered. "That's who you need."

"Please," Ryder said scornfully. "The guy you relegated to driving because you think he's too stupid for anything else?"

Even as he said it, Ryder remembered that it was Denny who had figured out he had some connection to Maria. Perhaps he'd underestimated the man. But he didn't think he'd misjudged his colleague's opinion of him.

"That's just it," Marco said, eyeing the knife Ana was now holding even more warily than the commandeered handgun Ryder held. There was something about a woman with a knife that made some men very nervous. He'd been there himself a time or two, where if the woman of the moment could have laid her hands on a blade he probably would have been minus some body parts he was exceptionally fond of.

"What's just it?" Ryder prompted.

"He's the one who drove. He always drove."

It hit him then, belatedly. Of course. If Denny drove, then he knew where they'd gone.

"Where is he?"

"At this hour? At home, I guess." When Ana shifted the knife in her grip and took a step toward him, the man scrabbled back in the bed like a frightened crab. "He lives behind the church, over on Boone Street."

The irony of that bit deep as Ryder grabbed a belt from the back of a chair. With it, he found some nylon shoelaces freed from a pair of worn shoes on the floor by the bed and tied the man up. He crossed the room to a small closet, searched it, then shoved the man inside and closed the door.

He searched the small apartment until he found another handgun and a cell phone—again not one of the ones with the Del Rio prefix—and took both. There was a landline phone on a table, and when he indicated it, Ana quickly severed the cord with her knife.

With a certain amount of relish, Ryder thought.

He smiled inwardly at the memory of Marco's expression when he'd seen this gloriously angry woman contemplating him with that lethal blade in her hand.

"I wonder," he mused aloud as they headed toward Boone Street, "if he thinks living behind a church means some salvation will seep into him."

"If so, he is a fool."

"The rest of them would agree with you that he's stupid," Ryder said. "But I'm not so sure. He's the one who figured out I…knew Maria."

He felt more than saw her gaze sharpen, something about the way she turned slightly toward him in the passenger seat of the truck, and then went very still and quiet.

"I am sorry I doubted you."

He wasn't sure what had brought on the change of heart. Perhaps she'd sensed that he'd been more than willing to follow through on his threat, if it would help them find Maria. The realization had startled him; for all his sins he'd never been one to treat human life lightly. Nevertheless, he knew it was true.

What he didn't know was why. And it was too big of a

tangle, sitting somewhere south of his heart near his gut, for him to try and sort out now.

As they pulled up to a stoplight—he didn't want to risk attracting any attention, even though the streets of little Esperanza were deserted at this hour—he flicked her a sideways glance. "You just keep right on doubting me, and everyone. Until you have your baby back."

After a moment she gave a short, sharp nod.

When they got to the small apartment above the garage behind the picturesque white clapboard building with the traditional steeple, there was a light on inside. At least, he thought there was; it seemed faint, and flickered oddly. A fire? Surely not, not in August. And not in this little place, that he doubted very much had any kind of a fireplace.

Unless it was…a fire.

Ryder tensed. This guy was their best lead, and Ryder wasn't about to let him toast himself before he talked.

He gauged the strength of the door; the building was old, and the paint on the door and the jamb was weathered, peeling. There was no lock other than the one in the doorknob, no dead bolt visible, something Ryder found odd for a man in his kind of business.

His final assessment was that he could probably take it down with one good hit. He didn't want to think what the effort would do to his already bruised body, but there was no other option. There were no balconies near the two windows, no other possible access points that he could see. He pulled the weapon he'd liberated from Marco free of his belt, then motioned Ana to stand back so he could back up on the landing for a running start.

"It is locked?" she whispered.

The man was apparently the main driver on the network

that smuggled stolen babies, Ryder thought, and whispered back, "Of course it's..."

His voice trailed away as he thought of all the times in his life when he'd overlooked the obvious. Tentatively he reached out and tested the knob.

It turned. Easily.

He gave her a sheepish look, but she didn't seem inclined to be critical. She merely nodded and waited.

But she had her three-times-great-grandmother's knife in her hand.

If I were the man who had her baby, I'd be a hell of a lot more worried about her than me, Ryder thought.

He backed to one side of the door, motioned her behind him, and when she'd moved, he reached out and turned the knob.

The door creaked open like the sound effects from some old spooky movie. Great burglar alarm. Maybe that was why he didn't bother with new locks. Nobody'd sneak through that door.

Nothing happened.

"Candles," Ana whispered, so close no one more than six inches away could have heard her. Her breath brushed warmly over his ear.

Ryder suppressed a shiver, and suddenly, inanely, realized the truth of the old joke, "Blow in my ear and I'll follow you anywhere."

But then he caught the scent that had made her say it, a sweet, warm aroma that reminded him of a woman in Amarillo, who had always wanted candles burning when they had sex. Which in turn reminded him that he hadn't thought that way of another woman since he'd met Ana, a realization that only furthered that tangle in his gut.

Get on with it, he told himself.

He inched forward, weapon at the ready, safety off, a round chambered. He didn't want to kill the guy before he talked, but he didn't want to die, either.

He made a quick, sharp move with his head, just enough to get a glimpse into the room. Ana had been right. Candles, a small row of them, were burning on a low table near the center of the room. They were also the only light in the room, which made it difficult to see into the shadowy corners. He'd have to—

He froze as he heard a sound from inside. Footsteps. His grip on the Mac 10 tightened.

Then there was a rustling, a slight thump, as if of something hitting the floor.

The voice that came out of the darkness startled him. But the words shocked him even more.

"I've been waiting for you. Come in."

Chapter 15

Denny was the only one who hadn't been surprised to see him alive.

In fact, he wasn't surprised to see him at all.

"You knew I wasn't dead," Ryder said.

"I knew."

"How?"

"Call it…instinct. Marco and the others, they have seen one or two dead men. I've seen enough to smell death."

"But you didn't tell them."

The man shrugged. "They don't care much for my opinion. And they figured if you weren't you would be soon enough, banged up as you were. Coyotes, cougars, something would have finished you off." He flashed an interested look at Ryder's battered face. "Obviously they underestimated you."

Ryder shifted his grip on the pistol. Denny was sitting— or rather kneeling—on the floor in front of the table that held the bank of candles. The thump he'd heard, he guessed. There was no weapon in evidence, but he doubted the man would have it in plain sight. He'd told Ana to wait outside until he assessed the odd situation, and so far, she was doing as he asked. But he also doubted she would stay there for long.

Just as he was doubting that this man was as stupid as his co-conspirators thought he was.

"So," he said casually, "how's the dumb-as-a-brick act working for you?"

For an instant, something flickered in the man's eyes. Or maybe it was the candlelight, making him look as if he were smiling.

"Are you after the baby, or the network?" The man asked it as if he were a salesclerk asking a customer which product he preferred.

"Yes," Ryder said, then added, "in that order."

The smile was real this time, then the man gave the barest of nods. "I suspected as much. Is it yours?"

"No," Ryder said. And then, he added the most important qualifier. "And yes."

Denny tilted his head sideways, in the same way he had when he'd been pondering Ryder's reaction to seeing Maria. As he thought of her name, Ryder realized with a little shock he hadn't even known it then.

Ryder wasn't even sure why he was talking to this man, as if there were some kind of rational discussion to be had, as if this were a civilized conversation instead of a dangerous meeting about a despicable act.

"I presume you already found Marco and Carl?"

"Yes."

Denny nodded again. "I'm guessing Marco directed you here?"

Again with the politeness, Ryder thought, on the edge of losing patience with this whole charade.

"If you want to call it *directed,*" he snapped out.

"Are they dead?"

"Not yet," Ryder said, deciding it might be wise to take out a little insurance. Not that he expected any of these scumbags to particularly care if another died, beyond some blow to their pride. "But if I don't make some calls by morning, it's a definite possibility."

Again Denny seemed to ponder this, and apparently decided he believed him. At least, once more he nodded.

At this point, Ryder had no idea how this was going to go. Wasn't even sure how to approach this lowlife with the odd demeanor.

And then it was taken out of his hands, as Ana walked through the door, bared blade glinting in her hand. Denny's head came up and, as he looked at Ana, his eyes widened speculatively. And then filled with understanding, as if it had all been explained to him.

"This is taking too much time," she said, eyeing the man, first with suspicion, then with comprehension. "If you think God will forgive you for a few prayers, you are misguided."

Denny nodded yet again. "How well I know. That —" Ryder tensed as he raised a hand, but Denny only gestured in the general direction of the door "—was my grandfather's church, once."

"Then he would be ashamed of you."

Ryder thought of Boots, wondered what he would make of this, if he would believe in this apparent paroxysm of guilt and repentance.

"I have no doubt he is," Denny said. Then, briskly, "The man you are looking for is Dr. Gary Breither."

"Bingo," Ryder whispered.

He'd long suspected the man, from the moment he'd heard that the notoriously incompetent physician was suddenly doing noticeably better financially. And had been making regular trips south of the border, declaring self-aggrandizingly that he was doing extensive charity work.

Ryder had thought this the perfect cover, and had wondered if the services he'd offered had been to poor, pregnant women, whose babies he had then offered up to the smugglers. But he'd hidden his tracks well—he might be inept as a doctor, but as a financial sneak he was stellar—and even the feds hadn't yet been able to trace his money trail.

Ana, however, was still suspicious. "Why should we believe you, when you give up so easily?"

Denny shrugged. "As you wish."

"Why *did* you give it up so easily?" Ryder asked, for the first time looking at Denny as a man rather than just one of the maggots feeding on the desperation of others.

"I suspect," Denny said, shifting his oddly steady gaze to Ryder, "for much the same reason you nearly threw your life away. Because the package was no longer just a package."

It flashed through Ryder's mind again, that moment when he'd unzipped the bag and realized the baby inside was the same one he'd brought into the world a few days before. Remembered the puzzled, almost bewildered expression that had crossed Denny's face as he worked to figure it out.

And again he thought of Boots. Of everything he'd spoken of, everything he'd tried to teach him. Going with his gut, Ryder slipped the safety back on the purloined Mac 10 and stuffed it back in his belt.

"You believe him?" Ana said, sounding a little startled.

"I do. Let's go."

"We are just going to leave him here? Free to call and warn this doctor?"

"I don't think he will."

"I will not," Denny confirmed.

Ana's hand tightened around the hilt of her knife. She was clearly not willing to trust Ryder's judgment on this.

"But," Denny said, eyeing her with something Ryder would have sworn was appreciation, "you may take my cell phone. It's on the table by the door."

Ryder nodded. Ana gaped at them both. "I do not understand. Why do you trust this man? He was one of the ones who beat you, is he not?"

"I'm not sure he ever really landed a blow. But he's got bigger problems right now. Because he knows—" he gestured at the candles "—that you're right. God won't forgive him, for a few prayers."

"So we are just going to leave him here?"

Again Ryder thought of Boots. "He'll punish himself more than we ever could. Or his God will."

Denny lowered his eyes, focusing on the candles. And Ryder wondered if he would choose to end his torture with a bullet to his head, or spend his life trying to atone, as Boots had.

Either way, Dr. Breither had lost his driver.

Ana wondered briefly if she were a fool for trusting this man, and his judgment about the man they'd just left. She watched him as he drove, studied his profile, the faint shadows of the marks on his skin where the men who had Maria had beaten him. She remembered the marks on his body as well, across that lovely chest and along the ribs above his narrow, flat waist…

The sudden heat embarrassed her. Even though she knew he couldn't see her in the faint light of the truck cab, she lowered her gaze and focused on what truly mattered, what it must be costing him to simply keep going through the pain.

For Maria, she reminded herself. And tried to quash the tiny ache inside, the burgeoning emotions that made her wish it was a little bit for her, too.

They were a couple of blocks from the church when her cell phone rang. Thankful she had changed the ring or she'd be sorting through the pile of phones they had accumulated, she grabbed it.

"It says restricted number," she told Ryder as she handed it to him as he drove, although she knew no one would be calling her at this hour except perhaps Jewel.

She felt a pang. On Ryder's instructions she had left a note saying only that she was well and with a friend, and would be in touch when she could. They had no way of knowing if one of the children had been manipulated into betraying Maria's existence to the smuggling ring.

But Ana knew that despite the note, the woman who had done so much for her would be beyond worried when she found both Ana and Maria gone unexpectedly. Ana had no real friends in the area, she could only hope Jewel would wait before telling anyone.

Ryder answered, listened, said nothing for what seemed like an endless stretch, then said, "Got it," and snapped the phone closed.

"Ryder?" she said when he didn't speak. Surely he wasn't going to refuse to tell her what his contact had said.

"They got the same name," he said after a minute. "Out of one of the couples who paid for a baby they never got."

It hit Ana then, that somewhere perhaps there was a desperate couple who had paid for Maria.

"Despreciable," she muttered.

"Yes, it would be despicable, if they knew," Ryder said. "But these guys are smooth, Ana. They have…well, salesmen on the other end, guys who convince people these are unwanted children, given up voluntarily. Or children who would be abused or abandoned—or worse—if left where they are."

"You are saying these people think they are saving these babies?"

"I can't say they all do, I'm sure some of them suspect it's not all legit, but yes, I think some do."

Ana pondered that for a moment. "I suppose," she said reluctantly, "I can understand someone wanting a baby so much."

Ryder made a sound, a male sort of grunt Ana had learned early in life served as an answer when a man had no answer for you.

"You do not believe in such a great need for a child?"

"I have to believe in it. This smuggling ring wouldn't exist if that need didn't."

"But you…you do not have this need yourself."

He shifted as if uncomfortable. But when he finally answered, she knew she was getting the truth. "No," he said. "I've never had it."

She turned this over and over in her mind, looking for a way to resolve the seeming contradiction. Finally, even knowing he would likely just grunt again, she spoke.

"Yet you risked your life for Maria. You could have died for her."

He did not even grunt. He said nothing. And she realized that she should have put it in the form of a question; another thing she had learned, belatedly, was that men tended to be quite literal, especially when dealing with aspects of emotion.

"Why?" she said, correcting her lapse.

She thought he still might not answer, but at last he said, somewhat lamely, "She's already here."

It made a strange sort of sense, Ana supposed. But she couldn't resist probing further.

"But if you feel nothing for children, why did you—"

"I didn't say I felt nothing. Just that I didn't feel the need to have them myself."

His mouth quirked, and she had the feeling he'd gone out of his way to make certain it had never happened. Odd, she thought. If she had fallen in love with someone like Ryder instead of Alberto, she would not be in this situation.

A burst of that unexpected warmth flooded her again as she sat in the dark cab of the truck, looking at the man behind the wheel. Despite his casual attitude and his protestations of a lack of interest in children, she had never forgotten the look on his face when he had held her baby in his hands.

And he had tried to save Maria, even knowing he had no chance against four armed men.

What would it be like to be in love with such a man? To have him love you in turn? Not an arrogant, unprincipled user like Alberto, but a man who, even if he was not happy about it, would help and not hurt?

He glanced at her then. "What is it with women and babies, anyway?" he asked, sounding almost exasperated.

"The continuation of the human race?" Ana said dryly, a bit stung by his tone.

He drew back slightly. And after a moment, she saw one corner of his mouth quirk. "Well, if you put it like that…"

Something about his reaction then made her say, almost shyly, "Thank you for trying to help Maria then, and for helping me now. It is good to know a man who will do the right thing."

For a moment he was very quiet. Then, softly, he said into the darkness, "Don't put your faith in me, Ana. I'll only let you down. It's what I'm best at."

"I don't believe that."

He laughed, a short, sharp, harsh sound. "Want a list of 'Ryder's-worse-than-useless' references? I can give you one. A very long one, with my brother, and probably my little sister, at the top. I'm the proverbial black sheep, in their book."

Ana could think of nothing to say to that. It seemed that, in his way, Ryder was as isolated from his family as she was from hers. He seemed to be saying he was the problem, not them. Yet she had no doubt that he was a good man, not anymore. She had had her doubts, even after the night of Maria's birth, but they had vanished by now.

"We're going to have to move fast," he said then, clearly changing the subject. "They're going to be right on my tail."

"We should have tied that man up as well," Ana said.

Ryder's mouth quirked again. "I didn't mean those guys."

It took her a moment to realize he meant the people he'd talked to on the phone.

"But…is that not a good thing?"

"Not for Maria."

Ana's breath caught. "What do you mean?"

"Their goal is to break this ring. To them, Maria's just another baby. If they get the job done in time to save her, fine, but that's not their focus."

She did not miss the subtext of that statement, that Maria was more than that to him. But this was not the time to dwell on that. She made herself concentrate on what he was saying.

"You mean that we must get the truth from this man, this doctor, quickly."

Ryder nodded. "I've suspected him for a while now, but

all I had was circumstantial. I could never find any solid evidence to tie him to the ring. And the feds, they're big on solid evidence. It doesn't do them any good to know who's guilty if they can't prove it."

"I do not care if they can prove it. All I want is my baby."

"I know."

"You think he is the leader of this baby-smuggling ring?"

"He's the most likely suspect I've come across."

"Then he will know where Maria has been taken. Who—" she stumbled over the horrible words "—has paid for her."

To her surprise, he reached out and took her hand, squeezed it. "We'll get her back, Ana. I swear we *will* get her back."

His hand felt warm, strong, comforting. Reassuring. And despite his warning not to put her faith in him, she found herself doing just that.

She hoped she would not regret it.

She prayed her daughter would not.

Chapter 16

Ryder had never had a wingman. He'd never needed one. Or so he'd thought. Now he seemed to have acquired one, albeit a wing-woman. And a beautiful, determined, and annoyingly smart one to boot.

He knew law enforcement people often worked with partners—even Furnell—and he'd always assumed it was for a very simple reason—two guns were better than one. But now he was beginning to understand the benefit of simply having someone else to bounce plans and ideas off.

And that's all it was. Nothing more than the benefit of having someone else there who called up odd feelings inside him. He didn't want to admit that because of Ana, he wondered what it would be like to have someone around all the time.

There was that forever thing again. He shoved it aside, but it was getting harder. He needed to focus, to concen-

trate. And he told himself to remember that Ana's determination to save her baby could well cloud what would
normally be a razor-sharp thought process.

Again he wondered how she'd gotten herself into her
situation.

"Where is Maria's father?" he asked bluntly. "Why isn't
he helping you?"

For a moment she didn't answer, and he felt she might
be too embarrassed, or simply deciding if he had the right
to ask. When she did finally speak, it was an answer, but
not exactly the one he'd been after.

"I would not accept his help."

"Why? You must have loved him."

He realized as soon as he said it that, on some level, he'd
already known Ana Morales would never sleep with a man
she didn't love. For some reason he didn't have time—or
the desire—to stop and analyze why he was so edgy.

He thought he had heard emotion rising in her voice, and
when she took a breath and went on, it burst through. "I
hope he will soon be in prison, where he belongs."

Something knotted up hard deep in Ryder's gut. The
anger, the scorn in her voice was unmistakable.

Well, now, he thought, there's a way to smash her trust
in you. Just tell her you're doing this to get out of prison.

"Why?" he asked carefully. Then, as a horrible thought
occurred to him, he slowed the car to look over at her. "Ana,
he didn't rape you?"

She laughed, harshly. "He did not have to. He was my
fiancé."

Ryder wasn't sure whether to be relieved or not. He put
his eyes back on the road. "So you did love him."

"I loved who I thought he was. He was not that man."
He heard an odd little sound in the darkness, realized she

was taking in a deep breath, as if fighting back tears. He wished suddenly he'd never started this. "He is a criminal, brutal, wicked and immoral. And he is in league with a man who is even worse."

"Worse."

"My father," she said, and for the first time, despite all she'd been through, there was bitterness in her voice.

"I'm sorry," he said, feeling stupid for not having anything better to say.

"It killed my mother when she found out. I did not know this, until I learned the truth myself, but then it became clear." She let out a harsh, compressed breath. "Do you have any idea what it is like to despise your own father?"

The old pain jabbed him unexpectedly; he'd thought himself done with that long ago.

"Yes," he said flatly.

He heard her suck in a breath. She obviously hadn't expected his response.

"Not," he added, "that I ever knew him. I know who he is, know that my mother was one of many women all over the country. Know that he fathered a few of us he couldn't be bothered to acknowledge. Know that he's—"

He stopped suddenly, shocked at the realization that he'd been about to tell her who his father was. What was it about this woman that had his mind and mouth running in such crazy directions?

He hastened to rein it in, redirect, something. Anything. "But as far as I know he's just a sleazebag, not a criminal. Not that it would surprise me, of course, but since I never knew him, it doesn't bother me much. But your father…"

He let his voice trail off, hoping she would accept the rerouting of the conversation. Not just to get it off of something he didn't dare talk about—the famous Colton name—but because he genuinely wanted to know. Which put him even more on edge.

When she spoke at last, her voice was controlled, level and coolly dispassionate.

"My father is sophisticated, charming, polished and gracious. He is also arrogant, ruthless and utterly evil. He cares nothing for the law, or for justice, only for his own gains. He controls a network of underlings, who all do his bidding."

When she paused at last, he hazarded a guess. "One of them being your fiancé?"

"Alberto was more of an…associate," Ana said. A trace of emotion broke through once more as she gave a small, rueful laugh. "At least, that is how he was introduced to me. As a business partner. At the time, I still believed my father was an honorable businessman, who would only deal with other honorable men."

"Ana—"

"I was no more than a pawn to both of them. To my father, to secure what Alberto could offer him. To Alberto, to secure my father's benevolence."

"A bargaining chip," Ryder said.

Ana considered this, as if she'd never heard the phrase. Her English was so perfect—better than his, he admitted wryly—she had him thinking about the complexity of idioms, hardly a topic that ever would have occurred to him in his life before.

Before Ana, that is.

It startled him that he would even think that way, that even casually he would divide his life into a before and after marked by the simple event of meeting a woman.

"Yes," she said after a moment. "As in the days of royalty arranging marriages for their children to political advantage. And my father thought of himself as a kind of royalty."

"Sounds more like a mafia don," Ryder muttered.

"A...godfather, is it? Yes. That is very like what he is. Except that he has no rivals."

Something he realized he should have thought of before now hit Ryder. "How did you get away from him? From them?"

"I used my pregnancy. They are the kind of men who shy away from anything having to do with such things, anything truly female. When I went to see my physician, I went alone."

"They let you?"

He heard rather than saw her shrug. "They did not know yet that I knew the truth about their dealings. I had only just found out, and I hid it from them while I decided what I must do. Then when I found out I was pregnant, that decision was made for me. I could never bring my child into their world."

Strong was too weak a word for her.

"So you decided to leave not just your home, but your country?"

"My father's reach is long," she said. "So while Alberto was out bragging about his manhood, and my father was lighting candles to ensure a grandson, not an unwanted granddaughter, I pretended to be more ill than I was with morning sickness. They became used to my absence for hours at a time."

"You bought yourself a head start," Ryder said admiringly.

"When I had done all I could to prepare, I feigned a serious bout of illness on a night when my father was hosting a glittering party. I knew he wouldn't miss me for hours, probably not even think about me until morning. By then I was far away."

Ryder didn't want to think what a young, pregnant

woman must have gone through to get here. Despite her courage, she must have been frightened.

"Is Ana Morales your real name?"

"It is, in part. Morales was my mother's name. I will never again use my father's."

The irony of that bit deep; here they were, two father-less souls, both using the names of mothers who had loved unwisely, thrown together in the midst of chaos. He had reluctantly gone along with Clay's change to *Colton* when the true identity of their father had been revealed, but he often reverted to *Grady* and was more comfortable with it.

"And," Ana added with emphasis, "I am in the process of doing things legally, to become a citizen. Jewel's family is powerful. They will help."

Speaking of the Coltons, Ryder thought wryly. But he pushed that aside for the moment.

"Maria," he began.

"She will never know," Ana said determinedly. "I will never tell her, about her father or her grandfather."

Ryder was grateful he had to pay attention to his driving for a moment, not because there was any traffic at this hour, but because they were nearing the turn they needed. It gave him a moment to ponder what Ana had said, and to wonder if he should tell her about a similar lie in his life.

And to wonder why he felt compelled to tell her every damn thing that popped into his head.

Finally, when he'd negotiated the turn and knew they only had a few more minutes to go, he spoke, the words he rarely said coming in a rush.

"For most of my life, I believed my father was an oil field worker, who died in an oil rig fire before my little sister was born."

Ana, as usual, did not miss his meaning. "But this was not true?"

"No. He was someone else entirely. Someone... wealthy, from a well-known family."

"Your mother must have had reason."

Ryder shrugged. "She did. We finally figured out that she was trying to protect us, that she knew he would never acknowledge us as his. He is..." He stopped the difficult flow of words, thinking there wasn't time now to list all the things Graham Colton was. And certainly not enough to list all the things he wasn't. "It doesn't matter. Point is, when we—my brother, sister and I—found out it was all a lie, that she'd died never telling us the truth, it was...hard."

It had been much more than that, of course. It had been stunning. So stunning that while Clay and Georgie had agreed to meet with the man who had fathered them, the man who had—for some reason Ryder had never trusted—finally reached out to them, Ryder hadn't wanted anything to do with him. And he was sure the father he'd never met would be happier that way. What Colton would want to acknowledge a reprobate like Ryder anyway? Even a slimeball like Graham Colton would think twice.

"You think I should tell her that both her father and grandfather are evil, terrible men?"

"I'm just saying that it was hard enough on us not knowing, and our father is just...pathologically self-centered," he said, using a phrase Boots had once used. "If your father and her father are as bad as you say, it could be worse for Maria. Maybe even dangerous."

Ana went still. "Dangerous?"

"I just mean that if it was me, and I had some connection to people like that, I'd want to know. So I could watch my back."

She said nothing for the rest of the drive, but Ryder could almost feel her thinking. He himself stayed quiet. He figured he'd talked more than enough. In fact, he'd talked about more things to this woman in the short time they'd known each other than to just about any woman he could remember that he wasn't related to.

Something about her—

He cut off his own thoughts when he realized they were nearing their destination. When he'd first suspected Breither was involved in the ring, he'd cased his home and office. He'd also located and checked out his old home, a vastly different place than the new, expansive, ostentatious residence he lived in now. Sitting regally alone on at least an acre of landscaped grounds, it was the kind of declaration of wealth that had always made Ryder think it would be easier to put up a sign saying "Hey, look, I'm rich!"

Envy, he'd told himself.

Recognizing a lack of class when he saw it, was what Boots had called it.

By then, he hadn't even seen anything odd in a convicted felon, sitting in a federal prison cell, discussing the finer points of class.

He parked near the edge of the property in the shadows of a tall pecan tree, something more common up in the hill country. For a moment he just studied the lay of the land.

He wondered what Ana thought of the place. If her father was as successful at his criminal undertakings as she'd said, she had likely grown up lacking nothing. Had she lived in a home like this one, or perhaps one even larger, more luxurious?

"Nice house," he murmured, not really wanting to open that door.

"Bought with the tears of mothers and babies," she said sharply.

"Yes," Ryder said simply.

She frowned, and after a moment said, "We must get inside, but how?"

He withheld any comment on her assumption that "we" would be going anywhere, and answered the last part. "When I was here before, I saw that there's a guesthouse and a pool with a pool house in the back, that would provide cover almost all the way up to the main house. It's only the last five yards or so that are exposed."

"But surely such a place will have alarms, perhaps dogs or armed guards?"

Armed guards?

With the realization that he had just gotten a glimpse into that prior life of hers he'd wondered about, Ryder said only, "No sign of dogs. Or guards. Alarmed, yes. But I can deal with that."

He was going to be glad he'd paid attention to his training that day, even if the thought had crossed his mind that being able to break into anywhere might come in very handy after he finished this job.

"What about others? Family?" She hesitated a split second, as if the idea that such a man would have children of his own was too much for her to conceive of. "Children?"

"Divorced. He lives here alone."

"Smart woman," Ana said sourly.

"I'm learning there's a lot to be said for smart women."

His own words startled Ryder; damn, the craziest stuff kept popping out.

"My father would disagree with you."

"His loss," Ryder said before forcing himself to turn his full attention to the task at hand. "Can you shoot?"

"If I must. My father had me instructed, for my own safety, he told me." Her tight smile was bitter. "Another of the many pieces I did not put together until too late, naive fool that I was."

"Not too late," Ryder told her. "You got out."

The smile she gave him then would stay with him forever, he thought. He handed her one of the liberated weapons. While she didn't look comfortable with it, she clearly wasn't afraid of it. She took a moment to look at it, while he pointed out the safety and told her how many rounds she had.

In the end, it was easier than he'd expected. Even though Ana insisted on going with him. She'd shown herself nervy enough and willing to let him take the lead. He was the one with the training, she'd said simply, so he hadn't had to waste time fighting her. They needed to move quickly; it was nearly dawn, a glance at his watch told him they had barely an hour of full darkness left, and what they had to do needed that cover.

As he'd told Ana, there were no dogs, no guards, but from his earlier surveillance, he noticed an up-to-date alarm system. An up-to-date alarm system that was, amazingly, not turned on. A red light flashed rhythmically, warning that the premises were unprotected.

So was Dr. Breither lazy, arrogant, stupid…or fiendishly clever? Had he gone off to bed so confident no one would dare mess with him that he hadn't bothered to set the system? Or was he just too stupid to remember?

Ana looked at him, and he saw the same questions in her eyes.

Not that it made any difference. No matter the reason, the answers they needed were inside this house, and there was no other way to get them except to go in.

At least the door was locked. Had it been open, every instinct Ryder had would have been screaming. But the combination of locked door but alarms not on left that final, most important question unanswered.

Had Breither been warned despite their precautions?

And was he smart enough to set a trap?

He pulled out the small leather case he called his break-in kit. It held a set of finely tempered lock picks, a tiny but powerful flashlight, and for situations that didn't require finesse, a glass cutter and a small suction cup.

A glance at the dead bolt told him it was a standard single cylinder, with a flip knob on the other side—cheap, for this expensive house, which said something, he was sure. He could probably pick it in a couple of minutes. But this back door that looked out on the pool area also had a large glass panel, and with the alarm off it only made sense to save that couple of minutes.

He placed the suction cup, cut around it in a circle large enough to allow his hand through, removed the glass, reached through to the dead bolt and flipped it open. He held back, waiting, watching, in case the apparently inactive alarm was instead an elaborate lure.

Nothing happened.

They stepped into the house, Ryder telling himself not to assume that their quarry was as stupid as this made him seem. He couldn't afford any mistaken assumptions.

Maria couldn't afford them.

Chapter 17

Ana had not known how she would feel when she faced this man Ryder suspected of being the leader of the baby-smuggling ring.

She felt utter contempt.

And disbelief. She was used to her father's urbane charm and air of strength and power. She had thought it would take at least that to put together this horrible endeavor. Was it truly possible that this skinny, cadaverous man with the beak nose, thinning hair and skittish eyes that refused to look straight at even inanimate objects, was the mastermind behind all this pain and heartbreak and anguish?

"But he is a cartoon," she exclaimed. "A caricature."

Ryder laughed. Ana liked the sound. An odd thought to have, under these conditions, but there it was.

It had taken him only a split second to get the locked door open through the hole he'd cut in the glass. They'd gone in quickly, but then Ryder made them both wait, something that went against the grain.

"Okay," he had finally whispered. "Not smart enough to set a trap."

She hadn't thought of that, that the disabled alarm system could have been a trap. She added cleverness and quick thinking to her growing list of things she admired about this man.

And upped her estimate of his courage and determination, since he had gone ahead anyway, even after thinking of the possibility.

Once inside, Ana had spared barely a glance at the furnishings of the house, thinking only that the entire place looked as if someone had hired a decorator and provided an unlimited budget for ostentation. Even her father had more taste; at least their home, luxurious though it was, appeared lived in.

The thought of the source of that unlimited budget had made her impatient. It also had her slipping Elena's knife into her hand once more; the gun Ryder had given her was at hand, but for a man like this she thought she might prefer the knife.

But now that she looked at him, a silly-looking, quivering man, cowering in the huge, ornate bed in a room that looked more like a high-end brothel, she felt only a pitying contempt.

"—it wasn't my idea," the man was saying his voice taking on a whine as his nervous eyes skipped from Ryder's weapon to hers.

"You're the last stop on this ugly railroad you've built. You're living—" Ryder gestured at the room "—on the proceeds."

"But I don't run it, I don't! I just needed the money, I—"

Ana lost patience. She stepped forward, leaning over the scrawny man as he held the covers with trembling hands, like some frightened virgin, as if they would protect him. Her knife glinted in the light from the overhead fixture Ryder had flipped on when they had first stepped in, startling the man into shocked stillness and giving them the edge.

Not that they'd needed it.

"You are unspeakably evil," Ana said. "You don't deserve to have ever lived, and certainly not to keep on doing so."

"Who are you?"

It came out as nearly a squeak, and Ryder laughed again. "She's who you should really be afraid of," he said. "You messed with the wrong mother, Breither. She'll carve you up like this silly bed if you don't talk. And she'll enjoy it, too."

Ana took an inward pleasure in Ryder's laughing threat, and in the way Breither's terrified eyes widened. "Mother…?" the man gulped out.

"I stand for all the mothers you have caused such pain and agony," she said, getting into the spirit of it. "Which is what I will deal to you in turn."

The man's already pale skin turned paler, and his muddy brown eyes suddenly rolled back in his head. He fell back onto the pile of pillows.

Ryder reached for him. "Damn," he said, but he was laughing. "He's out cold." He looked at Ana then. "You are amazing. And terrifying."

She reluctantly sheathed Elena's blade. "You do not seem terrified."

"I'm a man," Ryder said, his mouth quirking up at one corner in an expression she found oddly endearing, "not a mouse."

He certainly was that, she thought, and again the memory of his bare chest and flat belly flashed through her mind. She guessed that the rest of him was just as masculine, and wished she could some day find out for sure, a longing that startled her with its earthiness and power.

But he was definitely a different sort of man than she was used to in her life. He was strong, competent and clearly brave. Trustworthy? She thought so. He was doing the right thing, that was clear. But there was so much she didn't know. There were hidden depths to Ryder Grady that she did not understand, and she had no time to plumb them now.

That she wanted to unsettled her.

Her heart had betrayed her once, just as her mother's had betrayed her with her father. Yet she couldn't stop thinking that this, unlike her father and Alberto, was a real man. He was nothing like them, and that meant everything to a woman who had grown up under a very twisted vision of what a real man was.

Unlike this sham who had fainted at the mere sight of a woman with a weapon. Perhaps he knew he deserved to be separated from certain body parts.

"It is hard to believe he could be the person who organized this unspeakable thing," she said, voicing her earlier doubts.

"Yes." Ryder looked suddenly serious. "Yes, it's very hard to believe. It takes a certain amount of nerve to even consider an enterprise like this one. I don't think he has it."

She was gratified that he agreed with her, and so quickly. So she risked her second thought.

"But he knows who does."

Ryder nodded, something very like approval in his eyes. The expression warmed her unaccountably, and she felt a warmth rising in her cheeks that stunned her. She had sworn she would never hunger for a man's approval again, and yet here she was, basking in it. Was she becoming a fool yet again, and so quickly?

"We must find out," she said, her embarrassment at her own reaction sharpening her voice.

Ryder didn't take offense.

A real man, she thought again.

And this time no amount of internal chiding could dissuade her.

"That office down the hall," Ryder said, remembering glancing into the room as they searched for Breither.

She nodded. "I saw it."

"Put that blade to use on these fancy sheets."

She quickly did as he asked while he yanked the limp, unconscious man out of the bed and plopped him down into the wingback chair near the window. He took the strips of expensive fabric she handed him, twisted them into ropelike lengths and tied the man to the chair.

They were a good team, he thought as he tied off the last knot. He'd never been much of a team player, but this was different. This was the kind of thing he could get used to, more like having another part of yourself working in concert.

The old phrase, *My better half,* went through his mind, and his breath caught. He'd always thought that it was a joke used by housebroken men, but when he thought about Ana, there was no questioning that in any relationship, she would be the better half.

That he could see himself liking it that way, that he could imagine himself with her that way at all, rattled him so deeply he had to shake his head to clear it and get back to the matter at hand.

Moments later they were in the picture-perfect office.

"No computer," Ana said.

"Unless there's a laptop tucked away somewhere," Ryder said.

They began to search. They found no computer, but once Ryder had taken out his lockpicks and opened the heavy wood file cabinet against the wall, they found files upon files full of handwritten notes. Breither was apparently either old-fashioned, stuck in his ways, or too stupid to learn how to use a computer. Ryder's guess was it was some combination of all three.

"So much for the paperless revolution," Ryder muttered as he surveyed the files.

Ana didn't speak; she was flipping through the folder tabs quickly. "Nothing," she said, that edge still in her voice. If they found nothing and had to go back to Breither, Ryder didn't think much of the man's chances of holding out against her. He didn't have time to analyze why the thought made him smile inwardly.

"These are patient files," Ana said, closing the drawer, and adding grimly, "with an inordinate number marked with a sticker that says 'Deceased.'"

"Must be why he couldn't make any money as a doctor. His incompetence became known."

"Would he really keep papers to do with the babies in with all his old medical files?" she asked.

"This guy's squirrelly enough that I don't know what he'd do," Ryder said frankly.

But he kept searching, beginning with the bookcase behind a desk as heavily carved as the bed had been, while Ana kept going through files in another drawer of the filing cabinet.

"Maybe he's got a hidden compartment or something here," Ryder said. "These shelves aren't as deep as they could be."

Ana seemed to brighten at that thought and started helping him remove books from the shelves. Medical books, he noticed. Lots of them. How had someone who had done all the work to become a doctor become so perverted that he would go against every precept of the profession?

"'First do no harm,'" Ryder muttered.

Ana gave him a startled look. "Yes," she said, as if she'd been thinking exactly what he had. "That is what they swear. And yet he does this. It is abominable."

Ryder felt a small tug of satisfaction that they'd been on the same wavelength. But that didn't help the search. There was no trace of a hidden compartment. Ana was getting frustrated now. "We must find out. Do you think he is awake yet?"

Ryder stood there, holding the last book he'd removed from the shelves. Ironically, it was a four-inch-thick volume on obstetrics.

"If he's not, we'll wake him up," Ryder promised, dropping the book down on the pile they'd tossed haphazardly on the floor in their rush; Ryder had a certain respect for books, but no respect at all for anything belonging to this man.

Ana turned to go, then stopped when he didn't move in turn. He was looking at the book he'd just dropped, his mind racing.

"What?" she asked.

He shook his head. "I don't usually tackle books that big," he said, "but…"

He bent, reaching out to pick up the volume once more.

"It's not as heavy as it should be," he said.

He opened the cover. Flipped the first few pages.

The only real pages there were.

Ana gasped when he turned the next leaf to expose a compartment hidden inside the book, where the pages had been hollowed out. The interior had been coated with something to make the sides of the space stiff, providing a perfectly sized place for the papers inside, more handwritten notes and what appeared to be records. Names, places, records of payments. Dozens of them.

Ana stared. "This many? They have stolen this many babies?"

Ryder glanced at her. Her expression was both horrified and furious. He guessed that to Ana, this was suddenly about more than just Maria. He knew her determination to save her little girl was boundless, but her face revealed a fury that would demand nothing less than the total destruction of this reprehensible operation, and the people who were perpetrating it.

God help them, he thought. Or not, he amended, as he scanned the papers from the compartment and saw page after page that represented tiny, helpless babies like Maria.

"Here," Ryder said, handing her some of the handwritten notes in what looked to him like some form of Spanish, but one he didn't recognize. "I speak better than I read. Take a look at these."

Ana took the papers and scanned them rapidly. "It is not you. It is *Nahuatl*," she said.

"What?"

"It is the language of the Aztecs."

Ryder blinked. "Oh. Which means?"

"Nothing, perhaps. It might mean they were born or lived in Central Mexico, or their parents did."

"Anything else?"

"Some *Nahuatl* dialects are still spoken today, but mostly in rural areas. Some use it to show off their education, since it is among the most studied dialects in the Americas. It has existed since the seventh century."

He blinked again. "You sound like a teacher."

"It is what I hope to be. What I went to college to become."

College. Of course. Did you think her manner, her way of speaking, was learned on the streets of Mexico City?

Her father might be the Mexican equivalent of the God-father, but Ana herself had called him sophisticated, charming and polished. Of course he would want his child to exhibit those same qualities, even if he did consider her more of a possession than a daughter.

So much for being on the same wavelength. *She's way out of your league, Colton. Best remember that.*

She turned her attention back to the pages. Her brow creased more deeply with each one, and her anger grew visibly.

"What?"

"They have taken at least some of the babies from poor parents, who signed them over. For a pittance, a tiny part of what you say they receive for the babies here."

"That figures."

She looked up at him. "This cannot make it legal, can it? You cannot sell your child!"

Ryder nearly took a step back in the face of her ferocity. "I'm no lawyer. I don't know about any of that."

She turned back to the papers, went through some more, and began to frown. "There is someone who is mentioned here. Several times. As if he were in charge of everything."

Ryder went still. "Who?"

"I don't know," Ana said, frustration tingeing her voice again. "He is not called by name. At least, not a real name. It is a sort of nickname, I think."

"What is it?"

"There is no literal translation to English that I know of. The closest I can say would be he is called 'Big.'"

"Is there any clue as to who or where he is?"

She held up a hand as she went back to the first note and

began to read again, more slowly. When she finally reached the last one, her frustration broke loose.

"There is nothing! No indication of who he is, where he is from, nothing."

"How do they talk about him? As if he were a stranger, a local, what?"

She got his meaning quickly. "They speak of him as if everyone already knows who he is."

"That's something, then," Ryder said, although he had no idea what.

"He must know more," Ana said determinedly. "And we must find out."

Ryder wasn't sure she was right about Breither's knowledge, but he agreed that they had to try. Back in the bedroom, they found the man revived and struggling to get free. When they stepped into the room he let out a little shriek; clearly he thought they'd gone.

Confronted with what they'd found, the man paled anew. Ana held the notes she'd translated in front of him. "Who is this man they speak of?"

"What?"

"This 'Big' they talk of in these notes. Who is he? Where is he?"

Breither gave her a look so blank Ryder knew it couldn't have been faked. "I don't know what you're talking about. I only know it was the authorization from the parents."

"Authorization?" Ana nearly spat it out.

"Most of the transactions were legitimate," Breither protested. "Those papers say so."

"Which explains why you're hiding them and burning the evidence," Ryder said. The man winced at the biting sarcasm in his voice.

"I never knew—"

"Do not dare to claim innocence," Ana warned him. She held the notes in front of him again. "Tell me who this 'Big' is."

"I tell you, I don't know. I can't read that stuff."

"Then why do you have it?" she said, resting her other hand pointedly on the knife in her pocket.

He whimpered. "They told me to keep it all, somewhere safe. To burn the envelopes they came in, so they couldn't be traced."

Ana pulled out the blade, held it with a familiarity and ease even Breither had to notice.

"They?" Ryder prompted.

Breither kept his terror-widened eyes on the knife. When Ana turned it so it gleamed in the light he suddenly couldn't talk fast enough.

"The papers would arrive, anonymously, in a post office box, when a package was in the system and due to arrive that night. That's all I know. I never saw or talked to anyone except the man who delivered the package."

Ryder believed him.

He also believed Ana was on the verge of committing mayhem. It was the "package in the system," as if the babies were something to be shipped like a pair of shoes, that had done it, he thought.

"I understand, but he's not worth it, *mija*," he said softly. "He's just a cog in the wheel. And a sniveling coward at that. He just wet himself."

For a moment he didn't think she'd even heard him. But then she straightened, sheathing her ancestor's blade. She glanced at the dark stain forming on the expensive silk pajamas.

"The stench in here is foul," she said. "He does not deserve to live."

"Maybe he won't," Ryder said, injecting as much cheer as he could into his voice. "He doesn't strike me as the type who would have a lot of friends checking in on him when he doesn't show up for a couple of weeks."

The man whimpered again.

"I can no longer stand to be in the same room with him," Ana said and turned sharply. Ryder breathed again. He hadn't wanted to have to stop her, but he would have.

He was relieved that she'd backed off, he thought as he followed her out of the room. But he had no idea what she was going to do when she realized they were at a dead end.

When she realized that, barring a miracle, Maria was gone.

Chapter 18

"I am all right, truly," Ana said into the phone. "I will explain everything when I return."

"Your worthless fiancé didn't show up, did he?" Jewel asked, concern in her voice. She had been up for a couple of hours, even though it was just now six in the morning. Given her awful bouts with insomnia, Ana had guessed she would be awake, and therefore had risked the call.

Ana managed a creditable laugh at Jewel's question. "No. He considers himself well rid of us, I'm sure."

She doubted that. He was more likely furious with embarrassment at having his fiancée flee from him in the middle of the night. While her father was likely just furious, as he would be at one of his dogs who dared to disobey him. She didn't think he would have her put down, as he had one dog who had particularly displeased him, but sometimes she wasn't so certain of that. Especially since the dog had been her own favorite, and his misdeed had been to hesitate before leaving Ana's side when her father had called him.

"Is there any news of the baby smugglers?" Ana asked, trying to keep her tone casual.

"No developments. Adam was here early this morning, and he mentioned that they're getting very frustrated at the lack of progress."

Ana's heart sank. Not that she had expected anything different, but she had harbored a tiny hope that something might have changed.

The real purpose of her early-morning call was now accomplished, but she knew she needed to mask it with more normal chatter. She turned to the one most likely to distract Jewel—the besotted deputy, obviously checking on her in the early hours.

"And is there any progress on that front?" she asked, using the almost teasing tone she usually adopted when asking Jewel about the handsome Adam Rawlings, so clearly enthralled with her.

"Not as far as he's concerned," Jewel said. "He still wants more than I'm ready to give."

At the serious answer, Ana's voice became serious as well. "Then you are being wise."

Jewel laughed. "You're the only one who thinks so. Everybody else seems to think I should go for it."

"They only wish you to be happy. But no one knows what will do that better than you yourself."

"Ah, you are a wise one, my friend."

If so, it came much too late, Ana thought as she ended the call a few moments later.

"Nothing?" Ryder asked after a moment.

"Nothing," she confirmed. "You are not surprised."

Ryder shrugged as he drove. "The sheriff has a lot of other things on his plate just now. This is the only thing on mine."

She liked the single-minded sound of that, although so far even their combined determination had not accomplished the goal.

For the first time, she looked around, realized she did not recognize anything. "Where are we going?"

He seemed to hesitate for a moment before answering. "Back to my motel."

"Fine," she said. She wanted a quiet place to go through the notes again, where she could concentrate and perhaps find something she had missed in her rapid mental translation.

She heard him chuckle. It sounded rueful, and a glance at him showed a matching expression on his face. "I'm guessing," he said, "that does not have the same connotations in your world."

"I am not ignorant," she said, rather stiffly. "I presumed you did not mean it in that way."

His expression changed. "I'm not sure whether to be flattered or insulted," he said with a wry quirk to his mouth.

"I am sure there is a woman in your life who would take offense for you," she said. "Or at you, were you to pursue such a path."

To her chagrin, he laughed. "I love the way you talk when you're angry."

When she was angry, she knew her speech became more formal, especially in English. Although it was the language she knew best after her own, it was still not her first language. She tended to be extra careful when her emotions were roiled, to be certain she did not make any mistakes.

But that did not mean she appreciated being laughed at.

"I'm sorry," Ryder said. "I'm sure you're in no mood for jokes."

Having taken the wind right out of her anger—although she was fairly certain she had mangled that idiom—he was looking at her contritely.

"No," she agreed. "I cannot seem to find my sense of humor."

"It will come back with Maria," he said.

She gave him a grateful smile for that. He smiled back, and she thought it lovely, despite the fact that his face was still slightly swollen. It reminded her that this man had fought for Maria, was still fighting for her, going on when she was certain he would like nothing more than to lie down and rest what had to be an aching body.

A real man, she thought yet again.

"Ana?"

"Yes?"

He didn't look at her when he said quietly, "There isn't a woman to take offense."

"Oh."

She wondered why he'd felt it necessary to explain that. She wondered why she felt so gratified that he had.

She gave herself a mental shake; there was no time for such thoughts. She turned to look forward through the windshield again, to the east and the rising sun. The dawn of the first day without her baby in her arms.

She vowed it would also be the last.

Ryder was more than grateful for the plentiful hot water supply at the motel. He let it pour over his aching body. It seemed like a lifetime ago rather than just yesterday that he had stood here last. It had been routine, that last shower, not a matter of gingerly dodging the scrapes, sore spots, and developing bruises.

When he dried off and checked his chest and back in the

mirror, the wounds weren't as bad as he'd expected. There were going to be bruises all right, lots of them, but as he poked and prodded and took experimental deep breaths, he decided at the worst a rib or two might be cracked.

His face, on the other hand, was a lost cause. The left side was still swollen, and he had the beginnings of a brutal shiner to go with his split lip.

Looking like this, he'd have a hard time picking up a woman even in the worst roadhouse dive.

His lack of interest in every woman except for the one in the next room made him wince.

With a smothered sigh he turned away from the mirror. The last time he'd looked this bad was after he and Jorge Vega had crashed that motorcycle they'd taken for a joyride when he was thirteen. That had been the beginning of the end for Clay.

He felt a pang of sympathy for what he'd put his brother through; it couldn't have been easy to try and keep their little family together when he'd only been eighteen himself. But Clay had done it. Ryder began to think about the enormity of that task. Clay had had to fight some government agency that didn't think he was capable of handling a fourteen-year-old sister and a sixteen-year-old hellion of a brother. What kind of hard sell had his brother had to do to keep them all together?

And what good had it done? One ends up pregnant and dumped, the other in prison?

For one of the few times in his life, Ryder actually felt a pang of guilt. Clay had tried, more than most brothers would have, but Ryder hadn't listened. He'd developed the knack of tuning out his brother as he'd tuned out teachers at school, letting his mind wander to the next bit of fun on the horizon.

He pulled on his last clean pair of jeans, thinking he'd have to take Mrs. Sanchez up on her offer of laundry services, and grabbed the T-shirt he'd brought in with him. Pulling it on made him wince, but he didn't want Ana seeing his chest and back now that the bruises were rising to the surface.

He also didn't want to be half naked in the same room with her. The last time he'd been hurting too much. Now, he was hurting a little less…

Barefoot, he opened the door into the main room. When he'd gone in for his shower, she had been seated at the small table by the one window, the notes they'd found spread out before her. But although the papers were still there, she was not.

A tiny sound alerted him, and he stepped into the room and looked in that direction.

She was curled up on the bed in a tight little ball, her body shaking, and he realized that she was crying.

Ryder felt as if Mr. E had just delivered a knockout punch. He couldn't take this. Without faltering, she'd gone through a night of childbirth that would have left many men paralyzed.

"Ana," he whispered, sitting down on the bed beside her.

"I can find nothing," she gulped out between sobs. "There is all this talk in the notes about this person 'Big,' but there is nothing to tell us who or where he is. Nothing."

He reached out, unable to stop himself from touching her.

"Don't cry," he said, knowing even as he uttered the words how ridiculously inadequate they were. Why shouldn't she cry?

She lifted her head to look at him. Her eyes were reddened, her cheeks wet, and she was still beautiful.

"My baby," she choked out. "My baby."

Ryder saw with a sinking heart that it had hit her. That

she had realized they were at a dead end, that they had no leads, no clues, nothing.

Driven by a need to comfort unlike anything he'd ever felt for a woman before, he lay down beside her and pulled her into his arms.

"We're not giving up, Ana," he whispered against her hair. "We're not giving up."

She shuddered, sobs taking her once again. He wished he had even the slightest idea how he was going to keep the promise he'd made to this woman, and to a tiny little girl who was likely already lost to them.

He held her as she wept, and she let him. That alone was a bit of a wonder, he thought. Ana Morales was strong and fierce and tough when she had to be, and even as big an idiot as he was when it came to women couldn't miss the trust that implied.

Gradually she uncurled from her self-protective ball, and he could feel the soft, warm length of her pressed against him. If she'd been anyone else, if the circumstances had been any different, he would have made a move. He would like nothing more than to make love to this woman. He was good enough to make her forget her anguish, for a few moments at least, and perhaps allow her the peace of sleep for a few hours.

Again he told himself his self-control came because it was physically wrong for her that he wanted to make love rather than simply having sex. Also, the timing was wrong. Pressuring her at a time like this, with her full being focused on her daughter, would be one of the biggest mistakes of his life.

His worry about timing now—anytime had been the right time—was just another item on the growing list of things that were different with Ana.

But the reasons for it, whatever and however many there were, didn't change the fact that it was the hardest damn thing he'd ever done.

"We're not giving up, Ana," he said for a third time. And as she wept he held her, forcing himself to think, not of how good she felt in his arms, of how much he wished things were different and he could indulge the need that was threatening to rage out of control, but of what the hell to do next.

Chapter 19

When she had awakened in his arms, Ana had been amazed, then embarrassed that she had slept. She was not sure he had, since he had been awake and looking at her when she had opened her eyes. The smile he had given her then, even lopsided thanks to his obviously still tender lip, had warmed her in the instant before reality had flooded back. She felt guilty for sleeping while her baby was missing.

"You needed to rest," he'd said, accurately assessing her reaction. "And now we get back to it."

She had not been at all sure what there was to get back to, but she'd been encouraged that he apparently had some sort of plan, so she had hastened to quickly shower while he went out to find coffee. As she had showered, she had become aware of the aching fullness of breasts used to nursing Maria every few hours.

She dug through the pink bag and brought out the manual

breast pump that was in a side pocket. She had thanked Macy Ward—Yates now, she corrected herself—who had given it to her, but had also said she had no intention of being separated from her baby long enough to need it. Macy, who said she'd only gotten her sense of humor back since Fisher Yates had changed her life, had laughed and told her not to tempt fate with that kind of challenge.

She sent the tall brunette a silent apology for doubting her.

And chastised herself for tempting that fate to prove her wrong. Tears began anew as she went about the business of expressing the milk her baby should be having right now, and fierce worry at how Maria was being treated welled up inside her.

She had just finished when the door opened. She swiftly adjusted her bra and pulled her sweater down before Ryder stepped into the room. He stopped just after closing the door, two steaming cups in his hand, looking at the device in her hand curiously. She explained, expecting him to become embarrassed at the very thought. As she was embarrassed by the thought that if he had been thirty seconds earlier, he would have walked in on her with her breasts bared.

But Ryder just looked at her, an odd, almost wistful expression on his face. A distant, unfocused sort of look, as if he were picturing something else.

Then, suddenly, he was back, holding out one of the steaming cups to her.

"We're not giving up," he said yet again.

"I know," she said, eyeing the cup doubtfully.

"I got you hot chocolate," he said. "The lady said that was better than coffee for you."

Ana stared at him as she took the chocolate. Had the rakish, wild—and slightly battered-looking—Ryder actually asked some woman at a coffee shop what would be safe for a nursing mother to drink? Somehow that touched her as much as anything else he had done, and the tears threatened again.

She fought them down as she took the first sip, surprised at how good it felt, even knowing how hot it likely was outside.

While she drank, she watched Ryder gather up what appeared to be all his meager belongings. Or at least, all he had here in this motel room; she realized with a little shock that she did not even know where he really lived. She had trusted this man with the most important task of her life, and she did not even know if he lived in a house, an apartment, or a tiny room like this one in some other town.

"You are packing?" she asked as he stuffed things into a large canvas backpack.

"Don't know when, or if, I'll be back here. And some of it might come in handy."

She brightened at the implications of that. "You have a plan?"

He grimaced. "Nothing so organized. Just the only thing I can think of to do."

"Which is?"

"Shotgun," he said.

Ana blinked, wondering if this meant something other than the weapon it seemed to refer to, if it were some American English slang term she'd somehow missed.

"You fire a shotgun," he said, "the pellets spread out in all directions. You fire often enough, sometimes you get lucky and hit the right thing."

She soon understood what he meant, literally. The next few hours were a whirlwind of action, Ryder tracking down every person he thought might have a connection to the baby ring. Ana noticed he took a different tack with different people, angry and intimidating with some, persuasive with others, going from sharp and frighteningly forceful to gently coaxing. Shaking them down, he called it. But so far the results had been negligible.

When they confronted some of the clients of the ring, couples so desperate for a baby they had asked no questions, even Ana felt the stirrings of an unwelcome sympathy.

Ryder had told her her job with those people was to represent Maria. To show them the truth of what they had done in their vehement insistence on getting a baby. That she could do easily enough.

As they proceeded, she had the thought that they worked well together. It was unexpected, as so much had been with this man, but undeniable as well. And she could not seem to stop herself from wondering what it would be like to have this man in her life, the kind of man who would not see her as a possession but a partner, who would be proud rather than annoyed at her intelligence, and who understood her determination to raise her baby in a better place.

She told herself her yearnings, her imaginings of a long, golden future with Ryder were just that, pure imagination.

It was hard to accept when the solid, strong reality of the man was right before her.

He left the number of Ana's cell phone with each person they confronted. "You are hoping that they will have second thoughts or remember something after we leave? That they will call?" she asked when they'd made yet another stop. They were on the outskirts of San Antonio now, in a quiet residential neighborhood that seemed too peaceful and picturesque to harbor such evil doings.

"Or someone will," Ryder said, almost absently as he negotiated the ramp onto Interstate-35.

Someone? Ana wondered. It took her a moment to

realize he meant someone from the ring itself. That he thought one of the people they'd talked to—shaken down—would report to his bosses what had happened, that the man they had left for dead was not, and was now openly after them.

With his bruised face always before her, the risk Ryder was taking was never out of her mind. Yet she suddenly realized the danger he was putting himself in, that he was in fact asking for.

And yet he kept going. It was impossible to remain distraught in the face of Ryder's tireless pursuit.

And unaccountably, despite the fact that nothing they'd done so far had seemed to get them any closer to finding Maria, her spirits rose.

He was getting toward the end of his list of people to arm-twist, badger, and if necessary bite, Ryder thought. And so far he'd accomplished nothing but to advertise himself, not just blowing his cover but incinerating it and putting up a billboard to mark the spot.

Getting Maria back was the priority now. The baby ring was secondary.

Which meant he'd likely signed and sealed the orders that would send him back to prison himself.

"What was the deal you made?"

Ryder nearly choked on his own breath. He shot her a sideways look. "What are you, a mind reader?"

She lowered her gaze. "I am sorry. I should not have asked. You are helping me, helping Maria, that should be enough."

He fought the urge to reach out and take her hand. He hadn't meant to snap, she'd just startled him, so close was her question to what had just gone through his mind.

The idea that simply touching her hand, holding it, seemed like the thing he wanted most unsettled him anew. What the hell was happening to him? How had he gotten to the point where a mere look, a brush of skin, was enough, when it was from this woman? And why couldn't he seem to find the fortitude to back the hell off?

Maybe you can't, but I'll bet she can, he told himself.

"The deal I made," he said, his voice flat, "was to get out of prison. Happy now?"

If she was shocked, it didn't show. "Why were you in prison?"

She was so calm he would have thought she hadn't heard him right if she hadn't repeated the word back to him.

"It was the culmination of a misspent life," he said.

"In America, are not charges usually more...specific?"

What was with this woman? Why wasn't she cringing away from him instead of discussing this as if it were the weather?

"It doesn't matter. I didn't do what they put me in for—at least, not knowingly—but I've done enough to end up there anyway."

"Tell me," she said.

Right, he thought.

But he did. Somehow, in his efforts to avoid it, he ended up spilling it all, things he'd never talked about with anyone except Boots. Like some lovesick kid, he poured out his entire pitiful history to her. And she listened. Not that she had much choice, stuck here in the truck's cab with him, but she could have told him to shut up. And when he finally finished, he fervently wished that she had.

He waited, certain she sadly regretted that "Tell me," now. His life no doubt seemed a cakewalk compared to what she'd been through, and she probably thought him a whiner. He wasn't sure she wasn't right. He—

"Odd, is it not? That while my family was large and close, they were of no more good to me than yours to you."

Of all the things she could have said, nothing could have startled him more. "You mean I was no good to them."

"No. They obviously did not understand what you needed, just as mine did not understand—or care about—my needs."

"My brother tried," Ryder said, stirred to an uncharacteristic defense. "We just…always fought."

"I have two older brothers. They are very close. I believe they would die for each other. But they care little for the rest of the family."

"I guess we were just too different, my brother and I," Ryder said, wondering where that piece of understanding had floated up from. "We could barely stand each other. Maybe even hated each other."

She shook her head. "I doubt it is truly that way." When she went on, her tone was different, almost speculative. "The man who owns the ranch, Jewel's friend Clay, he also had a brother he always fought with. But when he learned that brother had died, he was devastated, as any brother would be. He is still fiercely grieving."

Ryder went ice cold. The oddity of suppressing a shiver in the August heat didn't even register.

"Died? Clay thinks…his brother died?"

"Yes. Seven months ago. Jewel told me."

When he got out for this assignment. That must be part of the cover. A part they hadn't told him about.

But he hadn't told anyone, except Boots, that he even had a brother. No one at the prison knew, nor did his new employers.

"How did he find out?" He couldn't help the hoarseness

of his voice, but Ana answered as if he'd asked a simple, normal question.

"He wrote to his brother, to try and make amends. It came back. He wrote again. The same thing happened. He called, and was given—Jewel called it the runaround?—so he went to see him in person."

Ryder swallowed tightly. "He went...to see him?"

"That is when he was told. He is still grieving deeply, and cannot forgive himself for waiting too long."

Ryder swallowed tightly. Emotions too deep and old to name swirled around inside him. But finally, belatedly, something occurred to him; there had been a very pointed note in Ana's voice as she'd told him this story. And then there were the details. More than seemed natural for the situation from her point of view.

So maybe you're wrong about her point of view, he thought. He looked at her, steadily, and at last she gave him what he'd suspected.

"He cannot forgive himself for giving up on his brother." She held his gaze. "For giving up on you."

Ryder let out the breath he hadn't even been aware of holding. "How did you know?"

"I was not sure, until now, when you said you and your brother might even hate each other. Jewel told me that was Clay's greatest regret, that his brother had...died thinking he hated him."

Ryder tried to wrap his mind around that. He could see Clay feeling responsible for the breach—after all, his brother felt responsible for damn near everything—but the image of a grieving, saddened Clay, over him of all people, was more than he could conjure up.

"Your brother is, by all I have heard, a good man."

"He always was. It was me who was the problem. I—"

The ring of her cell phone cut off his words and short-circuited the turmoil in his gut. He held his breath again as she picked up the phone and looked at the caller ID.

"It is not Jewel," she said, and he saw a tremor go through her. "It is a restricted number."

Had all his shaking yielded some fruit after all? Ryder took the phone and flipped it open.

"Talk," he said shortly.

"Back off." The voice was male, but so muffled, either by something over the mouthpiece or by electronic means, he couldn't tell anything more.

"Can't do that."

"You'll regret it."

"Probably," Ryder agreed. "But I want her back. Now."

The caller didn't pretend to misunderstand. "The baby?" The voice laughed then, giving Ryder a moment to focus on his way of speaking; he thought there was a trace of an accent, but as muffled as it was he couldn't be sure. "I grant you, her mother's a pretty hot piece of ass. But is she worth dying for?"

Initially, Ryder bridled at that description of Ana, even though, had he seen her for the first time without all the entanglement, he might have thought pretty much the same thing. She was, after all, incredibly attractive. He had the memory of long, aching hours of holding her and holding back to prove that.

But that reaction was blasted away by the realization that the question the voice had asked had provoked. Time was, he would have laughingly answered that there was nothing in this world he counted worth dying for. His life might not be worth much, but he still wouldn't give it up for something as stupid as a cause.

Or for someone else.

But now he wasn't so sure.

"Have to think about it, *cabrón?* Then I'll make you a deal. A trade. The baby…for you."

The voice laughed again as Ryder's mind raced. Was this Mr. E, looking for payback for that kneecap? Or was it Alcazar himself, demanding retribution for Ryder daring to infiltrate his operation?

"I'll call you back with details," the voice said, and the phone went dead.

It didn't matter who it was, Ryder told himself. What mattered was making sure whoever it was kept his end of the deal.

And it wasn't until that went through his mind that he realized he had every intention of making this devil's bargain. If it would put Maria back in her mother's arms, he would do a lot worse.

Besides, he'd escaped from them once. He could do it again. And even if it took some time, he'd survived prison, hadn't he? He could hold on long enough.

"What is it?" Ana asked, her voice shaking. "Was it the men who have Maria?"

"Yes."

She stifled a cry.

"It's all right," Ryder said, knowing he couldn't tell her the truth, it would only add to her burden. "We're starting negotiations."

"Negotiations?"

"We'll get her back, Ana. We *will* get her back. I promise you."

He hoped he wasn't telling the biggest lie of his misbegotten life.

Chapter 20

"Italy?"

Ana stared at the screen of the self-service check-in kiosk. The bustle of the San Antonio airport was simply background noise to her now, the people all around vaguely resented for not having such horror in their lives.

"So it seems," Ryder muttered.

Ana looked at him for a long, silent moment. When they'd parked the truck, he had stowed the weapons behind the seat with obvious regret. But he clearly knew there was no way he could get a weapon through security.

"They have taken my baby to Italy?" she asked, bewildered.

"Ana," Ryder said, "I don't know what they're doing. Maybe you should stay here, in case this is a false lead."

He had been trying to get her to agree to stay behind since the mysterious voice had called again, with the numbers for two e-tickets and instructions to be at the airport within the hour, and to board the plane without drawing any attention.

"But he said for both of us to take this flight. And if he has Maria, I must be there."

"If he does, I'll bring her back, Ana."

"I know you would," she said, believing it with a faith she was surprised to find was so strong. "But she is my daughter, and my responsibility."

"What if this is just a trick, to get us out of their way?"

As he voiced her worst fear, that while they were in Italy Maria would disappear irrevocably, Ana felt a shiver of pure terror grip her. It was a moment before she could control it and ask, "Do you believe that it is?"

Ryder shifted uncomfortably, and she read the answer in his eyes before he spoke. "No."

"Then we go to Venice."

Ana was thankful he did not argue with her. Perhaps it was because they did not have much time; they had to find the rental locker the mysterious voice had directed them to and still make it to the gate.

"Anna Giovanni," Ana read as he handed her a very real-looking Italian passport. "And you are?"

"Antonio Giovanni," he said. "Not too original. But I don't much like that they were able to find a photograph of you."

Ana shrugged; it was indeed a photo of her, not just someone who resembled her. "But it is from school, my graduation," she said. "It would not be hard to find, even to get from the university website."

"But they know who you are."

"They do now, yes. But that is not surprising, is it, after what we have done these last two days?"

"Maybe," Ryder said, but he didn't sound convinced.

"What of you? Your photograph?"

"That is a mug shot," Ryder said with a grimace. "Also public record. They just cropped it a little."

It was not until they were at their gate that Ana said, more than a little worriedly, "To do this so quickly…they are very efficient."

"Yes," Ryder agreed, and she did not think she'd mistaken the grim note in his voice.

"*Benvenuto,*" the flight attendant said cheerfully as they boarded.

"*Grazie.*" Ana thanked him for the welcome, automatically in Italian, earning her a sideways look from Ryder.

"Italian, too?"

"And French," she said. "And I can manage a bit of Greek, and a bit less German."

"Handy," he muttered, and she wondered why he didn't sound very happy about it.

She had many hours to think on the long flight. She tried to rest, telling herself she would need to be alert and ready when they landed. But she could only doze, never really sleeping, going just deep enough for awful imaginings about Maria's fate to shock her awake. It was only when Ryder put his arm around her after a particularly nasty one that she was finally able to relax.

When she woke that time, it was a gentler thing, and she found herself sleepily snuggling against his warmth. He was awake, and she wondered if he'd gotten any rest himself; he had to be as tired as she was, and must feel even worse, still aching from the beating he'd taken.

"Tell me about your family," she said impulsively.

"I don't have—"

He stopped suddenly, as if only now remembering that she knew who he really was. Would he refuse? She had poured out her sordid story, admitted to him the truth of her father and her fiancé. She knew this did not mean he had to do the same in return, knew that often men did not have the same view of sharing, bonding through the telling of secrets that many women had.

But still, these were hardly ordinary circumstances, she thought.

Just when she thought he indeed was not going to answer, he started to talk. It was clear from the awkwardness of it that he had not done this often, and she knew she would need to take care that he not regret it later.

That she was even thinking of later, and that they would still be together, was something she couldn't deal with just now. So she quietly listened to his halting tale of a free-spirited, fiery-haired rodeo rider who had fallen hard for the worst possible man for her, and ended up with three children whose father had never even acknowledged their existence until long after her too-early death.

"I think she worked herself to death," Ryder said, and Ana couldn't blame him for the bitter note in his voice.

She wondered if that was why he had shied away from settling down to a normal occupation, or if it was simply that he had inherited his mother's free spirit and couldn't handle settling down at all.

"Your father," she said, remembering what Jewel had explained when she'd first come to Hopechest Ranch, "he is related to the famous Colton, the man running for your presidency?"

"The black sheep brother," Ryder said sourly. "That would be dear ol' dad."

Ana hesitated before saying carefully, "You have called yourself this name as well, the black sheep. Do you see yourself as like your father?"

"No!"

The answer was so vehement that Ana had to hide a smile.

"Good. Because you are nothing like him."

He blinked, as if startled by her certainty. "How do you know?"

"A man who would go halfway around the world to help a baby who is not even his, would hardly abandon one of his own."

He stared at her for a long silent moment. "But I feel as if she's...partly mine."

"She is," Ana said quietly, admitting for the first time that some part of her daughter—and some part of herself— would always belong to this man who had come in out of the darkness to help them when they were most in need.

Ryder looked away then, quickly, as if he were embarrassed by the admission. Ana felt a flood of tenderness, and wished things were different so that she could show him how she felt. She had known that he wanted her, it had been impossible to miss his state of arousal when he had held her so gently for those agonizing hours in his motel room. That he hadn't even tried to act upon it told her many things, not the least of which was that he cared.

Had her body been healed already, would she have acquiesced? She did not know. She did not want to believe she would have fallen into bed with a man she barely knew, but she suspected it might have been a harder battle than she would like to admit.

Perhaps she was just destined to always fall in love with the wrong man, she thought.

Love?

Not, she told herself. Surely not.

She realized slowly that she was still leaning into him, loath to relinquish the closeness that had allowed her to rest.

Maybe not.

She stole a quick, sideways glance at Ryder. He was to her right, so she got the full impact of the beating he'd taken for Maria.

Maybe.

But she had no right to even consider such things until Maria was safe. Ana forced such thoughts out of her mind.

But she didn't move away from Ryder's warmth.

For a guy who'd never been farther away from the United States than Saltillo, Mexico, this should have been an exciting trip. Could have been, if you added in the beautiful, fascinating, incredibly courageous woman at his side.

He liked the sound of that "at his side" stuff. But it was the courageous part that threw cold water on the expedition. Much as he might—to his own bemusement—like the idea of a long, romantic trip with Ana Morales, the circumstances were what they were. They had a long way to go before he could let his thoughts turn to romance.

But he was willing to wait. That alone told him how much he'd come to feel for her.

Of course, he had to survive this first.

The mundaneness of being met by a driver holding a card with the names on their false ID nearly made him laugh. But that ordinariness was soon forgotten as, a few minutes later, the same driver ushered them from the car to a waiting boat, for which he was also apparently the wheelman. Ryder barely had time to glance around, marveling at this postcard image of buildings and canals, with the oddly shaped gondolas bobbing gently.

This boat was a racy-looking powerboat, however, and he had the thought that big houses in Texas weren't the only thing this smuggling ring had paid for.

It went so much against his nature to allow the driver to wrap a black cloth around his head as a blindfold that it took everything he had to sit still. His vision cut off, he heard the rustle of cloth as the man apparently did the same thing to Ana.

The boat began to move—surprisingly slowly and quietly, Ryder thought, until it occurred to him that perhaps there were laws here about speed and noise. The last thing these people would want was to attract attention. Not that that explained the fancy boat itself, but—

He heard Ana make a quiet, quivering sound that she was obviously trying to stifle. Instinctively he put an arm around her. She leaned into him, much as she had on the plane.

Despite everything, including the uncertainty of his own life span just now, he liked it just as much. Wanted nothing more than to have an endless string of such moments with her, forever.

And that he'd just thought once more of the word *forever* in conjunction with a woman came as only a minor shock this time.

They made several turns, and Ryder began to learn the pattern, the change in the sound of the water against the hull, the barely perceptible lean as the boat changed direction. He started out noting what directions they were traveling in and for how far, thinking about finding the place again. But when he realized that if he followed his mental map they would have gone in a big circle twice, he gave up.

Finally the boat slowed, and he heard the lap of water against stone much closer this time. Their driver called out, although in Italian. At least Ryder assumed it was Italian. Someone ashore answered.

"He wants them to tie up the boat," Ana whispered.

He tightened his arm around her in thanks; even now her quick mind never faltered.

Getting off the boat blindfolded was tricky, and his hands clenched into fists when he heard Ana say something sharply to one of the men, something that sounded like *"diavolo."* He could guess at the satanic reference, but didn't want to know what the man had done to earn it; he was having enough trouble allowing himself to be trundled along like so much baggage.

Like a duffel bag, he thought, and anger spiked through him, reminding him of exactly why they were here, because these people had thought of Maria, and dozens like her, as nothing more than baggage.

There was the sound and feel of stone beneath their feet as the two men now herded them along. Ryder could tell when they stepped inside a building by the change in the sound of their steps, by the echo of movement, by the very feel of the air around them. They kept going and the sounds changed again, echoed louder, as if they were walking down a hallway.

They turned to the left, and Ryder heard the sound of a door opening. Their escorts pushed them forward, he assumed into a room. He heard the door close behind them, and realized he didn't know if their two shepherds had come into the room with them or not.

A baby cried.

"Maria!" Ana's shout was joyous, but Ryder heard a thickness to it, wondered if she, too, was crying.

Ryder couldn't hear or sense the two men, so decided to risk yanking off the blindfold. He found Ana had already done the same, although he could barely see her in the darkened room. She threw down the cloth and started toward the crying baby; Ryder grabbed her and held her back.

"Wait, Ana. It could be a trap."

"But it is Maria! I know my baby's voice."

"I'm not saying it's not, just—"

A loud peel of laughter echoed off the walls, filling the room eerily.

"Have you not learned there's no logic in women?"

Ryder went still; it was the voice from the phone. The muffled effect must have been electronic, because it was the same here, coming over what had to be a speaker somewhere at the far end of the room.

"But I must thank you, Ana, for keeping your end of the bargain. I have been looking for this man."

"What does he mean? What bargain?" Ana asked.

"It doesn't matter," Ryder whispered to her. "Just don't agree to anything until you have Maria in your arms."

"No one crosses me and lives to speak of it," the voice said. "It simply isn't good for business."

"Ryder—" Ana began, but the distorted voice cut her off.

"There is a rope on the wall behind you, Ana. Get it, and tie his hands behind him."

"What?"

Ana sounded bewildered, but Ryder knew her well enough by now to guess that her mind was racing.

"It's all right," he said to her, almost absently as he surreptitiously fiddled with the belt at his waist. "Do what he says."

"But you—"

"If you want Maria back, do what he says."

There was a split-second's pause before he heard her breathe a low, reverent oath. "This is the bargain? You, for my baby?"

The voice laughed again. "You did not tell her that was the deal—your life for the baby's life? How noble of you.

How self-sacrificing." The laugh again, this time it sounded utterly gleeful. "How delicious."

"Do it, Ana," Ryder told her.

"I cannot," Ana said, urgently. "He will kill you, and I...cannot bear that."

The simple emotion in her voice made Ryder's chest tighten. Wouldn't it just figure that he would finally find the woman who made him want to mend his ways only to get himself killed before he'd so much as kissed her?

"Do it, Ana. For Maria. It will be all right."

He wished he was more certain of that himself. He'd never thought much about dying; he didn't guess people did at the ripe old age of twenty-four. Oh, there had always been the chance one of his risky escapades could have gotten him killed, but he'd always figured he didn't care.

And now that he did, now that, amazingly, for the first time in his life he was thinking about the future, a real future, here he was, likely going to die sooner rather than later.

And painfully rather than peacefully.

But at least it would be for a reason. A good reason, he told himself as the baby cried again. That was more than he would have likely gotten had he continued down his scapegrace path.

"Do it now," ordered the voice, "or I will quiet this baby permanently."

Ryder heard Ana stifle a tiny cry. "Do it, Ana," he told her again, still working at slipping his belt through the loops on his jeans.

She moved then, following orders she clearly did not want to obey. She tied his hands, loosely, then at the voice's order, retied them tighter; the man obviously had guessed she would do what she could.

For an instant her hands lingered over his.

"Step away now," the voice ordered.

Ana hesitated. And in that moment she leaned forward and kissed Ryder gently on his bruised cheek. There was a world of promise in that tiny kiss, and Ryder felt his pulse surge. He would get them out of this, somehow. For the first time in his life he had something he would die for.

But he was going to do his damnedest to live.

Chapter 21

"A loving little display. How touching," the voice said, the scorn practically bouncing off the walls.

Clearly he had no trouble seeing what was happening in the darkened room, Ryder thought. He suspected they used night goggles.

"Touching, but pointless," the voice said. "Leon!"

The man, who was apparently more than just a driver, stepped forward, crossing the room toward the voice. Moments later the lights in the room came on. Ryder had barely a moment to register the bare stone walls and floor of a small room in a very old building, because across the room stood the driver and in his hands was a duffel bag. A familiar duffel bag. A corner of a pink flowered blanket protruded from the unzipped opening.

"Maria," Ana cried.

"Don't move!" the voice shouted.

A heartfelt wail issued from the duffel, and Ryder's gut

knotted. She was so tiny, so helpless. His only consolation was that she didn't know enough to be afraid. But he knew she was in danger. His mind rapidly turned over possibilities as his hands worked at the rope binding his wrists, trying to get the proper alignment.

"How much do you want her back, Ana? What will you do to get her? How far will you go?" The disembodied voice taunted her.

"I will do anything to get my baby back," Ana said frantically.

"Ah, that is what I wanted to hear," the voice said. "Leon?"

The man holding the duffel stepped forward. Ana eagerly reached for it, but the man pulled it away. He set the bag down on the floor, then took a lethal-looking pistol from a side pocket. Ryder winced at the unseemly juxtaposition of the weapon and the innocent child.

Leon held the gun out to Ana. She stared at it, then at the man who held it, clearly startled.

"Take it," the voice ordered. "Show me how much you want your baby back. Will you truly sacrifice your noble lover?"

Ana gasped as Ryder's stomach clenched. Maybe he wasn't going to get out of this alive after all.

And without ever knowing what it would be like to be Ana's lover.

Oddly, that hurt more than the thought of impending death.

"Take it, sweet Ana. Take it, or I will have Leon use it on the brat."

With another gasp she grabbed the weapon, her gaze fastened on the splash of pink blanket.

"That's better. Now all you have to do is use it. Shoot him."

"You cannot mean that."

"Don't tell me what I can mean," the voice snapped,

sounding provoked. Interesting, Ryder thought. He'd been so blasé until now. Ana went very still, and he wondered if she'd noticed the change, too.

"You expect me to murder in cold blood?"

"I expect you to do what a good little mother would do. Save your child. Another man will come along for you to entice, seduce. You won't miss this one for long."

Ryder was watching Ana's face, trying to guess what she might do. At the same time he was working on the rope, hoping the melodrama playing out would give him cover. But for a moment he stopped sawing at his bonds, when he saw a familiar expression cross Ana's face. The expression he'd learned meant she was thinking, and quickly.

"Why are you doing this?" she asked.

"Do not question me!"

Again the snap, Ryder thought. He went back to working to free himself.

"Why do you wish him dead?"

Ryder wasn't sure what she was doing, asking all these questions, but since it was keeping Leon's eyes off him, he wasn't going to complain.

"He got in my way. Now do it, or you'll never see your baby alive."

"What will you do with her if I do not?"

The voice laughed. "Since she is female, I will train her to do what they are best suited for. And when she is old enough—perhaps thirteen or so—I will sell her to the highest bidder."

Fury spiked through Ryder. He fought it down, sensing that was exactly what the man wanted, that he wanted them provoked and angry...and helpless to do anything. He was feeding on that helplessness as a vampire would feed on the blood of his victims.

"Stop playing with us," Ana exclaimed. "You are like a cat with a mouse."

"Ah, but that is the fun of it, isn't it, *gatita?*"

Something flashed in Ana's eyes as the voice called her kitten. Some combination of knowledge, understanding, and anger that took Ryder's breath away. She looked as if the puzzle had suddenly fallen together in front of her eyes.

She knows, Ryder thought suddenly. She knows who this is.

And that quickly the entire landscape of the situation, and what had happened, shifted. Because there was only one explanation he could think of for her knowledge.

Ana's past had caught up with her.

"Shoot him now, or Leon will take that bag and throw it in the canal."

Ana's hands shook, but she lifted the gun. As if it had just occurred to her, she checked to see if it was truly loaded. Her face went pale, and Ryder guessed that meant it was.

She steadied the weapon with both hands. And slowly, she aimed it at Ryder.

He sucked in a breath, his gaze meeting hers over the sights of the weapon. Tears were brimming in her eyes, and he had the crazy thought that he had to make this easier for her. He couldn't bear the anguish in those beautiful dark eyes another moment.

"It's all right, Ana. I understand," he said.

And waited for her to do what she had to.

Anger, Ana thought, was a very useful emotion. Rage was dangerous, because it made you stop thinking. And she needed to think.

Gatita.

Kitten. Only one person in the world had ever called her that. A sweet, gentle nickname that had, in his hands, become an insult, a taunt, and finally a threat. And it had done so before today, in fact, from the moment she dared to question him, to ask for the truth about his activities, and his connection to her father.

Because she had no doubts; she knew with absolute certainty that her worst fears had materialized. That muffled voice belonged to Alberto Cardenas.

Her former fiancé.

Maria's father.

It was all clear now. Maria's kidnapping had not been a random happening, a crime of opportunity. It had been carefully planned and executed. Not because he wanted his daughter back—he had as little use for women as her father—but because she was his property. And no one stole from Alberto Cardenas.

She should have known better. Alberto would never accept that his woman had escaped from his grasp. It would be too big a blow to his manhood, and he would take it very personally. He had probably been looking for her, no doubt with her father's help, from the moment he'd discovered her gone.

And obviously their criminal network was very good at following orders. She had been a fool to think she could evade them.

But now there was more than her own life at stake. There was her child, the child she had promised to keep safe, to give a good life.

And Ryder.

God, Ryder. He had risked his life for her, and for Maria. And he had come here ready to make the sacrifice, to trade himself for her daughter. Even knowing what would likely happen, that it would probably mean his own death.

And in the moment when he had to believe she would kill him, he had thought only to ease her pain. To tell her he understood.

Determination flooded her. She might have been naïve once, but no more. And she knew she had one thing no one else had. Knowledge. Alberto didn't know for sure she'd guessed who he was. He might wonder if he had betrayed too much, but he thought her a fool and probably too stupid to pick up on it. But even if he did know she had guessed, it did not matter, because that was not the knowledge that mattered.

What mattered was that she knew Alberto, and knew exactly how to provoke him. She knew, as they said in America, how to push his buttons.

And push she would.

She could coax, she thought. Cajole, let him think she was cowed, and would show the proper respect now. He would enjoy making her crawl, she was certain. But would he believe her? She wasn't sure. And it would take too long. He would toy with her endlessly, and every moment with Maria so close and yet out of her reach was sheer agony.

Alberto's hair-trigger temper, on the other hand, was easy to provoke. And since he was obviously already furious with her, she had no doubt that even if she did coax him, the end result would be the same. He would kill Ryder—or make her do it. Then he would kill her, no doubt after reasserting his ownership in the worst possible, most painful and degrading way.

And Maria would be helplessly caught, destined for that horrific future her own father had planned for her.

Ana would not allow it. Alberto clearly thought her so useless, helpless, that he could put a loaded gun in her hands and make her follow his orders simply out of fear. So she would use his bad judgment against him.

"You are right," she said, as if after long consideration. "You are not a cat. Cats are at least brave enough to do their own hunting, kill their own prey."

The voice did not answer, but she heard a hiss as if he had sucked in a breath, coming over the speaker.

"You are a filthy vulture," she said, "a carrion eater, letting someone else do your dirty work."

"Quiet!"

Ana ignored the angry command. Ryder's eyes met hers again, and she saw understanding there once more; he realized what she was doing. She saw him glance around the room, as if noting the position of the two men who had brought them here. One was in front of them next to that priceless duffel bag on the floor and the other behind them, between them and the door through which they had entered. Then he looked at the only other door, the one at the far end of the room, over which the speaker the voice issued from had been placed.

"You hide behind this—" she gestured at the room "—afraid to even set foot in here, for fear a bound man and a useless woman will be too much for you to handle."

The voice swore at her in Spanish, a string of epithets she remembered well.

She heard Ryder whisper, too low for even Leon to hear. "I'm almost loose. Don't second-guess. Just shoot."

Ana's pulse leapt as adrenaline shot through her. She didn't know how he had done it, but it was both of them now, and the odds weren't quite so staggering.

"Coward." She spat out the word, letting every bit of her

contempt show. "Do you think your peons will not spread the word that you were too afraid to face a *woman?*"

Leon shifted uncomfortably, whether at being called a peon, or at the escalating tension Ana neither knew nor cared. She cared only about the black bag at his feet.

"Is that why you left Mexico? They found out your woman had gotten away from you, that you weren't man enough to keep her?"

"You are dead, *puta,* and I will do it with my own hands at your throat!"

She could almost hear the spittle as he shouted the word. Being called a whore again meant nothing to her; what mattered was that she heard the sound of footsteps over the speaker.

When the door beneath the speaker slammed open, things happened fast.

The man in front of them turned, startled to see his boss. Ryder, his hands somehow free, leapt at him, taking him down to the floor and rolling. Rolling him away from Maria, Ana realized as Alberto shouted.

"Shoot him!" he ordered the second man as he rushed toward Ana, his hands outstretched, fingers already curling as if they were around her throat. She wondered that she had ever thought him handsome; he was ugly, his face contorted by the evil at his core.

The second man hesitated, unable to get a clear shot. Ryder slammed the man who had given her the gun against the stone floor, knocking him out, then, in the same swift move, rolled once more and took the second armed man's feet out from under him.

Ana saw it only out of the corner of her eye; she was focused on the man coming at her across the room.

And on what she had to do.

Memories of all he'd done before, of what he'd done now flooded her, steeling her resolve and steadying her hand. She looked into the face of evil, and for a second, hesitated.

Don't second-guess. Just shoot.

She shot.

Chapter 22

Ana cuddled Maria to her breast, the hungry baby suckling with a fierce need that made her weep. She herself leaned against Ryder, sitting on the floor behind her, both she and her baby in the shelter of his arms.

"You're sure she's all right?" Ryder asked, sounding worried.

Ana had quickly checked the baby; she did not appear to have any injuries, but Ana would feel better when a doctor saw her and confirmed this.

"I think so." She smiled as the tiny fists kneaded her breast. She looked up at Ryder. He was watching her with such a rapt, gentle expression that she felt no embarrassment.

"I used to watch you, from a distance, when you would get up in the night to feed her. It was…beautiful."

Odd how the thought did not bother her, she thought. But there was a big difference between watching someone like a spy, and watching over her. She felt nothing but gladness that he had been there for them.

Again.

"I never intended to shoot you," Ana said, feeling suddenly anxious to be sure he knew that.

"If you'd had to, it would have been—" he began, but she hushed him.

"I would not. I knew you would do something, that you would not abandon Maria to such a fate."

He smiled then. "Good thing I learned about razor-edged belt buckles in prison. And that the room was dark enough I could slide the buckle to the back to get at the rope without being spotted."

"How strange, that if you had not been in prison to learn that, we would all be dead now."

He looked bemused all over again, then simply shook his head as if at the serendipity of life.

She frowned when the cell phone rang, destroying the moment. But she knew it was crucial that Ryder talk to the contact he had paged a few minutes before. When he answered, she heard him tell the man what had happened. She held her breath when he described the encounter that had resulted in the shooting; he had wanted to tell them he'd killed Alberto, but Ana refused to allow it, pointing out that a mother acting in defense of her baby was much less likely to be charged with a crime. His contact apparently agreed, as Ryder repeated for her benefit the man's assurances that no charges would be filed.

Ryder explained then what they had found here, not only the workings of the operation Alberto had begun here in Italy, but records outlining the entirety of the operation he had left behind on the Texas border, including names, dates—and most important the location of many of the kidnapped babies.

Ana heard him make arrangements to hand over everything to a local operative. Then he was silent, listening intently. His faced changed, and at last he said a quiet, "Thank you. I will."

He snapped the phone shut, and for a moment just sat there, looking at it.

"What did he say?"

"They're ecstatic," Ryder said with a crooked grin that took her breath away; she'd never seen him look like this, so carefree. "And I'm free."

Ana's eyes widened. "It is done? He said so?"

"He said 'You've got a second chance. Make it good.'" He reached out to stroke her hair. Then, gently, he brushed the back of his fingers over Maria's cheek. "I intend to do just that."

Ana's throat tightened. Soon, they would be busy, she guessed. Talking, explaining, showing what they'd found here. It would take time, no doubt. But she had that now.

And she had Ryder.

Ana sighed, and snuggled up to his warmth.

"I don't understand what happened the night she was born," Ryder said, sounding bemused. "But I feel like…"

"As if she is yours?"

He nodded, looking as if he were about to blush, Ana thought. She found it impossibly endearing.

Just as she found endearing that he'd wanted to take her for that symbol of romance in Venice, a gondola ride. She had to admit there was something quite romantic about it.

But nothing nearly as romantic as Ryder's assumption that of course Maria would come with them, because there was no way he was letting the baby out of his sight again for the foreseeable future.

"I have thought of her that way," she admitted. "As if there would forever be a connection between you and her."

There was a long, silent moment before Ryder said quietly, "And you, Ana?"

She hesitated for a moment, but only to search for the right words. There was no doubt in her mind that she had finally found what she thought would always elude her, a man she could love and trust completely. A man who would always be there for her and for Maria.

And no woman in the world could have had better proof of that than she had received today.

"I can only hope for that for myself," she said at last. "It is up to you."

He kissed her then, and it was everything she had known it would be; passionate, yes, and hot and arousing, but also achingly sweet, and full of a promise that was unlike any she had ever known, because this one she knew she could believe in.

When at last he broke the kiss and drew back, she could barely breathe.

"Do you want me, Ana?"

"So much," she answered, meaning it with all her heart and body, looking up into the dark, piercing eyes that had been the thing she remembered most about him from the night Maria was born.

He tightened his arms around her then, and she felt a tremor go through him. It thrilled her in a new sort of way, and she realized that this was only the beginning.

"When the doctor says it's all right…it will be good, Ana. I promise."

"I already know this," she said, feeling lighthearted enough to tease him a little.

As the oddly shaped boat moved along the canal, the

gondolier maintaining a discreet silence and distance, Ryder held her quietly for a long time.

"Do you believe in miracles, Ana?" he finally asked.

"I believe in you," she said.

"I've never been worth that," he said. "But now…"

"You have changed."

"I have." He shook his head. "I have my life back. And you and Maria to share it with. How lucky can one guy get?"

"You will be luckier yet," Ana promised.

"Can't be," Ryder said with a chuckle.

"Yes," Ana insisted. "Because soon you will have your brother and sister back."

Ryder went still.

"They will know what you have done, and they will see the man you have become. And they will accept you for who you are now, and forgive whatever you might have been in the past. You will have the homecoming you deserve. This is my promise to you, Ryder Grady Colton."

For a long, silent moment he just looked at her. She held his gaze, letting every bit of what she was feeling show.

He threw back his head and laughed, a loud, joyous laugh unlike anything she'd ever heard from him. It lifted her heart and her hopes, told her she was right, that together they could conquer anything.

"If anyone can do that, you can," he said.

"I will," she said determinedly.

"Damn. Boots is going to give me that smug, I-told-you-so look again," Ryder said.

She wasn't sure what that meant, but she was too content at the moment to ask. Later. Nothing mattered just now except that the three of them were here, together, and safe.

It didn't matter, Ana thought as the sunset turned the

water to fire and they floated under the famous Bridge of Sighs, that they were at the moment living a romantic cliché.

Clichés, she thought, became clichés because they were the best way to express something.

And the best way she could think of to express what she was feeling right now, was to kiss the man she loved.

So she did.

"…Colton campaign's swing through Texas is being anticipated with great excitement, now that disgraced Governor Daniels is out of the election picture."

The man watching the television report grinned. A dark, roiling sort of joy filled him. He nearly laughed aloud with glee as he watched the video clip of the candidate moving through the crowd, shaking hands, smiling, eating up the adulation like the pig he was.

It was all coming together. The two people at the top of his list, the two people he most wanted within his grasp, were both going to be within reach at the same time. Obviously he was on the right track, this was meant to be.

This was the time, and the place. All his work, all his planning, was finally going to bring him his soul's deepest desire.

He would finally have his payback.

* * * * *

A HERO OF HER OWN

BY
CARLA CASSIDY

Carla Cassidy is an award-winning author who has written more than fifty novels. In 1998, she won a Career Achievement Award for Best Innovative Series.

Carla believes the only thing better than curling up with a good book to read is sitting down at the computer with a good story to write. She's looking forward to writing many more books and bringing hours of pleasure to readers.

Chapter 1

Jewel Mayfair shot up, heart pounding and panic suffocating her with a thick press against her chest. Her bedroom was dark except for the glow from a nightlight plugged into the socket on the wall opposite her bed.

She stared at the light, willing her heartbeat to slow and drawing deep, even breaths to calm down. She'd had the dream again. No, not a dream, it was a nightmare that had plagued her for over two years, ever since the car accident that had taken the life of her fiancé.

Andrew! Her heart cried his name as she remembered the last night they'd had together. Everything had been so perfect. She'd picked him up in her car

and they'd gone to their favorite restaurant where
he'd surprised her with a proposal, complete with a
beautiful ring. And she'd surprised him with some
news of her own.

Her hands moved to her flat abdomen. The accident hadn't just taken Andrew from her. It had also
taken Andrew's child, who had been growing inside
her. Grief pierced her, as rich and raw as it had been
when she'd awakened in the hospital after the accident and been told of all that she had lost.

Slowly her breathing returned to normal and she
glanced at the clock on her nightstand. Just after
midnight. She'd been asleep for less than an hour and
she knew from experience that sleep would be a long
time coming again.

She slid her long legs over the side of the bed and
grabbed the thin robe on the chair nearby. She belted
the robe over her short nightgown, then opened the
doors that led out of her master bedroom and onto a
covered porch.

Despite the hour, the late August heat fell around
her like an oppressive veil. Ahead of her was the
pool and beyond was the woods that was part of the
Hopechest Ranch estate.

In the last six months since coming to Esperanza,
Texas, she and the woods had become intimate
friends. It was among the tall oaks and thick brush
that she spent hours each night when she couldn't
sleep. And lately that had been almost every night.

The chlorine scent of the pool hung in the air as

she walked around it to the gate in the back. Opening the gate she paused and looked at the house.

It was still hard for her to believe that she was here in Esperanza, running a ranch for troubled children. The Hopechest Ranch was housed in a beautiful Spanish-style structure made of adobe with a tiled roof.

Jewel had her own quarters and there were four additional bedrooms for the children and a married couple, Jeff and Cheryl Cookson, who were part of the staff.

Seeing no lights on and knowing that if any of the children awakened, the Cooksons would take care of things, she walked out of the gate and into the cooler air beneath the trees.

A light breeze ruffled her short, sun-streaked brown hair as she walked down a well-worn path. She tried to erase from her mind the horrifying visions that haunted her sleep far too often. She was exhausted. Her insomnia was getting worse instead of better.

It was ironic that her job as a psychologist at the ranch was to help children heal from trauma and deal with problems, but for the life of her she couldn't figure out how to heal herself.

She stopped walking and leaned with her back against a huge oak trunk. Closing her eyes, she wondered if she'd ever get a full night's sleep again, if the haunting dreams would ever stop. She'd hoped that by moving from Prosperino, California, she'd leave behind the haunting memories of that accident and her loss. But they'd chased her here and if anything had gotten more intrusive over the last five months.

"Jewel."

Her eyes popped open and she froze, every muscle in her body rigid. Had somebody just uttered her name? Or had it been the wind and an overactive imagination? Her heart banged a more rapid beat as she gazed around her.

The warm night turned icy around her as she cocked her head to listen, narrowed her eyes to see. "Hello?" she said, the word no more than a whisper.

The moonlight was full, spilling down enough light to illuminate the path, but not able to pierce the darkness of the thick woods.

"Jewel."

She gasped. Even though she knew it was impossible, that deep male voice sounded like Andrew's.

"Andrew?" she half whispered his name as tears stung her eyes. She sensed more than saw a form just off to her right. "Andrew, is that you?" Her head filled with wild thoughts.

He hadn't really died in the car accident. It had all been a terrible mixup, a case of mistaken identity. Somehow he'd survived and he'd come here to find her.

"Andrew, wait!" she exclaimed as she saw the shadowy form moving deeper into the woods. Her heart was now pounding so hard it made her half-breathless.

Her mind went blank as she waded through brush and stepped around tree trunks. She had to find him. She was certain the voice she'd heard calling her name was Andrew's. She didn't know how that was possible, didn't care. All she wanted to do was to get to him, to feel his arms around her once again.

Goose bumps rose on her skin and she was half-dizzy as she fought the underbrush, felt the prickly bite of it against her bare legs.

She stumbled into a low-hanging branch. The whack of the limb across her forehead jarred her back to reality. And the reality was that she was in the middle of the woods chasing after a ghost.

The figure she'd been chasing was gone…or had never been there, she thought. Fighting back new tears of despair, she turned and screamed as she bumped into a solid male chest.

"Jewel. It's me. Quinn Logan." His big hands grabbed her shoulders. "Are you all right? I heard you scream."

"I bumped into a tree branch." Her voice sounded far away and she mentally shook herself in an effort to get grounded.

"Come on, let's get back on the path," he said. He dropped his hands from her shoulders, but took one of her hands in his and led her back to the path.

As her mental fog lifted, she jerked her hand from his and stared at him, his handsome features visible in the full moonlight.

He had a mane of brown hair, with flecks of gold and auburn that enhanced his lean features. A scar across one of his cheeks did nothing to detract from his appeal. His topaz eyes glowed feline and, as always when Jewel looked at him, a crazy fluttering went off in her tummy.

"What are you doing out here in the middle of the night, Dr. Logan?" she asked warily. Quinn was the local veterinarian. At six foot three, he had broad shoulders and a quiet simmering energy and strength that made people believe he could handle anything a large animal might do.

"Quinn," he said. "Please make it Quinn, and unfortunately sometimes animals don't get sick during normal business hours. I've been over at Clay's place dealing with a colicky horse." Clay Colton was Jewel's cousin and he lived on the large spread next to the Hopechest Ranch.

"Is the horse all right?" she asked, and wrapped her arms around herself, unable to get back the warmth she'd felt before she'd heard that ghostly voice. Had Quinn been the shape she'd seen in the woods? Had he softly called her name?

"The horse is fine. I'm more concerned about you. You said you hit your head?" He placed two warm fingers beneath her chin and raised her face toward the light. Butterflies went off in her stomach at his touch.

"I'm fine," she said stiffly, and backed away from him.

He reached up and shoved a strand of his hair back from his eyes, gazing at her curiously. "What are you doing out here in the middle of the night?"

She hesitated a moment, then decided to be truthful. "I was having some trouble sleeping and thought maybe a walk outside would help."

"How about I walk you back to your place and see you safely inside?"

"No, thanks. That isn't necessary," she protested. She felt off balance, shocked to find him wandering the woods and still confused by thinking she'd heard somebody call her name.

All she wanted to do was get back to the house and into the safety of her own room. At the moment she felt distinctly unsafe, even though Quinn didn't appear threatening in any way.

"I'll just say good night now," she said. She whirled around and hurried back in the direction of the house, grateful when he didn't try to stop her.

She didn't relax until she was settled in her room with the doors locked. She lingered at the door, peering outside, but there was no sign of anyone—ghosts or otherwise.

Moving away from the door, she took off her robe and climbed back into bed. Her heart still thudded with adrenaline and she knew sleep would be far off, if at all.

She'd gone a little crazy out in the woods, thinking that she heard Andrew's voice calling her, believing for a moment that he was someplace out there in the dark woods.

Or was it possible that Quinn had been playing a cruel game with her? She frowned as she thought of the handsome vet. She'd only run into him a half a dozen times since her arrival in town and usually that was out at Clay's place. But, on each of those occasions, she'd been acutely aware of him, had felt more than a little bit of attraction.

There had been a moment when his warm hands had been on her shoulders when she'd wanted to throw herself against him, feel the heat and strength of his arms enfolding her in an embrace.

She closed her eyes and remembered the sensation of his fingers beneath her chin. It had been so long since a man had touched her in any way. Was it any wonder she'd reacted to his simple touches?

She didn't know what worried her more, the fact that she might be losing her mind or that she was attracted to a man who might, for whatever reason, be playing games with her sanity?

Mornings were chaotic at the Hopechest Ranch and the next morning was no different. The sounds of childish laughter awakened Jewel just after seven and she blessed Cheryl and Jeff Cookson who would be in the kitchen preparing breakfast for the seven children who were currently residents.

The children's ages ranged from ten to thirteen, the eldest a girl who had arrived the previous day from Chicago.

Jewel would have a session with the girl, named Kelsey Cameron, this morning. Jewel had official therapy sessions with each child twice a week, but at the Hopechest Ranch therapy never stopped. Every activity, every conversation provided therapy to heal wounds, buoy self-confidence and get the children on the road to happy, healthy lives.

As Jewel showered and dressed for the day, her mind wandered back to those minutes in the woods with Quinn. Even though she was relatively new to the town, she knew Quinn's story. Clay had told her about how several years ago Quinn had diagnosed one of Clay's horses with a disease that had threatened the rest of the stock. Clay had been forced to put down the prized stud. At the time most of the other local ranchers had thought Quinn's diagnosis was wrong.

Ultimately, Quinn had been vindicated, but not before both his reputation and his practice had taken major hits. Clay had stood by his friend and never missed an opportunity to tell Jewel that Quinn was a great guy.

So what was that great guy doing skulking around the woods last night? If he'd gone to Clay's to take care of a sick horse, why hadn't he driven his truck over instead of making the long trek by foot from his place to Clay's?

Once she left her room, there was no more time for thoughts of Quinn. Breakfast was followed by the counseling session with Kelsey Cameron. The young teenager had come to Hopechest Ranch after four years of being shuttled from family member to family member. Her mother, a drug addict, had just awakened one morning and decided she didn't want to be a mother anymore. One of Kelsey's aunts had contacted Jewel. She was worried about the girl, who had become more angry and withdrawn with each passing day.

Jewel got little from Kelsey, but hadn't expected much in the first session. Besides, today was riding-lesson day, something the children all enjoyed. It was a perfect way for Kelsey to start feeling like a member of their "family."

After lunch, when the children all piled into the minibus, Jewel drove next door to Clay Colton's ranch, the Bar None. As she went the short distance, the kids chattered with excitement, talking about the horses they would ride and Burt Walker, their instructor. She glanced in the rearview mirror and saw that Kelsey sat, staring out the van window, looking as if she'd rather be anywhere else.

The three-hundred-acre Bar None ranch was one of the most successful horse ranches in the area. Clay Colton was one of three illegitimate children of Graham Colton and a pretty rodeo rider named Mary Lynn Grady. Clay was a solid, responsible man and since coming to town Jewel had grown to love him like a brother.

She drove past the two-story ranch house and headed toward the stables. Her stomach did a crazy two-step as she recognized Quinn's black pickup parked nearby. She raised a hand to her hair, momentarily wishing she'd taken more time with it that morning. The thought irritated her and she quickly dropped her hand and parked the bus in front of the stables.

As the children piled out of the bus, Burt walked over to greet them. He was a slender man who'd once been a champion barrel racer. He now worked for Clay and conducted the riding lessons.

"The horses have been waiting for you," he exclaimed to the kids. "They told me last night how much they were looking forward to giving you all a good ride today."

Barry Lundon, a ten-year-old with anxiety issues, widened his eyes. "They talk to you?"

Sam Taylor nudged Barry with his shoulder. "Don't be a baby," he said with his twelve-year-old wisdom. "Horses don't talk."

"Of course they do," Burt said. "They just don't use the same kind of language that we do. Come on, let's get inside and get you all saddled up and I'll tell you about horse language." He winked at Jewel, then led the kids to the second stable.

They'd all just disappeared when Clay, Tamara and Quinn walked out of the building directly in front of her. "I thought I heard the chatter of little voices," Clay said with a warm smile.

"We were just headed to the house for some lemonade," Tamara said. Tamara Brown was Clay's ex-wife. They'd divorced five years ago and she'd become a CSI agent in San Antonio. They'd reunited when a body had been found in a ravine on Clay's ranch and Tamara had been part of the investigating team.

"How are you, Jewel?" Quinn's deep voice evoked memories from the night before when his strong, warm fingers had touched her chin and she'd felt the ridiculous need to jump right into his arms.

"Fine. Just fine," she replied. He looked as attractive this morning as he had the night before in the moonlight. The sun shimmered on his long, thick brown hair finding blond highlights that looked warm and soft. Jewel knew that he was forty-four years old, five years older than she was, but he had an underlying energy that made him seem younger than his years.

"Beautiful day," he said.

"Yes, it's lovely," she replied.

"Before you know it, winter will be here."

Tamara released a tiny sigh of impatience. "You two can stand out here in the heat and talk about the weather until the cows come home. I'm going up to the house for a glass of lemonade." She turned on her heels and headed for the house.

Clay stared after her with the eyes of a man who loved what he saw. *Andrew once looked at me that way,* Jewel thought. She didn't know if she'd ever be ready to pursue a relationship with another man, but she had to admit there were times she missed having somebody look at her that way, as if she were the most important person on the face of the earth.

Clay turned back to face them. "You two coming?"

"I can't," Quinn said as he glanced at his watch. "I've got an appointment in about fifteen minutes.

I've got to get going." Once again he turned his gaze to Jewel. "It was nice seeing you again."

She nodded, those crazy butterflies taking wing in her stomach once again. "You, too."

She and Clay watched as he got into his pickup truck. She was grateful Quinn hadn't mentioned their midnight meeting. She didn't really want Clay to know that she often walked the woods between their places because she suffered nightmares. Her job was healing. She didn't want anyone to find out that she couldn't heal herself.

"He's such a nice guy," Clay said as Quinn's pickup headed down the gravel lane. "And such a talented vet."

"Speaking of vets, I heard you had a horse down last night," she said.

He frowned at her. "A horse down last night? I don't know where you heard that, but it's not true. My stock is all healthy."

He'd lied. Quinn had lied to her the night before. The warmth of the sun on her shoulders couldn't quite warm the chill that suddenly gripped her.

What had Quinn been doing in those woods the night before, and why had he lied?

Chapter 2

From the moment Jewel had first stepped inside Clay's white wood-frame, two-story home she'd felt the warm welcome it offered. She followed Clay into the wide entry hall and to the rear of the house where a farm-style kitchen opened into a family room.

The family room held two leather couches that faced each other in front of a massive stone fireplace. Western antiques dotted the room, a wagon-wheel coffee table, two lanterns from the 1800s and a framed torn Texas flag that was reported to have flown at the Alamo. The end result was a feeling of old and new, of warmth and permanence.

They didn't go into the family room but instead

stopped in the kitchen, where Tamara had already poured lemonade for them.

"Where's Quinn?" she asked as Clay and Tamara sat at the round oak table.

"He left. He said he had an appointment," Clay explained.

Tamara served their drinks, then joined them at the table. "Did I see a new little face out there this morning?"

Jewel nodded. "Kelsey Cameron. She arrived yesterday from Chicago. Mother a drug addict, father unknown, poor thing has been shuffled from relative to relative for the last four years."

"You'll work your magic, and when she leaves here, she'll have a new sense of self-worth and be wonderfully well-adjusted," Clay said.

Jewel smiled. "You make it sound so easy."

"That's because you make it look easy," Tamara exclaimed. "Your rapport with those kids amazes me."

Jewel waved a hand to dismiss the topic, embarrassed by their praise. "Have you heard that Joe and Meredith are planning a visit?"

Clay leaned back in his chair and nodded. "One of the last stops on the campaign trail."

"I have a feeling the Coltons will be spending Christmases at the White House," Tamara said.

"Uncle President," Clay mused. "Has a nice ring to it."

Jewel laughed. "He's still a few months from winning the presidential election."

"Shouldn't be a problem, especially now that Allan Daniels is out of the running," Clay replied.

Allan Daniels was the current governor of Texas and had been Joe Colton's hottest competition for their party's nomination until his true character had been exposed. Dirty dealing and bribery had effectively neutralized Daniels's threat to Joe's candidacy.

For the next fifteen minutes they talked about the election and how well Joe Colton was doing in the polls. That led to a discussion of politics in general and then the talk turned to more family news.

The Colton family tree was a complicated one. Joe and Meredith had five children of their own and had fostered seven. Jewel's mother, Patsy, who was Meredith's twin sister, had kidnapped Meredith and pretended to be Joe's wife for ten years, giving him three more children. Graham, Joe's brother had two children with his wife, Cynthia, then had indulged in an affair with Mary Lynn Grady and they'd had three children.

Sometimes when Jewel thought about the history of the Colton clan her head hurt, especially when she thought of her own mother, Patsy, who had done horrible things and eventually died in a mental hospital.

Jewel tried not to think of her mother too often. She preferred to think about Charlie and Ruth Baylor, the couple who had adopted her and given her a wonderfully normal Midwestern upbringing. Unfortunately, the couple had since passed away.

"Hello! Anybody home?" The familiar female

voice was followed by the sound of boots against the tile entry floor.

"In the kitchen," Tamara yelled.

Clay's younger sister, Georgie, strode into the kitchen, bringing with her the high energy that was as much a part of her as the waist-length red braid that bobbed down her back. Following at her heels was her husband, Nick Sheffield.

"Georgie, Nick." Clay motioned them toward the table. "Have a seat, we're just enjoying some lemonade and local gossip."

"Hi, Jewel. Saw your kids outside in the corral. Got any future champion riders in the bunch?" Georgie asked. Georgie had spent most of her life on the rodeo circuit as a champion barrel racer. Even the birth of Emmie, her daughter, five years ago hadn't stopped her from competing.

"I don't think so." She laughed. "From what I've seen of them, most are just hanging on to the saddle horn for dear life."

Georgie's green eyes seemed to sparkle with more liveliness than usual as she looked back at her brother. "I've got a surprise for you."

"You know I don't like surprises," Clay returned.

Georgie laughed. "You'll like this one." She turned in the direction of the front door. "Come on in," she yelled.

Jewel's eyes widened as Clay's brother, Ryder, appeared. Next to him was Ana Morales, a Mexican woman who had worked for Jewel before her baby was kidnapped in a black-market ring. Ana held the baby girl in her arms and wore the smile of a woman in love as she gazed up at Ryder.

Clay stood, his face reflecting myriad emotions. Jewel knew the history between the two men, that Ryder's bad-boy lifestyle had led to Clay washing his hands of his younger brother. Jewel knew how painful it had been for Clay to shut his brother out, how tormented he'd been by the difficult decision. But Ryder had turned his life around when he'd been sent to a correctional facility and offered a chance to work undercover for the CIA. He'd cracked open a black-market baby-trafficking operation, saving Ana's little girl and falling in love in the process. During this time, Clay had thought his brother was dead, had grieved for his and the family's loss. Now they had a second chance.

"Hi, Clay," Ryder said, his voice husky with emotion.

There was a moment of charged hesitation, then Clay took two steps forward and embraced his brother. Tears filled Jewel's eyes. Tamara's eyes were suspiciously bright, as well.

Jewel jumped up and hugged Ana. "I've missed you so much," she said. She and Ana had formed a friendship while Ana had worked for her. Jewel cooed over the baby, then stepped back.

It seemed that suddenly everyone was talking at once and in the melee Tamara shocked everyone by confessing that she and Clay had eloped and were married.

As a new round of hugging and backslapping began, Jewel slid out of the room and then out of the house, wanting to leave the family alone for their reunion.

She had a feeling that the issues that had torn Clay and Ryder apart were behind them and the brothers were on their way to building a new, close relationship. She was thrilled for them, but as she walked toward the stables a new sense of loneliness weighed her down.

Clay and Tamara were married and it had been obvious by the glow on Ana's face that she and Ryder were probably not far behind. There seemed to be a marriage epidemic breaking out in Esperanza. But Jewel had not caught the bug, and felt immune to anything even remotely romantic.

On more than one occasion Deputy Adam Rawlings had made it clear that he was interested in pursuing a romantic relationship with her. They'd seen each other socially several times but, try as she might, she just didn't feel more than friendship for him. Besides, with the nightmares she'd been suffering on a regular basis, she was probably better off alone. No man would want to spend his nights with her while she was haunted by ghosts from her past.

She dismissed all thoughts of romance from her mind as she entered the stables. The kids were just finishing up brushing down their horses and Burt approached her with a friendly smile.

"They're just about done," he said.

"How did Kelsey do?" she asked, hoping the new girl had opened up a bit.

"Never said a word to anyone, but she's got a natural seat in the saddle. She grow up around horses?"

"No, just the opposite. She's an inner-city kid, probably has never been on a horse in her life," Jewel replied.

Burt looked over to where Kelsey was working on the horse, a look of fierce concentration on her face. "She shows all the signs of being a born rider. I hope she sticks around long enough for me to work with her more extensively."

"She's not going anywhere for a while. We've got lots of work to do with her," Jewel replied.

It took another half an hour to get all the children loaded into the bus and headed back the short distance to the Hopechest Ranch. The noise level was just below that of a jet engine as they all chatted about their horses and the riding experience. The only one who didn't say a word was Kelsey, who stared out the window as if she were lost in a world of her own.

Jewel was determined to break into that world. It wasn't just her job, it was a calling from her very soul.

"Everybody out and you can have free time play in the garage until dinnertime," Jewel said as she parked in front of the house. One section of the three-car garage had been turned into a playroom, complete with toys and games and craft items.

All the kids headed for the garage except Kelsey, who lingered behind. "Is it okay if I just go to my room?" she asked.

Jewel would have preferred she go with the other children and interact, but she also knew it was going to take some time for Kelsey to feel safe here, to feel as if she were part of the group.

She placed a hand on the girl's shoulder. "That's fine. Dinner is at five-thirty so make sure you're in the kitchen by then."

Kelsey nodded and headed inside. Jewel lingered outside, fighting a wave of exhaustion. The restless nights and bad dreams were getting more frequent, and more difficult to handle.

She raised her face to the warmth of the sun and once again thought about romance. Maybe she was incapable of loving anyone. Maybe the love she'd had for Andrew had been all she had and once it had been given she'd been left empty.

Of course, that didn't explain the odd tingle of excitement she felt whenever she was around Quinn. Female hormones reminding her that she was alive—that's all it was, she told herself.

It was impossible for her to fall in love again, especially with her past visiting her every night in the form of nightmares.

Voices in the night. Visions in the woods. Equally as haunting as the dreams was the fear that somehow she was slowly falling into the mental illness that had consumed her mother.

* * *

"She should be just fine," Quinn assured Ralph Smith, a local rancher who had called him about a cow who had gotten caught in some barbed wire. "All the wounds are superficial and now that I've cleaned her up and applied antibiotic cream, she shouldn't have any problems."

He slapped the rear of the big animal and with a low moo she headed back toward the pasture. "I'd definitely do something about that barbed wire."

Ralph frowned toward a stand of trees and brush. "I didn't even know it was there, just tangled up in all the weeds, but I'll get it out of here today."

Together the two men walked toward the gate in the fence. Initially, coming out here and meeting up with Ralph had been awkward. Ralph had been one of the loudest, most critical ranchers when Quinn had been forced to put down Clay Colton's prized stud.

It had been the second-darkest time in Quinn's life. The darkest had been when he'd lost his wife, Sarah, to cancer.

Even though Quinn had been proven right in his diagnosis of the disease that had infected Clay's stud, even thought his decision to put the horse down had probably saved the rest of the stock, Quinn had never quite gotten over how quickly some of the locals had turned on him.

The fact that Ralph had called him to come and check out the cow was an olive branch he had extended to Quinn. It had been a long time coming, but Quinn wasn't a man to hold a grudge. Life was too damned short.

"Just let me know if the wounds begin to ooze or look infected and I'll come back out," Quinn said as he reached the door of his pickup truck.

"I appreciate it, Doc." Ralph held out his hand and the two men shook.

Minutes later as Quinn drove away from the Smith ranch and back toward town, he thought about those dark days when many in the town had turned their backs on him, made darker because he was still grieving for his wife. At the time all he had was his work and when that took a hit, he considered packing up and leaving Esperanza.

Instead, with the support of the Coltons, Clay in particular, he'd stayed and held his head high. When his decision to put the stud down had been vindicated, he'd put the whole ordeal behind him and got on with his life.

As he drove down Main Street, he decided to stop for dinner at Miss Sue's Café, where he took many of his evening meals. He told himself it was because he hated to cook, but the truth was he dreaded the evening hours spent alone.

An old-fashioned cowbell heralded his arrival as he entered the quaint café. "You're a bit early today, Quinn," Becky French, the owner of the establishment, greeted him with a warm smile.

He smiled at the short, plump woman. "It's never

too early for a good meal." He walked over to one of the wooden tables by the window and sat in a chair where he could easily see out the window.

"Got some new pictures," Becky said as she poured him a cup of coffee. There was nothing Becky loved more than to show off pictures of her grandchildren. She set the coffeepot down and dug into her apron pocket to withdraw a handful of photos.

Quinn took them from her and studied each of the smiling childish faces. "They're beautiful," he said.

Becky smiled and nodded. "They are." She tucked the photos back in her apron. "I'll just give you a few minutes. The special is smothered steak and mashed potatoes."

"Then I don't need a minute. That sounds good." He returned the menu and leaned back in the chair to sip his coffee. She scurried away, the gray bun on top of her head bobbing with her brisk walk.

Kids. At one time Quinn had hoped to have a house full, but fate and cancer had stolen that dream from him. He and Sarah had never had a chance for children.

Even though it was early, there were already other diners in the café. Quinn had never been in the place when there weren't at least a handful of people. Most mealtimes the place was packed.

He'd just finished his coffee when Georgie Sheffield, her husband, Nick, and her daughter, little Emmie, came through the door.

"I hear we just missed you this morning at Clay's,"

Georgie said to him. "We had a reunion. Ryder and Ana are back in town and we took them to Clay's." Georgie's green eyes sparkled brightly. "It was wonderful."

Emmie sidled up next to Quinn. At five years old, the little girl was the spitting image of her mother. Her red hair was cut pixielike to frame her face and she was dressed just like her mama in jeans, a Western-style shirt and cowboy boots.

Emmie was bright and precocious and had spent most of her young life on the rodeo circuit with her mother. The little girl considered Quinn a special friend because he fixed horses when they got sick and there were few things Emmie loved more than horses and cowboys.

"Excuse me, Mommy, but I want to talk to Mr. Quinn," Emmie said. Georgie smiled with amusement and nodded. "Guess what happens next week?"

"I can't imagine. What?" Quinn replied.

She leaned closer, bringing with her the scent of sunshine and childhood. "School begins."

"Ah." Quinn smiled at her. "And what are you, in the second grade, the third?"

"Maybe I should be because you know I can already read," Emmie exclaimed. She leaned even closer. "But, truly it's going to be my very first day of kindergarten." A fierce look of determination crossed her petite features. "And I'm going to make one new friend, even if he or she isn't a cowboy."

"I think that sounds like a wonderful plan," Quinn said.

Emmie turned to her mother and Nick. "And now I'll go pick us out a table."

As she left the adults behind, Georgie offered Quinn a weak smile. "I can't believe she's starting school. She's so comfortable around adults. Her friends have always been rodeo cowboys. I just hope she fits in okay." Her eyes clouded and sparkled with sudden tears of worry.

"I'm sure she'll be just fine," Quinn said.

"Of course she will," Nick agreed, and placed an arm around Georgie's shoulder. "She's as strong as her mother and almost as pretty."

Georgie laughed and leaned into Nick. He grinned at Quinn. "You just wait, maybe someday you'll have to live through the trauma of the first day of school."

As the two of them joined Emmie, who had chosen a table toward the back of the café, Quinn thought about what Nick had said.

He and Sarah had talked about having children one day, but before that dream had been realized she'd been diagnosed with the malignant aggressive brain tumor that had taken her in six short months. They'd had only nine months of marriage before her diagnosis.

Sarah had been a quiet, thoughtful woman and when she died, she did so as quietly and unassumingly as she had lived. He'd grieved deep and hard for a long time. Now when he thought of Sarah, the sharp despair was gone and he was left with a loneliness and a growing desire to get on with his life.

"Here we are," Becky said as she delivered his

meal. "Anything else I can do for you?" she asked as she poured him another cup of coffee.

"No, thanks. I'm good."

"You're not good," Becky replied, her blue eyes sparkling with the liveliness that was her trademark. "You know I'm not happy unless I'm minding everyone's business but my own. You need a woman, Quinn. You spend far too much time at this table all alone—no offense."

He laughed. "None taken. I was just sitting here thinking the same thing."

"We've got a lot of nice single women in this town who'd love to see you socially. You're that strong, silent type. A little bit of that is quite romantic, but too much of it puts off the ladies."

"I'll keep that in mind," Quinn replied. It was impossible to be offended by Becky's advice because he knew how well intentioned it was.

As she left his table, his thoughts turned to the woman he'd met in the woods the night before. Jewel. From the moment he'd first met her, she'd intrigued him.

Certainly he found her amazingly attractive with her short, tousled, streaked golden-brown hair and big brown eyes. Although slender, she had curves in all the right places and legs that seemed to go on forever.

Last night wasn't the first time he'd seen her wandering the woods around the Hopechest Ranch, although it was the first time he'd let her know he was there.

Quinn had a feeling he and Jewel suffered from the same afflictions—insomnia and loneliness. Quinn often spent the nighttime hours at Clay's place where he boarded his horse, Noches.

What he didn't understand was what had made Jewel scream in the woods the night before and why she'd looked positively haunted when he'd encountered her.

Chapter 3

As the purple shadows of twilight began to deepen, a responding tension filled Jewel. It wasn't natural for the coming of night to bring something that tasted very much like suppressed terror into the back of her throat.

Jeff and Cheryl were in the process of getting the kids ready for bed and Jewel sat at the kitchen table making a list of school supplies she needed to purchase before school began next week.

When she finished her list, she would tuck each of the children in for the night. Those minutes just before bedtime, when she connected with each of the children with a good-night kiss and a wish for sweet dreams, was an important part of the routine of love that abounded at the ranch.

A knock sounded on the front door and she looked at the clock. Although it felt much later, it was only just after seven.

She hurried to the front door and opened it to see Deputy Adam Rawlings. As usual not a strand of his dark brown hair was out of place and he was impeccably dressed in his khaki uniform. "Hi, Adam."

"I was just out making rounds and thought I'd stop by and say hello," he said.

Jewel flipped on the outside light and stepped out on the porch to join him. "Quiet night?" she asked.

"Most of them are quiet," he replied. "Not that I'm complaining. I heard you've got a new boarder. How's that working out?"

She nodded. "A thirteen-year-old girl named Kelsey from Chicago. If you'd asked me yesterday how things were going I would have said not well. She was quiet and withdrawn. But today she appears more open. She loved the riding lessons at Clay's yesterday and wanted to know when we'd be going again." She broke off as she realized she was beginning to ramble.

"How's everything else going?" he asked. His gaze narrowed slightly. "You look tired."

"I am," she admitted. "I was just sitting at the table, thinking about everything I need to buy for the kids to start school next week." She smiled. "Trying to figure out school supplies for seven kids in seven different classes is enough to make anyone tired."

"I'll let you get back to it. I just thought I'd check

in and see how you were doing." He shifted his muscular body from one foot to the other. "If you get a minute to yourself and want to get dinner out or maybe see a movie, you know all you have to do is just call me."

She smiled. "Thank you, Adam. I'll keep that in mind."

They said goodbye and then she watched as he left the porch and walked back to his patrol car. He seemed like such a nice man, good-looking and obviously interested in her. Unfortunately, she just didn't feel anything for him except a mild friendship.

As his car pulled away, she went back inside to the kitchen table. She finished making her list and by then it was time to kiss the kids good-night.

She went into the boys' bedroom first. The room held two bunk beds and at the moment all four sleeping places were occupied. Barry and Sam, the two older boys, had the top bunks and eight-year-old Jimmy Nigel and seven-year-old Caleb Torrel had the lower bunks.

"All tucked in?" she asked Barry as she approached him first.

He nodded. "Will you keep the nightlight on?" he asked anxiously. "I'm not scared or anything, but I just don't like the dark."

Jewel smiled at the dark-eyed boy. They had this same conversation every night. "The nightlight will be on until morning. Sleep tight, Barry."

As she moved from Barry to Sam and then to the

two younger boys, she couldn't help but think of the baby she'd lost. She'd desperately wanted to be a mother, had been thrilled to discover she was pregnant. The minute the doctor had confirmed what she'd suspected, her heart had filled with a happiness she'd never known before and hadn't known since.

As she moved from the boys' room to the girls', she shoved away thoughts of the baby she'd lost and dreams of what might have been.

There were three girls in residence at the moment. Kelsey slept on the top bunk of one of the beds and on the lower bunks were Lindy Walker and Carrie Lyndon, both ten years old.

Jewel went to Kelsey first. She didn't touch the girl in any way, wouldn't invade Kelsey's personal space unless she was invited to do so. "Ready to call it a night?"

Kelsey nodded, her green eyes less guarded than they'd been the day before. "I'm not used to going to bed so early."

Jewel smiled. "We believe in the routine of early to bed, early to rise around here. Besides, with school starting next week, it's important that all of you get plenty of sleep."

Jewel moved to the other beds, where the girls demanded good-night kisses and hugs, then she left the room and turned out the light. As in the boys' room, a small nightlight burned in a wall socket.

She met Cheryl in the hallway and smiled tiredly. "Another day done," she said.

Cheryl returned her smile and swept a strand of her long, dark hair behind an ear. "I wanted to run an idea by you. Jeff and I would like to plan a day trip for the kids in the next couple of weeks. There's a Native American museum two hours from here and we thought it would be fun to visit the museum and have a picnic lunch at a nearby park."

"Sounds like something they would enjoy," Jewel replied.

"We haven't finalized a day yet, I just wanted to put a bug in your ear about it."

"Let me know what you and Jeff decide and we'll work out the details."

Cheryl nodded. "Then I'll just say good night."

As Cheryl headed toward the front bedroom where she and Jeff slept, Jewel returned to the kitchen. She tucked into her purse the list of supplies she needed to buy, then once again sat at the table to make notes in the files she kept on each of the children.

Busywork. In the back of her mind she knew that's what she was doing, creating work to keep her mind off the fact that soon it would be time to go to bed.

To sleep.

To dream.

Again the taste of dread mingled with a simmering terror. If only she could have one night of peaceful sleep and happy dreams. If only she could wake up in the morning well-rested and happy.

If only Andrew hadn't died in the car accident.

She sighed and focused back on the files in front

of her. These were her children, the ones who came to Hopechest Ranch in need of stability and love. They were all she needed. And maybe a good night's sleep was vastly overrated.

She didn't know how long she'd sat working when she heard a strange scratching sound. She got up from the table and followed the noise to the front door. Definitely sounded like something scratching for attention.

Equally curious and wary, she unlocked the door and cracked it open. The door shoved inward and a chocolate-colored dog jumped up at her. In surprise she stumbled backward and fell on her behind. The dog licked her face as if she were a long-lost friend that he was thrilled to see again.

"Okay, okay," she said with a burst of laughter as the dog continued to lavish her with kisses. She looked up to see Quinn standing in the doorway. Her heart jumped with a quickened beat.

He stepped inside and took the dog by the collar. "Sorry about that," he said as she quickly got to her feet. "He's a Lab and just a puppy so he hasn't learned his manners yet."

"It's okay." Jewel reached up and self-consciously raked her fingers through her hair. As always the sight of Quinn sent an electrical tingle through her. "He's a cutie. Is he yours?"

"Actually, I was hoping he'd be yours," Quinn said.

"Mine?" She looked at him in surprise.

The dog sat on the floor next to him, looking first

at Quinn, then at Jewel, as if aware that they were talking about him.

"It might be presumptuous of me, but I thought maybe you could use a companion, especially when you decide to take a walk in the woods late at night." Quinn shoved a strand of his thick, wavy hair away from his eyes, and shifted from foot to foot, as if suddenly extremely uncomfortable. "Maybe it was a stupid idea."

"No, it was a lovely idea," she replied, touched by the thoughtfulness of the gesture. "Actually, we've talked about getting a dog since I first opened the doors here, but we've just never gotten around to it. What's his name?"

"He doesn't have an official name yet." Quinn's eyes were a warm topaz. "I have to warn you, he's only twelve weeks old. He's not quite housebroken, but he's a big lover and has a terrific personality. Most important, he's great with kids."

"Then how can I possibly turn away such a wonderful gift?" she replied. The children would be positively thrilled with this new addition to the family. "Maybe we'll put him in the garage for tonight. Do you think that's okay?"

He nodded and clipped a leash to the collar. "I'm sure that's fine. Why don't you take him and I'll unload the supplies from the truck."

"Supplies?"

He smiled, a warm, beautiful gesture that detracted from the scar across his cheek and trans-

formed him from slightly dangerous-looking to more
than slightly wonderful-looking. "In the truck I've
got a doggie bed, food and water bowls, a couple of
toys and several bags of kibble."

"Quinn, you didn't have to do all that," she protested as she took the leash from him.

"It wouldn't be fair to give you a gift that cost you
a ton of money," he replied. "And along with the gift
comes free veterinary services for the life of that
guy. Consider it my donation to Hopechest Ranch."

She started to protest once again at the generosity
of the gift, but then changed her mind and smiled.
"Thank you."

Together they walked out of the door. She headed
for one of the three garages as he went out to his
truck. The first garage was the playroom for the kids.
The second was where she parked her car and the
third was currently empty. It was to the empty one
that she led the puppy.

As she waited for Quinn she crouched down and
stroked the puppy's back. "We'll let the kids give you
a name," she said. He gazed at her with big, brown,
adoring eyes.

Her heart expanded with warmth. Quinn had
brought her a dog to walk in the woods. It was one
of the most thoughtful things anyone had ever done
for her. He thought she could use a companion.

Had he sensed the deep, abiding loneliness that
had been her constant companion for the last couple
of years? A loneliness that never went away, no mat-

ter how many people surrounded her, no matter how the children filled her days and nights.

She stood as he approached with two big sacks of dog food over his shoulder. Although he was tall and lean, he had broad, strong shoulders that easily managed the heavy bags.

"I can't believe you did this," she said. As he drew closer, a new spark of electricity swept through her.

"I figured maybe if you're grateful enough you might invite me in for a cup of coffee." He set the bags on the garage floor.

"I think maybe we can work something out," she replied. She told herself that the crazy buzz she felt at the very idea of spending some time with him was nothing more than the pleasure of having somebody fill these hours of darkness before she finally called it a night.

It took him only minutes to unload all the items from his truck. She got the pooch settled for the night, then Quinn followed her inside and to the kitchen.

The kitchen was one of the largest rooms in the house, but as Quinn took a seat at the long wooden table, she felt as if the room shrank. He possessed a simmering energy beneath his calm, cool exterior, an energy that seemed to shimmer in the air around him.

"I'm not keeping you up, am I?" he asked as she made the coffee. "I didn't realize how late it had gotten until I got to your front door."

"It's not a problem," she assured him. "I normally don't go to bed too early." It was only when she turned away from him to check on the coffee that she remembered what had happened the night before— their encounter in the woods and the lie he'd told her about what he'd been doing there.

Quinn wasn't sure what happened, but one minute her brown eyes were warm and inviting and the next minute they chilled and held a new wariness.

"You lied to me last night," she said. "You told me that you had been over at Clay's because he had a horse down, but I asked him about it and he said all his stock was healthy."

So that's what had caused the change in her expression. She'd obviously just remembered what he'd told her the night before.

"Yeah, I lied," he admitted. "It was a stupid thing to do. I was embarrassed that I'd bumped into you, embarrassed to tell you the truth."

She remained standing by the counter next to the coffeepot. The coffee was finished brewing but she made no move to get cups. He had a feeling that she was waiting for his explanation and if she didn't like it, then the offer of coffee would be rescinded.

And he didn't want that. It had taken him all evening to work up the nerve to come here. In fact, it had taken him months to work up his nerve to be here. He wanted to have coffee with her. He wanted to know more about her.

"And what, exactly, is the truth?" she asked, the coolness in her voice strong enough to frost his face.

"I don't sleep well, haven't for years. On the nights when I know I won't be able to sleep I go to Clay's and spend time with my horse, Noches. I board him there and right now he's my favorite nighttime companion."

She searched his face, as if on his features she'd discover if he was telling her the truth or not. "Jewel, why else would I be out in the woods in the middle of the night?" he asked.

She turned her back on him to reach for two cups in the overhead cabinet, but not before he saw a flash of emotion in her eyes, an emotion that looked something like fear. "You should have just told me that last night," she replied. She poured the coffee then joined him at the table.

"I haven't been eager for it to get around that the town vet suffers from insomnia. The first time an animal dies for whatever reason everyone will say it's my fault because I don't get enough sleep," he said.

She took a sip of her coffee, her brown eyes gazing at him curiously over the rim of her cup. "It must have been difficult for you," she said as she placed the cup back on the table. "When you had to put down Clay's horse and so many in the town turned against you. Clay told me all about it."

"It was difficult," he agreed, "but it's over and done with, and I try to keep difficult things from my past firmly in the past." As thoughts of Sarah drifted through his mind, he decided a change of topic was in order. "I understand I missed a big reunion over at Clay's place this morning."

"You did." A smile curved her lips and Quinn felt the beauty of the gesture in a starburst of warmth in the pit of his stomach. "It was wonderful to see Clay and Ryder together again. Finally, I think they're going to have the relationship they both want."

Quinn nodded. "I know how badly Ryder's lifestyle hurt Clay, the bad choices his brother made when he was younger, but it sounds like he's turned it all around."

"How did you hear about it—the reunion, I mean?" she asked curiously.

"I ran into Georgie and Nick and Emmie at the café this evening." He smiled. "Emmie told me she's excited to start school next week and she's determined to make one friend who isn't a cowboy."

Jewel laughed and again Quinn's stomach filled with a welcome warmth. She had a nice laugh. "That one is a pip," she said. "I know Georgie has been worried about her fitting in at school. Emmie has spent her whole life on the rodeo circuit with adults as her peers, but I keep telling Georgie that Emmie is going to be just fine. She's so bright, she shouldn't have any problems."

There followed several long moments of uncomfortable silence. Quinn felt like a teenage boy on a first date as he desperately searched for an interesting topic of conversation. He'd been wanting to get to know her better ever since she'd come to town, but it had been years since he'd done the dating dance.

"I'll bet your kids…" he began.

"How did you get…" she said at the same time.

"Go ahead," he said.

"I was just going to ask where you got the dog."

"I helped deliver a litter of four and the owner insisted I get pick of the litter for helping out. I already have a dog and so figured I'd just try to find him a good home. I think this will be a great place for him."

She smiled. "The kids will love him and taking care of him will be therapeutic for them."

He leaned back in his chair, some of his tension beginning to ebb. "You like what you do here."

She nodded, her golden-brown hair sparkling beneath the artificial light. "I love it. I was working for Meredith Colton at the Hopechest Ranch in Prosperino, California, and when she offered me the opportunity to come here and open up a ranch, I jumped at the chance."

"Was it a tough change? Moving here from California?" He took a drink of the coffee.

"Not really. I was ready for a change and, of course, Clay has been very supportive."

"He thinks a lot of you," Quinn said.

"He thinks a lot of you, too."

"He's been a good friend and a great support over the years." Quinn took another sip of his coffee.

"You know, I have the same problem you do with insomnia," she said. She wrapped her slender fingers around her coffee cup and looked more vulnerable than she had moments before. "I start dreading the coming of night just after dinner."

He wasn't surprised by her confession. "Have you seen a doctor? Maybe you could get a prescription for some sleeping medication."

She waved one of her hands. "I don't want to do that. I don't want to medicate myself to sleep. What about you? Have you seen a doctor, Doctor?" she asked lightly.

"No, I'm like you. Eventually after a couple nights of restlessness I manage to get in enough sleep to keep going." He hesitated a moment, then added, "From what Clay has told me, that's not the only thing we have in common."

"What else do we have in common?" One of her eyebrows danced up quizzically.

"We've both lost people we cared deeply about. Clay told me about your fiancé. I'm sorry for your loss."

Her eyes darkened as her complexion paled. "Thank you. It was a tragedy, but it's in the past."

It was obvious by the tightening of her lips, the paleness of her skin, that even though it was in her past, she still felt deeply the grief of the loss. She cleared her throat. "What about you? Who did you lose?"

"My wife, Sarah."

"I'm sorry. I didn't realize you'd been married." Some of the color returned to her cheeks.

"We weren't married long before she was diagnosed with a brain tumor. Six months later she was gone."

To his surprise Jewel reached out and covered his hand with hers. "Oh, Quinn. I'm so sorry."

Her touch sizzled through him and he turned his hand over so that he now grasped her hand. "The only reason I told you this is because I want you to know that I understand grief, that if you need somebody to talk to, I have a good ear and strong shoulders."

She pulled her hand from his as if suddenly uncomfortable by the physical connection. "I appreciate the offer, but I'm doing okay. Tell me about Sarah. What was she like?"

"Quiet and sweet. We met while I was in school. I was getting my degree in veterinary medicine and she wanted to be a nurse. It began as friendship and grew into love. She loved animals almost as much as I did and we talked about having a dozen kids and twice as many dogs and cats. What about your fiancé, Andy…wasn't that his name?"

"Andrew, never Andy," she replied, her eyes going soft. "He owned an accounting firm. He loved numbers and puzzles and he'd asked me to be his wife on the night that he died."

"Clay told me it was a car accident."

She nodded and once again wrapped her fingers around her cup, as if seeking warmth from the coffee it still contained. "We were driving home from the restaurant where we'd eaten dinner. It was misting and the road was dark. A Hummer seemed to come out of nowhere and steered right into the driver side of our car. I was knocked unconscious." One of her hands moved to splay on her stomach. "The driver of the Hummer was never found."

Quinn wanted to reach out to her, to pull her into his arms and hold her until her haunted, vulnerable look went away. "Even though you can't ever prepare yourself for the death of somebody you love, I had six months to prepare myself for saying goodbye to Sarah, but you had no time to prepare yourself for saying goodbye to Andrew."

She shrugged. "It happened. It's over and life moves on." She glanced at the clock on the stove.

"It's getting late," he said, taking it as a hint. "I should get out of here." She didn't argue and he stood and carried his cup to the sink. "Thanks for the coffee," he said as they walked to the front door.

"Thanks for the dog," she replied. "It was a very thoughtful thing for you to do." She opened the front door and leaned against it.

He knew she was waiting for him to walk out, but he was reluctant to leave. "Jewel, I'm sorry if our conversation brought back bad memories." He'd finally gotten an opportunity to talk to her one-on-one and the topic of conversation he'd chosen was their painful pasts.

To his horror her eyes misted with tears. "I'm sorry," she said as the tears spilled onto her cheeks.

He stepped toward her then, unable to stand by while she cried, feeling guilty because he was responsible for her tears. He should have talked about the weather, or about town politics, about anything but loss.

He opened his arms to her and to his surprise she walked into them and laid her head against his chest.

He embraced her, the scent of her soft, floral perfume eddying in the air.

The last thing he'd expected when he'd arrived here tonight was to have her in his arms, but when she raised her face to look up at him, he knew he wanted to take it one step further. He desperately wanted to kiss her.

Chapter 4

Jewel knew he was going to kiss her. His intent shone hot in his amazingly gorgeous eyes. In the back of her mind she knew this was crazy, that she didn't know this man well enough to kiss him and she certainly wasn't interested in a relationship of any kind.

Still, that rational part of her brain was no match for the wave of sharp, visceral desire that swept through her as she gazed up at him. She parted her lips as he dipped his head to take her mouth with his.

Crazy. It was pure madness that possessed her, but she gave in to it. His mouth was hot, the kiss sending a shaft of warmth up and down her veins. She welcomed the feeling, welcomed him as she opened her mouth more to him, allowing him to deepen the kiss with his tongue.

She knew she should step back and call a halt to things, but it had been so long and Quinn's arms were so strong around her and his kiss made her ache for more.

His hands stroked the length of her back as his mouth continued to ply hers with fire. She wrapped her arms around his neck and tangled her fingers in his soft, sexy mane of hair.

She swirled her tongue with his, felt her knees weaken and threaten to buckle. She clung to him more tightly, her heart beating a rhythm of desire.

His mouth finally left hers and moved down the length of her neck, nipping and teasing with slow, deliberate intent. She dropped her head back, allowing him to kiss her throat, and trail his hot mouth along her collarbone.

It didn't matter that she'd only known him on a casual, social level until now. She didn't care that this was probably one of the most foolish things she'd ever done. For right now, in his arms, she wanted to be foolish and abandon herself to being held by Quinn, being kissed by Quinn.

Once again his mouth captured hers and as she pressed more tightly against him she realized that he was aroused. This knowledge only made her desire flame higher.

She wanted to make love with him. She wanted

to lose herself in his caresses, in the very mindless sensations of sex.

She'd heard enough about Quinn from Clay to know he wouldn't hurt her, that she was safe with him. She wasn't concerned about consequences. The most she'd have to worry about was perhaps a little embarrassment the morning after. But she didn't care about the morning after—all she cared about was here and now.

"Miss Jewel?"

Jewel and Quinn shot apart like two guilty teenagers at the sound of the young voice drifting down the hallway. Jewel recognized the voice. She drew a deep breath to steady herself, not looking at Quinn. "Lindy, what's wrong?"

"You'd better come quick, Kelsey is packing her suitcase and says she's gonna run away."

"I'll be right there." Jewel finally looked at Quinn as she felt the heat of a blush warm her cheeks. Okay, so her embarrassment hadn't waited until the morning after.

"You need help?" he asked softly.

"No, I'll be fine. Please, just go." Now that the heat of the moment had passed, she was appalled by what had just happened between them...what had almost happened between them.

She was grateful that he didn't argue but simply nodded and left. She closed the front door behind him then hurried down the hallway to the girls' room where Kelsey was throwing her clothes into the battered cloth suitcase she'd arrived with.

"Kelsey, what's going on?" Jewel asked.

The girl didn't stop her activity and kept her eyes downcast. "Nothing. I just don't want to be here anymore."

"Has something happened? Did somebody say something to upset you?" Jewel took a step closer to the young teenager.

"No. I just gotta go, that's all. I've got to leave." She glanced up at Jewel, tears filling her bright green eyes.

Jewel stepped toward her and held out her hand. "Come on, let's go someplace where you and I can have a little private chat."

Kelsey hesitated a moment, then slipped her hand into Jewel's. "Lindy, Carrie, back to bed and lights out," she said as she led Kelsey from the room.

She took the girl into the kitchen and gestured her to the chair where Quinn had sat. "Want a glass of milk? Maybe a cookie?"

Kelsey shook her head, her face radiating abject misery. Jewel sat in the chair next to Kelsey's and took the girl's cold, small hands into hers. "Honey, I can't help you if you don't talk to me," she said softly.

Kelsey caught her lower lip in her teeth, then released it and sighed. "I like it here. That's the whole problem."

"I'm sorry. I don't understand," Jewel replied.

Kelsey frowned. "Every time I get someplace where I like to be, then somebody makes me leave. I figured this time I wouldn't wait around for somebody to kick me out. I'd just go, before I like it so much that it hurts to leave."

A sob escaped her. "What's the point of staying here and being happy when I know sometime I'll have to leave and won't be happy again?" she cried.

Jewel leaned forward and gathered the girl into her arms. "I never turn up my nose at happiness," Jewel replied as she stroked Kelsey's hair. "What you have to do with it is grab it and hold it as close as you can for as long as you can. Then when it's gone you have special memories to help you through the bad times. Besides, one of the things we want to do while you're here is teach you some skills so that you can learn to be happy wherever you are."

Kelsey raised her head and looked at her through tear-glazed eyes. "I'm afraid to be happy because it hurts so much when it goes away."

Jewel held her close, her heart aching for the girl. "I know, honey. But I'd like you to stay here with us and grab on to all the happiness we can give you. Let's not talk about when you leave. Heavens, you've only been here for one day."

Kelsey laughed as Jewel released her. "I really don't want to leave," she admitted. "I want to ride the horses some more and I like the other kids, too."

"Good, then how about we get you back into bed? There are a bunch of activities on the schedule for tomorrow and you don't want to start the day tired. You can unpack your things in the morning."

Kelsey nodded and together they walked back to

the girls' room. "Good night," Kelsey said. Jewel watched as she moved her suitcase off the bed and then climbed into the bunk.

With the crisis handled, Jewel returned to the kitchen where she turned out the lights then headed for her own quarters.

Her head filled with a vision of Quinn, and she couldn't believe what had happened between them before he'd left, couldn't imagine what might have happened if they hadn't been interrupted.

Or maybe the problem was she *could* imagine all too well what might have happened. Her mouth heated as she remembered the kisses they'd shared. In another minute she would have led him to her bedroom, allowed him—no, encouraged him—to make love to her.

God, was she so desperate, so lonely that she'd just fall into bed with anyone? She entered the dressing room and stripped off her jeans and T-shirt and threw them into the hamper, then stood in front of the wall mirror and stared at her reflection.

She raked her fingers through her short sun-streaked brown hair and frowned as she saw the tired lines that radiated outward from her eyes.

No, she wasn't desperate enough to fall into bed with any man who showed an interest in her. If that were the case, she would have slept with Deputy Adam Rawlings by now. He'd certainly make it clear he was interested in a romance with her, but she had never wanted to kiss him. Not like she'd wanted to kiss Quinn.

It was Quinn who stirred her like no man had for a very long time. She turned away from the mirror and reached for her nightgown. From the moment she'd first seen him, something about him had drawn her not only on a physical level, but on an emotional level, as well.

There was a solid gentleness about him that attracted her and nothing he'd done this evening had changed her mind. Still, she was a bit embarrassed by how quickly she'd responded to him.

Clad in her nightgown, she went into her bedroom and pulled down the covers on the bed, surprised to realize she not only felt tired, she felt sleepy.

Maybe the conversation with Quinn had relaxed something inside her, or maybe it had just been his calm, steady presence that had created an unusual sense of peace inside her.

She crawled into bed and glanced at the clock on her nightstand. Almost eleven o'clock. Maybe tonight she could actually sleep. She turned out the light on her nightstand, then closed her eyes.

A vision of Quinn at the table filled her mind, his topaz eyes shining with an inner strength, his mouth curved up into a gentle smile. Almost immediately she felt the heaviness of sleep overtaking her and she gave in to it.

The dream began almost immediately. She and Andrew were seated in the restaurant. It was their favorite place to eat, an Italian café with traditional checkered tablecloths and candles in the center of each table. The food was impeccable and the atmosphere conducive to romance.

They had just finished eating when Andrew smiled at her, his blue eyes holding suppressed excitement. "I've spent the entire day today trying to figure out a wonderfully romantic way to do this, but I'm an accountant at heart and that means I'm not very creative." He reached into his shirt pocket and withdrew a ring box.

It was magic. The man, the ring and the moment. The scene shimmered in a golden haze as it played out in her dream. The engagement ring sparkled as he reached for her hand and slid it onto her finger.

And the magic only grew stronger, brighter when she told Andrew her secret, that she was pregnant with his baby. Andrew had been thrilled and they'd excitedly talked about wedding plans and baby names. They'd laughed as they'd left the restaurant.

"Here, baby, you drive," she'd said, and handed him the keys to her car. She'd picked him up at his office and driven to the restaurant. "That way, I can sit and admire my new ring," she's said with a laugh.

The scene shifted abruptly, as dreams often do, and they were in her car, Andrew behind the wheel. The golden light that had shimmered was gone and everything was in the sharp colors of harsh reality.

Even in sleep Jewel knew what was coming and she fought to wake up, not wanting to see the images. But the dreamscape held her captive and she saw the

Hummer appear out of nowhere, a bright yellow monster with sharp silver gnashing teeth.

"No!" she cried, but the monster didn't listen. She watched in horror as those scissor-sharp teeth slammed into their car, then snatched Andrew and shook him like a rag doll.

As the monster tossed Andrew aside, it came for her, biting into her stomach, killing her baby, killing her dreams.

Her screams woke her. She shot straight up in the bed, her heart stuttering so fast in her chest she thought she was going to die. Deep sobs wrenched through her, making it difficult to breathe.

She grabbed her stomach, as if to protect, to save, but she knew it was a futile gesture. The monster had won. He'd managed to take everything away from her, leaving her empty inside.

She remained in the center of her bed, shivering and silently weeping as the nightmare lingered in her head. Why hadn't the driver of the Hummer stopped? Why hadn't he tried to help?

If medical help had been summoned immediately, would Andrew have been saved? Would her baby have lived? These were haunting questions with no answers.

Finally, tears spent, she reached over and turned on her nightlight, knowing that it would be a very long time before she fell asleep again.

She rolled to the side of the bed to get up, and frowned as she heard the crinkle of paper. Puzzled, she slid over and spied what looked like a page from a newspaper.

She picked it up and stared at the headline: Tragic Accident Kills Accounting Executive. She dropped it as if it burned her fingers. It was the original article that had appeared in the paper years ago when the accident had happened.

Her heartbeat, which had finally slowed to a normal pace, now crashed and banged so painfully she couldn't catch her breath. How had the article gotten in her room, in her bed?

Somebody had been in her room. Had someone crept in while she was sleeping? Earlier in the night while she and Quinn had been in the kitchen?

Was he still here now?

She jumped off the bed and grabbed the baseball bat that leaned against the wall in the corner of the room. She didn't want to alarm anyone else in the house, but she needed to make certain that nobody was here who didn't belong here.

Heart pounding so loudly she could hear it in her head, she went back into her quarters, flipping on the lights in the dressing room, the bathroom, then her bedroom. She checked closets and behind doorways. When she'd cleared her quarters, she went through the rest of the house. She checked all the doors and windows, but found nothing out of place and nobody there who didn't belong. The doors and windows were locked tight and showed no breach of any kind.

She finally crept back to her bed. It was just after

one. There would be no more sleep for tonight. She sat with the baseball bat clutched in her hands, and waited for morning to come.

"Rover," Barry exclaimed. "That's a good name for a dog."

"That's a dumb name," Sam replied. "We should call him Champion or Bruno. Those are good dog names."

They were all in the kitchen, where the dog was running from child to child, his tail wagging with happiness. He lavished kisses on everyone he met and Jewel wasn't sure who was happier—the dog or the children.

"He looks like a cup of hot cocoa," Kelsey said.

"That a good name—Cocoa." Carrie clapped her hands. "Here, Cocoa." The dog ran to her and nearly knocked her down.

"I think Cocoa is a wonderful name," Jewel said. Her eyes felt gritty from her lack of sleep and the fear that had gripped her when she'd seen the newspaper article on the bed still simmered just beneath the surface of her consciousness.

"And now what we need to do is divide up the responsibility of taking care of Cocoa," she said, trying to stay focused.

As the kids talked about who would be responsible for feeding and providing fresh water for him, and who would take the dog out for walks, Jewel's thoughts once again returned to the night before.

It had been just before dawn that the idea of something other than a mysterious intruder struck her. On the top shelf in her closet was a cardboard memory box. Inside it were family photos and memorabilia from her past.

She'd had several copies of the newspaper article inside the box. While she had no way of confirming that the copy that had been on her bed had come from her box, she suspected that it might have.

Maybe she'd gotten up in the middle of her nightmare and had taken the article from the box and laid it on the bed. She wasn't sure what frightened her more—the idea of an intruder whose motive apparently was to torment her, or the possibility that she was unconsciously haunting herself.

Was this the way it had begun with her mother? Was this how true madness began? She remembered reading an article in a psychology magazine once about a woman who believed she was being stalked. She received threatening notes in the mail, her car tires were slashed. One incident after another plagued her and the truth was only discovered after her family hired a private investigator. The truth was that she was doing it all to herself with no conscious knowledge of her actions.

"Can we walk him now?" Barry's voice intruded into her disturbing thoughts.

"There's a leash for his collar out in the garage. Sam, why don't you run out and get it, then you can all take turns walking him in the front yard," Jewel said.

As Sam went off to retrieve the leash, Jewel

looked at Cheryl. "I've got some things to do in town today. It's possible I'll be gone most of the day."

"Not a problem. Jeff and I can keep things running smoothly here on the home front," she replied.

"Don't forget that at two today Mark Potter is coming to give an art lesson." Jewel had hired a local artist to come twice a week to give the kids art lessons. She believed in the therapeutic quality of art.

Sam returned with the leash and within minutes all the kids were out in the yard with Cocoa and under the supervision of Jeff.

Jewel went to her bedroom and grabbed her purse, then left the house and got into her car. She waved as she drove down the driveway and smiled as she saw Cocoa, with an exuberant leap, knock Carrie on her behind. Carrie laughed and wrapped her arms around the dog.

The dog had been a great gift from Quinn. Quinn. As she headed toward town, the handsome vet filled her thoughts.

She knew what his mouth tasted like, had felt the silky softness of his amazing hair and his strong shoulders beneath her fingertips. But she didn't know where he came from, what kind of family he had or even what kind of food he liked.

The whole kiss thing had been crazy and as she thought of seeing him again she wasn't sure if the thrum of nerves that tingled inside her was dread or anticipation.

She dismissed him from her mind as she pulled

into a parking space in front of the town library. At some point in the early morning hours, with sleep deprivation weighing heavy, she'd wondered if maybe her unconscious mind was trying to tell her something important, something about the accident that had taken everything she loved away from her.

In those dark predawn hours, she'd realized there was a lot about Andrew and his work she hadn't known. There had always been a small part of her that had believed the accident wasn't an accident at all. The Hummer hadn't attempted to swerve to avoid hitting them. The driver hadn't jammed on the brakes or taken any action to prevent the accident.

Although the authorities had ruled it an accident, due to the mist that had made the country road a bit slick, Jewel had never completely embraced the notion that it had been nothing more than a tragic accident.

She could have done some research on the computer at the ranch, but for some reason she'd felt it was important to keep this separate from her life there. One of the library computers would do just fine for a little research into Andrew's business.

As she entered the library, she was surprised to see sixteen-year-old Sarah Engleleit behind the counter. The teenager had spent some time at the Hopechest Ranch two months ago when she'd run away from home.

"Sarah," she exclaimed. "I didn't know you were working here."

"I just started last week. It's just part-time but I really like it. How are things at the ranch?"

"Busy, as usual." Jewel smiled. "I'm just going to use one of the computers for a while. I'll see you later."

Jewel made her way to one of the computer stations, a new burst of nerves attacking her as she realized she was about to go backward in time, back to where dreams held possibility and the horror of having that possibility stolen away.

For a moment she sat in the chair and fought the impulse to rub her eyes, knowing they were already red enough for somebody to mistake her for a vampire.

She couldn't remember the last time she'd felt so exhausted. It was as if all the nights of insomnia had finally caught up with her this morning, making concentration difficult.

Long and Casey Accounting had been a powerhouse in the business world in California. Andrew had owned the firm and Gray Casey had been a junior partner. When Andrew died, his younger brother stepped into the position Andrew had held and the company had continued to thrive.

The first thing she researched was the accident. There had been several news articles about the tragedy in the days following the wreck.

She tried to maintain an emotional distance as she read over the articles that had been in the local papers, but she learned nothing new from the printed accounts.

By keying in the search words *Long and Casey*

Accounting she got over two hundred results. The morning turned to afternoon as she checked each one, unsure what she was looking for, but compelled to continue. She took notes of things she thought might mean something.

It was three o'clock when Sarah came over to where Jewel sat. "I'm leaving and just wanted to say goodbye," she said.

Jewel got up and gave her a hug. "You know you're welcome out at the ranch anytime."

"I know. Maybe one day after school I'll drop by for a visit."

"I'd like that," Jewel replied. As Sarah headed out the front door, Jewel returned to her reading. Her eyes, which had burned earlier, now felt raw.

She was just about to give up the search when she hit an article that caused her to sit up straighter in her chair.

Successful Entrepreneur Indicted for Tax Evasion, the headline read. She scanned the page, wondering why a news report about a James Corrs had been brought up by her typing in Andrew's firm's name. She found her answer on the second page of the article. It had been Andrew who had turned in James Corrs to the Internal Revenue Service.

The date on the newspaper was three weeks before the car accident that had taken Andrew's life. Could this James Corrs have sought revenge against Andrew? Certainly he'd had a lot to lose by battling a tax-evasion charge.

Dear God, was it possible the car accident hadn't been an accident at all, but rather a murder?

As a firm hand fell on her shoulder, a scream of surprise escaped her.

Chapter 5

"I'm sorry, I didn't mean to startle you," Quinn said as he took a step closer to Jewel.

She hurriedly closed the folder in front of her and hit the button to return the computer to the home page. It was as if she didn't want him to see what she'd been doing. "I didn't mean to yell," she replied. "I was just so engrossed that I didn't see you there."

"Engrossed in what?" he asked lightly. She looked both beautiful and terrible. She wore a pair of jeans and a sleeveless blue blouse, but it wasn't her clothes that captured his attention. It was her eyes. They were so red they looked as though, if she opened them wide enough, they'd start to bleed. That, coupled with her drawn, exhausted look, had him worried about her.

"Just a dry psychology article," she replied. Her

gaze didn't quite meet his. "What about you? What are you doing here?"

He held up two books and tried not to think about the searing kiss they'd shared the night before. "I ordered a couple of books from the library in San Antonio and they came in this morning."

"Must be interesting material for you to order it all the way from San Antonio," she replied. She looked nervous, on edge as she clutched the file folder to her chest.

He smiled. "Yeah, *Animal Husbandry and New Medicine for Old Health Problems in Animals.* If I try to read them before I go to bed, they just might solve my insomnia problem."

She laughed, but even that sounded stressed and tired. "I've tried reading before bedtime to get sleepy, but it doesn't work for me." She released a small sigh as she set the folder down on the desk. "Lately, nothing seems to be working for me."

"Ah, but I'll bet you haven't read *Animal Husbandry.* You want to go get a drink?" The invitation sprang from his lips almost before his brain had formed the intention.

She looked so miserable and he was reluctant to just say goodbye, turn and walk away from her.

To his surprise, she hesitated only a moment then nodded. "Actually, a drink sounds great." She got up from the computer station and grabbed her folder from the table. "Where do you want to go?"

"There's a new Mexican place down a block on Main. It's got a nice little bar inside. It's called Joe's Cantina."

She frowned, the gesture emphasizing the tired lines across her forehead. "I haven't heard of it before."

"It's only been open about two weeks. I checked it out last week. The margaritas were great and the food was terrific."

"Okay, sounds good to me," she agreed.

"If you want, we could walk from here."

A moment later they walked out into the late-afternoon sunshine. Quinn dropped off his books in his truck and she put her folder in her car, then together they headed down the sidewalk toward the restaurant.

"Did everything go okay after I left last night?" he asked. "The girl who was going to run away? Did you get her settled down?"

"She didn't really want to run away," she replied. "Poor thing was just scared because she likes the ranch and she didn't want to get attached and have to leave. She's afraid to be happy because she knows what it feels like to have happiness vanish."

"That's a tough thing to know so young."

Jewel nodded, the sunshine catching and sparking on the gold highlights in her hair. "It's tragic. That's the problem with most of the kids who come to the ranch. They've already experienced things that no child should have to go through. Oh, by the way, the dog now has a name. Cocoa."

"Nice," he replied. "So the kids were happy with him?"

She smiled. "Happy is an understatement. They were overjoyed."

"I'm glad. I know Cocoa will be happy there."

As they reached the door to the restaurant the scent of salsa, tortillas and spicy meat filled the air. Quinn opened the door for her, then followed her into the establishment.

On the right side was the seating area for diners and on the left was an intimate bar with small round tables and low lighting. They settled at one of the bar tables and both ordered margaritas.

"I usually don't drink before dinner," she said, as if it were important that he understand that. "And until last night I've never kissed a man who brought me a dog." Her cheeks flamed pink.

Quinn's blood heated as he thought of that kiss. It had taken him a long time and an icy shower after he'd left her ranch to cool down and given the opportunity to kiss her again, he wouldn't hesitate. Even now the thought of kissing her again created a ball of tension in the pit of his stomach.

"Jewel, if you're worried that somehow I think you're a fast woman because of what happened last night, put that worry out of your head. Neither of us planned for it to happen. It just happened, but I'd be less than honest if I didn't tell you that I wouldn't mind if it happened again."

She was saved from having to respond by the waitress, who delivered their drinks and a basket of chips with a bowl of salsa.

"You mentioned last night that you knew a lot about me from Clay, but I don't know much about you," she said once the waitress had left. "Where are you from? Do you have other family?"

"My family lives in Oregon and it's a big one. I have three brothers and two sisters."

"Wow, that *is* big. Are you close?"

Quinn reached for a chip. "We're very close. A day doesn't go by that I don't get a phone call from a brother or sister or one of my parents. All my siblings are married with families of their own and they hate the idea that for the last five years I've been alone." He dipped the chip into the salsa, then popped it into his mouth.

"So how did you end up in Esperanza?"

"I went to school in San Antonio and fell in love with Texas. When I graduated, I started looking around the area for a small town that needed a veterinarian. Esperanza fit the bill. The vet at the time, Dr. Eliot Patterson, was about to retire and he invited me out here for a visit. I fell in love with the town and the people. What about you? Are your parents still alive?"

"The story of my parents is a twisted, sordid tale." She paused to take a sip of her drink, her eyes darkening. "My father was a used-car salesman named Ellis Mayfair who came through town twice a month to see my mother. At that time my mother was living in Sacramento. The short story is she got pregnant and Ellis wasn't happy about it. I was delivered by Ellis in a motel room. When my mother fell asleep Ellis gave me to a doctor who adopted me out in an illegal adoption. When my mother woke up and found out what he'd done, she stabbed him. He died and she went to prison."

"My God, Jewel." As he thought of his own family closeness, he wanted to grab her to him and hold her until he figured out a way to somehow change her history. As if losing her fiancé weren't enough, this bit of information made him realize just what kind of a survivor Jewel Mayfair really was.

"It's all right," she said hurriedly. "The story has a happy ending. Charlie and Ruth Baylor adopted me and raised me in a small town in Ohio. They couldn't have kids of their own and were loving, wonderful parents."

Although her smile was genuine as she spoke of her adoptive parents, the darkness that had deepened her eyes when she'd first spoken of her real mother and father didn't lift.

Quinn had a feeling there was more to the story than the thumbnail sketch she'd given him, but he was reluctant to pry too deep too fast. Still, he couldn't stop himself from probing a little more.

"Did you ever get a chance to know your real mother? Is she still in prison?"

Her fingers tightened around the stem of her glass. "No, she eventually got out of prison, and we managed to meet, but she passed away soon after that."

"I'm sorry." Once again he wanted to wrap his arms around her and hold her until the haunted darkness in her eyes receded. Instead, he decided a change of topic might be more appropriate. "So, how did you get involved with the Hopechest Ranch?"

Some of the tension left her face as she took another sip of her drink, then relaxed into the back of the chair. "Originally, I had my own small practice. Then when the accident happened, I pretty much fell apart. I gave up the practice and sort of drifted in a deep depression. It was my Aunt Meredith who suggested I spend a couple hours a week at the Hopechest Ranch in Prosperino, and when she decided to open the ranch here, she offered me this position and I jumped at the opportunity."

"It must be amazingly rewarding working with the children."

"It is, but I'm sure you feel the same way about your work with animals."

He nodded. "It's very rewarding and at times heartbreaking."

She smiled. "That defines my work at the ranch perfectly."

For a moment they were silent, but it was a comfortable silence. It lasted only a short time, then they began to speculate on Joe Colton's run to become president and talked about how excited Jewel was about Joe and Meredith's upcoming visit to Texas and the Hopechest Ranch. At some point during their conversation he noticed the stress that had lined her face easing and the shadows in her eyes backing away.

Quinn glanced at his watch, then back at her. "Look, it's almost six. I don't know about you, but smelling all the food cooking suddenly has me starving. How about we move to the other side and get some dinner."

"I'd like that," she said. Her immediate acquiescence both surprised and pleased him. He wanted to know more about her. He wanted to know everything about her and it had been a long time since he'd felt that way about a woman.

For the last five years Quinn had grieved deeply for the wife he'd lost, but now he was more than ready to share his life with a special woman. From the moment he'd seen Jewel, he'd had a feeling she might just be that woman and everything he'd learned about her and in the kiss they'd shared only made him more certain.

But there was no question that Jewel had secrets. He saw them in the dark places in her eyes and her quick movements to hide whatever it was she'd been doing in the library only emphasized that.

Quinn was a patient man and he was determined to unlock all the secrets that Jewel Mayfair possessed.

It's just dinner, that's what Jewel told herself. They were simply two adults enjoying the pleasure of each other's company over a meal.

Still, she couldn't deny that being in Quinn's company relaxed her, that the quiet steadiness of his nature drew her and calmed the chaotic noise inside her head.

Even with the rich scent of the Mexican food in the air, she could smell the scent of his cologne, a masculine woodsy scent that she found wonderfully appealing.

It was impossible for her not to think about the kiss they'd shared the night before. Just looking at his mouth made hers heat with the memory.

"Another margarita?" he asked as the waitress arrived to take their orders.

"No, thanks. One is definitely my limit." Instead they both ordered soft drinks to go along with their meals.

"I haven't had enchiladas for a long time." She placed her napkin in her lap.

"Mexican food is one of my favorites," he replied. "Along with Italian and Chinese and good old-fashioned American cuisine."

She laughed. "You sound like a man who just likes to eat."

"Guilty as charged." He reached up and pushed back a strand of his magnificent hair.

She smiled. "I've been thinking about getting some animals for the ranch, petting-zoo kinds of animals. Caring for them would be terrific therapy," she said.

"That's a wonderful idea," he agreed. "Unconditional love is what you get with animals. They don't care where you've been or what you've done. When you decide to do that, let me know and I'd be glad to go with you to purchase the animals you want."

"I'd appreciate it. I was thinking maybe some baby lambs and goats to start." No question, she was physically attracted to Quinn. There was a simmering sexuality about him that was even more appealing because he seemed so oblivious to it.

By the time the waitress arrived with their meals, he was entertaining her with stories about the various animals he'd encountered over the years.

She couldn't remember the last time she'd laughed as much and she'd forgotten how wonderful it was to share laughter with a good-looking man.

"Cocoa is the first animal I've ever owned," she confessed.

He looked at her in mock horror. "No dog when you were growing up? No pet rabbit or kitty or turtle?"

She shook her head. "Nothing. Ruth was allergic to pets and when I finally got out on my own, it just didn't seem that important."

"I've had a dog all my life. Right now I have a schnauzer. Sabra has been the only woman in my life for the last four years, but I'm hoping that's going to change."

There it was, that whisper of heat flashing in his eyes, a heat that said he liked what he saw when he looked at her. A responding warmth swept through her. Was she ready for a new relationship? The possibility shot a little thrill through her.

"Is Sabra the jealous type?" she asked in an attempt to keep things light.

"Not that I know of, although I've never had another woman in my house."

His words surprised her. "I would think all the single women in Esperanza would be banging down your door."

He grinned. "I have to admit, I have had a few questionable casseroles brought to my doorstep by some of the local women, but I just wasn't interested until lately in pursuing anything."

She had the distinct impression he was courting her.

He leaned forward. "I know I'm not the most exciting man on the block. I'm forty-four years old. I know my limits when it comes to drinking. I take my friendships very seriously and, except for last night, I usually don't kiss on the first date."

He was definitely courting her, and it was working. He didn't seem to have a clue that the picture he painted of himself was far more appealing than a wild bad boy. Solid and dependable—that's what Jewel wanted in a man.

As the waitress came to remove their plates and ask them about dessert, she declined, but Quinn insisted she needed some coffee and sopaipillas to complete the meal.

Laughing, she settled back to enjoy dessert with him. Her research into Andrew's death had long ago left her mind and being in Quinn's company made her feel as if somehow everything in her life was going to be all right.

They took turns dipping the puffed pastry into a bowl of honey and split the vanilla-bean ice cream that Quinn had added to the dessert order.

The conversation remained light and easy. They talked about their favorite foods, movies they liked and didn't like and mutual acquaintances they knew.

It was after eight when they finally left the restaurant and walked back to where their vehicles were parked at the library.

He walked her to her car and she leaned against the side and smiled up at him. "Thank you for dinner, Quinn. It was an unexpected pleasure."

He stepped closer to her, invading her personal space, but she didn't mind. Remembering how she'd felt the night before when his big strong arms had surrounded her, when his mouth had plied hers with heat, she definitely didn't mind at all that she sensed he wanted to kiss her again.

"I'd like to do it again," he said.

For a moment she thought he was talking about kissing her, then she realized he was talking about having dinner together.

"I'd like that," she replied. She found something almost hypnotically peaceful about being in his company, but it was a peacefulness coupled with a huge dose of an emotion that felt strongly like desire. And it had been so long since a man had moved her on any level.

"There's something else I'd like to do again." He took another step closer to her and this time there was no mistaking what he was talking about.

Her heart two-stepped as he reached out his hand

and with his index finger traced the outline of her lips. "Do you mind?" he murmured.

"No." The single word whispered out of her with a sigh of anticipation.

He leaned forward and took her mouth with his. He tasted of honey and coffee and a passion that was contagious.

Before things could spiral out of control, she ended the kiss. "Dr. Logan. I think you could be a dangerous man."

He stepped back from her and smiled. "If we were someplace more private, I'd like to be a lot more dangerous." His smile fell away and he gazed at her intently. "I like you, Jewel. You're the first woman since my wife whom I've wanted to spend time with and get to know better." He shifted from one foot to the other, as if uncomfortable as he waited for her to reply.

"And I'd like to get to know you better, too," she replied. "I'll tell you what. Sunday I'm planning on taking the kids on a trail ride at Clay's. With school starting Monday, I thought it would be a nice way to end the summer vacation. Why don't you plan on joining us?"

There was no better way to judge a man's true character than to see him interacting with children, she thought.

"I'd love to share a trail ride with you and the kids," he said without hesitation. "In fact, why don't you let me bring a picnic lunch for everyone?"

She laughed. "Are you out of your mind? I mean, I do have seven kids in residence at the moment."

"Then it's lunch for nine. Just tell me what time and I'll take care of the rest of the details."

"Okay," she said, helpless to turn down what appeared to be a heartfelt offer. "Why don't we plan on meeting at Clay's at eleven? We can ride for two hours then have lunch around one." As he nodded his agreement she opened her car door and slid in behind the wheel. "Good night, Quinn."

As she pulled out of the library parking lot and onto Main she couldn't stop herself from taking a quick glance in her rearview mirror to get one last look at him.

He stood by his truck watching her drive away and once again her heart fluttered with a sense of anticipation, of sweet possibility.

She turned on her headlights against the approaching darkness of night and wondered if it was possible that she was finally ready to look ahead instead of dwelling on a past she couldn't change.

Had her grief over Andrew and the baby ebbed to where she could entertain the idea of a new man in her life? She tightened her hands on the steering wheel. Maybe, she thought. Maybe it was the right time.

She liked Quinn and the more time she spent with him the more she liked him. He stirred up a desire inside her that half stole her breath away.

She glanced at her watch as she turned into the lane that led to the ranch. Good, she'd be just in time to tell the children good-night.

Funny, how the exhaustion that had weighed so heavily on her as she'd gone through the morning, the same exhaustion that had burned her eyes and ached in her shoulders at the library had disappeared while she'd been in Quinn's company.

He excited her and energized her while at the same time bringing to her a kind of inner peace she hadn't felt for a very long time. It was a heady combination.

Cheryl was in the kitchen when she got home. Jewel made the nighttime rounds to say good-night to the children, then she sat at the table and listened as Cheryl filled her in on the day.

"Mark had the kids do some acrylic oil painting today. He brought birdhouses for each of them to paint. The kids loved it and we now have seven interesting-looking bird houses to hang in the trees," Cheryl said.

"We'll have to see about getting them up this weekend. Maybe we can hang them in the trees out there so they can be admired while we have our meals." She pointed to the kitchen window.

"That would be nice," Cheryl agreed. "Barry had a bit of a meltdown this afternoon. His mother called and started talking about all the things that would be different when he got home. He got anxious, had a panic attack, then got angry. Jeff took him for a walk so he could cool down."

Jewel made a mental note to have a session with Barry first thing in the morning. She and Cheryl talked for a few more minutes, then they said their good-nights and parted ways.

Jewel went first into her sitting room, which served as her office and took a few minutes to make notes in Barry's file. Calls from his mother always upset him. Barry's father had died a year ago and within a month his mother had remarried. Almost immediately Barry had started having panic attacks with bursts of extreme rage. His mother seemed to be clueless that she hadn't given her son time to grieve the loss of his father.

She closed the file and yawned, her thoughts immediately shifting back to Quinn. She wondered how he had gotten the scar on his cheek. It actually enhanced his attractiveness, giving his face interesting character.

She was curious to see how he'd be with the kids. It was easy to enjoy the company of children who were well-behaved, but the children at the Hopechest Ranch were here because their behavior wasn't perfect.

Yawning again, she went into her master bath and got ready for bed. Maybe she'd read for a while. It was just after nine and she was in the middle of a new book by a famous psychologist detailing her work with borderline personality disorder.

Minutes later, snuggled in her bed with the bedside lamp on and her book in her arms, she tried to focus on the words, but her mind kept drifting back to the time she'd spent with Quinn.

There had been a time following Andrew's death and the loss of her baby that Jewel hadn't wanted to live, when the depression had been too huge for her to stand. The incapacitating grief had passed, but it wasn't until Quinn had gazed at her with his simmering topaz eyes that she felt as if she were truly alive again.

Even now, just thinking about him, her heart quickened and a smile curved her lips. She closed her book and placed it on the nightstand. Maybe if she went to sleep right away Quinn would fill her dreams. That would be so nice.

She shut off the light and burrowed back down beneath the crisp sheets. "No bad dreams tonight," she whispered in the dark. "Please, no bad dreams."

She closed her eyes and listened to the ordinary sounds of the house at rest, the soft hum of the air conditioner, the faint tinkle of the wind chimes that hung outside on the back patio. Familiar sounds, comforting noise that lulled her into that twilight state between consciousness and unconsciousness.

That's when she heard it—the sound of a baby crying—and even though she knew it was impossible, she knew it was *her* baby crying. She felt the mournful cries in the depth of her womb, in the center of her soul.

No, not again. Not tonight. The cries seemed to come from all around her and pierced through her with the sharpness of a needle.

"It's not real," she said aloud. But it sounded so real she wanted to leap out of bed and go searching for the baby she'd lost, the baby who cried for her from the beyond.

This had happened before. She'd heard this sound

before and had jumped out of bed and tried to find
the source. She'd wandered the woods in search of
the baby who needed her, who cried for her, and had
found nothing.

She refused to leave her bed tonight. Instead, she
clapped her hands over her ears as deep, wrenching
sobs escaped her.

She knew the cries weren't real and yet they
echoed through her with an authenticity that was
heart-wrenching.

"Go away," she whispered. "Please, stop crying."

It seemed to last forever, but as suddenly as it had
begun, it stopped.

Tears ripped from the very depths of her and she
realized they weren't just tears for the baby she'd
lost, but also because she realized now that she could
never have anything with Quinn Logan. She could
never have a relationship with any man.

There could only be one explanation for the
baby's cries that haunted her, for the sound of
Andrew's voice calling to her from the woods.

She was losing her mind.

Her mother had died in a mental institution, the lines
between reality and madness so blurred and undefined
that in the end she hadn't even known her own name.

As sobs racked through Jewel, she feared that was
her future, that eventually the lines would blur for her
and she'd wind up like her mother, alone with only
her mental illness and locked away from the world.

Chapter 6

Jewel had just finished the early morning watering of the flowers when an unfamiliar truck pulled up to the front of the house. The truck might be unfamiliar, but the man who climbed out of the driver's seat wasn't.

"Ryder!" She greeted him with a surprised smile.

"Hi, Jewel." His long legs carried him to where she stood. "Hope it's not too early for a visit."

"Of course not. Mornings start early here at the ranch. You want to come in for a cup of coffee? Some of Cheryl's blueberry muffins are probably left over from breakfast."

"No, thanks, I just finished breakfast." He raked a hand through his shiny black hair. "Actually, I'd like to talk to you about a job. You probably heard that

Ana is going to be teaching at the bilingual school. She starts in two weeks."

"No, I hadn't heard, but good for her. I know that's what she's always wanted to do. She'll make a wonderful teacher."

He nodded. "And I've decided to go back to school." His ebony eyes glittered with a newfound pride. "I want to be the best husband for Ana, the best father for Maria that I can be, and I've decided an education is the first step."

Jewel placed a hand on his forearm. "Good for you, Ryder. I'm sure Clay is proud of your decision."

"He is, but more important, I am. I'm committed to turning things around for myself. I'm here for a couple of reasons. I was wondering if you could use some part-time help and if there's a possibility that while I'm in school you'd be available to add Maria to your group of kids. To be honest, Ana and I wouldn't trust her in anyone else's care."

Jewel thought of the sweet baby girl and her heart expanded. "I think we could definitely work something out," she replied. "I've been thinking of having a pen built for some goats and lambs and small animals. Think you could handle that?"

He grinned. "Not a problem. I won't be starting school until the spring semester so until then I was hoping you could use me twenty to twenty-five hours a week."

She nodded and for the next few minutes they worked out the details of his employment and baby

Maria's care. She showed him the area on the side of the house where she wanted the pen and assured him that Jeff would be available to help.

As he got back into his truck to leave she waved, wondering if it had been a simple case of maturity or finding the love of a good woman that had turned the bad boy into a good man.

After he left, Jewel went back inside to grab her car keys and the list of school supplies that needed to be bought. "I'm off," she told Cheryl who was in the kitchen. "Thank goodness I can get this shopping done today and not have to be in town tomorrow. I hate shopping on Saturdays."

"Jeff and I have a whole day of shopping planned for tomorrow. I told him I want to drive into San Antonio and get me a good pair of shoes. All you can find around here are cowboy boots and sneakers."

Jewel smiled. "Make him take you out to lunch at one of those fancy restaurants on the river walk."

"I plan to," Cheryl replied.

Minutes later Jewel was in her car, headed toward Main Street. Since the moment she'd gotten out of bed that morning, she'd thought about calling Quinn to cancel the plans for Sunday.

After the horrible trauma of the night before, she didn't feel it was fair to give him false hope, to allow him to think that they could ever have a real relationship.

He'd made it more than clear that he was interested in her and, under different circumstances, she would have reciprocated. She liked the solidness of him, the gentle nature that she sensed he possessed. And if she were truthful with herself, she'd admit that she also loved the width of his shoulders, the simmer of sensuality that lit his eyes.

But how could she, in good conscience, follow her heart when she suffered visions of a dead man, heard the sounds of her baby crying out from the grave?

It would be best to call him and cancel, to stop whatever might happen between them now before one of them got hurt. The problem was she wasn't sure how to gracefully withdraw the invitation she'd extended. She could cancel the trail ride altogether, but that wasn't fair to the kids.

She sighed as she pulled into a parking space in front of the local discount store. It took her over an hour to get everything for the kids to start school Monday morning.

She was juggling her bags to the car when she saw Quinn walking toward her. Despite her desire to the contrary, her heartbeat raced a little faster at the sight of him.

"Let me help you with those," he said as he took two of the bags from her.

"School supplies," she said. "It's amazing what's required by the teachers these days."

He opened the back car door and put the bags he'd carried inside, then took the other two from her and stowed them, as well. When he turned to look at her, his eyes glowed with a warm light. "I just came from Miss Sue's café where I arranged for lunch for nine to be ready for Sunday. She's working on a real picnic menu—fried chicken and coleslaw and butter-milk biscuits."

"You shouldn't have done that," she protested in dismay. There was no way she could uninvite him knowing the trouble he'd already gone to.

"I don't mind. In fact, I'm really looking forward to it and you know I've never met a kid who didn't like fried chicken." He checked his watch. "Unfor-tunately, I've got to run. I've got an appointment with a horse. I'm looking forward to Sunday, Jewel." He said her name as if it were a caress.

She nodded and watched as he hurried off. Okay, so much for canceling Sunday's plans. Deciding to stop into Miss Sue's for a cup of coffee and a cin-namon bun, Jewel headed down the street toward the café.

As she walked, she realized that a part of her hadn't wanted to cancel, but instead yearned to spend another day in Quinn's company.

The kids would be with them, there would be no opportunity for him to kiss her again, to touch her in any way. She'd give herself that time with him and after Sunday she'd make sure they had no time alone together again.

A sadness swept through her as she realized that she was making the choice to be alone, but what other choice did she have? She would embrace her work, spend her life helping and loving other people's children. It would be enough because it had to be enough, but that didn't mean it didn't hurt.

Quinn Logan had suffered tremendously in burying a wife. She wouldn't want to add to his heartache by getting close to him, allowing him to care for her and in the end having to tell her goodbye as mental illness overwhelmed her.

What she hoped was that the auditory hallucinations were just a manifestation of her grief. Right now they only seemed to affect her at night, just before she fell asleep. She hoped that eventually they would stop, but feared what the future might bring.

The cowbell tingled as she walked through the door of the café. Immediately she saw Olivia Halprin and Sheriff Jericho Yates at one of the tables. They waved her over and insisted that she join them.

Olivia had appeared in town a couple of months ago, suffering from amnesia, and it was Jericho who had taken in the injured young woman. Jericho had taken her to his log cabin in the woods and there love had blossomed.

It was discovered that Olivia had worked for Governor Allan Daniels, the man running against Joe Colton for the party nomination. Olivia had uncovered a trail of crooked deals and bribery, and when her memory had finally returned, Allan Daniels had tried to silence her...permanently. Jericho had managed to save her life and the two had been inseparable ever since.

"How are things at the ranch?" Jericho asked as Jewel sat at their table.

"Fine. And how about your place? I heard through the grapevine that Olivia had been doing some decorating at the log cabin."

Jericho gave a mock frown. "She's put in some fu-fu things that have destroyed the rustic character of the cabin."

Olivia laughed and gave him a playful punch in the arm. "Don't let him fool you. He loves the changes I've made."

Jericho reached out and covered her hand with his. "Actually, that's true. She's made it a home."

"So do you know yet if it's a girl or a boy?" Jewel gestured toward Olivia's tummy.

"The doctor thinks it's a girl," Olivia replied. She smiled at Jericho and then looked back at Jewel. "And if it is, the sheriff has already told me we'll get right to work on a boy."

"That's nice. I'm so happy for you both. And is there a wedding in the future?"

"Absolutely," Jericho replied. "In the very near future."

As Jewel ate her cinnamon bun and drank a cup of coffee, she visited with the couple. There was no question that the two were deeply in love, and while Jewel was happy that they'd found each other, she felt the bittersweet pang of her own loneliness.

It was just after noon when she pulled back into the ranch and reminded herself that she needed to have a session with Barry that afternoon. She smiled as she saw all the kids out in the yard with Cocoa.

Jeff sat on the porch, watching as the kids chased the dog and the dog chased the kids. Jeff approached as Jewel got out of the car.

"We figured a little exercise would be good for Cocoa," he said as he grabbed two of the bags from the backseat.

"I'm not sure who's getting more, the kids or the dog," Jewel replied with a laugh.

"I'll tell you one thing, that dog is smart, but I don't think he's going to make it as any kind of a watchdog. He likes everyone too much. Deputy Rawlings stopped by earlier and I thought Cocoa was going to lick him to death."

Jewel laughed. "That's okay. He's not meant to be a watchdog. Did Adam say why he stopped by?"

"I got the feeling it was just a social visit. I'll take these bags inside for you." He grabbed all the bags while Jewel walked out in the yard to join the kids and Cocoa.

As she played with the dog and the children's laughter filled the air, she reminded herself that this was what was important. She told herself that she didn't need what Jericho and Olivia had found together, she didn't need anything but this ragtag family of troubled kids and the love of her family to sustain her. Maybe if she repeated that mantra enough times, she would actually believe it.

* * *

Quinn arrived at Clay's place early on Sunday. It should have worried him, how anxious he'd been for this day to arrive. But instead he embraced his anticipation, for the first time in years feeling ready to move on with his life, ready to fall in love and fulfill the dreams he hadn't been able to fulfill with Sarah.

And he wanted to do it with Jewel. She both excited and intrigued him. When he was around her, he felt the expectation of something special about to happen, saw a glimpse into a future he desperately wanted to grab.

The food he'd picked up from Miss Sue's was packed in two large coolers and he arranged with Carlos, one of Clay's hands, to have it delivered to a specific place in the pasture around one o'clock.

He was in the stables, saddling up Noches, his black stallion, when Clay walked in. "I heard through the grapevine that you and Jewel were seen looking quite cozy at a certain Mexican restaurant the other day."

Quinn grinned. "Normally I'd tell you that you know better than to listen to the grapevine, but in this particular case, it's true."

"You'll never find a better woman than Jewel," Clay said. "She's had some tough breaks in her life. She deserves some happiness." There was an edge to Clay's voice, as if he was warning Quinn not to toy with Jewel.

Quinn clapped his friend on the back. "Down boy,

you know me better than to think I'd ever intentionally do anything to hurt her."

"I know. I just worry about her." Clay stepped
back and leaned against the stable door. "But it
sounds like you have a fun day planned for today."

"It should be fun." Quinn finished cinching the
saddle and gave Noches a pat on his rump.

"And you talked to Carlos about the lunch details?"

"Yeah, thanks for letting him help out." Their conversation was interrupted by the sound of the minibus
from the Hopechest Ranch pulling up.

Quinn stepped out of the stable and got a blood
rush as he saw Jewel. She looked beautiful with her
tousled golden-brown hair shining in the sun. Her
brown eyes sparkled and her features were relaxed
in a way he hadn't seen before. Worn, tight jeans fit
her long legs to perfection and her pink T-shirt deepened the chocolate hue of her eyes.

In the first fifteen minutes Quinn tried to put faces
with names as she introduced him to all the kids.
Then it took another half an hour to get everyone on
his or her horse and out of the stables.

They followed a well-worn horse trail across the
pasture. The kids were in the lead and Quinn and
Jewel brought up the rear, their horses side by side.

"You look great today," he said.

"Thanks, I feel pretty great. I've been looking forward to today, kind of a final celebration with the
kids before school starts tomorrow."

He hoped she'd also been looking forward to

spending more time with him, but he didn't ask, was afraid of sounding too forward. He had a feeling he needed to take things slowly with her, that she was like a wounded animal that needed to be gentled. And that was one of Quinn's specialties.

It was impossible to have a real conversation with her during the ride. The kids yelled back and forth to one another and the horses whinnied and nickered as the sound of their hooves on the hard earth filled the air.

Still, Quinn always enjoyed riding Noches, who had just enough spirit to be challenging yet not enough to be unmanageable. And there was the additional benefit of being able to look sideways and see Jewel on the horse next to him.

She was a good rider and looked at ease in the saddle. She flashed him a bright smile and urged her horse into a trot, quickly moving to the front of the pack.

Quinn nudged Noches faster to catch up with her. Noches tossed his head, wanting to run like the wind, but Quinn held tight to the reins, refusing to give the stallion his head.

The trails led through the woods, across a small dry creek bed and then into open pasture. It was only then that Quinn allowed Noches to run. He flew ahead of the group with the wind in his face. The horse responded to his most subtle command. Quinn pulled in as he reached the far edge of the pasture and waited for the group to catch up with him.

"Pretty fancy riding, Dr. Logan," Jewel said.

"Maybe I'm showing off in an attempt to impress you," he replied.

She laughed. "Consider me impressed."

"Me, too," Carrie said as she rode up next to them. "Someday I want to ride that fast, but this dumb old horse won't do anything but walk."

Jewel smiled. "When you've had a little more experience on a horse, maybe we'll find you one that runs."

The ride continued until they came to a stand of trees where Carlos sat on a tractor with a small cart behind it containing the lunch coolers. Carlos unfastened the cart and with the promise to return for it later, he drove away.

They let the horses go to graze and Quinn pulled several large tablecloths from the first cooler and spread them on the ground.

Lunch was chaos and laughter. The kids talked almost as much as they ate and it was obvious they all adored Jewel. Jewel remained relaxed. She laughed often and the sound was music to Quinn's ears.

After lunch Quinn pulled several Frisbees from the cooler and led the kids in a game of catch. Jewel remained on the tablecloth and played cheerleader.

As the kids continued to toss the Frisbees back and forth, Quinn walked over and collapsed next to Jewel. "You're the cutest Frisbee cheerleader I've seen in a long time," he said.

"Have you seen a lot of Frisbee cheerleaders in your life?" she asked teasingly.

"Hundreds. Maybe thousands," he replied. "I travel the countryside seeking Frisbee cheerleaders."

"We both know you're full of beans, as the kids would say."

He laughed and looked over where the kids were playing catch. "They're a nice bunch," he observed.

She smiled. "They know you are responsible for giving us Cocoa so they're on their best behavior with you. Trust me, they aren't always this easy to get along with."

"Kelsey doesn't seem to be having as much fun as the others."

Jewel frowned as her gaze went to the dark-haired girl who stood slightly separated from the others, hands shoved in her pockets.

"Kelsey has spent the last couple of years being shuttled from relative to relative. She's terrified to embrace any kind of happiness because she's afraid it will be taken away from her."

"That's the way I felt right after Sarah died."

Jewel turned to look at him, her gaze curious. "You're so much more open than I thought you'd be. Clay had told me you were the strong, silent type."

He smiled. "Normally I *am* pretty quiet, but I've been working on changing that." He looked back at the kids and frowned thoughtfully. "After Sarah died I realized there were so many things I hadn't said to her, so many thoughts I hadn't shared. I decided I'd never let that be a regret again."

Their discussion was interrupted as Lindy joined

them on the blanket, her face flushed from her exer-
tions. "I've gotta rest," she exclaimed. "I'm pooped,
but I think maybe another piece of chicken would
give me my energy back."

Quinn grinned at her. "There's only one thing
better than a piece of fried chicken." He reached
into the cooler and pulled out a container of chocolate cupcakes.

Lindy's eyes lit up and she turned to where the
other kids were still playing with the Frisbees. "Hey,
guys, we got cupcakes," she yelled, sparking a
stampede as they all ran for dessert.

It was almost five by the time they made their
way back to the stables. "They'll all sleep well tonight," Jewel said as she brushed down her horse.

"Nothing like fresh air and sunshine to bring on a
good night's sleep," Quinn replied. He didn't want
the day to end. While he'd enjoyed his interaction
with the kids, he didn't feel as if he'd had enough
time with Jewel.

He led Noches into his stall, then returned to where
Jewel was finishing up with her horse. "I have an idea.
Why don't you take the kids home and get them set-
tled in then meet me back here for a sunset ride."

She looked up at him and in her eyes he saw indeci-
sion. "Come on, Jewel," he urged. "There's nothing
more beautiful that a horseback ride at sunset. Meet
me back here about seven-thirty." He smiled at her. "I
promise you it will be a painless experience."

She smiled then and nodded. "Okay, you talked me into it."

"Great, then I'll meet you back here."

A few minutes later Jewel went with the kids and Quinn left to go home to check on the animals either boarding with him or recovering from illnesses.

Quinn lived in a three-bedroom ranch house. It was simple and efficient but he spent most of his time in the front building, which was the heart of his veterinary practice. The building was divided into four areas—a small office, an area for boarding animals, an examination room and an operating room.

He checked on the boarders, made sure they had food and water, then decided to shower the day's dirt off before the ride with Jewel.

As he redressed in a clean pair of jeans and a navy T-shirt, he tried not to think about what he'd really like to do with Jewel. He'd love to take her on their sunset ride, then dismount and make love to her beneath a starry sky.

She'd confused him today. There had been a distance in her eyes. She'd been more closed off than before, as if afraid to share too much of herself with him.

He didn't want to screw up by pushing her too fast and yet a part of him thought she needed a nudge back into life. He was so ready to embrace her, to embrace love again but, more than anything, he wanted to discover the source of the darkness he sometimes saw in her eyes, a darkness that worried and confused him.

Chapter 7

Jewel hadn't intended to agree to the sunset ride. She knew Quinn liked her, but it wasn't fair to make him think that there was any chance for a romance between them.

But she felt such deep loneliness and so enjoyed his company. It was difficult to deny herself the pleasure of spending more time with him. Maybe they could become good friends.

She stood beneath a hot stream of water in her shower and tried to imagine just being friends with Quinn. It would never work. Friends didn't want to kiss friends and now that she knew what Quinn tasted like, how she felt in his arms, she would never be satisfied with just a simple friendship. And she had a feeling he wouldn't be, either.

"You're overthinking," she said aloud as she stepped out of the shower. That was the problem with being a psychologist, sometimes she analyzed way too much.

She put on a clean pair of jeans and a short-sleeved cotton blouse. Even when the sun went down, it was still warm, despite being the beginning of September.

She was just ready to walk out the door when Adam Rawlings pulled up. As usual, not one of his dark brown hairs was out of place as he got out of his car and ambled toward the porch.

She stepped outside to greet him. "Evening, Adam."

"Jewel." His brown eyes gazed at her intently. "Haven't seen you around lately."

"I've been busy, you know with school starting to-morrow and all."

"You need to take some time off." He smiled, his brown eyes warm and inviting. "Maybe see a movie with me or go out for a nice meal."

"I appreciate the thought, Adam, but now just isn't a good time for me. Maybe when things calm down around here." This wasn't the first time he'd asked her out and he never seemed offended that she never agreed to go out with him.

Perhaps she should. He'd certainly be a safe date for her because she felt absolutely no sparks with him. Unlike Quinn, who by merely looking at her could set her very skin on fire.

"You need to focus on yourself, Jewel," he said,

concern radiating from his eyes. "It's a great thing what you do here for these kids, but you should remember that you're a young woman who should have a life of her own."

"Thanks, Adam. Actually, I was just on my way out." She couldn't very well tell him she was on her way to meet another man, so she offered no other explanation.

"Then at least let me walk you to your car," he replied.

She nodded and stepped off the porch. "Everyone has been talking about the Coltons coming to town," he said as they walked to the garage. "It's not every day we get the man who's probably going to be president, and his wife in Esperanza."

"I can't wait," she exclaimed. The thought of seeing Meredith and Joe again filled her with warmth. "I'm planning a good old-fashioned Texas barbecue here during their visit."

"Sounds like a good time. I'm sure you'll want Jericho and all of us deputies here for additional security."

"I want you here as guests, as well," she replied. She punched the button on her remote to raise her garage door. "It will be a wonderful day filled with family and friends."

"Those are the best kind of days," he agreed. "I'll just say good night now and let you get on your way."

"Thanks, Adam."

He cocked an eyebrow upward. "For what?"

"For always checking in with me...for caring."

He smiled and there was a fierce intensity in his gaze. "I do care." He nodded a goodbye, then turned on his heels and went back to his car.

Jewel got into her car and backed out of the garage as Adam disappeared into his. He was a nice man. He had a great body for a man who was forty years old. Funny, she'd never heard him talk about any family. She assumed he was no stranger to loneliness, either.

The minute she pulled out of her driveway, thoughts of Adam disappeared as Quinn filled her mind. The sun hung low in the sky. Another thirty minutes and it would be sunset.

When she pulled up in front of Clay's stable, Quinn was already there, both his horse and the one she'd ridden that afternoon saddled and ready to go.

She couldn't help the way her heart leapt at the sight of him, so tall, so strong-looking and with that smile that made her feel as if she were the most important person in his world.

As she got out of the car and approached him, she couldn't help the lightness that filled her heart, the emotion that felt remarkably like joy.

"Hi," he said.

"Hi, yourself. Looks like you've got us all ready to go."

"I've even got a bottle of wine and a couple of glasses tucked into my saddlebag for a sunset toast."

"Wine and a sunset—sounds like the perfect ending

to a day," she said. And of course, there was also the handsome hunk to add to the heady combination.

She was glad she'd come. As they mounted the horses, she told herself not to think, not to analyze, but rather just to enjoy the beauty of the night and Quinn's company.

At a leisurely pace, they followed the same trails that they'd ridden earlier in the day. For a few minutes, neither of them spoke. It was a peaceful silence, one that didn't demand to be broken.

Birds flitted from tree to tree, emitting their last melodic songs of the day and a faint breeze provided a pleasurable relief from the afternoon's heat.

"I enjoyed the kids this afternoon," he said, finally breaking the silence.

"They think you're awesome," Jewel replied. She'd been impressed watching him interact with the kids. He'd treated each of them with respect and kindness. He'd listened patiently to all of them and she'd known instinctively that it hadn't been just an act for her benefit.

"Kelsey seemed a bit standoffish."

Jewel nodded. "She's afraid to be happy. I'm trying to teach her that happiness isn't a constant state of being and you need to grasp it when it comes and hold tight."

He frowned. "It's a shame a child that young has to have that kind of fear."

"You like kids." It was a comment rather than a question.

He nodded. "I do. I always wanted a big family

of my own. Unfortunately, it just wasn't in the cards for me."

"You still have time," she protested. "It's not as if you're over the hill."

He grinned and reached up to sweep his hair away from his eyes. "No, but sometimes I feel like I'm halfway up that hill."

She laughed. "If you're halfway up the hill, then I'm right behind you."

For the next few minutes they kept a slow pace and talked about the afternoon and each of the children. "Carrie told me she loved Cocoa but she really, really loved kittens," he said. "And Barry told me he'd love to have a lizard." He flashed her a grin. "I think I may have started something."

Jewel laughed again. "Maybe I can satisfy them with the goats and sheep I intend to get once I have a nice pen ready. I hired Ryder to work on building the pen."

"What's the story on Ryder and Clay's father? I've always gotten the feeling that things weren't great between them all."

"Ryder, Clay and Georgie are Uncle Graham's children from an affair he had while he was unhappily married to Cynthia, who was an extremely wealthy woman. Although everyone said he truly loved their mother, Mary Lynn Grady, he loved money more and so refused to leave his wife."

"It's a foolish man who would choose money over love."

"Uncle Graham has been on the outs with the family for a long time," she continued. "I think Uncle Joe tried to be close to him and gave him one opportunity after another to do right, but Uncle Graham continued to make bad choices and I think it hurts Uncle Joe that the two don't have any kind of a relationship now." She smiled ruefully. "Aren't you sorry you asked?"

"Not at all. To be honest, I find the Colton family history fascinating. It makes me realize how truly boring my family is."

"I'm sure the Coltons would have gladly taken a little more boring over the years," she replied.

They rode to the spot where they'd had lunch earlier in the day, then dismounted. Quinn pulled a blanket from his saddlebag, along with the wine and two glasses.

They sat side by side as the sun dipped lower in the sky, spreading out the last gasp of daylight in vivid pinks and oranges.

"To a beautiful sunset and a beautiful woman," Quinn said as he raised his wineglass to hers.

The toast might have sounded cheesy coming from any other man, but the light in his eyes told her the words came from his heart.

She stretched out on her side on the blanket and propped herself up on an elbow. "You should find a nice woman, Quinn."

He laid down facing her and crooked an eyebrow upward. "I have," he replied.

She shook her head. "You need somebody without baggage. Unfortunately, I have a ton."

"I don't know if you've noticed or not, but I have big, strong shoulders."

"Trust me, I've noticed," she replied dryly.

"Then why don't you trust me?" His eyes held her gaze intently.

She broke the eye contact and instead took a sip of her wine and stared at the sunset slowly fading into a night sky. "It's not that easy," she replied softly.

He reached out and covered one of her hands with his. "You can trust me, Jewel. You can tell me whatever is on your mind, anything, anytime."

She pulled her hand out from beneath his, finding his touch far too pleasurable. "You don't know anything about me. You have no idea where I come from."

"Then tell me. But hear me, Jewel. I can't imagine anything you'd tell me that would change my mind about you." His deep voice held a certainty that sent a rush of warmth through her.

"Did you know that my mother and Meredith Colton were twins?" she asked.

"No. I hadn't heard that," he replied. He showed no surprise at her seemingly abrupt change of topic.

"After my mother got out of prison for killing my father, she attacked Meredith. Meredith had amnesia and my mother switched identities with her. My mother impersonated Meredith for almost ten years while Meredith suffered amnesia and in those ten years my mother wreaked havoc on Joe's life."

"And what does this have to do with you, Jewel?" His tone was as gentle as the night breeze that caressed her skin. He moved closer to her, so close she could smell the scent of his cologne, feel the heat from his body radiating over her.

"Your mother was obviously a troubled woman, but I've seen you with your kids, I know the kind of heart you have, and if you thought by telling me about your mother I'd back off, then you were wrong." He set his wineglass aside.

This man was killing her with his heated eyes and his open heart. She wanted to tell him that she heard voices in the night, that phantom baby cries ripped at her guts. She wanted to warn him that she might be as unstable as her mother had been, but at that moment he reached out and touched her lips with his index finger.

"I want you, Jewel and the only thing that will make me back off is if you tell me that you don't want me." With a slow deliberation, he took her wineglass from her and set it just off the blanket.

She knew he intended to kiss her and even though she told herself she shouldn't let it happen, she shouldn't want it, want him so badly, she did.

He gathered her into his arms and kissed her. Soft and gentle, his lips whispered against hers and her heart fluttered in response.

Was it wrong of her to want him even knowing that she wouldn't, couldn't have a long-term relationship with him? If it was wrong at this moment, she didn't care. All she wanted was for him to hold her forever, for him to keep kissing her until she lost the capacity to think.

She opened her mouth, urging him to deepen the kiss. His tongue touched her bottom lip, then delved deeper to swirl with her own.

His hands moved up and down her back, caressing lightly as she tightened her arms around his neck. She leaned into him, wanting full contact with his lean, hard body.

Night shadows deepened and still they kissed, the only noise the sound of the horses shuffling their hooves nearby and Jewel and Quinn's quickened breathing.

She wanted more. The yearning that filled her was so intense that she could think of nothing but Quinn and her need to have him make love to her.

Her fingers found a button on his shirt and she unfastened it, wanting to run her hands over his bare chest. He released a small gasp as she unfastened another button, but his mouth didn't move from hers.

She used both hands, eager to get the shirt unbuttoned, and when she did, she slid her hands over his sculpted, hard chest. His skin was fevered heat and she loved the feel of his muscles, his bare flesh, beneath her fingertips.

He slid his hands up beneath her blouse, his palms warming her from the outside in, firing a desire in her to have more from him. His mouth lifted from hers but only to move to her cheek, then to the sensitive spot just behind her ear.

She was lost…lost in his touch, lost in the sensations that he evoked inside her. She wanted to stay in this pasture with him forever, with his mouth on hers, with his hands warming all the cold places in her heart and the night air surrounding them. But without warning he dropped his arms from around her and sat up.

He raked a hand through his thick mane of hair and released a deep sigh. "Not like this, Jewel," he said. "I want you so badly it hurts, but not like this. Not in a pasture. I want you in a soft bed with sheets to cuddle beneath and the entire night stretching out before us."

"Then take me home, to my bed and stay the night with me," she replied. She was shocked by her own words, but that didn't mean she wanted to take them back.

Just one night. She wanted just one night with him, with no sense of reason interfering, no common sense at play. She wanted one night of not thinking, of keeping the ghosts at bay.

He placed his palm on her cheek, the heat in his gaze igniting a faster burn inside her. "Are you sure that's what you want?"

"I've never been more sure of anything in my life," she replied.

In one fluid motion he stood and held out a hand to her. She reached for his hand and he pulled her to her feet and back into his arms. "I think I've wanted you since the very first time I laid eyes on you."

She looked up at him. "I feel the same way."

He released her and without saying another word he grabbed the wine bottle and glasses, then the blanket and stowed them back in his saddlebag.

As they rode back to the stable, she waited for a whisper of caution to flit through her head, a protest against what she was about to do, but all she felt was a calm peacefulness sweeping through her as she thought of spending the night in Quinn's arms.

Stars had begun to twinkle overhead, along with a half-sliced pie moon. The horses moved quickly toward home, as if they sensed their riders' eagerness.

When Jewel and Quinn reached the stables, it took only minutes for them to unsaddle the horses and get them into the appropriate stalls. Jewel then got into her car and headed for home with Quinn following in his truck.

She wouldn't be able to write this off as a crazy, impulsive move made in the heat of the moment. At any time during the ride back from the stables she could have changed her mind, but she didn't.

She wasn't giving him forever; she wasn't promising a thing. Consenting adults slept together all the time—it didn't have to mean anything except a single night of pleasure.

When she reached the ranch, she pulled into the garage, then stood by the door while Quinn parked and got out of his car.

He walked toward her and she felt the thrum of sexual excitement singing through her veins. She didn't remember feeling this intense hunger for Andrew. Making love with Andrew had been warm and fuzzy, not hot and edgy and that's exactly how Quinn made her feel.

When he reached where she stood by the front door, she felt his hesitation. "I'm only going to ask you this one last time," he said. "Are you sure about this? I've got to warn you, I'm not the kind of man who wants to make love to you then sneak out like a thief in the night."

She answered him by opening the front door and pulling him inside. The house was quiet and she led him through the entry and into her private quarters.

When she'd left the room hours earlier she'd had no idea that Quinn would be here with her, in her private, intimate space.

Although the room was quite large, he filled it with his presence. He held her gaze as he unbuttoned his shirt once again and shrugged it off his shoulders. His muscled chest gleamed in the light on her nightstand. He sat on the edge of the bed and took off his boots and socks, then stood once again.

Her throat went dry and her knees threatened to buckle as his hands moved to the button on his jeans. A rush of heat went through her, watching him step out of his jeans, leaving him only in a pair of low-riding navy briefs.

He came toward her with slow, deliberate movements, then unfastened the buttons on her blouse. When he was finished, he shoved the material off her shoulders and it fell to the floor behind her. His lips claimed hers once again and he cupped her breasts through the thin lace of her bra.

She unhooked her jeans, wanting nothing more than to be naked with him, to feel his hot, firm flesh against her own. He broke the kiss as she peeled off her jeans, then she walked over to the bed and slid in beneath the covers.

He grabbed his wallet from his jeans, set it on the nightstand, then joined her in the bed and wrapped her up in his arms as their lips met in a fiery kiss of desire.

The kiss continued while he unfastened her bra, swept the garment away as if it offended him, then captured her breasts in his hands. She hissed with pleasure as his thumbs raked over her taut nipples.

"You are so beautiful," he murmured, his mouth laving hers. He raised up just enough to stare down at her face. "You have no idea how much I want you."

"It can't be anymore than how much I want you," she replied.

He dipped his head and captured one of her nipples with his mouth. Sweet sensations of both pleasure and want crashed through her as she tangled her fingers in his thick, soft hair.

It didn't take long for them to rid themselves of the last of their underwear and their caresses grew even more intimate. She loved the smooth skin on his chest, broken only by a smattering of hair in the center. She loved the smell of him, a scent of the outdoors coupled with woodsy cologne and clean male.

He seemed to be in no hurry as he nibbled on her ear, slid his hot, hungry mouth down her throat, explored her inner thigh with his hands and moved her closer and closer to explosive peaks.

Refusing to be a passive partner, Jewel discovered that he moaned with pleasure when she ran her hand across his lower abdomen, close but not touching where she knew he wanted her to. He gasped as she licked his flat male nipples.

They caressed and tasted each other like two people who had been sensory-deprived for an eternity. His fingers finally found the very center of her, sliding against her moist heat, and she arched to meet him, need clawing at her, taking her up to new heights.

As she felt the approaching climax, she clung to him. Every muscle in her body stiffened and tremors of pleasure rocked through her, leaving her gasping and spent, yet wanting more.

She reached down and encircled the hard length of him, reveling in his moan of pleasure as she stroked him. He only allowed her touch for a moment, then he rolled her over on her back and reached for his wallet on the nightstand.

It took him only seconds to put on a condom, then move on top of her and between her thighs. For just a moment he remained poised above her, his eyes glowing like those of a wild animal.

In that moment, she felt more loved, more cherished then she ever had in her life. It was in the tenderness, in the hunger of his golden-brown eyes.

As he eased into her she closed her eyes, giving herself to the magic of his lovemaking. And it *was* magic. He entered her and paused to kiss her with a gentleness that stole her breath away.

He began to move against her, back and forth with slow, even strokes intended to produce the most pleasure. She raised her legs and locked them around his back, urging him deeper and faster as she felt the build once again begin.

Crying his name over and over again, she was lost in the act, in him. They moved faster, frenzied, and their pants and gasps filled the room.

She was there again, crashing down with earth-shattering tremors. He cried out her name as his own release washed over him. He shuddered once... twice, then remained still, his weight supported on his elbows as he sought to catch his breath.

He placed his hands on either side of her face and kissed her. "I'll be right back. Don't go away." He rolled out of the bed and padded into the adjoining bathroom.

Jewel felt weak with sated pleasure. She felt as if she had melted into the mattress and only an atomic bomb could force her to get up.

Quinn returned to the bedroom, and she turned off the bedside lamp. She was glad he wasn't dressing to leave but instead slid back into the bed and pulled her into his arms.

She lay with her upper body across his chest and she reached out a finger and touched the scar on his cheek. "How did you get that?"

He smiled. "Her name was Molly and she was the meanest mare I've ever met. I was working on her shoulder, where she had a sore, and she reared up and knocked me in the face then stomped on me."

She looked at him, horrified. "I had no idea being a veterinarian was so dangerous."

"I was young and careless and wasn't as wary as I should have been. It was as much my fault as it was hers."

"I'm glad you didn't jump back into your clothes and backpedal out of here." Jewel released a soft sigh and placed her head on his chest where the sound of his heartbeat was strong.

He stoked her hair with his big, strong hand. "As far as I'm concerned, the cuddle time afterward is almost as important as making love."

She sighed again, surprised to find her eyelids heavy with sleep. Her body fit perfectly against his and each caress of her hair brought sleep closer and closer.

"Quinn? Sometimes I have nightmares," she said, feeling as if she needed to warn him in case she had a bad night.

He slid his hand from her hair down her back, his palm like a miniature heating pad against her skin. "You won't tonight, Jewel."

He said the words with such confident assurance that she believed him. They shifted positions. She turned on her side and he spooned around her back, an arm flung over her as if in protection. Feeling more safe than she had in years, Jewel slept.

Chapter 8

Jewel awakened to early morning sunlight filtering in through the curtains at her window. Her first thought was that there had been no dreams, no ghostly cries from the beyond. She had slept deeper and longer than she had since the death of Andrew and their unborn child.

Her second thought was of Quinn. She turned over in the bed and found herself alone. He must have crept out earlier and she was almost grateful. She would not have to explain to Jeff or Cheryl and the children why the handsome vet was in the house before breakfast.

Rolling over on her back to stare up at the ceiling fan, her head filled with visions of the night she'd shared with him. Just the memory caused her to tingle from head to toe.

He'd been a wonderful lover, both gentle and commanding and it frightened her more than a little how much she would love to repeat the experience.

But she couldn't. She'd already been unfair to him by allowing last night to happen. She knew Quinn wasn't the kind of man to take his relationships lightly and that would make everything more difficult.

She couldn't date Quinn knowing that she would never, could never fully commit to him. It wouldn't be fair to him and ultimately her.

Time to distance herself, she thought as she got out of bed and padded into the bathroom, then got into the shower. Even though she had slept dreamlessly last night in his arms, that didn't mean that she would no longer be haunted by Andrew and the baby she had lost.

It wouldn't bother her so much if she only heard Andrew softly calling her name and the baby crying in her dreams, but there had been far too many nights when she'd been wide-awake and had heard them.

And that's when the true haunting began, when she remembered her last visit with her mother in the mental ward. Patsy had been lost to the world, muttering incoherently and laughing inappropriately, hearing voices that weren't there, answering questions that nobody had asked.

As Jewel dressed she heard the sound of the children in the kitchen getting ready for breakfast. They were louder this morning, their voices filled with first day of school jitters.

Initially, Jewel had considered having her kids homeschooled, but ultimately she'd decided that interacting with the kids in town would be far healthier for them than isolation and the feeling that they were different. Besides, she wanted the town residents, who had harbored reservations about a ranch for troubled kids, to see that these kids weren't a threat.

An hour later she stood by the road that ran in front of the Hopechest Ranch, waiting for the school bus to appear. The sun overhead was brutal even at this time of the morning. The morning weather report had indicated that for the next week or two the temperatures were supposed to be well above normal.

"And the bus will bring us right back here after school, right?" Barry asked for the fourth time.

"The bus driver will drop all of you off at this very same spot," Jewel assured him.

"I hope my teacher likes me," Lindy exclaimed.

"Don't worry," Kelsey said, and placed a hand on Lindy's shoulder. "What's not to like?"

Jewel's heart warmed as she saw the older girl reassuring Lindy. It was the first sign she'd seen from Kelsey that she was reaching out, forming bonds, and that was important.

The bus lumbered into sight, spewing up a cloud of dust. It was only eight in the morning and already Jewel felt as if she could use another shower.

She saw the kids off, waving until the bus roared out

of sight, then she turned and walked back to the house. She'd just reached the porch when Ryder arrived.

Maria wasn't with him and he explained that Ana was home today with the baby. Her school wasn't to start until the following week.

"Gonna be a hot one today," she said.

"Supposed to be vicious for the next couple of weeks," he replied. "I've got the supplies coming for the pen this morning."

"Great, but make sure you stay hydrated while you're working out here," she cautioned. "Come inside and cool off whenever you need to."

He flashed her a grin. "Don't worry, I won't let the heat defeat me."

"I don't want to push you, but I'd love for the pen to be up and functioning by the time Meredith and Joe come to town."

"That's what, two weeks from now? I'm hoping Jeff and I will be able to have it knocked out by next weekend. That will give you a week to get the animals you want for the kids."

"Sounds perfect," Jewel replied.

With a wave he headed toward the area where the pen would be constructed. Jewel went back into the house.

"If it's okay with you, Jeff and I would like to take the kids on that field trip we talked about next Saturday or the Saturday after that," Cheryl said as the two women sat at the table and sipped a cup of coffee.

"The week after would work out perfect for me,"

Jewel replied thoughtfully. "While you're all gone, there are some things I want to do around here to prepare for the barbecue I'm planning for Joe and Meredith."

"Great! I'll tell Jeff we're on," Cheryl replied. The phone rang and she jumped up to answer it. She held out the phone to Jewel. "It's Quinn Logan for you." She covered the mouthpiece as Jewel hesitated.

"Tell him I'll call him back," she finally said. Her heart ached as Cheryl delivered the message. She'd love to hear his voice this morning, to tell him that she'd slept better in his arms last night than on any night since she'd arrived in Esperanza. But what was the point when she intended nothing more between them?

"Everything all right?" Cheryl asked, hanging up the phone.

"Fine, I just didn't feel like any social chitchat this morning. I'm going to go back to my office and catch up on some paperwork," she said, feeling the need to escape Cheryl's skeptical gaze.

Once she was at her desk, she leaned her head back against the chair and forced herself to think of anything but Quinn.

That day in the library—when she'd been researching the accident that had forever changed her life—seemed like months ago. She realized that she hadn't followed up on any of the information she'd learned that day.

What ever happened to James Corrs after Andrew

had turned him in for tax evasion? She hadn't gotten that far before Quinn had interrupted her.

With the kids at school and no fear of interruption she logged onto the Internet and searched for news articles related to James Corrs. It didn't take her long to find what she was searching for. James Corrs had gone to prison for federal tax evasion. He'd been sentenced to fifteen years. That was a long time to spend behind bars.

Before going to prison had he paid Andrew back by ramming into her car? What she wanted to do was call the authorities in California and have them reopen the case, investigate fully James Corrs as a suspect in the fatal hit-and-run.

But she knew what they would say. The accident had been ruled just that, they had other crimes to investigate and couldn't spend the time or manpower on a hit-and-run that had happened almost three years ago.

Wrapping her arms around her shoulders, plagued by a chill despite the warmth of the room, she thought about that moment when she'd awakened from one of her nightmares and had found the news clipping lying next to her.

It was crazy to think that somebody had snuck into the house and placed the clipping on her bed for her to find. But it was no more crazy than the logical explanation that she'd gotten up in her sleep and had dug the clipping out of a box of keepsakes.

Quinn had kept the ghosts at bay last night. It had been the first time in a very long time that she hadn't suffered any nightmares or heard voices or crying in the night.

Once again she found herself fighting the impulse to pick up the phone and return his call. Instead, she got up from her desk and decided to head over to Tamara and Clay's. They'd pulled a fast one eloping. Jewel wanted to hear all the details from Tamara and hadn't had an opportunity to talk to Tamara since learning the news.

Maybe part of the reason she wanted to talk to Tamara was because she knew her friend had never really warmed up to Quinn. By talking to her, Jewel could get the man out of her brain and would be able to forget the crazy yearning she had to fall back into his arms.

She drove the short distance to Clay's and parked in front of his house. She stepped out of the coolness of the car and the midmorning heat slapped her in the face.

Tamara answered her knock, her pretty face lighting with a smile. "Jewel, what a pleasure. Come on in."

"Thanks, I just thought I'd pop in for a quick visit. Is this a bad time?"

Tamara linked arms with her and walked her toward the kitchen. "Actually, it's a perfect time. I was just getting ready to have a glass of iced tea."

"Sounds wonderful. I can't believe how hot it is."

Tamara unlinked her arm with Jewel's and pointed her to the table. "And according to the weather reports it's only supposed to get worse. So I guess you're at loose ends today with the start of school."

Jewel smiled. "It's going to be strange having the kids gone during the weekdays."

"And I hear you have a new houseguest." Tamara set a glass of tea in front of Jewel then poured herself one and joined her at the table.

Jewel frowned. "A new houseguest?"

"Woof woof," Tamara replied.

Jewel laughed. "Ah, you mean, Cocoa. Yes, it was Quinn's idea." It was a perfect segue into the topic she most wanted to discuss. "I always got the impression you didn't much like Quinn."

Tamara smiled. "I have to confess that when he had to make the decision to put down Clay's stud, I hated the man. It was purely an emotional response. I saw how that decision hurt Clay and I guess it was kind of like killing the messenger. But since I've been back here I've changed my mind. Clay is constantly telling me what a stand-up guy Quinn is and I have to confess, I agree."

She raised an eyebrow. "Do I sense some interest there? Is it possible Adam Rawlings has some competition for your affections? Adam certainly hasn't hidden the fact that he has the hots for you."

"Unfortunately, the feeling isn't mutual and no, there's no interest with Quinn." The lie left a bad taste in her mouth. "I think I'm one of those women who are best alone."

"Human beings are not meant to be alone,"

Tamara countered. "We're built to thrive when loved and when loving. Trust me, Jewel, I tried it alone and it's not all it's cracked up to be. If you have an interest in the handsome vet, I say go for it."

For the next three days Jewel thought of Tamara's words. Quinn called several times each day and if Cheryl didn't answer and take a message, Jewel let the machine pick up.

She knew it was only a matter of time before she had to face him. What worried her was that she knew she was weak as far as he was concerned and for both of their sakes she had to stay strong. She had to stay away from him.

It had been four days since Quinn had heard from Jewel and he didn't intend to let another day pass without speaking with her.

It was obvious that she was avoiding his phone calls, so this morning he refused to give her a chance to escape him. At eight o'clock he parked his truck at the end of her driveway, where he assumed the school bus would pick up the kids.

He got out of the truck and walked around to the back, where he sat on the edge of the bed and waited. He wasn't sure what was up with her. When he'd left her bed in the predawn hours after making love with her, he'd believed that they were on their way to building something meaningful, something magic.

He couldn't accept that he'd simply imagined the

way she'd responded to him, not only in bed but also on their sunset ride when they'd shared pieces of themselves with each other.

Something had spooked her and he was determined to get to the bottom of it. She was the first woman who had captured his interest since his wife's death, and he wanted her to be the last.

The sun beat down on his shoulders as he watched the house. Maybe he'd rushed things with her. They'd gotten intimate so fast. Maybe he should have spent more time courting her. But there was no question that he felt an enormous passion for her, a passion that was hard to deny.

He sat up straighter as he saw the front door open and the kids began to spill out. Jewel followed them with Cocoa on a leash and he saw the exact moment she spied him. Her shoulders went rigid and she slowed her pace as if dreading what lay ahead. He was shocked by the quick stab of pain that coursed through him at her reaction.

Cocoa, on the other hand jumped and leapt with eagerness as soon as the dog saw him. "Dr. Quinn." Lindy greeted him with a wide smile. "Did you come to see us get on the bus?"

Sam tapped her on the back. "Duh, he's here to see Miss Jewel."

"I got here extra early so I could see all of you," Quinn replied.

"See, he wanted to see us get on the bus," Lindy exclaimed in triumph.

Quinn smiled at Jewel. "You've been a difficult lady to get in touch with the last couple of days." *Keep it light,* he told himself. He took a step toward her and petted Cocoa.

"Things have been crazy around here this week," she replied, her gaze not quite reaching his.

"Too crazy for a quick phone call?" A note of censure crept into his voice.

Before she could reply, the bus appeared. It wasn't until the kids were loaded and the bus pulled away that he spoke again. "Did I move too fast?"

She finally looked at him. "No, it's nothing you did wrong. It's me. I've just realized I'm not ready for any kind of a relationship."

"You seemed more than ready for one before we fell into bed with each other," he replied.

Her cheeks turned pink and she looked away from him, staring back at the house as if longing to run inside and escape him. "It was that night that I realized I just wasn't ready for this…for you."

"And when will you be ready? Because I'll wait. Ask around town, Jewel. People will tell you I'm a very patient man, especially when it comes to something…someone I think is important."

She looked up at him again and in the depths of her chocolate eyes he saw a yearning and he knew for certain that they were worth fighting for. All he had to figure out was exactly what he was fighting against.

"If we moved too fast, we can slow things down," he continued. "I'll take you out to dinner. We can see a movie and I won't touch you, won't kiss you again unless you give me express permission."

A half laugh, half sob escaped her. "Oh, Quinn, you're making things so difficult. That's why I didn't want to talk to you—because I knew you wouldn't just accept what I said without question."

"I accept things when they make sense, but so far you haven't told me anything that makes sense." He placed a hand on her shoulder. "The other night was amazing and confirmed for me that you're the woman I've been waiting for all this time. I thought I could be the man you were waiting for, too."

She stepped away from his touch, as if finding it painful and that only confirmed his feeling that she cared about him and was running away from him for another reason.

"Talk to me, Jewel. Tell me what's really going on." He'd thought he'd never find love again when Sarah died. He'd believed all chance of happiness had died with his wife.

But after spending time with Jewel, after making love to her, he knew she was his second chance for happiness and he wasn't about to let her walk away without an explanation that made sense.

She straightened her shoulders but her gaze didn't quite meet his. "You're a nice man, Quinn. And I got caught up in the moment with you, but I'm just not ready for any relationship with a man. I'm sorry if I led you on, but there's nothing else to say."

She didn't wait for his response, but rather turned

and headed toward the house with Cocoa running at her side.

Quinn watched her go, his heart a leaden weight in the pit of his stomach.

Quinn had never been an egotistical man, but he didn't believe her. He didn't believe that she'd gotten caught up in the moment and now realized she didn't care about him. When he'd touched her, he'd seen a flare of desire in her eyes. She wanted him still.

Jewel Mayfair had secrets. He'd sensed that since the moment he'd met her and he was determined to get to the bottom of things, to discover the secrets that kept her from a life of happiness with him.

Chapter 9

The night wrapped around Jewel like a lover with a fever, the heat of the day maintaining its grip long after night had fallen.

She'd spent the last two hours tossing and turning in bed, unable to find sleep no matter how hard she tried. She'd finally given up and decided to take a walk in the woods.

This time it wasn't ghostly voices or baby cries that had kept her from falling asleep. Rather, it had been thoughts of Quinn.

Seeing him that morning had been far more difficult than she'd thought it would be. Telling him she didn't want a relationship with him had been sheer torture. All she'd really wanted to do was rush into his arms, hear his deep, reassuring voice telling her that they were going to have a wonderful future together.

But as long as she questioned her own sanity, she would never allow herself to be with any man who would have to go through with her what she'd lived through in the final months of her mother's life.

It had taken her years to connect with Patsy and even though the Baylors had raised her with love, she'd needed something from her mother that they hadn't been able to give her. Unfortunately, she'd never gotten it. Patsy had been incapable of giving love to the daughter she rarely recognized and could no longer remember giving birth to.

It had to be like what family members of Alzheimer's patients went through and Jewel wouldn't consciously choose to put somebody she loved through that.

The brush rustled to her left and she caught her breath in surprise. Slowly she breathed again as she realized she must have disturbed some poor creature's slumber. Nice that somebody could get some sleep tonight, she thought ruefully.

Even though she was dressed only in her night-gown and a lightweight short robe, the heat was oppressive, pressing in on her from all sides. There had been a number of power outages over the last couple of days due to the heat and the overload on the electrical grid. And there was no break in sight.

She heard a rustling from someplace behind her. She froze again. It hadn't sounded like a little night creature. It had sounded big. The sound came again, this time a little closer, a loud crashing as if something or someone was running toward her.

She thought of all those times she'd felt as if somebody was watching her and a lump of apprehension jumped into her throat. A burst of adrenaline shot through her and then came the taste of fear.

As the noise grew closer, she ran blindly down the narrow path, her heart pounding. She threw a glance over her shoulders and although she saw nothing on the path behind her, she saw movement in the tangled woods and brush just off the path.

There was no question in her mind. Somebody was after her and the fact that he hadn't said a word, was rushing at her out of the dark, terrified her.

She was afraid to run full tilt on the dark path. If she banged into a tree or tripped over an exposed root, then whoever was behind her would catch her. If she ran fast enough and far enough, she'd eventually reach Clay's place and safety, but the crashing noise let her know that whoever was chasing her was getting closer.

Tears filled her eyes, making vision even more difficult. She tripped and painfully smashed a knee to the ground. She scrambled back to her feet and kept moving, a sob escaping her lips.

"Jewel?" The deep voice boomed from just ahead of her.

She sobbed in relief as Quinn appeared on the path in front of her. His tall, lean silhouette in the near-darkness appeared like an island in a sea of shark-infested waters. She didn't hesitate but ran directly into his arms. "S-Somebody chasing me." Her teeth chattered despite the warmth of the night.

He tightened his arms around her. "It's okay. You're safe now."

She hid her face in the front of his clean-smelling shirt and after a moment had passed she didn't hear any noise except the beating of her own heart, and the beating of his. Here was safety, in his big, strong arms.

Looking up at him, she saw his gaze taking in the woods around them, felt the slight tension that filled his body, the tension of a man ready to fight whatever might crawl out of the darkness. It only made her feel even safer.

"I don't see or hear anything," he finally said. "Whatever it was or whoever it was is gone. Come on, I'll walk you back to your house," he said as she finally stepped away from him.

He took her by the arm, as if to keep her close to him as they began to walk back to the ranch. She welcomed his touch, the reassuring feel of his warm hand on her arm. "Why don't you have Cocoa with you?" he asked.

"I was afraid he'd bark at everything that moved and disturb the kids," she replied. With each step she took with Quinn at her side, her heartbeat slowed to a more normal pace.

"Quinn, I didn't imagine it. There was somebody

chasing me," she said as they left the path and entered the gate that led into the pool area.

In the moonlight his gaze held surprise as he looked at her. "It never entered my mind that you imagined it," he said. He motioned her toward one of the pool chairs. "Let's sit for a minute, let you calm down before you go inside."

The idea of sitting and talking to him was much more appealing that her going back to her bedroom alone with only her thoughts as company. She sat in a chair and Quinn next to her, close enough that she could smell his familiar scent.

"Better?" he asked after a minute of silence.

"I was better the minute you appeared on that path," she confessed.

He leaned forward and took one of her hands in his. "I get the feeling that there are things you aren't telling me and I wish I could make you realize that it's okay to trust me. I don't want to give up on you, Jewel. Nothing you said to me makes me believe we can't have a future together."

She felt as if her heart were being ripped in half. "Did you know I lost a baby?" The words tumbled from her lips before they had fully formed in her head.

He drew in an audible breath and his hand tightened on hers. "No, I didn't know that."

"It was in the accident that killed Andrew. I was four months' pregnant when I left the restaurant with Andrew that night. Then the accident happened and I was knocked unconscious. When I regained consciousness the next morning, both Andrew and my baby were gone."

"I'm sorry, Jewel. I'm so damned sorry for you."

The grief in his voice oddly enough eased some of her own. *Tell him about the cries,* a little voice whispered inside her. *Tell him that you hear Andrew calling your name during the night.*

But she didn't. She couldn't. What if he told somebody else and word got out that Jewel Mayfair was unbalanced, that she heard and saw ghosts in the night. She would lose her position here at the ranch, and that, along with the children here, were all that kept her from utter despair.

"Jewel, I know that what you went through was horrible and there will always be a place in your heart for all you lost, but isn't there a place for me, as well?"

Again a new pain ripped through her as she gazed into his beautiful eyes, felt the warmth and caring radiating from his hand holding hers.

"You're too young a woman to allow grief to forever rule your heart. There can be other babies. You can have a life filled with love." He leaned back a bit. "Maybe what you're suffering is a bit of Kelsey-itis," he continued.

She frowned. "What do you mean?"

"You're desperately afraid to grab on to happiness again because you know that it can be stolen away. You told me that you've told her that you need to grab on to it when it comes and hold tight so that you at least have memories of happiness if it goes away.

Maybe you need to take your own advice. You need to let go of Andrew to make room for new happiness."

Was it possible that the voice and the cries of a baby were nothing more than her trying to keep Andrew and that distant happiness alive? Was it possible that in embracing what Quinn offered, in allowing him into her heart, the cries from the grave would finally be silenced forever?

For the first time since arriving in Esperanza, her heart filled with a fragile hope. She wanted to reach out to Quinn. She wanted him in her life.

"We can take it slow, Jewel," he said. "We can take it as slow as you want. I know you have a lot of things on your mind right now with Joe and Meredith coming to town next weekend and I realize your job here takes up a lot of your time. I'll take whatever you can give me. Just don't cut me out."

"I don't want to cut you out," she said softly, and this time it was she who tightened her grip on his hand. "Maybe I *have* been afraid to let go of the past," she admitted slowly.

"Trust me, I understand. After Sarah died, I grieved for a long time. I was afraid that if I let go of the grief I'd have nothing, be nothing. It defined me for a long time. Then one morning I woke up and the sun was shining and the birds were singing and I decided I wouldn't let my grief define me for another moment. It was time to start living again."

"Have you ever thought about being a psychologist?" she asked teasingly.

He laughed, that low, deep sound that wrapped around her heart and warmed her from the inside out. "I have enough problems figuring out the psychological problems of animals. I wouldn't attempt to try to analyze people. I'll leave that to you." He released her hand. "Now why don't you try to get some sleep?"

She nodded and stood. As always she found Quinn a rock of steadiness, a source of calm that she welcomed. He walked with her to her back door then he took her in his arms and she stepped into the embrace.

"If I call you tomorrow, will you take my call or at least return it if you're out?" he asked.

"Absolutely," she replied. What he'd said about her being a lot like Kelsey had made sense. She was willing, at least for now, to reach out for happiness, reach out to him and see where the path led.

"And if I invited you to have lunch one day this week?"

"I think we could arrange something like that," she replied.

"Good." His eyes gleamed and he pressed a kiss to her forehead. "Then I'll just say△ good night."

"Good night Quinn," she replied. She watched as he went back to the gate and then disappeared into the darkness of the night.

She went inside and hoped she wasn't making a mistake. Maybe the haunting she'd been experiencing since arriving here was simply her mind refusing to let go of the past. Perhaps now that she'd made a decision to go forward, leaving her past behind, the haunting would stop.

It wasn't until she was back in bed that she realized that one question hadn't been answered. Who had been chasing her through the woods?

"It's looking good," Jewel said to Ryder the next morning. The pen was almost complete and the kids had spent most of breakfast discussing what kind of animals they'd like to have.

Barry had wanted a hippo and Lindy had her heart set on a baby elephant. It had taken some fast talking to bring them back to reality.

Ryder wiped a handkerchief across his sweaty brow. "We should have it finished in the next day or two."

"Terrific. I'm heading into town. Is there anything you need?" she asked.

"No, I'm good." He picked up his hammer. "I think the kids have the right idea today."

Jeff and Cheryl had the kids out by the pool. The sounds of splashing and laughter rode on the hot, steamy air. "Feel free to join them," Jewel said. "I think they plan on being out there all afternoon. In the meantime, I'm off. I'm meeting Ellie to talk about the plans for next Sunday."

"Have fun," he replied.

Minutes later, as Jewel drove into town, her mind whirled with all the things she needed to check out with Ellie. Weeks ago, when she'd first found out that

Joe and Meredith intended to stop here on the final leg of their campaign trail, she'd spoken with Ellie about a tent rental, chairs and tables and all the functional things that were needed to accommodate a big crowd. Today she wanted to discuss the menu.

As she thought of seeing Joe and Meredith again, her heart filled with joy. When Jewel had learned about her real mother and had found Patsy in the mental ward, Patsy had told her of her other two children, Joe and Teddy. Patsy had said she never knew the identity of her first son's father and had hinted that Teddy's father was a member of Joe's family.

Jewel hadn't known what to believe or whether she would be welcome into the Colton family after all that her mother had done. But Joe and Meredith had opened their loving arms to her and embraced her as one of their own. With Patsy gone and her adoptive parents also deceased, Joe and Meredith had become like parents to her.

It was Meredith's loving support that had gotten Jewel through those dark days after the accident, and it was Meredith who had given her a new start here in Esperanza.

Jewel couldn't wait to see them both again and she wanted everything perfect for their visit. She wanted to prove to her aunt Meredith that trusting Jewel with the Hopechest Ranch had been the right thing to do.

Ellie's shop was on Main Street, a tiny storefront with artificial flower arrangements, wooden trellises and a champagne fountain for rent in the windows.

"Ellie?" Jewel cried out as she entered the shop.

"I'm back here." Ellie's voice drifted out from the back room. "I'll be right out."

Jewel sat in the chair in front of the desk and waited for Ellie. The store was a fantasyland of party supplies and Jewel never tired of looking around.

Ellie appeared, her brown frizzy hair looking wilder than usual and her cheeks flushed a bright pink. "Sorry, I was getting things together for a wedding that's taking place tomorrow. I swear, something's in the air around here lately. I've never been so busy." She flopped down at her desk and blew a strand of her hair out of her eyes. She grinned. "Now, let's talk about your big deal next Sunday."

For the next hour they went over the menu and checked and rechecked the lists of things that Ellie and her crew would be providing for the day.

"Your guests are arriving around five, right?" Ellie asked. Jewel nodded and Ellie continued. "My crew will be at your place no later than ten in the morning to start setting things up."

It was after two when Jewel left Ellie's. The heat slammed her in the face as she walked out of the cool store and she was eager to get back to the house and maybe join the kids in the pool. With this heat, no other place sounded the least bit attractive.

As she walked to her car she got that feeling again, the prickly sensation of somebody watching her, of something not quite right. She glanced around, seeking the source of the odd feeling.

Although there were other people on the sidewalks, nobody was paying any attention to her. They were hurrying toward stores, going about their lives.

She dismissed the feeling and got into her car, relieved as she drove away to see nobody following her.

An hour later Jewel was in her modest one-piece bathing suit and playing a game of water volleyball with the kids. Jeff and Cheryl sat in the shade of one of the umbrella tables, Cheryl calling out encouragement.

It was right before dinner that Jewel thought about Jeff Cookson. He was a quiet man, good with the kids, but he always appeared vaguely uncomfortable when interacting with Jewel.

Was it possible that it had been Jeff who had chased her through the woods the night before? Before hiring the couple, who were originally from San Antonio, where they had worked at a juvenile facility, Jewel had checked and double-checked their references and found them impeccable.

She dismissed the idea of Jeff skulking around after her in the dead of night, but that left her with the question that had plagued her since she'd awakened that morning. Who had been in the woods with her?

After dinner Jewel and the children had a group therapy session in the playroom. She talked to the kids about good and bad emotions and the appropriate way to express them. They followed up the session with a movie and then it was bedtime.

With the house quiet and at rest, Jewel curled up

in bed with a book. She'd only been reading a few minutes when the phone rang.

"Good day?" Quinn's deep voice washed over her and she smiled with the simple pleasure of hearing it.

"Great day," she replied. "I finalized things with Ellie for the barbecue on Sunday and spent the rest of the day in the pool and doing therapy with the kids. What about you?"

"I operated on a dog with kidney stones, checked out a horse that had rubbed a sore spot on her flank and spent the rest of the day reading the books I got from the library the other day. It was just a normal day in the life of a small-town vet, a normal day made better now that I've heard your voice."

She smiled into the phone. "I feel the same way about hearing your voice. It's a perfect way to end the day."

"Are you ready for bed?" he asked.

"Actually, I'm in bed. I was just doing a little reading. The house is quiet and after all the fun in the sun this afternoon I actually feel like I'm going to be able to sleep."

"Good. Then I'll let you go. I just didn't want the day to pass without talking to you. Can you work me in for lunch one day this week?"

"Maybe Thursday would be good, but I'll have to let you know the first of the week." She had no idea what the week might bring with all the preparations for Joe and Meredith.

"Okay, I'll check in with you tomorrow or Monday. Good night, Jewel, and sweet dreams."

As she hung up, a pleasurable warmth remained. If she let herself she could easily fall in love with Quinn Logan. She was already more than halfway there. She just wasn't sure if she should allow herself to take the full leap.

Yawning with sleepiness, she turned out her lamp and got settled for the night. As she fell asleep she filled her head with thoughts of Quinn, of how it felt to be held in his arms, how endearing it was when he shoved that mane of beautiful hair away from his eyes.

There was something so solid about him, a quiet confidence that made her believe he could handle anything life might throw his way. He'd gotten through both the death of his wife and the damage to his professional reputation with dignity and grace. She fell asleep remembering the feel of his warm lips against hers.

She jerked awake abruptly and sat up, unsure what had pulled her from a dreamless sleep. A glance at the clock told her it was just after two.

Her heart pounded unnaturally fast and she wasn't sure why. Had it been a dream that had awoken her? A nightmare she now couldn't remember?

Maybe a glass of water would calm her racing heart. She slid her legs over the side of the mattress and reached for her robe at the end of her bed. She didn't need her bedside lamp to make her way to the kitchen. The path was lit with nightlights in case one of the kids got up and wandered in the night.

She'd just reached the doorway into the living room when she heard it—the sound of several heavy footsteps coming from the family room/kitchen area.

Her heart leapt into her throat. Those footsteps didn't belong to one of the children, nor would Jeff or Cheryl be wandering the house in a heavy pair of shoes at this hour of the night.

She slid back into her bedroom and grabbed the bat she kept near her bed. With this being a ranch for children she refused to have a gun, but at this moment she wished she were holding something more lethal than a baseball bat.

If there was an intruder in the house, her sole concern was for the safety of her charges. Gripping the wooden weapon tightly in both hands, she advanced through the living room. She stifled a small gasp as she passed the front door and saw it cracked open.

Somebody was in the house!

Somebody who didn't belong.

Her mind whirled a thousand miles a minute as she crept forward, searching the shadows of the room for potential danger.

When they'd first opened the ranch, there had been some people who weren't thrilled at the idea of a place for troubled kids here. Had somebody who had a problem decided to act on it?

From the living room she walked to the doorway that led to the family room and kitchen area. Her heart hammered so hard in her chest that she felt as if she might pass out. She kept the bat on her shoulders, ready to hit a home run if it became necessary. Her eyes had adjusted to the near-darkness of the house.

She saw nobody in the family room and was beginning to think that maybe whoever had been inside was now gone. She had no idea what they might have been looking for or what they'd been doing, but a tiny edge of relief whispered through her. She relaxed her grip on the bat handle.

Turning, she looked into the darkened kitchen and froze, every nerve and muscle screaming inside her as she saw the tall, dark form of a man. She must have made a noise for he turned to face her, his features covered by the dark material of a ski mask.

"Who are you? What do you want?" The words barely escaped her lips before he rushed toward her.

Chapter 10

Everything seemed to move in slow motion. His heavy footsteps rang on the floor as he came toward her. She gripped the bat tightly and swung.

Strike.

She missed him and stumbled backward. *Three strikes and you're out,* she thought as she fought back a wild, hysterical burst of terrified giggles. But the giggles died a quick death as he once again advanced toward her and tried to grab her by the throat.

She ducked and evaded his grasp, her heart hammering with flight-or-fight adrenaline. She tried to discern his features beneath the ski mask, desperately looking for something familiar, a clue to his identity, but she couldn't even tell the color of his eyes in the narrow slits.

She didn't have to know his identity to recognize that he was dangerous. She could sense an evil intent wafting from his big body. A scream rose to her lips but she fought it back, bit it away. The last thing she wanted was to scream and have one of the children stumble sleepily into the room.

He growled, like a wild animal let loose after months of captivity. The ominous sound raised the hairs on the nape of her neck, washed through her a terror she'd never known.

As he rushed toward her again, she swung the bat wildly and felt the whomph of it connecting with some part of his body. He grunted in obvious pain then pushed her to the side so hard she crashed to the floor. He ran past her and out the front door.

Jewel scrambled to her feet, ignoring the pain in her hip from the fall. Once again with the bat held ready to hit a home run, she advanced toward the open front door.

Her heart hammered.

Was he there?

Just outside? Waiting for her to run after him? Heart pounding so hard she could hear it banging in her brain, she moved closer. When she reached the door, she slammed it closed and locked it, then leaned weakly against it as a sob choked out of her.

Who was he? What had he wanted? She needed to call somebody. Sheriff Yates. She had to report this. She shoved away from the door and immediately turned on all the lights in the family room. Deep tremors possessed her as she stumbled toward the telephone on the end table.

It took her shaking fingers two tries to finally punch in the right numbers and connect with the dispatcher for the sheriff's office. She told him she needed somebody out here, that there'd been an intruder in the house. "And no lights or sirens," she exclaimed. The dispatcher told her somebody would be out as soon as possible.

She hung up the receiver and leaned back, the bat still clutched tightly in one hand. What would have happened if she hadn't had the bat? She didn't even want to think about it.

Was the man who had been inside the house tonight the same one who had chased her through the woods? Was he the one she'd sensed watching her?

There had been such rage in that growl he'd released. He'd been like a marauding bear, who wanted nothing more than to rip her limb from limb.

She shivered and rose on shaky legs to go to the front window and watch for Jericho Yates or Adam. Was the intruder still out there? Hiding in the night? Waiting for another opportunity? She checked the lock on the front door, making sure it was engaged.

How had he gotten in? Was it possible the front door had been left unlocked when they'd all gone to bed? She frowned and tried to remember if she'd locked it or not. She just couldn't be sure.

She was vaguely surprised that nobody had heard anything, but then she realized that the assault had all been relatively silent. Other than those initial few words that she'd spoken aloud when she'd first seen him and that horrible low growl, there had been little noise.

She breathed a small prayer of thanks that none of the children had awakened. Not only could they have been physically harmed, but it was vital to their mental well-being for them to believe that they were safe and secure here in their temporary home.

It seemed like an eternity before she saw a car coming down the road. When the vehicle turned into the driveway she saw that it was from the sheriff's office.

The car parked in front and as the door opened she recognized Adam. As he got out of the car she unlocked the front door and opened it to meet him.

"Are you all right?" he asked as he reached her, concern darkening his eyes.

She nodded, for a moment too overwhelmed to speak. Hot tears burned at her eyes, rose up in the back of her throat. Now that she knew she was safe she realized that she was precariously close to breaking down.

Adam gripped her arm tightly. "Is somebody still inside?"

"No." She finally found her voice. "No, he ran out the front door."

"Go back inside. Lock the door. I'm going to do

a sweep of the area and I'll be back in a few minutes to talk to you."

She nodded, closed the door and relocked it. Her heartbeat was slowing to a more normal pace and some of the trembling that had possessed her body had finally stilled.

Standing by the window, she saw Adam's flashlight as he searched the front yard. He disappeared from sight around the side of the house and she drew a deep breath to steady her racing emotions.

Although it soothed her to know that Adam was out looking, she didn't expect him to stumble upon the intruder. He was probably long gone…and hopefully with a cracked rib or a broken leg to boot.

What she'd like to do was pick up the phone and call Quinn. She knew the sound of his deep, calm voice would anchor her, soothe her. But she wouldn't wake him in the middle of the night, hated herself for her weakness in needing him, wanting him.

"Jewel?"

She gasped and whirled around to see Cheryl standing behind her, her robe clutched closed, brown hair in sleep disarray and her eyes wide in alarm. "You scared me to death," Jewel exclaimed.

"Sorry. What's going on?" She eyed the bat that Jewel had refused to release.

"Somebody was in the house. A man. He tried to attack me but I hit him with the bat and he ran out the door. Deputy Rawlings is here now, checking out the area."

"Oh my God." Cheryl moved closer to Jewel. "Are you sure you're okay?" Jewel nodded. "Do you know who it was? What he wanted?"

"I don't have a clue," Jewel replied.

"How did he get in?"

"By the front door." Jewel frowned. "I can't remember if I locked it before I went to bed or not."

At that moment a soft knock sounded at the door. Jewel opened it to allow Adam inside. "Unfortunately, I didn't find anything," he said.

"Let's go into the kitchen," Jewel suggested. She finally let go of the bat, leaning it against the family-room wall. "I'd rather not wake the children."

With Jewel leading the way, they filed into the kitchen area. "This is where I first saw him," Jewel said. "I'm not sure what woke me up, but I thought I heard the sound of footsteps and I grabbed the bat and I saw him."

Cheryl placed a comforting arm around Jewel's shoulders. "You should have called to us. You should have called for Jeff."

"Where is Jeff?" Adam asked.

Cheryl gave them a sheepish expression. "He's still asleep. But if you would have screamed, he would have woken up."

"I didn't want to scream," Jewel replied. "The last thing I wanted was one of the kids waking up and coming into the room."

"Did you recognize him? Did he say anything to you?" Adam asked.

"No, nothing. He had on a ski mask. I didn't recognize him and he didn't say anything to me."

"What about height and weight?" Adam pulled out a small notepad from his shirt pocket.

For the next few minutes Jewel described her assailant, although there was precious little she could tell him. Adam made a sweep of the house, then there was nothing more he could do. "It sounds to me like you probably interrupted a robbery," Adam said.

Jewel nodded. "I think you're right. He probably wouldn't have tried to attack me if I hadn't confronted him." She wanted to believe this. It was the only thing that made sense.

It was after three when she walked with Adam out on the porch. "I'd like to tell you that I'm certain we'll catch this guy, but with the sketchy information you gave me, I don't have a good feeling about it," Adam said. "I'll check with the local doctors to see if anyone shows up with broken ribs or unusual bruising, but the man would be a fool to do that unless you seriously hurt him."

Jewel sighed and tied the belt of her robe more tightly around her. "I hope I busted his spleen," she exclaimed as she wrapped her arms around herself to ward off an inner chill.

"Jewel, I could stay the night if it would make you feel better," he said. He moved to stand next to her and put his hand on her forearm. "You should know by now that there's nothing I'd like more than to have a permanent place here at the ranch with you and the kids."

She realized it was time to be truthful with the handsome deputy. From the moment he'd arrived in town he'd made it clear to her that he wanted a relationship with her. It was time he knew the truth.

"Adam, you're a wonderful man and I'm sure someday you'll make somebody a great husband, but that somebody won't be me. I like you. I like you a lot and I hope we can remain friends, but I just don't feel that way about you. I'm sorry."

He dropped his hand from her arm and stepped back from her, a look of disappointment crossing his features. "No need to apologize. If it's not there, it's not there. I can't say I'm not disappointed, but I also can't say I'm surprised." He offered her a smile. "If we'd both been on the same page, we would have been dating for the last couple of months."

He jammed his hands into his pockets. "I'll let you know what I find out in the next day or two about what went on here tonight. Take care of yourself, Jewel, and if you ever change your mind you know where to find me."

She watched from the door as he walked to his car and got in. She had a feeling there would be fewer impromptu check-ins by him in the future now that he knew there was no hope for them.

When she returned to the kitchen, Cheryl had made a pot of hot tea and sat at the table. "Come on, have a cup of tea. I know well enough that you probably won't sleep for the rest of the night." Cheryl got up and fixed her a cup of tea, then put it on the table.

Jewel sat down wearily. Now that the excitement was over and Adam was gone, she was aware of the throb of her hip and a headache pounding at her temples. "Thanks," she said and cupped her hands around the warmth of the cup.

"Are you sure you're okay?" Cheryl asked as she gazed at Jewel with concern.

"I'm fine. I just have a headache." She took a sip of the tea, hoping the hot liquid would ease some of the pain in her head. "I just wish I knew why that man was inside, what he wanted here."

"Maybe it was a local kid who thought you had psychiatric drugs," Cheryl offered.

"Maybe, but if it was a kid, he was definitely a big kid. I just don't want anything to happen to mess up the big barbecue next Sunday," Jewel said worriedly.

"Don't worry, everything will be fine for Joe and Meredith's visit," Cheryl assured her.

"I hope so." Jewel took another sip of the tea, welcoming the warmth that helped banished the chill that had been with her since the moment she'd opened her eyes and realized something wasn't right in the house.

"Is there anything else I can do for you?" Cheryl asked.

"Yes, go back to bed," Jewel replied with a tired smile.

"Are you sure? I don't mind sitting with you if you want me to."

"No, I'm fine. I'm just going to finish this cup of tea then I'm going back to bed myself. Wait, I changed my mind, there *is* something you can do for me. Would you wait by the front door while I go get Cocoa? I think it's time our furry friend moved from the garage into the house." Jewel got up from her chair and carried her teacup to the sink.

"Sounds like a good idea," Cheryl agreed. "I doubt that dog would bite anyone, but if somebody comes in who doesn't belong he could sure raise a ruckus by barking."

Jewel stopped in the family room to grab her bat, then Cheryl followed her to the front door, where Jewel grabbed the leash hanging on a hook by the door and flipped on the outside light. As she stepped onto the porch, her heart began to bang with apprehension.

Was the man who'd been inside out here lingering in the night? Had he watched from some safe place while Adam searched for him, then left? It suddenly seemed like a long trip between the house and the garages.

"If you see anything or anyone, scream like hell," she said to Cheryl.

"Don't worry. And trust me, I can scream loud enough they'll hear me in town."

Jewel nodded. With the bat gripped in one hand and the leash in the other, she began the long walk toward the garage.

The night was silent and she listened for any sound that might forewarn her of anything amiss, but she arrived at the garage door without incident.

It took only moments to fasten Cocoa's leash then hurry back to the house where Cheryl waited at the front door. Cocoa danced with excitement, obviously thrilled to have his sleep interrupted by human interaction. He had lavished her with kisses as she connected the leash, then pranced next to her as they went back to the house.

"Thanks, Cheryl," she said once they were back inside with the door locked securely behind them. "I'll see you in the morning."

Jewel was thankful that Cocoa didn't bark as she led him to her quarters and closed the door behind them. She took the leash off him and he ran around the room, sniffing every corner and huffing with excitement.

Jewel set the bat against the wall next to her bed, then took off her robe. She was certain she wouldn't get any more sleep, but her aching body yearned for the softness of her mattress.

As she got into bed, Cocoa jumped up next to her and curled up as if he'd spent every night of his life sleeping in the bed with her.

"Don't get used to that," she said to him. "Tomorrow we'll bring in your bed."

He hunkered down and released what could only be described as a deliriously happy sigh. Jewel reached out a hand and stroked his soft fur. The feel reminded her of Quinn's hair, soft and silky to the touch.

As she continued to stroke the dog, she felt her heartbeat slowing and her tension ebbing. It had to have been a botched robbery attempt.

Although the attack had felt personal when he'd emitted that growl and had reached to grab her around the neck, surely it hadn't been personal at all. She'd trapped him and, like a wild animal, he'd sprung to get free.

She'd made no enemies that she knew of since coming to Esperanza. Some of the townspeople hadn't initially been thrilled with the idea of a ranch for troubled kids in their midst, but the last couple of months of the ranch's smooth running had quieted even the most vocal of critics.

Even though she had no intention of falling asleep, she must have, for she awakened to Cocoa licking her arm. A glance at her clock let her know it was a few minutes before seven, time to get up and face a new day.

"Okay, just a minute," she said to Cocoa, who jumped off the bed and began to run in circles near her closed bedroom door. "I'm hurrying." She got out of bed and pulled on her robe, afraid that Cocoa's obvious need to go outside wouldn't wait until she showered and dressed for the day.

She fastened the leash on his collar, then opened her bedroom door. The scent of freshly brewed coffee and frying bacon greeted her. Cocoa stopped in his tracks and sniffed the air, momentarily distracted from his run to the front door by the delicious scent.

"Come on, boy. First things first," she said as she tugged him toward the door. Once she was at the door, she released his leash and let him run while she stood in the yard and watched. He disappeared around the side of the garage and was gone for a minute or two, then came running back to her.

"Good boy," she said. "Cocoa is a good boy." She patted his neck, then reattached the leash and led him to the garage.

She had quickly discovered that having him in the house while the kids got ready for school was too much of a distraction. He chased the children and barked for them to play with him while they were trying to get dressed.

Once the kids were on the bus, she'd let him back into the house. After last night, she was determined to acclimate him quickly to being inside rather than in the confines of the garage.

Returning to her quarters, she showered and dressed for the day and by the time she got to the kitchen the kids were up and the house was filled with the usual chaos of morning.

Once the kids had left for the day, Jewel returned to the kitchen for another cup of coffee. Jeff sat at the table with her while Cheryl bustled around, clearing the last of the breakfast dishes.

"Cheryl told me about what I slept through last night," Jeff said, his hazel eyes narrowed in concern. "I can't believe you tried to take on an intruder by yourself."

"In the light of day I can't believe it myself," Jewel admitted, a coldness seeping through her as she thought of those terrifying moments the night before.

"The only good thing is that I managed to hit him hard enough to hurt."

"Still, what good is it to have a man in the house if you don't holler for him when you need him?" Jeff replied gruffly.

Cheryl turned from the sink and grinned at Jewel. "He's having a hero meltdown this morning. He wanted to be the hero and instead you took care of the situation yourself."

"Trust me, if something like that ever happens again, I'll scream," Jewel said. "Thank goodness it was a case of all's well that ends well."

"Maybe Deputy Rawlings will be able to figure out who it was," Cheryl said.

"Probably some kid looking for drugs," Jeff replied.

"That's what I think," Jewel agreed. "He probably thought he could find some good psychiatric drugs in the house."

"On another topic, we're still on to take the kids Saturday for that field trip, right?" Jeff asked.

"Absolutely. That will work perfectly with me. While y'all are gone I'm going to clean this place from top to bottom to have it ready for the barbecue on Sunday." Jewel finished her coffee and stood. "And now I'm going to go get Cocoa and let him back in here. I also want to move his bed from the garage to my bedroom. From now on he'll be in the house at night."

"Need any help?" Jeff asked.

"No, thanks. I can take care of it," she replied.

"Then I'm going to do a little yard work before it gets too hot to breathe outside." Jeff pushed his chair away from the table and stood. "And if my wife loves me, she'll bring me out something cold to drink in the next hour or so."

Cheryl smiled at him and for a moment Jewel felt like a third wheel as she sensed the love radiating between the two.

As she walked outside to the garage, a deep yearning slid through her and her head filled with thoughts of Quinn. She felt as if she were being selfish in pursuing a relationship with him and not telling him about the voices she heard at night, the haunting cry of a baby that made her doubt her own sanity.

But the idea of not grasping on to the happiness he brought into her life was devastating. All her words of wisdom to Kelsey would mean nothing if she didn't embrace the philosophy of reaching out for happiness herself.

She opened the side garage door and stepped inside Cocoa's temporary quarters, expecting to be met as usual with a tail wag and a tongue lavishing, but Cocoa didn't greet her at the door.

He lay on the floor in a pool of vomit. As he saw her he struggled to stand, but his legs buckled and he collapsed back to the floor.

"Oh my God," she cried, and whirled to the door. "Jeff! Come quick. Something is wrong with Cocoa." Her heart leapt into her throat as she crouched down beside the dog. Tears washed from her eyes. "It's okay, baby. You're going to be all right. We just need to get you to Quinn's."

She stood as Jeff entered. "He was fine this morning," she said.

"Definitely not fine now," Jeff said with grim expression.

"Let's get him loaded in the car and take him to Quinn's."

They used a worn blanket and wrapped Cocoa up in it, then placed him in the backseat of Jewel's car. "Want me to come with you?" Jeff asked as she started the engine.

"No. Stay here. I'll let you know what's going on." She didn't take time to say anything more, but quickly tore down the driveway and onto the road to Quinn's.

She kept up a steady stream of chatter as she drove, unsure if she were trying to calm herself or the dog. "Quinn will take care of you. It's going to be okay." It was shocking to her how quickly the dog had crawled into her heart and she knew how deeply he'd already ingrained himself into the hearts of the children.

He had to be okay. He just had to be! She roared down the highway and breathed a sigh of relief as she turned into Quinn's place.

Quinn's house sat back from the road, an attractive ranch-style house with hunter-green shutters. But she pulled in front of the building closest to the road and parked. That one-story building was where Quinn's veterinary practice was housed.

Hank Webster, a local rancher was just leaving as she got out of her car. "Please, could you help me? I've got a very sick dog and I need help getting him inside."

With Hank's help they managed to get Cocoa inside where Quinn's receptionist, Brenda Lopez, quickly gestured them into an examining room.

With Cocoa on the table, Jewel thanked Hank, who then left. She stroked Cocoa's head and frowned as she smelled the strong scent of garlic emanating from the dog's breath.

"It's okay, boy," she said as tears misted her vision.

He whined, a pathetic little noise that broke her heart. What was wrong with him? What had happened? He'd been fine two hours ago.

She turned as the door to the room opened. Quinn walked in, one leg dragging in an unmistakable limp. He flashed her a quick smile. "What happened?" he asked as he went directly to Cocoa.

"I…I don't know." A chill swept through her, one that had nothing to do with worry for Cocoa. "What happened to your leg?" Her voice felt as if it came from someplace very far away.

"Molly the horse not only managed to tear up my face, she also got me in the knee. It sometimes acts up." He leaned closer to Cocoa's face. "Smell that garlicky scent. That's arsenic poisoning. I need to get him treated. Why don't you wait out in the waiting room?" He ushered her out then called for his vet tech to come into the room to help him.

On wooden legs she moved to one of the chairs

and sank down, her worry for Cocoa momentarily banished from her mind.

She felt blindsided. Last night she'd struck somebody in the lower body with a bat and today Quinn had a pronounced limp. There was no way to escape the icy chill that swept through her as she wondered if it had been Quinn in her house the night before.

She desperately wanted to believe that it was nothing more than a coincidence, but all she wanted to do was run and escape from him and from the terrible possibility that it had been his knee she'd hit the night before, that it had been his hands reaching for her throat.

Chapter 11

Jewel felt as if she might throw up. An hour later as she drove home, her head whirled and nausea rolled in her stomach.

Cocoa had been poisoned with arsenic and Quinn had a mysterious limp. Any trust she'd felt toward the handsome vet had been shattered, leaving her feeling sick and making her realize just how much she cared about him.

She'd been more than half in love with him and given just a little more time she would have allowed herself to fall completely, head-over-heels. But the thought that she'd been the one who'd given him that injury with her bat filled her with coldness.

He'd managed to get Cocoa stabilized, but had

told her the dog needed to stay for a couple of days to make sure there were no residual effects from the poison. They decided he would keep the dog until after the barbecue on Sunday.

She deserved an Oscar for her performance with him. Even when the emergency was over and he'd asked her when they were going to be able to have lunch together, she'd managed to keep her cool and not betray that anything was wrong. She'd told him that until the barbecue was over, they could not get together. She simply had too much to do.

Thankfully he'd had an appointment with a sick cat and with a squeeze of her hand he'd told her they'd talk later. She hadn't been able to escape fast enough.

Tightening her grip on the steering wheel, she thought about that moment when she'd seen the intruder standing in her kitchen. Had he been as tall as Quinn? Were Quinn's shoulders as broad as that man's had been? It could have been Quinn beneath that ski mask.

By the time she reached her place, none of the questions had been answered and the sickness that had gripped her had only grown more intense.

Jeff greeted her as she parked the car. "I found part of a steak in Cocoa's part of the garage," he said when she got out of the car. "I think maybe your intruder left it for the dog."

She nodded. "Quinn said he thinks it was arsenic poisoning, so I guess that makes as much sense as anything right now."

"How's the dog?"

"Serious, but stable," she replied. "If you'll excuse me, I'm going to my room to clean up a bit."

Her intention was to shower again and change her clothes, which smelled like dog vomit. She had no intention of crying. But as she stripped and got beneath a hot spray of water, the tears began.

At first she thought she was crying for Cocoa, but as the tears increased she realized that she was weeping for what might have been with Quinn.

There was no going back. She would always wonder if he had been the man who had broken into the ranch, the man who had growled at her with such hatred, the one who had reached out to grab her around her throat.

Would Quinn, a man devoted to the health and well-being of animals, poison a dog? Why would he break into her house? What possible motive could he have? No matter how she twisted and turned the questions, she couldn't come up with any logical answers.

But she couldn't get that limp out of her mind. That physical injury of his had effectively killed any chance the two of them had for a future.

She refused to love a man she didn't trust. She leaned weakly against the shower stall and wept a lifetime of tears. She cried for the happiness she'd lost when Andrew and her baby had died. She sobbed for the happiness she might have found with Quinn. Finally, she cried because she didn't understand the twists and turns that life had thrown at her, beginning the day of her birth, when she'd been stolen away from her mother and sold in an illegal adoption.

The week passed in a haze for Jewel. She took care of the children, conducted therapy sessions and once again met with Ellie for the final preparations for Sunday's festivities.

Quinn called daily to update her on Cocoa's condition. They'd got the poison in time and Cocoa was doing just fine. She kept the conversation brief and light, although her heart had disengaged. She couldn't allow him back into her heart. She couldn't love him now, with all trust broken and a sliver of fear of him finding purchase in her heart.

It was just after nine on Saturday morning when Jeff and Cheryl rounded up the kids for their day trip away from the ranch.

"Make sure you all behave for Cheryl and Jeff," Jewel told each of the kids as they got into the minibus. "I want perfect behavior reports on each of you when you get home this evening."

"We'll be good," Barry promised, and they all echoed his words.

Although it was still early morning, the sun sizzled in a cloudless sky, promising no relief from the intense heat that had gripped the region for the past three days.

"Make sure they all get plenty to drink," Jewel said to Cheryl once they were all loaded and ready to pull away.

"Don't worry, Mother Hen. We'll bring your chicks home safe and sound," she assured Jewel.

Jewel forced a smile. "And call me if there are any problems," she said. She waved as they drove off and continued to wave and smile until the bus disappeared from sight.

Instantly her smile fell away. She was grateful that at least for the remainder of the day she wouldn't have to force a fake cheerfulness. She wouldn't have to pretend that everything was right in her world.

Sooner or later she was going to have to tell Quinn that there was no hope for them. The only reason she hadn't done so yet was because he would be attending the barbecue and she didn't want any unnecessary tension between them.

Once the barbecue was over and Joe and Meredith had left town, she'd tell Quinn that she wasn't available, that he needed to look elsewhere for a life partner.

The one thing she hadn't done was tell anyone about her suspicions. She'd considered calling Adam and telling him that Quinn was sporting a suspicious limp. The only thing that had stopped her was the possibility that Quinn might have been telling the truth about how his knee got injured.

Quinn had already lived through much of the town turning against him. He'd already faced false accusations that had nearly destroyed his life. She didn't want to be responsible for doing it all over again. She had no real proof, just a coincidental limp.

Just an awful limp that had destroyed everything.

As she stood there alone in the yard with the top of her head boiling beneath the hot sun, a sudden prickly feeling lifted the hair on the nape of her neck, raised goose bumps on her arms.

It was the crazy, inexplicable feeling a person got when she thought she was being watched. Jewel whirled around, eyeing the house behind her, then looked toward the nearby woods.

Nothing.

"Silly goose," she murmured to herself, but that didn't make the feeling go away. If she stood out here long enough, she would totally freak herself out.

She had a million and one things she wanted to accomplish today while the kids were out of the house. Standing in the front yard giving herself the heebie-jeebies wasn't on her to-do list. She headed inside and carefully locked the door behind her.

Although the children were responsible for cleaning their own rooms, Jewel wanted to give each room a thorough once-over. She knew there would be people with Joe and Meredith who had never been to the ranch before and would be looking closely at Meredith's pet project. Jewel wanted to make certain everything was perfect.

The morning passed quickly as she vacuumed and dusted each of the bedrooms, then tackled the bathrooms that the kids used.

The busywork kept her mind blank and for that she was grateful. Her brain felt fried from all the analyzing and thinking it had done over the past five days. She didn't want to think about anything but Joe and Meredith's visit the next day.

Not only would the day convene family and friends, it would also be an early celebration of Joe's political success. The polls and pundits were all forecasting a Colton presidency.

At noon Jewel stopped her work and sat at the table to enjoy a sandwich of the chicken salad Cheryl had fixed early that morning.

It was only as she sat eating that she realized just how quiet the house was with everyone gone. The silence pressed in on her from all sides. It wasn't a comfortable silence but rather an oppressive one.

And, as always when she had a moment of peace and her head was relatively empty, it filled with thoughts of Quinn. More than once she'd felt as if she were being watched. Was it possible Quinn had been stalking her long before they'd gotten close?

Had he merely stumbled on her that first night in the woods or had he been there all along, watching her? He'd known she often walked at night, had guessed that she suffered from insomnia.

She stifled a laugh of irony. She hadn't wanted to involve herself with him because she'd feared she was losing her mind. What if he was the one who was mentally deranged? An obsessed stalker, who had her in his sights?

Was it possible he had poisoned Cocoa with the intention of saving the dog and being a hero? The very idea sickened her.

She'd just finished eating and had put her dishes in the dishwasher when the doorbell rang. Grateful for a break in the silence and her racing thoughts, she hurried to answer.

She opened the door to Georgie and was ridiculously pleased to see the woman. "What a nice surprise!" she said as she opened the door to let her in.

"Nick and Emmie are having a bonding day. He took her to lunch and then was going to buy her a couple of pairs of new jeans for school. I was at loose ends so I thought I'd drop in and see if there's anything you need for tomorrow's big party."

"Come on in and have a glass of iced tea with me," Jewel said. "I think I have things under control for tomorrow. Ellie and her crew are going to arrive at ten in the morning to set up tents and chairs and everything we need to make the day a success."

As Georgie sat at the table, Jewel poured them each a glass of iced tea. "How does Emmie like school?" she asked as she joined Georgie.

"She loves it." Georgie's expression was a blend of happiness and wistfulness.

Jewel smiled. "Spoken with the bittersweet expression of a mother."

Georgie grinned. "She's already made friends with a bunch of kids and has assured me there isn't a cowboy in the bunch. She loves her teacher and she gets up every morning eager to go."

"And even though you want her to have friends and love school, it breaks your heart that she's expanding her horizons and doesn't need you quite as much as she did."

Georgie leaned back in her chair and sighed. "Exactly."

Jewel laughed. "Don't worry. You're still the most important thing in her world and will continue to be until she gets to be a teenager. Then she'll think you're the dumbest person on earth and wonder how you ever survived without her wisdom and knowledge."

Georgie laughed and shoved her long red braid over her shoulder. "God, I needed to hear that."

"How's Nick?"

"Bored. He's put in an application with the sheriff's office for a position as deputy, but so far there are no openings in the department. You can take the man out of the Secret Service, but you can't quite take the protect and serve out of a former Secret Service man."

"I think it's so romantic that he gave up his position with the Secret Service to come here for you," Jewel replied.

"Speaking of romance. I hear through the grapevine that you and Quinn have been seen around town, looking pretty cozy together."

It was impossible not to feel a stab of pain at his name. "Just friends," Jewel replied.

"Too bad. You two would have made a great couple."

Jewel took a sip of her tea then said, "I'm really not interested in being part of a couple right now."

"I highly recommend it," Georgie replied.

Jewel forced a laugh. "Why is it that every woman who has recently fallen in love thinks that every other woman on earth should be in the same state?"

"Because loving somebody makes you be more than what you were before you loved." Georgie paused to sip her tea, then continued. "Because loving is what we're made for, why we're on this earth." She gave Jewel a wide grin. "Loving somebody and riding horses, that's my idea of heaven."

This time Jewel's laughter was genuine. For the next few minutes the two talked about the Colton clan and everyone who would be at the barbecue the next day.

"Is Uncle Graham going to show up?" Jewel asked.

Georgia shrugged. "Who knows what Dad is going to do. He's really trying to turn his life around, but sometimes I wonder if it's a case of too little, too late. It would be nice if he and Uncle Joe could somehow put the past behind them and build a new relationship, kind of like what Ryder and Clay have done, but I'm not holding my breath for any miracles."

The two women visited for another half an hour, then Georgie stood. "I'd better get home, if you're sure there's nothing I can do to help with tomorrow."

"Pray for a break in this heat," Jewel said as she walked with Georgie to the front door.

"Isn't it terrible? I heard that a bunch of people were without electricity last night because of an overload of the system. Thankfully, the electric company got things back up and running in a couple of hours."

"I wouldn't even want to be a couple of hours without the air conditioner on days like these." Jewel opened the door. "Thanks for stopping by, Georgie. I really appreciate it."

"We all appreciate what you're doing tomorrow. It will be terrific to have so many of us in the same place at the same time. I'm really looking forward to it."

A few minutes later Jewel stood on the porch and watched as Georgie pulled away. She'd welcomed the distraction, but now it was time to get back to work.

The afternoon passed quickly and about five she started looking for the kids to return. She knew they'd be eager to share their day with her and hopefully they'd be exhausted enough to go to bed early. Tomorrow was going to be a big day for them all.

By six she decided to go ahead and eat something instead of waiting for everyone to return. Jeff and Cheryl had probably treated the kids to dinner in a roadside café.

As she ate leftover meat loaf with green beans and a salad, she thought of the conversation she'd shared with Georgie.

There had been a moment when she'd felt love for Quinn, when he'd filled her heart and soul and she'd never wanted to leave his arms. There had been an aching moment when she'd been brimming with the possibility of him…of them together, but with the possibility gone, she was left empty.

Once again the silence that surrounded her was suffocating. She couldn't wait for everyone to get back where they belonged, for the house to be overflowing with lively chatter and laughter.

It's better this way, she thought, once again thinking of Quinn. Even if he hadn't been the one who had

broken into the ranch, even if his limp really was
from an old injury, she wasn't in a place to tie her life
to somebody else's.

As long as she suffered from those haunting memories after midnight each night, as long as Andrew
and the baby she'd lost cried out to her from the
grave, called her from the woods, there was no place
for another man in her life.

But if she were going to pick the man she'd want
to spend her life with, it would be the Quinn Logan
who had laughed with the kids in the pasture on the
day of the picnic. It would be the Quinn who had
made love to her with a gentleness and a passion that
had her believing in happy-ever-afters.

And tomorrow she'd have to see him and social-
ize with him and wonder if he was some sort of
psycho stalker or the man she should never have let
slip through her fingers.

By seven, all thoughts of Quinn had disappeared
as she stood at the front window and stared worriedly out at the road. They should have been home
by now. She'd tried to call Cheryl's cell phone twice
but each call had gone directly to voice mail.

She opened the front door and stepped out on the
covered porch. The heat was like a sickening slap in
her face. With the sun beginning to set, it should
have cooled off, but the heat was as fierce now as it
had been at noon. Not a breath of air stirred around
her. It was even too hot for the insects to have begun
their nightly hum and whirr.

Where were Jeff and Cheryl with the kids? The plan had been for them to be home for dinner. What could have happened and why wasn't Cheryl answering her phone?

It wasn't long before she felt it again…that disquieting sensation of being watched. She backed closer to the door and wrapped her arms around her shoulders, chilled despite the heat of the night.

Was there somebody out there?

Watching her?

Somebody who knew she was all alone?

Stop it, she mentally commanded. Those kinds of thoughts would only freak her out.

The sound of the ringing phone pulled her back inside and she raced to grab the receiver in the living room. It was Jeff.

"We've got a busted alternator and a dead cell phone," he said. "Don't worry. We're checked into a motel for the night and the local mechanic has promised me he'll have us back on the road by ten tomorrow morning."

Jewel breathed a sigh of relief. "What happened to the cell phone? Did you just forget to take the charger?"

"Actually, it kind of got crushed. We were stuck on the side of the road for a while. It was hot and Barry got nervous. He had a little meltdown and stepped on the phone. He's fine now," Jeff said hurriedly. "I've got insurance on the phone and everything is okay."

"I was getting so worried."

"I'm sorry. We just didn't have a way of calling until now."

"And you're sure the kids are okay?"

Jeff laughed. "They're calling it the big adventure and we're all in one room with roll-away beds wall to wall. We'll feed them a good breakfast in the morning and we should be there in plenty of time to get them cleaned up for the party."

"Keep all the receipts for everything and you'll be reimbursed," Jewel said.

"I'm not worried about it. We'll see you tomorrow and don't you worry. We have everything under control."

Jewel breathed a sigh of relief as she hung up the phone. Even though she'd known that Jeff and Cheryl would have things under control, she was grateful that everything was fine, that the bus would be fixed and they'd be home in the morning.

Now all she had to do was get through the night alone. Normally, she didn't mind time alone, but she'd been on edge all day and would have much preferred her "family" home with her where they belonged.

Exhausted from her day of work, she took a shower and got into her nightgown and robe. She carried a book into the family room and curled up on the sofa. She turned on a lamp as the darkness of nightfall encroached, stealing the light in the room.

She started to read, but the silence bothered her. She punched on the television and found an old movie that she'd seen several times before. She wasn't interested in watching it again, but welcomed the noise as she returned her attention to her book.

The lights and the television went off as the power failed. The abruptness of the power failure made her heart double-jump in her chest. For a long moment she remained unmoving in the darkness of the room.

Dark energy charged the air, as it often did before a terrible storm, but there were no storms forecasted, even though the area desperately needed some rain.

The heat, she thought as she got up from the sofa. Georgie had just mentioned that the power company was having problems because of the intense heat. There must be an overload of the system somewhere.

She turned off the television, not wanting the electricity to come back on in the middle of the night and wake her suddenly. She grabbed her book and went into her quarters.

The first thing she did was make her way through the darkness to her bathroom, where she had a stock of emergency candles on a shelf. She took out several, lit them and set them on the nightstand next to her bed, then with the candlelight creating flickering shadows on the walls, she got into bed and opened her book.

Abe Lincoln might have been able to read by candlelight, but Jewel found her mind wandering away from her book and back to the past.

The loneliness etched into her heart had existed long before the loss of Andrew and her baby, although that particular devastation had certainly deepened the wounds.

The loneliness had begun at a time when she'd been desperate to connect to her mother. When she'd been old enough to learn the truth about Patsy, all she'd wanted was to help the woman who had given her life, to find that bond of love that surely had to exist.

The need to help her mother was part of what had driven Jewel into psychology. The fact that she'd been too late to help Patsy had begun the hole of loneliness that gnawed inside her.

Quinn had filled that hole. Quinn had taken away her loneliness for a little while, until she'd seen that limp, until the trust she'd started to give to him had been destroyed.

She closed her eyes and tried to conjure up a picture of Andrew, for a moment surprised when the only man whose vision filled her head was Quinn.

Quinn with his beautiful topaz eyes.

Quinn with that wonderful mane of hair and the endearing habit of brushing it out of his eyes.

She squeezed her eyes more tightly closed. She didn't want to think about him. There was no point in regretting what would never be.

She'd rather think of that moment of sheer happiness in the restaurant with Andrew, when he'd placed the ring on her finger and she'd rubbed her hand across the place where his baby grew inside her.

Tears stung her eyes. God, she'd wanted to be a mother. She'd wanted the scent of baby powder and formula, the sound of baby coos and the joy of kissing a sweet belly as she changed diapers. She'd wanted that more than anything in her life.

Although she loved the children who were under her care at the ranch, she never lost sight that her job was to heal them and then send them back to their real lives and to their own mothers and fathers.

She opened her eyes and blew out the candles, knowing she wouldn't read anymore tonight. Hopefully, in the next couple of hours, the power would come back on, for already she felt the coolness of the air-conditioning vanishing beneath the weight of the heat outdoors.

Maybe she should crack a window open. It wouldn't take long before the house would be stifling. She crept from the bed and opened the window and that's when she heard it—the mournful cry of a newborn baby.

Chapter 12

Something had changed.

Quinn saddled up Noches and while he sweet-talked the black stallion, his mind was filled with thoughts of Jewel.

Something had changed with her in the last week and he couldn't quite put his finger on it.

He knew she was busy with the preparations for Joe and Meredith's visit and the barbecue she'd planned, but what he sensed in her tone wasn't preoccupation with everything that was going on; rather, it was as if she were emotionally distancing herself from him.

She'd been pleasant enough, but there was an edge in her voice that cut through his heart, that definitely concerned him.

He'd thought about stopping in at her place when he'd driven by it a little earlier to go to Clay's, but as he'd passed he'd seen that all her lights were out and assumed everyone was already in bed. The last thing he wanted to do was disturb her if she was getting some much-needed sleep.

The moon overhead was nearly full, spilling down enough light that a nighttime ride had sounded appealing. Besides, concern about Jewel had kept sleep at bay the last couple of nights and he didn't think tonight would be any different.

Noches left the stable with a spirited shake of his head, as if eager to run despite the heat of the night. Quinn held the reins loosely, allowing the horse to lead the way across the moonlit landscape at a quick pace.

The night air made Quinn feel as if he wore a blanket around him even though he was clad only in jeans and a short-sleeved navy T-shirt. Noches didn't seem to mind the heat as he pranced energetically along the path that led to open pasture.

These night rides were Quinn's contemplation and relaxing time. After his wife's death and during those dark days when he'd felt as if the town had turned against him, riding in the evening had kept him sane.

All the aches of the day faded, all the disappointments that life had heaped on him melted away as he just enjoyed the simple pleasure of the motion of the horse beneath him.

But tonight was different. Thoughts of Jewel kept

him from finding the peace and relaxation he normally found on nights like this.

He thought he'd finally broken through to her, had gotten past the defenses she'd erected around her heart after Andrew's death and the tragic accident that had taken the baby she carried. Quinn had believed he finally had Jewel trusting him, believing that they had a future together, but now he wasn't so sure.

What she didn't know was that he was a man who didn't give up. He needed her in his life. He wanted her there. And he would do whatever it took convince her that it's where she belonged.

"No."

The word fell as a whisper from Jewel's lips as the baby's cries seemed to grow louder and heartbreakingly plaintive.

She clapped her hands over her ears. The sound made her dizzy and sick with fear. It pierced her very soul and made her want to both scream and hide in a closet where the sound couldn't find her.

Only a shaft of moonlight that danced in the window broke the profound darkness of the room. But in that moonlight she could see her bed with its rumpled sheets. She could see the book she had been reading flat down on the nightstand.

She was awake.

She wasn't dreaming the sound.

She was either crazy or the sound was real. She lowered her hands from her ears and cocked her head to one side, for the first time really focusing on the noise as unemotionally as possible.

So many nights she'd suffered through this, so many nights she'd curled up in her bed and consciously willed the sound away. She'd always assumed it was the cries of her dead baby haunting her from the beyond.

But what if it wasn't?

What if it was real?

Her mind whirled as she thought of the black-market baby ring Ryder had infiltrated a month before. Was it possible the baby she heard crying was real and not a figment of her imagination?

She stood at the window and stared out into the night, her muscles tensed and her heart pounding wildly. Always before, the sound had stopped as abruptly as it had started. She remained frozen, waiting, praying for it to end, but the sound continued...and continued.

She had to know the truth. She had to find the source. For the first time she recognized the possibility that it might not be in her mind, that she just might not be crazy. She acknowledged that the baby might be real.

Whirling away from the window, she stepped into her bedroom slippers and grabbed her bat, then opened the door that led outside.

She walked around the edge of the pool and to the back gate where she paused and cocked her head to listen. Nothing.

She couldn't hear the baby anymore. The heat wrapped around her, suffocating her, and the night offered an ominous silence, as if every insect and night creature held their breath in anticipation, but anticipation of what?

The hairs on her nape rose and a chill slivered up her spine. Her body tensed in alarm. She sensed something…somebody nearby.

"Jewel." The voice rode a breeze like a hot whisper.

She gasped and gripped the bat more tightly in her sweaty hand. Andrew. It had sounded like Andrew. Her mind felt sharper, clearer than it had in months.

It couldn't be Andrew. He was dead. But the voice was real. She felt it in her very bones. The voice was real and it wasn't Andrew's.

Somebody was stalking her, somebody was making her think it was her dead fiancé calling to her in the night. She couldn't imagine why anyone would do such a thing, couldn't imagine who might be responsible, but she was determined to find out.

"Jewel, come to me." The voice came again, low and hypnotic, but this time she steeled herself against it. She couldn't be sure where exactly it came from. The trees and brush played tricks with the sound, making it appear to come from all around her.

The moonlight momentarily disappeared as a cloud chased across the sky. She unfastened the gate and walked through it and onto the path that led to the Bar None. "Where are you?" She kept her voice soft and low as she walked deeper into the woods.

She sensed that she was not alone. Every tensed muscle in her body, every taut nerve she possessed told her that somebody else was in the woods, something who wanted her to believe that she was haunted by the dead.

She hadn't walked far on the path when she saw a figure ahead of her. She jumped off the path and hid behind a tree, her heart banging against her ribs.

Leaning around the tree, she looked at the figure and as the moonlight once again appeared, she recognized the tall man with the mane of hair.

Quinn.

She wanted to fall to her knees and weep. Only now did she realize a part of her had held out some hope that he truly was the man she'd wanted to believe he was, that he wasn't the person who had broken into the ranch and tried to hurt her. The pain that ripped through her as she stared at him on the shadowy path nearly destroyed her.

A hand fell on her shoulder and she screamed, but the scream was cut short as the same hand slid up and over her mouth. She half turned to see Adam. He indicated for her to keep quiet and removed his hand from her mouth.

"Follow me," he whispered. He grabbed her bat and tossed it aside. "You're safe now," he said, and took her by the hand.

She wanted to ask him what he was doing out here, but she didn't speak until they had gone some distance and she knew Quinn wouldn't be able to hear their voices.

"What are you doing out here, Adam?" she whispered.

He dropped her hand but continued to walk. "Since the night of the break-in I've been watching your place. I saw Logan skulking around and then I heard him call your name. I knew he was up to no good. Now, I need to show you something."

"What?" she asked, struggling to keep the tears at bay as she thought of Quinn.

He shook his head, his expression grim. "You have to see it to believe it."

Heart thudding in a combination of pain and apprehension, Jewel continued to follow Adam, wondering where on earth he was taking her. She could tell that they were on Bar None land, but they were headed to an area of the property where she'd never been before.

They finally broke out into a clearing where an old barn with gray weathered boards stood, listing precariously to one side. "You've got to see what's inside," Adam said.

The door opened with a creak of rusty hinges. A small work light hung from the rafter, creating a small pool of light inside.

The first thing Jewel saw was a tall pole embedded in the ground in the center of the barn. Around the bottom of the pole, brush and dry wood had been gathered.

"Oh my God, what is this place?" she asked.

She turned to look at Adam, his features taut and almost frightening in the dimness of the light and the play of shadows.

He drew his gun and smiled, his eyes gleaming with an ominous light. "This is the place where you'll pay for the sins of your mother."

Quinn had decided to go to Jewel's place and see if he could talk to her. The distance he'd felt from her over the past week gnawed at him and he wanted to talk to her before the barbecue the next day. He needed to make sure that things were okay between them.

He'd gotten halfway to her place when he'd hesitated. What if she were sleeping soundly, peacefully? Knowing that sleep was an issue for her, did he really want to wake her up, knowing that she had a full day ahead of her tomorrow?

He'd stopped on the path and that's when he heard it, a sharp, quick scream that sounded as if it had been cut short. He froze, all his senses on alert. There was only one woman he knew who often walked these woods at night and that was Jewel.

He raced down the path, his heart pounding as he looked left and right, afraid of what he might see, afraid of what he might not see.

Reaching the gate that led to the pool area of the Hopechest Ranch, he saw that it was open and beyond that the door that led into Jewel's private quarters was open, as well.

As he ran around the pool and to the door, he knew instinctively that she wouldn't be inside sleeping peacefully in her bed, not with the door open.

Still, he didn't slow his pace until he stood in the door leading into her bedroom and saw the empty bed. "Jewel?" he called softly, not wanting to awaken anyone else in the house. "Jewel, are you in here?"

He could smell her, that fresh floral scent that went right to his head. He flipped on the light switch next to the door, but nothing happened.

What the hell? He tried another light with the same result. He knew Clay's place wasn't without power and guessed that his place and this one would be on the same circuits, so why wasn't Jewel's electricity working?

This, coupled with the sound of that half scream had alarm bells shrieking inside his head. "Jewel," he called one last time although he knew in his gut she wasn't here. He ran back to the door and peered outside. She was out there someplace and what scared him more than anything was that something...or someone had made her scream.

"Adam, what are you talking about?" Jewel stared at him, then at the gun he held on her. She grappled to make sense of what was happening.

My God, was this somehow because she hadn't gone out with him? "I'm sorry if I've somehow hurt your feelings by not going on a date with you." This was Adam...Deputy Adam Rawlings. He was supposed to protect her. What was he doing holding a gun on her?

He laughed and the malevolence in the tone shot a shiver of icy terror through her. "Don't be stupid, Jewel. Do you really think this is because you wouldn't see a movie with me or share a meal?" The laughter faded and his features formed an expression of tense determination. "Turn around." He pulled a length of rope from his pocket.

"Adam, please, tell me why you're doing this. You said something about my mother? How do you know my mother?"

He motioned for her to turn around and, afraid of what he might do if she didn't comply, she did. He quickly tied her hands behind her back, then whirled her around to face him. His eyes were filled with the dark demons of rage.

"Why am I doing this? Because the Coltons have destroyed everything in my life." He grabbed hold of her bound hands and pulled her toward the upright pole. "Heard any babies crying in the night, Jewel? Has Andrew been calling to you from his grave?" He laughed and a new terror soared through Jewel.

"What do you know about Andrew? What do you know about my baby?" Oh God, this couldn't be happening. Her heart beat a rhythm of dread as she stared at him.

He smiled. "I know exactly what his face looked like right before I rammed into your car that night on the road. I saw his surprise, then his horror." His smile disappeared. "But it was supposed to be you behind the wheel. You were the one who was supposed to die that night."

Bile rose up in the back of her throat as she realized that this was the man who was responsible for Andrew's death, for the death of the baby who had never had a chance.

She struggled against the bonds that held her, wanting to get loose, wanting to kill him for what he'd done to her, to Andrew and to their baby.

But he held tight to her and roughly yanked her toward the pole with the dried brush and wood around the bottom, like a pyre for a witch.

He was going to burn her at the stake. The sudden knowledge shot a new wave of terror through her.

"Adam, please, don't do this. For God's sake, I don't understand. Tell me why you're doing this!" Tears blinded her as he forced her through the dry tinder and tied her to the upright pole. When he was finished tying her hands, he leaned down and tried to capture her legs.

She kicked her legs, trying to smash him in the face, at the same time screams ripped from her throat. He ignored her legs, and grabbed a handkerchief from his pocket and shoved it into her mouth. "Shut up," he screamed, the cords in his neck bulging out. "Just shut up."

Once again he reached down to grab her legs. She twisted and kicked, but to no avail as he managed to grab them and tie them to the pole. After trussing her, he leaned back on his haunches. "I haven't properly introduced myself. My name isn't Adam Rawlings. It's Adam Mayfair. Ellis Mayfair was my father. It's nice to officially meet you, sis, and let me tell you, I've got one hell of a reunion planned for all of you."

Chapter 13

Quinn raced back down the path to where he'd tied up Noches, thankful for the bright moon overhead. The scream he'd thought he'd heard coupled with Jewel's open back door moved him quickly down the path.

When he reached his horse, he dug into his saddlebag and pulled out his cell phone. He had no idea what had happened to Jewel, no real evidence that anything bad had occurred except his gut instinct, and his gut instinct was screaming with alarm.

As he'd run back to his horse he'd searched the path where Jewel usually walked on the nights she couldn't sleep and she was nowhere to be found. He'd called her name out over and over again, but had gotten no reply. If she were out here, she would have answered. If she'd just been out walking, she would have made her presence known…unless she couldn't.

He couldn't get that half scream out of his mind. If it hadn't been Jewel, then who would it have been? And where in hell was Jewel?

He punched in the number for Jericho Yates at the sheriff's office, knowing he might be raising an alarm for nothing, but he'd rather be made to look like an anxious fool than do nothing at all.

Yates answered on the second ring.

"Jericho, it's Quinn Logan. Look, I might be over-reacting here but I just walked by Jewel's place. Her back door was open and the gate leading to the woods was open, as well, but she's noplace to be found. The house is dark and I think the electricity isn't working and I thought I heard a scream coming from the woods a few minutes ago."

"Whoa, slow down," Jericho exclaimed. Quinn drew a breath and started again, this time more slowly even though each and every second that passed filled him with agony.

"I'll head out now and see if I can figure out what's going on," Jericho said. "In the meantime if you find her and everything is all right, call me back on the cell." He gave Quinn the number, who quickly memorized it.

As he ended the call, Quinn remounted Noches. He intended to search the property until he found her. She needed him.

And he needed her. It had taken him five long

years to find a woman he wanted to spend the rest of his life with, and he knew without question that woman was Jewel.

But she was in trouble. He felt it in his heart, in his very soul. She was in danger and unless he found her, for the second time in his life he'd lose the woman that he loved.

Quinn knew there were three hundred acres of Bar None ranch land and he wouldn't rest until he and Noches had covered every square mile in an effort to find Jewel.

Quinn. His name roared through Jewel's head. She'd thought it was him who had tormented her, who had broken into the ranch. She hadn't trusted him, had been afraid to trust him. But he'd been the one man she should have trusted, the one man she should have believed in.

Adam told her that it had been him who had broken into her house, him who had gaslighted her with a recording of a baby crying and by whispering her name on the nights she went out walking.

And all Jewel could think about was that she'd never get the opportunity to love Quinn the way she wanted to, she'd never be able to accept the love he had for her. She'd been such a fool. She'd refused to listen to her heart and what it had been trying to tell her.

He'd been right. She'd been trapped by the same emotions Kelsey suffered, afraid to reach out for happiness, afraid that it might be snatched away. That fear had kept her from seeing the truth, that Quinn was exactly the man she wanted in her life.

And now it was too late.

"Your mother stole my father from me," Adam railed, once again the cords in his neck standing out with his rage. "And if that wasn't enough Joe Colton has managed to destroy everything that was ever important to me."

Jewel stared at him, unsure what he was talking about. Adam saw the puzzled look on her face and it only seemed to increase his anger.

"I had a cushy life in Reno. I worked as a security guard and one night I saved the life of the owner. Lola Justice was so grateful, she took me in, set me up in high style, then Joe Colton's newspaper the *Register* broke a story about her embezzling from the casino and ruined it all."

He paced back and forth in front of her as she desperately worked to try to loosen the rope that tied her to the pole. "Then I met Rebecca. She was nothing but a barmaid, but she loved me. You remember the story, don't you? I set her up in Georgie's house while Georgie was out of town. We took everything Georgie had and used a computer to start a hate campaign against Joe Colton. But Colton sent Nick Sheffield to check it out and Rebecca ended up dead. Everything…Joe Colton and your mother have destroyed everything in my life."

Tears raced down Jewel's cheeks and she tried to stop the sobs that wanted, that needed to be released, afraid that if she allowed them out, she'd choke to death on his handkerchief.

Half of what he said she didn't understand and certainly wasn't responsible for, but his hatred had obviously festered for years, an irrational, all-consuming hatred of her and the entire Colton family.

Her eyes widened in horror as he pulled a book of matches from his pocket.

No! She screamed the word over and over again in her head. *No! No!* She didn't want to burn to death. The very idea of dying by fire horrified her.

He pulled off one of the matches and lit it, then laughed as she struggled against the ropes, choking as she attempted to scream around her gag.

He blew out the match, then pulled off another, obviously enjoying tormenting her. "Tonight you'll pay for the sins of your mother and tomorrow I have a little surprise ready for Joe Colton. He won't be making it to the White House. Hell, he won't even see next Monday morning. It was nice meeting you, baby sister." He threw her a mock kiss.

Once again he lit the match, only this time he tossed it at the dry brush at her feet. For a moment nothing happened, then smoke began to swirl up in the air.

"Nice knowing you, sis," Adam said, and then he disappeared out the barn door.

A thousand thoughts shot through Jewel's head. She hadn't been losing her mind. Adam had been be-hind the voice that called to her in the night, the baby cries that had ripped at her soul. She wasn't crazy like her mother. Adam had been playing with her head.

As she thought of those nights when she'd been haunted by what she'd thought was Andrew's voice, when she'd been certain it was the baby she'd never had who cried out to her, she wanted to weep. All the doubts, all the worries that she was losing her mind—they had all been the responsibility of one hate-filled man.

The smoke drifting up from her feet grew blacker. The barn door that Adam had left open allowed in a faint night breeze and with a crackle some of the brush on the outer edges of the pile burst into flames.

A horror she'd never known suffused her. She was going to die here. The heat from the flames began to toast her feet and the smoke burned her eyes. Choking, she was racked by coughs and managed to dislodge the gag he'd shoved in her mouth.

Her screams were a combination of coughs and sobs as the flames at her feet grew hotter and bigger.

It wasn't enough that she would die here. Adam intended to kill Joe. Somehow he'd make sure that Joe never left Esperanza alive and there was nothing she could do to stop this vicious, malicious man.

Quinn. He would be her final regret. He'd told her she could trust him, but she hadn't believed him and now she was going to die because she'd trusted the wrong man.

I'm sorry, Quinn. I'm so sorry. She would die

with her regret, with the knowledge that she might have found her happy-ever-after with him.

A new spasm of coughing gripped her, leaving her lightheaded. Her chest ached and her throat burned as she continued to struggle to get free, but Adam had done a good job in making sure she couldn't escape.

She closed her eyes, hoping the smoke killed her long before she felt the burn of the flames. A weary resignation consumed her as the smoke filled the barn and the flames at her feet edged closer to the pole where she was tied.

Her eyes flew open as she heard the sound of a horse whinny. Quinn rode into the garage on Noches, who reared up, nostrils flared and eyes wide in fear at the sight of the fire.

As the stallion landed on all four legs once again, Quinn jumped off his back and Noches turned and ran out of the burning barn.

Jewel sobbed at the sight of Quinn. He raced to her and, stomping out the flames behind her, he managed to untie her feet, then her hands. He scooped her up in his arms and ran outside, into the hot night air, air that smelled amazingly sweet after the smoky interior of the barn.

When they were far enough from the barn not to be in danger, he placed her on the ground and cupped her face with his hands. "Are you all right?" He reached down and touched her slippers, as if to assure himself that her feet hadn't been burned.

"I'm okay," she replied, and coughed. "It was

Adam…Adam Rawlings, but his real name is Adam Mayfair. He's my brother, Quinn, and he tried to kill me. He's going to kill Joe. Tomorrow when they arrive in town." She was babbling and coughing at the same time. "We have to stop him. We can't let him hurt Joe."

"I know." Quinn pulled her against his chest and held her tight. "It's all right. He won't hurt anyone ever again."

She looked up at him and he continued. "I saw him sneaking away from the barn. He didn't belong here and I had a bad feeling about it, so I took him down. He's now handcuffed and tied to a tree."

They both turned to look as a whoosh went through the air and one side of the barn caught on fire. "We'd better call somebody," Jewel said.

"Jericho should be here any minute and I already asked him to call the fire department. Hopefully, they'll be here soon."

He helped her to her feet and once again pulled her into an embrace. "Oh God, Jewel, I thought I'd lost you forever."

"Quinn, I've been such a fool." She told him about the break-in at the ranch and believing that it had been him when he'd limped into the examining room. She also told him about thinking she was losing her mind, about how Adam had been gaslighting her.

She told him about the kids being gone and that it had been the sound of a baby crying that had pulled her from the empty house where Adam had been waiting for her. By the time she'd finished, Jericho had arrived along with a fire truck.

The rest of the night flew by as Jericho took statements and the firefighters kept the flames contained to the old structure that eventually collapsed in on itself.

Clay showed up and jokingly told Jewel that Adam had saved him the time and trouble of having the old barn taken down and carted away.

Adam Mayfair was led away by Jericho. He didn't say a word to anyone, but his eyes burned with his hatred for them all. He'd be jailed and would be facing enough charges to keep him away for a very long time.

Dawn was just beginning to peek over the horizon as Jewel and Quinn left the area and began the long walk back to the Hopechest Ranch. They didn't speak as they walked, although Quinn held her hand firmly.

It was enough, his hand holding hers. She didn't need his words to know what was in his heart. She'd seen it in his eyes every time he'd looked at her through the long night. She'd felt it as she'd leaned against him, absorbing his strength and calm.

He loved her.

His love filled her up, warmed her in a way the hot night never could.

And she didn't have to look too deeply into her own heart to know that she was in love with him, as well. When they reached the Hopechest Ranch, they went in through the gate and to the back door where she turned and faced him.

"It's going to be a big day for you," he said.

She nodded. "The first thing I need to do is call an electrician. Adam must have cut some wires or done something last night to make sure the electricity stopped working and I'd be in the dark."

He reached out a hand and placed his palm on her cheek. "I can't believe how close I came to losing you."

She covered his hand with her own. "I'm sorry, Quinn. I should have known that I could trust you. My heart told me I could, but I refused to listen. The worst part of all was thinking that I was going crazy, that I'd end up like my mother, locked away in a mental ward. I didn't want that to be your future with me."

He dropped his hand and instead pulled her tight against him, so close she could feel the strong, steady beat of his heart against hers.

"Even knowing that might be someplace in the future, I'd take the time with you now," he said. "I'd grab on to the happiness we could find together and hold tight to it, build memories of it and those would sustain me when things got rough. That's what I want, Jewel." His eyes flamed with emotion. "You're the woman I've been waiting for, the one I want to spend my life with. I love you, Jewel."

She'd told herself she didn't need the words, but they soared through her, bringing with them a joy that filled her up. "I love you, too, Quinn."

He leaned down and took her mouth with his in a kiss that emphasized the words he'd just said, a kiss that held all the emotion in his heart. And she kissed him back with that same emotion, with all the love and passion she felt for him.

She'd been searching a long time for the place where she truly belonged and she realized now that the place was in Quinn's arms.

When the kiss ended, he reluctantly let her go. "Is there anything I can do to help you with today?"

"No, it's all under control," she replied.

"Then I guess I should go and let you get some sleep or whatever."

She didn't want him to go. She felt as if she'd waited an eternity for her life to really begin and now with her love for him burning bright in her heart, she didn't want to put off starting to build memories.

"You know, Jeff and Cheryl and the kids won't be home until around ten," she said. "You could come in and help me with…whatever."

He grinned, a slow, sexy smile that shot straight through to her heart. "Why, Miss Jewel, I thought you would never ask."

Epilogue

Meredith Colton sat on one of the lawn chairs next to the house beneath the huge tent that had been erected for the day's activities. The tent was packed with people and for a moment she was grateful that everyone seemed to have forgotten her, giving her a chance to just breathe and to sit and observe.

In the months since Joe had thrown his hat into the ring for the presidency, there had been little time for herself, but she'd supported him every step of the way. He had a vision of hope, of prosperity that the country desperately needed.

She gazed into the crowd, seeking her husband. She spied him in a group of men, his handsome face animated as he talked. Her heart swelled. Even after all these years the mere sight of him could make her pulse beat faster.

He would be the next president. There was no doubt in her mind, nor were there any doubts in the minds of Washington's most popular pundits. Short of a personal catastrophe, come January he would be sworn in as the new president of the United States.

A shiver raced up her spine as she thought of the catastrophe that had nearly occurred. Jewel had filled them in on everything that had happened the night before. Adam Mayfair had intended to somehow find a way to kill Joe during the barbecue today.

Meredith's thoughts drifted to her sister, Patsy. Patsy had spent much of her life trying to hurt Meredith and it appeared that her legacy of hatred had lived on after her death in the form of her son. But Adam was in jail now and hopefully that was the end of Patsy's reign of terror.

As always, when Meredith thought of her sister, conflicting emotions roared through her. She felt bad that no matter how many times she'd reached out a hand to her twin sister, instead of gripping it and holding tight, Patsy had bitten it.

A hand touched her shoulder and she turned her head to see Georgie. "You need anything? Want some food, something to drink?"

Meredith smiled and shoved away her sad memories of the sister she'd never really known. "No, thanks. I'm fine."

"I'm better than fine," Georgie exclaimed, her eyes shining brightly. "Nick just had a talk with Jericho. With Adam's arrest, Jericho has a deputy vacancy to fill. It looks like Nick is going to get his wish and be part of law enforcement here in Esperanza."

"That's wonderful. I'm so happy for you both," Meredith exclaimed.

"Uh-oh, I see Emmie bending the ear of one of the servers. I'd better go rescue him."

Meredith laughed as Georgie hurried away. Little Emmie had been charming the crowd all evening as she enthusiastically shared stories of school and new friends.

She wasn't the only little person charming the crowd. Jewel's children had been well-behaved and equally charming as they mingled and tried to help out where they could.

A new warmth filled Meredith, the warmth of happiness for her family. Clay had found his happiness with Tamara and Ryder had become the man they all knew he could be in loving Ana.

All of their children had come to the party and the tent was filled to the brim with Coltons and their families.

Jewel approached Meredith with a smile and a glass of iced tea. "I thought maybe you could use this," she said as she handed Meredith the cold drink.

"Thank you, dear." Meredith patted the empty chair next to her. "Sit for just a minute."

Jewel sat and Meredith reached for one of her

hands. "I can't help but notice that the attractive veterinarian hasn't been able to take his eyes off you."

Jewel's cheeks flushed pink and her eyes shone so brightly Meredith felt the sparkle in her own heart. Oh, she knew that look, it was the one she saw in her own mirror when she thought of her Joe.

"He's wonderful, isn't he?" Jewel exclaimed.

"He makes you happy." It was a statement rather than a question. If it had been a question, the answer was on Jewel's face. Meredith squeezed her hand. "I'm so happy for you, honey."

She'd worried about Jewel, who had suffered such a tragedy when she'd lost Andrew and her baby. When she'd sent her here to Esperanza, it was with the hope that she would heal, and it seemed that she had. The shadows that had darkened Jewel's eyes the last time Meredith had seen her were gone, replaced with the shining light of a woman in love.

They visited for a few more minutes, then Jewel left her to tend to some of the other guests. Meredith smiled as she saw Quinn reach Jewel's side and give her a quick kiss on the forehead.

The two of them were going to be just fine, and Meredith was grateful that Jewel had finally found what she'd been searching for, the love and support of a good man.

Once again Meredith glanced around and spied Graham standing just inside the tent opening. He stood alone, backed against the tent as if unsure of his welcome. His blond hair had gone almost completely gray and he looked sad.

Meredith knew her husband's brother lived in a big house in Prosperino and she suspected that the empty house rang with the hollowness of his life.

Graham had made decisions that had long ago driven his brother from his life, and after that, his children. Meredith had heard that he'd been reaching out to Ryder, Clay and Georgie, attempting to make amends for his poor choices and his absence during their formative years.

Meredith glanced over to where her husband stood and she saw the precise moment he spied Graham. Joe's back stiffened and for a long moment the two men stared at each other from across the room.

Go to him, Joe. She consciously willed her husband to move across the room, to go to the brother she knew he loved, a brother who looked hungry to belong.

Go to him. The past was gone and couldn't be fixed. All they had was the future. She didn't realize she was holding her breath until Joe began to walk to where Graham stood. It was only then that she released a sigh.

She watched as the two men talked and when Joe held out a hand to Graham and Graham grasped it with a smile, Meredith felt a wave of peace sweep through her. It might just be a handshake, but it was a beginning.

Meredith knew that she and Joe were about to embark on the biggest adventure of their lives. Joe would be the next president of the United States and she would be the first lady.

It would be a time of dreams realized, not just for herself and Joe, but hopefully for the nation. There would be successes and failures, laughter and tears, but she wasn't worried about it. The Coltons were survivors and whatever the future held, they'd see it through.

Tonight was about family and friends. It was about embracing this shining moment of happiness that filled her heart and soul. She and Joe would survive and grow with their love for each other and the love of their family to sustain them.

* * * * *

Snow, sleigh bells and a hint of seduction

Find your perfect Christmas reads at
millsandboon.co.uk/Christmas